Black Harvest

ALSO BY M. C. PLANCK

BLACK HARVEST

WORLD OF PRIME BOOK FIVE

M. C. PLANCK

Published 2019 by Pyr®

Cover illustration © Shutterstock.
Cover design by Jennifer Do
Cover Design © Start Science Fiction

This is a work of fiction. Characters, organizations, products, locales, and events portrayed in this novel are either products of the author's imagination or used fictitiously.

Inquiries should be addressed to

Start Science Fiction
101 Hudson Street, 37th Floor, Suite 3705
Jersey City, New Jersey 07302
PHONE: 212-431-5455
WWW.PYSF.COM

Paperback ISBN: 978-1-63388-558-5
Ebook ISBN: 978-1-63388-559-2

10 9 8 7 6 5 4 3 2 1

Printed in the United States of America

CONTENTS

6   CONTENTS

1

GONE GIRL

He caught her with a word.

A single, elegant syllable, an orchestra of chimes in a gentle wind, and the woman paused in a movement that did not end. A waitress, serving afternoon ale in a quiet tavern; her dark hair loose around her shoulders, softening the hard cast of her face; the old and faded dress worn nonetheless with a sense of style. The spell held her as still as a statue, leaving only her eyes under her control. It was an artistic tableau, save for those eyes.

Eyes that burned in fury, hatred, and . . . fear.

The first two Christopher expected. The last settled on him like a weight.

He had spent a year murdering seven-foot-tall dog men at the point of a sword. A bloody and horrifying business, that, especially when their cubs bit as fiercely at his ankles as their females did at his throat. He had destroyed their entire civilization, broken the remnants to servitude, and then accidentally delivered them into the hands of goblins, who treated them even worse. The ulvenmen had fought with insane bravery to defend their way of life. Since that way of life included slavery, cannibalism, and regular attempts to commit genocide against the human realm, Christopher had met them on equal terms. Yet they had never shown fear. Even as they bled out at his feet, they had broken their fangs on his blade in glorious rage.

The goblins had hated, deceived, and betrayed him at the first opportunity. If they had been frightened at any point, it had been thoroughly masked by their sneering contempt.

He had dethroned and destroyed a king without ever piercing the man's arrogance.

None of them had been afraid. Only he had trembled in those encounters, his Earth-borne birth a poor preparation for this world of unrelenting violence.

In retrospect, he could see all of that had been the easier part of his task.

On the other side of the room, Lalania pulled off her wig. Her natural hair, golden and wavy, spilled around her shoulders. It didn't matter that there was not enough space under the short black cap for all that blonde glory; her disguises were mostly magical these days. The bard walked through the nearly empty tavern, silencing the questioning looks of the handful of customers by ignoring them. The tavern owner, who had paused in the act of washing a pitcher, now paused in the act of asking a question, leaving him standing almost as still as the woman held in magical stasis.

The blonde girl studied the frozen one carefully. With relief so subtle Christopher doubted anyone else could see it, she spoke. "I don't know her."

They had discussed the possibility that this woman might have once been a student of the College.

He had to stop thinking of her as a woman. Use her real name, her real title. *Assassin.*

The woman—the *assassin*—had tried several times to kill Christopher. Arguably, she had succeeded at least once, as he had left her company as a corpse, although by his own hand. This had been her only mistake. Of all those she had killed, only Christopher had come back. She had been more careful with the others.

Some by the simple expedient of obscurity. He had no idea who all her victims were. Many by the clever stratagem of making them his enemies, so they died on his blade or at the hands of his allies, where naturally revival would not be extended.

And two by learning the rules of magic, its provisions and limits, faster than he had. First had been a child in Carrhill. Revival did not work on the exceedingly young, as he had been horrified to discover.

Second had been the old man. Revival did not work on the exceedingly old, as he had been grieved to discover. For two long years, his greatest triumph had been tainted by unexpected sorrow; the man who had done the most to prepare him for greatness had died before seeing him on the throne. The guilt was doubled because Christopher had not merely been too busy to travel out to see his friend and mentor in those first few months after the final battle, he had actively been avoiding Pater Svengusta, afraid of what he would see in the old man's eyes. The first casualty of Christopher's war had been Saint Krellyan, beloved leader of Svengusta's church. So much fear and sadness in a world where magic could banish sickness, madness, and even death.

Within limits.

Christopher pulled off his own wig, dissolving the illusion Lalania had laid over him. Several of the customers choked on their ale to see their ruler and liege lord in a tavern of such low repute. The room emptied quickly as the guests fled, fearing whatever justice he had come to dispense might rub off on them. The tavern keeper dropped his pitcher and opened his mouth. Lalania cut him off with a peremptory gesture. He bent down behind the counter to pick up the jug and then quite sensibly stayed there, out of sight.

The assassin did not react. Of course not, because she was paralyzed, but her eyes showed no change. She had known who he was from the word.

She had not known him when he had entered the room, dressed like a common workman. She had not known him when he grunted incoherently and raised a thumb to order a mug of ale. Lalania had not trusted him to speak despite all her coaching. She had not known him until the spell.

He had not known her, had not been able to confirm Lalania's suspicion, until she placed the mug of ale on the table. Once before she had done that and then stabbed him in the neck with paralytic darts. The face she wore now was foreign to him; she was at least two inches taller than the last time he'd seen her; her voice was not one he had ever heard before. But the simple act had revealed her. The overt flirtation of her too-close stance, the female vulnerability hidden in plain sight like a false lure, the contempt underlying the whole performance—those he instantly recognized. Those he would never forget.

Lalania had found the woman. She and her peers from the College had tracked the woman—the *assassin*—to this town. They had singled out one suspicious barmaid in a kingdom of barmaids through careful and keen observation, two long years of work. There were spells he could have used that would have been faster, but magic was quite literal. It would have found his target and nothing else. Lalania wanted to pluck this thread gently to see whether it could lead them to their greatest enemy. In the end, the bards had concluded the trail stopped at the Gold Throne. There was no lead here to drag the hidden foe into the light.

Now she was just a murderess pretending to be a barmaid, not an enemy of the state serving powers of ultimate darkness. His realm was full of people who had killed at someone else's command. He punished them as slowly as he could, hoping that given time they would see the value of a new way of doing things. Only the worst had to die, and most of them had already done so on the battlefield beside the Gold Apostle, who had worked at the behest of another, the dark and hideous *hjerne-spica*, who had run the kingdom from the shadows. Feudalism was not unmade in a day. He was kind of hoping for a decade, but even that looked optimistic.

Time had run out for the assassin. It remained to be seen whether she had learned anything new.

"Let me bind and search her," Lalania said. "Then we can send for the local watch and have her transported."

"No," Christopher said. "I'll do it here."

He stood and drew his sword. There was no reason for delay. Her fear was a burden he did not want to carry another step.

The words of another spell rang in the air. He leaned forward, holding the sword between them, its killing point aimed at the ground, the hilt shared against both their foreheads. A token of his god, a promise of justice, and a binding on both of them. The naked edge was an honest symbol; the power of the atonement spell would bind him as much as it bound her.

He was in a different place now. He stood beside her, a mere shadow, while she crept through a dark and quiet village. Not just a memory; she spoke over her shoulder to him, narrating without affecting the action, like the director's commentary on a movie.

"This is what you wanted to see, I presume."

He did not answer because he could not lie. As much as he wanted to avoid what she would show him here, there were worse things she could have chosen. Such as the child.

The details were unimportant. Only she cared about the skill with which she entered through a locked window on the second floor, glided noiselessly down a creaky wooden hall, and slipped unknown into an old man's bedroom. She stood over the white-haired sleeper for a moment and then struck, the dagger sinking fast and true through the scraggly beard and into his throat.

The old man was a priest, merely first rank, but that still granted him inhuman vitality. He opened his eyes and struggled. She held him down, his voice silenced by steel. He could not call for help, either mundane or divine.

She had learned, after all, from her mistake with Christopher.

The old man looked up into his killer's eyes. Recognition dawned; although he had never seen her, still he knew who she must be. Here there was neither fear nor anger. Only sadness. And something else—a crinkle of smile, at the very end, before the light faded altogether.

Christopher felt tears running down his face. A remarkable feat for a man who was merely shadow at the moment but no more remarkable than the old man's wisdom. He had guessed, then, that someday Christopher would be standing here, watching through his killer's eyes. He had deduced, through sheer faith, that she would be caught and Christopher would extend the chance of atonement. He had done all of this while silently bleeding to death. And taken the chance to say goodbye.

"Goodbye, old friend," Christopher whispered to the fading face. Svengusta had been the first ally Christopher had made in this world. He had saved Christopher's life, invited Christopher into his home and family, sheltered Christopher from missteps, and invested gold and hope in Christopher's revolution.

And not lived to see it with his own eyes. Because of this woman.

"He can't hear you," she said.

"I know." Christopher felt weary, already drained to the bottom. "He didn't have to. He knew what I would say. He knew I would see this. You understand that, right?"

"Next you will tell me he begged for my redemption with his last breath."

There were no lies here. Christopher could only speak the truth. "He did."

She sprang up from the body, throwing her shoulders back. The memory froze as she railed off-script. "And will you grant it? Will you give me my freedom, after all of this?"

"Only if you will take it."

"I bow and I scrape, I grovel and promise to behave, and off I go as free as a bird?" She cloaked her words in mockery, which was as close to falsehood as she could get in this place.

"You know it is not that simple."

"Oh, my lord, how exalted your wisdom! Explain it to me, a simple peasant girl, a foolish child, a lost and stray lamb. Show me the path I should tread to please your mewling gods."

"You can't hide behind bravado here. I know you know the truth when you see it. You were the first to tell me the ugly ones." When he had lain in a dungeon, bound and broken, at her nonexistent mercy.

"I did that to hurt you," she said unnecessarily. Both of them already knew that.

"But it was truth all the same. And it helped me. It set me on this path."

"Don't you dare," she hissed, struck to the core. "Don't you dare redeem me against my will. I did what I did for your pain, and if it rebounded to your profit, it was entirely unanticipated and undesired. You cannot take my agency from me."

Given all the extraplanar beings that had manipulated Christopher's career so far, he was not entirely sure the concept of agency was as clear as she suggested. That was too abstract a point to raise at the moment.

"Nonetheless, we are here. I can redeem you, if you let me. I will, for the sake of an old man."

She spat in his face. "You will for the sake of your vanity. You sit on that throne, handing out judgment like beggars' coins. This one for life, that one for the noose, as you will. You dress up your whimsy in fine clothes and call it justice, and yet at the end of the day, the gallows still bears its heavy fruit. Now you extend mercy to your most hated foe, the wickedest woman in the kingdom, solely so you can wear your virtue like a crown. As if it will wash away the sea of blood you have guzzled."

As always, her words were true enough to cut. But he already knew these truths. He already bled from them daily.

He shook his head gently. "Is that why you did it? Just to climb to the top of my enemy's list? Did you think I would hate you more for a dear friend than for an innocent child? Did you think I would ever fear you more than a *hjerne-spica*? Is all this wickedness merely for *your* vanity?"

Her fist passed through him, insubstantial as a shadow.

"How dare you!" The shriek cut through his anger and tore at his heart. Any creature in pain is still in pain, even if it is a wicked, dangerous thing.

She turned and fled, running through memories like backstage sets, old and musty. He followed behind, a ghost over her shoulder, bound to her without choice.

So many memories, each hastily thrown together from backdrops, only to crumble away as she tore through them, fleeing what could never be outrun.

In the end, they ended where they had to end. Together they stood over a terrible scene, while a terrible man did terrible things to a child. Christopher would have been sick if he had a stomach in this form; he would have been enraged if he did not know these events were already done and dusted years ago. He would have been moved to pity if not for the knowledge of what she had done to a child even younger and more helpless.

"Give me a name," he said, "and if he still lives, I will give him a measure of my justice."

"You are too late," she said. "He was my third kill. When I was eleven, I found a dagger and hid it beneath a loose floorboard. It was my dolly, my secret friend, my first lover. When I was twelve, I stabbed a younger boy to prove myself to a traveling mummer. He was impressed; he finished the boy off and took me on. Two years later, we passed through the same village again. I was experienced enough to do it on my own this time. Despite the drink, he was still too strong for me to toy with, so I had to make it quick. The event was not as satisfying as I had hoped." Simple facts she recited in a calm, measured tone.

"Have any of them been?"

"No." She was thinning, turning translucent, as if the absence of spite were dissolving her form. "I murdered and robbed and loved, and yet this moment never changed."

"I cannot change it either. Nothing can undo the past. But I can take it from you. I can build a cage around it so that it will no longer poison you. Or I can erase it from your mind."

"No," she said. "No vessel could contain this bile. Nor can you pluck it from my soul, for what would be left? This moment has cast its burning light over the whole of my life, coloring every hope before it and every choice after it. I am what it has made me. What I would be without it I cannot imagine. Some poor, guileless creature, merely waiting for another tragedy. I would rather the mercy I gave that child in Carrhill. She will never grow up to be someone else's plaything. She will never succumb to the fire and cast it out to burn others, over and over again without surcease."

"It doesn't have to be like that," he said, but the words were hard because they were perilously close to a lie.

She shrugged, almost invisible now. "You came too late," she whispered, and then she was gone, a wind blowing away in the night.

Stunned, Christopher opened his eyes and caught the falling body, dropping his sword heedlessly to the floor despite the danger of its sharp edge. The woman was dead in his arms. He opened his clenched fist. It contained a bright purple pebble, the tangible remains of her soul.

Lalania stared at him. "I did not know that death was a possible result of this spell."

He sighed. "Nor did I." Just another truth he had not had time to learn.

2

ARBITRARY VALUE

"**W**hy can't I revive him?"

"You already know."

"Tell me again."

Lalania sighed. They were alone in the throne room for a few moments, a rare respite from the steady stream of petitioners, salesmen, and complainers. That Christopher chose to spend that time rehashing this old argument should have annoyed Lalania, but he suspected her sigh was only for appearance's sake. It had become a comforting ritual for them both. In the light of the death of the assassin, this might be the last time.

"He has lived his span. Threescore and ten, and the magic stops working. It is the fate of all children of men; it is the time allotted to them upon the stage of the world."

"That's . . . ridiculous." He glared at his sword, the tangible symbol of his patron, its hilt high and ready in the scabbard attached to the cold marble throne. "That's a completely arbitrary number. It doesn't apply to elves, and they're so biologically compatible they can mate with humans." Or so he had been told; the bards were more than willing to gossip about that race of creatures whose exalted nature made them largely insufferable.

"On the contrary," she said, happy to have a chance to contradict him. "Elves cannot be revived; your power does not extend to them. The compact they made with the Gods for their extended life is not without cost."

He transferred his glare to her, through lowered brows. "They can be reincarnated, which for them means the same thing as revival in the end." The Lady Kalani had mentioned the cost of reincarnation—a life trapped in a nonhuman body—even as she explained her mitigation. For a shape-changing elf, it amounted to no penalty at all. And all elves could shape-change.

"Then how much more you must pity the ulvenmen, whose span is measured in single years rather than scores."

She said it only to distract him. It worked, however, because he did pity them. The wolfmen, with their savage claws and staggering appetites, were ill-equipped to deal with the complexities of a moral life and robbed of the time to learn.

She watched him brood in silence only for a moment. As usual, she could not bear to let him wander in the weeds without her direction.

"It may be arbitrary, but is it not necessary? The old oaks must eventually fall; else the saplings would never have their day in the sun."

"But it's not necessary. That's what arbitrary means. Somebody picked that number just because . . . There's no reason for it to be so short."

She pulled a dubious face. "How would you know what reasons they did or did not have? Do you think the gods should appear before you and make an accounting of their wisdom?"

He thought about it but only out of habit. The answer was obvious. "Yes."

The laughter burst out of her despite her thespian discipline. "I would say the throne has made you prideful, but I know you thought the same when you were only a first rank."

"Long before that," he muttered.

They were spared by the entrance of the next court case. As the sovereign, Christopher sat in judgment over the peers, but as lord of Kingsrock, he also judged the commoners of his county. This was his least favorite duty. The nobles were entitled, wealthy, and possessed of supernatural powers. Knocking them down a peg or two was generally satisfying. The common people were just poor. He had never realized that the only building with more misery than a hospital was a court-room. A steady stream of tragedy flowed through his door, and there was surprising little he could do about it.

A large, lumpy man in craftsman's clothes took his place in the docket. The bailiff swore him in using the peculiar customs of this land.

"State your name."

"Throd Morkmonten," the man grumbled. Such an absurd appellation would normally have made Christopher suspicious of mockery. But not here.

"State your crime." The bailiff glowered until the man answered.

"Household discipline." A euphemism for domestic violence.

"State your innocence," the bailiff instructed.

The man opened his mouth and wrestled silently with his tongue for a moment. Christopher rolled his eyes. They always did this, every time, despite knowing his rank. There were, of course, people who could defeat the truth-spells of a twelfth-rank priest, but this man was manifestly not one of them. No commoner had a chance against the magic lain upon this courtroom in Christopher's annual ceremony of dedication.

A torrent of words burst out. "How else am I to maintain my household? The woman forgets; she is not right in the head. I could easily throw her out and get a younger one. A cuff to the ear is only kindness. And within my right, by ancient law and tradition." Notable among the words was the absence of any protestation of innocence.

"It is also within my right, by law and tradition, to sentence you to the lash, is it not?" Christopher asked.

The man squirmed only briefly. "Of course, my lord."

"Then perhaps three lashes is only kindness. Since you seem to have forgotten my law."

The doughty Throd had more to him than met the eye. His face turned to the floor, his eyes cast down in submission, he nonetheless stood his ground. "Yet the question remains, my lord: how am I to maintain my house? The woman drinks and neglects her duties; the children sometimes go without a noonday meal."

Christopher almost smiled. "You seem a clever fellow. I'll trust you to figure it out. If it turns out the fist is occasionally necessary, then I shall accept that. Just as you must now accept that occasionally the lash is necessary to maintain my kingdom. Three lashes for every blow of the fist. If you don't like the price, find another method."

Justice was a star in the distance. The best he could do was the pale light of mercenary economics.

Lalania intervened. "The Bardic College holds classes every ten days. Make time to learn a different way or grow a thicker hide." That was his criminal justice diversion program: a series of conflict resolution lectures by professional prostitute-spies. Attendance was surprisingly high, but that was probably due to lecturers being beautiful young women in skimpy clothes. How much of the lesson sank in was a question he had not figured out how to ask yet. Still, it couldn't hurt.

The bards had done far more for the crime rate by simply asking questions. Nobody had dared to lie to the previous king, either, but Treywan was known to not care overmuch about dead bodies in alleyways as long as the corpse's tael was still intact. Between the bard's investigations and Christopher's affiliation, the murder rate had dropped to merely impulse crimes. These put Christopher in a terrible bind since he could usually revive the victim, but at a price he did not care to pay. The old system had allowed the perpetrator to make restitution, but this meant exchanging gold for tael. Christopher did not want to part with tael. Nor did he want a judicial system where the rich could simply buy their way out of thoughtless violence. Consequently, he had passed an absolute law: any killing other than self-defense led to the noose. Everybody hated it, from the peasants to the nobles to Christopher himself. But after he hung a knight for chasing down and slaughering a boy who had thrown a stone at him, they abided by it.

There was a lot of abiding. Pretty much everyone expected his reign and its many and varied insults to tradition to be temporary. They stored up their passions and grit their teeth. The nobles plotted and the commoners seethed.

Except for his soldiers. Their status and privileges had gone up, not down. They served under honest and fair commanders for a lord who revived them, were paid decent wages, and fought with guns instead of swords. They had gone from the most despised class—commoners serving as expendable monster bait for the nobility—to police with the power to arrest the peerage. Consequently, they were extremely loyal and obeyed every order without hesitation. Christopher's nascent democracy was in fact a theocratic military cult maintained by armed force.

This was not even remotely what he had intended, and yet it was such an improvement over the previous administration that he could not walk away. So here he sat, trying to beat mercy into brutish illiterates at the end of a whip, and hanging them when he failed.

"You understand, right?" Christopher asked as Throd began to leave. "I will keep hitting you until you stop hitting other people. Because it's the only way I can get you to stop hitting."

Throd looked up at him curiously. "To live is to suffer. The strong thresh the weak until stronger arise. How else shall mankind survive in this vale of tears? You apply the lash to thousands; someday one shall wield the whip in his turn. Just as King Treywan harried you into his throne."

Nothing was as it seemed in this world. His dirty peasant apparently was a philosopher of rhetoric in disguise. This annoyed Christopher unreasonably.

"Dark take it," he swore. "How can you be so smart and still not see? Bailiff, make it six lashes. The quicker to harry our good man into wisdom."

"You can't do that," Lalania said. "Never mind the illogic; it violates your precedent."

This was what proved he was other than a tyrant. This was all that kept him sane. He leaned back in his chair and nodded his surrender. The bailiff led the doughty Throd out of the courtroom to carry out his original sentence.

"Every time you allow me to correct you in public, you look weak." Lalania was frowning at him.

There were arguments he could have made. That the public needed to see even their liege bound by the rule of law; that they should think of him as a man rather than the incarnation of pure good; that sound arguments should defeat moments of passion. The truth was simpler and more personal: he needed her disapproval. He needed her to frown at him. It was the only thing that kept him from falling into her arms. He could not say these words, so he said nothing.

Rescue came clad in green leather. A party of Rangers approached the throne. Their arguments were always sharp and hard, but he appreciated them. He didn't have to pull his punches. The Druidic counties were the only real threats to his rule as, they could defeat his riflemen in guerrilla warfare or simply decamp into the far Wild. Their constant demands for more Ranger promotions were a source of never-ending strife, and every time he lost the argument, he got raked over the coals by the Blue church for not promoting more of their knights. He leaned forward, looking forward to saying "No," forcefully and repeatedly.

The faces of the men before him gave him pause. They were troubled rather than angry, hesitant rather than demanding. Christopher would have named it fear except that the word did not seem to apply to Rangers.

"We apologize, my lord," said their leader, "for interrupting your court. But we must report. The realm is in danger."

A welter of emotions flitted through him: relief, for an external threat to unite the realm and justify his army; outrage, for the peasants who must surely die, viewed as nothing more than treasure to be harvested; fear, for whatever fantastic predator this turned out to be. At the last came anger. Whatever it was, it was surely a product of the *hjerne-spica*, the squidotian nightmare that lurked in the dark, provoking strife to advance its goals. Because those goals included his own rapid rise through the ranks, he was often the beneficiary of those peasant souls. A gift he dared not refuse, since he would need the power their lives bought him to defend them from the next threat. And ultimately from the Black Harvest, the cataclysmic doom when the *hjerne-spica* would consume every soul in the kingdom, having judged it ripe for the plucking. Consequently, the last four years had taught him to run toward danger, the sooner to end it.

He rose from the throne, calling for his horse and armor.

3

WELCOME TO GRACELAND

The riders came to a stop at the edge of the clearing. Each wore varying styles of armor, from the traditional knightly plate-mail, to the overlapping serpentine scales Christopher had liberated from the ulvenman chieftains, to simple chainmail. They were armed equally eclectically, with swords ranging from rapiers to great two-handed cleavers to katanas. The only unifying element was the guns: rifles and revolvers bristled in profusion. Christopher alone did not carry one.

Several of the horses were destriers, huge fighting beasts who glared at each other and snorted in warning if any got more than a nose ahead. Their riders were of similar temperament, although they did not snort.

"It's a trap," Cannan said. The big man glowered over the forest to the south from the back of his equally big horse.

To Christopher, it didn't look any more dangerous than Central Park. The trees were gently spaced, the grass neatly cut, the ground free of leaf-litter and weeds. All that was missing were some park benches and a few streetlights.

On the other hand, the part of his brain that had become acclimatized to this world was screaming. Nobody here had a riding mower. So who cut all this grass?

The Rangers had been less than helpful. Their explorations had mapped only the northern edge of the park. They avoided the area, fearing that even spying on it would in turn reveal too much information to whatever lived inside. As long as the border did not expand, the Rangers were content to leave well enough alone and trust their neighbours to do the same.

"Of course it's a trap," Christopher answered. That much was obvious. The problem was that he did not know whose trap. Had the Rangers lured him out here to kill him off on a hunting trip? The plan had precedent after all. Was the whole thing a setup by the Wizard of Carrhill and the Witch of the Moors, using magic to disguise the true nature of the forest? Those two certainly wouldn't object to a stack of dead Rangers as collateral damage. Or was the *hjerne-spica* testing him by setting monsters against the realm? For all he knew, the thing had run out of patience and wanted to eat him now.

The only way to find out was to walk into it. Christopher wasn't entirely stupid; he wasn't walking in alone. Behind him was a column of infantry, cavalry, and artillery, a thousand men and several hundred horses, wagons, and guns. At his side were people of rank in addition to his normal retinue. Both the Lord Ranger Einar and Duke Istvar accompanied him today, with squadrons of their own cavalry. For magic he had his own priests and Friea the Skald, head of the Bardic College, riding on a well-formed and lively roan mare. Lalania was careful not to outshine her boss, which meant that the most attractive woman in the column was actually an aged spy with a mind as sharp and devious as a panther. Not that anyone could tell; the woman looked barely eighteen and simpered like a schoolgirl whenever a man so much as glanced at her. Christopher found the whole thing ridiculous, but apparently it worked. Istvar kept going on about breeding a foal off Friea's mount, talking about the various qualities of stud horses he had at home.

He could divide his kingdom into the loyal and disloyal simply by glancing over his shoulder. The leaders of the loyal faction were here with him, risking their necks, and the disloyal were at home, waiting for him to die. For the most part that was fine. He didn't need any more knights and rather wished Istvar hadn't brought his. They were expensive to revive because they generally expected to have their ran restored. However, he would have appreciated the company of eith the Witch or the Wizard. He barely understood divine magic, arcane magic was an entirely different beast, as Master Sigrath had made clear just before being consumed by his own demon.

"I will lead the way," Istvar announced. His knights perked themselves up because riding into mysterious forests to face unknown monsters was apparently something to look forward to.

"It would be wiser to send infantry first," Karl said. "They will search the ground for snares that might injure horses."

"Good point," Christopher agreed, and waved a squad forward. Istvar's face darkened, and Christopher realized he'd fallen into Karl's trap. The young man's reasons were sound—not only were the infantry cheaper to fix, but armed with rifles and grenades they were as powerful as the knights—but that was not why he had suggested it. Heroes were the first to advance into danger. Karl was taking that job away from the ranked men and giving it to farm boys. And reminding Istvar that a commoner outranked a Duke in this army.

That was itself another good reason. Christopher swatted his own mount, Royal, on the side of the head to bring it back into line. It was as upset over the infantry advancing first as Istvar was. Both the horse and the man would just have to get over it.

"If you would seek snares, you should send those who can set them." Einar was grinning, or as close as that granite face could get to it. He was clearly enjoying watching Karl and Istvar spar, since his own Rangers were vastly superior for this task than either of their troops.

"I'm sure there will be plenty of dangers yet to come," Christopher said, managing not to sigh. Lalania's public speaking lessons were having an effect on him. "Everybody will get a turn."

"Fairness in round," Friea said, "and round again. And yet, my lord, perhaps you should not be entirely fair. The realm would be sorely grieved to lose you."

"It would miss any of us, my Lady." That seemed like the diplomatic thing to say.

She shrugged, managing to make her chainmail jiggle in inter-esting ways. "Not myself. Uma already chomps at the bit; she should take the reins before inaction dulls her spirit. If I fall in battle, I beg you only to return the trappings of my office to her."

As usual, everything the woman said had multiple meanings. In this case, she was clearly telling him that she had also passed the magical cutoff date. She was too old to revive despite her current appearance. That such a fact should be revealed to him here and now, as a response to a simple pleasantry, was typical. Christopher would have called a conference and put all his secrets on the table, but that was not how the bards worked. A direct meeting would be too easy to magically spy on. So information had to be coded and dribbled out bit by bit to those who could only understand it in context.

That was one thing he could thank the goblins for. Deep in the heart of their fortress, surrounded by the magic of their evil god, he'd been able to have a straightforward conversation with an elf. Not that he was going to thank them; that conversation had been painful. For that matter, the only other honest conversation he'd ever had here—with Friea when they were surrounded by an anti-magic field—had also been incredibly painful.

There was a lesson here that he was stoutly trying not to learn.

"Impossible," Istvar declared. "You have much ahead of you and more to offer." Istvar did not know the Skald's true age—although he had to know she was older than she appeared—but Christopher sus-pected the motivation was more personal. They were all getting older. Magic could not stop that. At some point, Istvar would have to accept that even his ranks could not keep him in the saddle when facing younger men. That point would be a lot further away here than it would have been on Earth, but it would still come.

As it would eventually come for Christopher. And he had a lot do before then.

"Step it up," he called out to the infantry squad. They stopped poking every square foot of ground with their bayonets and advanced quickly but still warily into the park.

Nothing happened. Karl waited until the squad was a hundred yards into the woods and almost out of sight before he signaled them to stop. With a frown, he turned to Christopher. "When worms sun-bathe, the robin must be wary."

Meaning that whatever monster was smart enough not to take this easy lure was smart enough to be dangerous. No simple maw of teeth and hunger but an intelligent and cunning mind. A hawk, soaring about the ground, waiting for the unwary bird to follow after the worms it disdained. Christopher, of course, was the robin in this scenario.

"You spend too much time around those bards," he replied, and spurred his horse forward.

~~~~~

The column marched three miles before Karl ordered a halt. The land was still manicured and neat. It was also devoid of any creature larger than a squirrel. The only distinguishing feature was the large open plain in front of them, the first clearing they had seen that was large enough to decamp an army.

Christopher sat on his horse and stared at the plain while his soldiers tromped through it, beating the ground with poles. Rangers roamed to and fro, occasionally stopping to examine a bush or flower with intense scrutiny. Nothing happened. Nonetheless, he could not shake the feeling that he was staring at a guillotine. When he glanced at Cannan, the man just shrugged.

Friea rode out, accompanied by Istvar. She circled the area on horseback, peering through the ring of her thumb and forefinger. When she returned to Christopher, there was admiration hidden in her face. "I swear to you, my lord, this field is free of magic."

"I equally swear it free of snares, pits, poison, and ambush," Einar said, although he had not moved from Christopher's side.

Christopher nodded his head. "So whatever their trap is, it's really amazing."

"Phenomenally so," Einar agreed. "This is why the area is proscribed by our law."

"It can't be that dangerous," Gregor said. "The Gold Apostle came down here and acquired those giant ants he gave to Joadan. He had to sleep somewhere."

"Yet he came only once," Friea noted. "And we do not know what price he paid. Whatever rogue magic made monsters out of insects will not be without cost."

"Do you want to move on?" Christopher asked Karl.

The young officer struggled with an answer. Christopher knew it was cruel to put so much responsibility on him, but it was in fact his job. Christopher ran the kingdom, the church of Marcius, and the county of Kingsrock. Karl ran the army. That was why he now wore the rank of general. The first commoner general in the kingdom's history and, in Christopher's opinion, the best. Certainly better than Christopher.

"If we flinch from shadows we will exhaust ourselves to no purpose. This is the most defensible position we have seen for a camp. Absent any compelling reason, we should make use of it." Karl looked over at Lord Einar, clearly trying to pass the baton.

"The only contrary reason I can give is common sense. Although a toddler would be smart enough not to fall into this trap, expertise and magic agree with your decision." The man was enjoying this far too much. "Rangers would never camp here. But Rangers would never bring an army here."

Christopher decided to argue. "Perhaps the inhabitants did not expect an army. Perhaps they use this field for games and are mystified that we are standing here arguing about it. Perhaps they just wanted a place to plant strawberries."

Everyone but Friea and Einar seemed relieved at his words. The Skald smiled in appreciation for his sophistry even while she clearly did not fall for it. The Ranger just grinned harder.

"Why haven't we seen crops?" Gregor asked. "Even the goblins had wheat fields."

"My apologies," Einar answered. "I thought you knew. Everything here is a field. The mown lawn we have been walking through is cultivated rye grass. Not plowed, as we would do, and not organized into discrete and uniform parcels for convenience, but still of sufficient density to support half the kingdom. We tried to emulate it once, but the method is exceedingly labor intensive."

"So you're saying there are a hundred thousand peasants hiding in those trees?" Gregor asked, looking out at the forest.

"More, I would assume. Yet that is not cause for concern. One presumes that their peasants are no more dangerous than ours. The role of peasants is to produce, not fight."

"I have learned to fear peasants," Gregor said darkly. Einar had not been there when the goblins had tried to drown Christopher's army in corpses.

"Set a fire line," Christopher told Karl. "All around the perimeter. We'll want a ring of fire in case they try to swarm us. A lot of fire."

"I shall look to my defense," Karl said, staring at him with hard eyes. "You must look to yours. Should you need to flee, you must do so. The realm can survive the loss of an army. It cannot survive the loss of its liege." Only half the power of the kingdom had marched here. There were another thousand men back in Kingsrock, under the command of the battle-seasoned Curate Torme and supported by the spell-power of Cardinal Faren. Yet the price of Christopher's rank made him irreplaceable.

"He's not wrong," Gregor agreed softly. "Keep your flight spell handy. There will be no dragon rides this time."

4

BURNING RING OF FIRE

The men devastated the nearby forest for firewood, piling it in a ring surrounding the clearing. They placed incendiary charges among the lumber, thus negating the issue of whether the wood was too green to burn. Setting things on fire was not a problem for Christopher's army.

Ironically, Christopher grew more disturbed as the defenses took shape. Where was the trap? He watched the men raise his command tent with dismay. The idea of taking off his armor and laying down for a nap struck him as absurd.

"They're probably waiting for nightfall," Gregor said. "I mean, doesn't everybody?"

It was true. So many of the monsters seemed able to operate in darkness. Christopher still hadn't succeeded in refining white phosphorous, so his dream of parachute flares lighting up the night was as empty as wishing for search lights or night-vision goggles. All of those things could be had with magic, of course, but magic was something you gave to individuals, not armies.

A principle apparently belied by the hundred magical lightstones scattered throughout his army. Each was the size of a ping-pong ball and gave off as much light as a torch. These were the cheapest of all magical items, yet six of them still cost as much as a human soul. They were also ridiculous, in that they flickered exactly like real torches. What possible point was there in such fidelity? Nonetheless, their convenience was undeniable. Electricity would have to wait for this world's Edison because what Christopher knew about it wouldn't light a Christmas tree bulb.

As the sun set over his camp, the men began to light real torches at the perimeter. The lightstones were reserved for the interior of the camp, where the wagons full of black powder were gathered. Christopher's one secret weapon was explosives. He had brought a lot of them. The tension thrummed along his spine. He looked over to Cannan, whose instincts were generally reliable in these situations. The man had his huge sword in both hands and looked like he was about to hit someone. Cannan often looked like that, but he usually kept the sword sheathed when he wasn't actually hitting people. Gregor seemed wary, although that might only have been because of the proximity of Cannan's blade. The red knight's sword was ridiculously sharp. Christopher had seen it cut an anvil in half.

Einar and Istvan joined them, both men strolling calmly as though they were at a picnic.

"Can't you tell something's wrong?" Christopher asked them.

"We will be attacked soon, yes. So much is obvious, although I am not sure it is wrong," Einar answered.

"Sooner would be better," grumbled Istvar. "While we are awake, armed, and gathered together."

It was true. All of the principals of the camp were here now, save for the two bards and the Prelate Disa. The bards would participate in any battle from behind the lines, where their spells could achieve the most effect. Christopher and Istvar would use their magic to win the fight; Disa would use hers afterward, along with the dozen young priests and priestesses accompanying the army. Injuries were only temporary in a camp with so many priests.

"We should not be so convenient a target," Cannan grumbled. This was odd for several reasons, first of which was that normally the man complained that Christopher's ranks were too dispersed. Concentrating everything into a single powerful blow was standard military doctrine here. The other reason it was odd was that Cannan seemed to actually rumble while he grumbled, quivering enough to jingle the overlapping scales of his armor.

Christopher realized the ground was shaking. He had time enough for one word, and that was spent starting a spell. Then the earth opened up and swallowed them all.

~~~

He fell into darkness, surrounded by dirt and tent poles and his companions. It seemed like forever, but before he could finish his flight spell, the ground slammed into him. Detritus from above clattered on his head.

Light flared. Istvar, shaking off a pile of dirt, raising a lightstone over his head with one hand and a sword with the other. This collapse would have killed any mortal man, but none of Christopher's retinue was mortal anymore. It would take more than this.

More was apparently on the menu. The light revealed them to be in the center of a shaft, perhaps forty feet deep and twenty wide, with three narrow but tall tunnels opening onto it at the bottom. From these tunnels crawled giant black shapes, ants flowing forth from an anthill.

Which was not a metaphor. They were ants, the size of cows, with mandibles like scythes. Already one latched onto Christopher's thigh, squeezing like a vise. Instinctively, he smacked it with his sword, knocking off one of its legs. It kept squeezing.

Then it broke in half, the head spasming as it fell away, mandibles clicking at random. Cannan, roaring, his massive sword flashing, spun in a circle, chopping up ants. Christopher paused long enough to cast a blessing on his sword and then joined him. Now his blade bit with more effect, although not nearly as much as Cannan's.

As his hearing recovered, he realized Cannan was trying to communicate something.

"Get out of here!" The man paused long enough to jab upward; an ant took the opportunity to bite him on the ankle. It held on while three more crawled over themselves to lunge at Cannan, now unable to move out of the way.

The situation was not as bad as it appeared. Christopher had three entirely separate ways to escape this trap. He could fly, he could enchant his feet so that he could walk on air, or he could turn to mist and blow out like steam. Unfortunately, all of these would leave some of his companions behind.

Instead, he cast the strength spell on Cannan. Empowered, the man sliced through all three lunging insects and kicked the one attached to him so hard it fell over and waved its legs in the air. Christopher moved into the center of the shaft and looked for someone else to help.

It was mildly humiliating. Despite his armor and sword, he spent most of the battle throwing spells. The other men all had varying ranks of the warrior profession. Casting strength on them, and then healing, and then endurance when they began to flag, was a better use of his time. Dead ants began to pile up. His men climbed on top of the bodies and fought from there. Eventually, they would reach the surface on a stack of corpses.

Then Christopher noticed that the queen was coming in by crawling on the roof of the tunnels, while dead ants were being dragged out along the floors. The pile stopped growing. The ants could cycle an infinite number of attackers through this chamber. Eventually, Christopher would run out of spells, and then the swordsmen would fall to attrition.

Flying out seemed like the better part of wisdom after all. The battle had bought them time and space. Christopher, protected from interruption, put the air-walking spell on Cannan, Istvar, and Einar while they fought.

"Carry Gregor," he shouted to Cannan. Then he cast the flight spell on himself. Only once his feet left the ground did the other men take off. Christopher could float, whereas the others had to stomp up, like climbing a flight of stairs, and that in heavy armor. Cannan had Gregor hanging off his back by one arm, huffing like a draft horse. Gregor slashed at the ants that crawled up the walls after them.

Christopher began to worry about all of these ants boiling up into his camp. He flew faster, moving to the edge. Men rushed to him as he pointed into the hole.

"Fire!" he shouted. The ants were actually gaining on the air-climbing men. They were as fast on the walls as on the ground. Riflemen leaned over and blazed away. A layer of ants tumbled back to the ground.

The next wave replaced them, but now Christopher's retinue had cleared the surface.

He spent his speech on a spell. Fortunately Istvar recognized which one it was and started bodily pulling men away from the edge of the hole. They got the message in time, and when the column of flame filled the shaft, it caught none of his men. The ants, however, burned with an acidic tang and a horrible crackling.

Still flying, Christopher hovered over the shaft and looked down. Nothing moved. Either the ants had learned their lesson or they were preparing something new.

In the distance, he heard a rifle shot. He couldn't sit here and babysit a hole in the ground while his army was under attack.

Captain Kennet appeared at the edge of the hole, rolling a barrel of powder. He called orders to several other men, who were manhandling more barrels. Behind him stood Quartermaster Charles with a lit torch. Kennet had taken to dynamite from the very beginning. He could handle this. Christopher flew off to find Karl and learn what other dangers had struck while he was burning ants.

<hr />

He was relieved to see there were no more sinkholes. Instead, the ants had made a rush at the edges of the camp. These ants were half the size of the others; Einar declared them to be workers, not soldiers. Apparently they were only a diversion. Once the strike against the principals failed, they withdrew, having inflicted little damage, held off by rifles and fire.

The casualties came from flying ants spitting globs of acid several hundred yards. Christopher was horrified at the results. The men were not just dead; they were disfigured, some missing hands or chunks of their torso, some with half their faces eaten away. He could bring them back from the dead, but he could not fix this. The Saint's ability to regenerate flesh was still denied to him for another rank, and even then it was frightfully expensive.

There had only been half a dozen of the fliers, most of which had been shot down. Presumably they were the ant's spell-casters, thus expensive, and therefore limited. If the ants had a hundred more in reserve, Christopher would have to retreat. His men had signed up for death, not a lifetime as hideous cripples.

The men did not seem to understand this yet. They kept looking at the ground, terrified of being swallowed up.

"Fill bowls with water," Christopher told Charles, his quarter-master. "Spread them around the camp. If the ants are tunneling under us, the water will shake."

"Yes, sir," the young man said. As part of his salute, he threw a con-cerned glance at one of the acid-burned corpses.

Christopher turned away before his face could betray him. Charles was smart; Charles had also been the recipient of the Saint's magic. The young soldier understood the problem. Christopher could not lie to him, could not even order him to lie to the men, so for the sake of morale, he simply did not answer the unasked question. This was a kind of dishonesty, of course, but just another one of the many diplomatic silences sitting on a throne compelled. He had never lied so much in his life and all without saying a word.

Also unsaid was what the soldiers should do if the bowls did start shaking. Christopher didn't have a plan for that. He just wanted to stop them from feeling helpless. He returned to his new command tent, trying not to feel helpless himself.

"An unsatisfactory engagement," Istvar complained. "Although our casualties were light, our winnings were lighter. The vast majority of the enemy's tael has returned to them." The fliers had been shot down outside the ring, and the soldier ants had drug away their fallen, leaving only a few hundred peasants to harvest.

"Not entirely without merit," Einar replied. "Our lord has perhaps learned something of great worth." The Ranger knew his audience reasonably well. He followed up with a necessary hint. "Namely, the value of tradition."

Christopher paused to think. The obvious inference was that he should have honored the Ranger's law and not come here in the first place. That didn't make a lot of sense, though. The Rangers had brought him here. Peasants and livestock had gone missing from the border, and no one the wiser, despite the Ranger's formidable tracking skills. This was a problem that had to be solved before panic set in. If the peasants refused to go into their fields the realm would starve. So what tradition was he supposed to be valuing?

"Are you so keen for adventure, my lord Einar?" Friea smiled seductively, which seemed about the only affect she could achieve dressed as she was. "Do you long to serve your lord in battle, side by side, through epic journeys into unknown realms?" Then, with a salty glance, she ruined it all. "Or do you merely think he'll share the tael with his retinue?"

"He doesn't do that," Gregor said. "We all know that. None of us expects a promotion until the great work is finished."

"Not entirely true," Einar said, still looking like a cat on a particularly warm rug. "He promotes his priests."

Christopher defended himself. "We need their magic." The priests provided justice, healing, and fertilizer, which was an interesting but exceedingly useful combination.

"As you now need our strength. Surely you see there are no other options. Now we understand the danger. No wild magic or deranged wizard created Joaden's ants. They were bred and born that size. We are faced with a threat that our lore places among the greatest to any realm: a Formian nest. There are only two possible reactions. One is to run away, abandon our fields and farms, and flee as far and fast as possible."

The Ranger paused rhetorically. That was only an option for his own people, and even then only in theory. As much as the druids played at living in harmony with the land, their people's health and prosperity would be decimated by becoming nomads. Meanwhile, the peasant farmers and townsmen of the rest of the realm would simply die on the march.

Einar shrugged gently, acknowledging these truths without speaking them. "The other is to form up, shoulder to shoulder and rank to rank, march into that hole, and extirpate the queen. Nothing less will end this infestation. Your commoners and their tricks cannot help you here."

Istvar's face brightened, which Christopher thought was an insane reaction to the proposition of crawling into a giant anthill. "For once you will see the need of our profession. Steel and tael will see you through. Mere flesh and blood cannot stand here, no matter how brave."

They were right. In the dark and close confines of the tunnels, all that mattered was density. Like a bodkin-point arrow piercing mail, the concentrated power of rank would succeed where a hailstorm could not. His men would die faster than they could reload.

"At least it will be better than the goblin keep," Cannan said.

"How so?" Gregor looked at the red knight curiously.

"We can start killing right away."

5

JOURNEY TO THE CENTER
OF THE EARTH

Christopher had done a great many stupid things as a young man. He had done a great many dangerous things since coming to this world. Standing in front of the dark hole in the ground, he reflected that this was surely the stupidest and most dangerous of them all.

Gregor was apoplectic. "Not even the dragon would be so foolish. What if they collapse the roof on your head? Does your rank let you breathe dirt?"

"The Lyre of Varelous can dig a tunnel as easily as it can build a fort. I will accompany my lord, as is my right." Lalania was hiding her fear well. Christopher doubted anyone else could see it. Yet she was correct. No one else could use the lyre.

"Speed will be our defense," Lord Istvar said. "We will not remain in one spot long enough for such a simple snare. We have here the greatest swordsmen in the realm. Ser Cannan, by virtue of the blade he bears, and myself, by virtue of the fact that the Saint has shot anyone who could challenge me." At the end, Istvar remembered to be polite and turned to Christopher. "And yourself, of course."

Cannan was having none of it. "Saint Christopher only defeated you by magic. He will have better use of it than sword-slinging today."

The red knight was right. Backed by healing spells, the two warriors could destroy an army, as they had demonstrated at the bottom of the sinkhole. Christopher healing the two men was a better use of resources than Christopher turning himself into one of them for a short while.

"My bow would be of limited use," Einar said, "yet you may find my skills helpful. I will accompany you, with your permission." The Ranger wore a pair of short swords and was seventh rank. He was almost as dangerous as Istvar.

"I don't want to strip the camp of all rank," Christopher said.

"Why not?" Karl shrugged. "They will concentrate their attacks wherever you go. They will not turn on us until you are dead. We are only treasure to them, not a threat."

So simply had they deprived Christopher of his greatest asset. A few tunnels under the earth and his scientific revolution was reduced to a side-show.

Friea shook her head. "You underestimate yourself, Goodman. Their champions remain underground out of fear of your fire sticks. Were Christopher interested in a war of attrition, you might well win it for him."

"The price of occupation would be paid in corpses," Istvar growled. "I am not willing to bleed my counties for such an end."

Nor was Christopher. If he spent all his tael raising dead soldiers, he'd never gain in rank.

The Skald acquiesced gracefully. "By your leave, my lord, I will remain above and put my talents at your General's disposal. If nothing else, I will be able to communicate with you through Lalania."

"Okay," Christopher said. "So it's just the five of us."

"Six," Gregor interrupted. "I'm coming with you."

The man was as competent as Cannan, although he lacked the advantage of the royal sword. Still, Christopher had planned on leaving him with the army.

He started to say this but stopped at the look on Gregor's face. The truth was that the army did not need him. Karl was their undisputed commander, and Disa was their chief healer. Gregor was as outdated and useless as the rest of the knights. He had only a single rank of priest, the rest of his ranks being in the warrior class. The army already had a dozen first-rank healers.

"Okay," Christopher said. "The six of us."

The Rangers had found an entrance a few hundred yards into the forest. It had the look of regular use, so they chose it instead of going back into the sinkhole. After moving aside a few bits of brush apparently intended to disguise the entrance, Christopher and his party stood facing a wide tunnel that appeared to be plastered in concrete and sloping down sharply.

Walking into the darkness of the goblin keep had been hard. This was harder. The smell of dirt was borne out of the tunnel on a surprisingly warm breeze, rising an atavistic fear of being buried alive in his throat. The scent was tinged with acid, calling to mind the clicking mandibles of impossibly sized insects. Walking forward felt like walking into a nightmare.

"Not this again," Cannan grumbled.

"It's not as bad as the goblin's," Lalania said. "This spell only bars against chaos. I presume Duke Istvar will not even notice."

"Notice what?" the Duke asked.

Lalania did not answer. She was staring at the ground, an actress preparing for a dramatic entrance.

"The rest of us will require some degree of healing on the other side," Einar suggested.

"Perhaps," Cannan said, and stepped forward, crossing an invisible threshold.

Nothing happened. Cannan looked at Christopher and shrugged minimally. It was an awkward moment, like walking in on a man in the bath.

Gregor grimaced and forced himself over the same edge. Golden mist wreathed over the knight for an instant. He turned around and thrust his hand back across the border.

Disa, white as a sheet, crept forward and touched his hand. She spoke a healing spell softly.

Einar strode across, suffered the same mist, and bowed in appreciation to Disa while extending his hand for healing.

Christopher steeled himself and followed. The pain was only a portion of the goblin's version of this spell. Disa replenished his tael with a single spell.

Lalania and the Duke came across, both free of mist.

"I don't like this," Christopher said to Lalania. "Drop your guard and let Disa heal you. Get it over with."

"You forget your exalted rank," she answered with a provocative smile. "This would still slay me instantly." Then she ignored him to fiddle with her new toy, a gift from Einar: a hooded lantern, although powered by a lightstone instead of whale oil. It cast a roughly focused beam of light sixty feet like a spotlight. Christopher felt bad for not having invented it, but he had thought of the lightstones as magical rather than physical sources of light. It had not occurred to him that their light could be reflected and directed.

Istvar and Cannan were advancing side by side into the dark, not waiting for the lantern. Cannan's sword glowed as brightly as a torch when he wanted it to. Christopher and Lalania had to hustle to catch up with them, Einar and Gregor bringing up the rear.

Fifty feet in, they came to a branch. Cannan jerked his head and led Istvar off in the new direction. Christopher started to follow, but Einar stopped him with a hand on his shoulder.

"Clear . . . I think," Cannan called out.

The rest of the party followed his voice into a large room packed with black barrels and a cupboard. It took Christopher a moment to resolve what he was looking at.

Ants. Half the size of the soldiers, with mandibles no larger than his hand, stacked six deep. In the midst of them was a boxy, square-headed ant the size of a tractor. It looked like a piece of farm machinery more than an ant. A specialized creature, bred for a special purpose. If Christopher squinted, he could see it as a weird version of a combine harvester.

One of the lesser ants trembled. Its mandibles clacked once and then went silent again.

"I believe we have found their peasants," Einar said. "I regret my earlier disregard; they look somewhat more disconcerting than I had anticipated."

"There must be a hundred," Gregor whispered. "Why aren't they attacking?"

"Why bother? We would easily destroy them," Istvar answered. "The queen acts with due regard for the lives of her subjects."

"Then ask, why are they here?" Einar asked. "Instead of fleeing deeper into the tunnel?"

"An offering," Lalania said. "She hopes we will take their tael and be satiated."

Istvar frowned in disappointment. Lalania took pity on him. "It is still wise. It spares the rest of her subjects and, not incidentally, allows her time to prepare an attack. Such as this one."

The floor trembled slightly under the weight of soldiers rushing up the tunnel.

"My comment was meant to be rhetorical," Einar complained, letting the knights charge past him.

Istvar and Cannan threw themselves against the flood. The ants charged four abreast. Only the strength spell Christopher had cast on the two men allowed them to hold the line. Their glowing swords swung and swung, throwing up ant parts in their wake. Limbs, claws, mandibles, parts of heads, and whole heads in a spray.

"Watch the rear," Einar said, leading Gregor past him. Lalania did something with her lantern, and now it cast in all directions, like a normal torch, although with only a normal radius. Still this was better for close-quarter sword fighting. The Ranger and the knight took up places behind the first two men, just in time. Another wave of ants came crawling on the ceiling, trying to flank the front. Einar and Gregor fended them off at sword point. One fell from the ceiling onto

Cannan. The red knight shrugged, flipping it off in front of him, and then cut it in half.

Christopher forced himself to turn his head and look at the worker ants. They remained still, cowering in their hovel, like any peasant. He could not wholly quell a pang of sympathy.

Lalania looked at him and rolled her eyes. "Fear not. They will give you cause to regret your kindness soon enough."

After a moment, it was all over. The flood vanished, leaving the hallway choked in insect corpses.

"It's now or never," Cannan said. "Standing here to collect our treasure will only result in worse."

"Okay," Christopher said. Cannan and Istvar took that as a command and ran farther down the tunnel, wading through the corpses like snowplows. Lalania focused the light forward again and followed. Christopher had to rush after her or be left in the dark.

Again Einar and Gregor brought up the rear. They traveled another hundred yards, the tunnel curving and twisting. Two more branches led off into rooms full of ants. They ran past them without stopping.

"Three, two . . . one," Einar said, counting down on his fingers. The ground trembled above them.

"Did they . . ." Christopher asked, not really wanting an answer.

"Yes," Lanalia said. "Do not worry. The lyre will reopen the way in but a moment when we choose to leave."

"Assuming you are still alive," Einar said conversationally. "No offense, Minstrel, but I would have preferred the company of the Skald."

"A tale I have heard my entire adult life," Lalania said sweetly. "And yet, in the clutch of darkness, one woman is much like another."

"That's not true . . . ," Gregor started to argue before he thought better of it.

Another ant attack spared them all the pain of conversation. This battle was short, the swarm of ants drying up quickly. Around the next curve, they discovered why. The tunnel branched three ways, but each branch was half the width of the main tunnel. The men and ants would have to travel single file now.

"Left," Einar called out.

Lacking any better choice, Christopher nodded his assent. Cannan moved forward, but Istvar blocked him with his steel shield. The red knight let the Duke go first.

A dozen yards on, Istvar dropped to one knee. The ants came at them on two levels again, one line crawling on the ten-foot-tall ceiling and one line on the floor. Istvar held back the press with his shield, slowly dismembering the ant in front of him. Cannan knocked them off the ceiling, the glowing sword slicing the creatures into segments.

After a moment, the tunnel was too choked with bodies and parts of bodies for any more ants to get through.

"Back out. Take the center passage this time. And run!" Einar was issuing commands like he knew what he was doing. Christopher was grateful for the reprieve. However, it meant the Ranger and Gregor were now the front of the column, running single file down another tunnel. When they encountered more soldiers, Einar did the brunt of the work, chopping through the ants like a blender. Gregor, behind him, merely had to deal with the ones clinging to the top of the tunnel. Even so, Einar advanced so quickly he could not keep up. Several ants slipped past the blue knight's blade. Lalania ducked and squealed, bouncing the light crazily, while Christopher hacked desperately. Finally, he realized all he had to do was keep them off the woman. Once they slipped past, Cannan and Istvar easily plucked the ants from the ceiling.

Their impetuous advance paused when the tunnel opened up again to wider dimensions.

"If you don't mind," Einar said politely. His leather armor was rent in a dozen places, marking where ants had bitten, stung, or clawed him. The man had fought without thought to defense. Christopher consumed several small spells restoring the Ranger's tael.

"What next?" Istvar asked, reclaiming the front of the party.

"They have lost at every martial encounter." Einar answered. "They will try magic soon."

The tunnel had a gentle slope. The party followed it down, ignoring the smaller tunnels branching off the sides and occasionally the ceiling, moving at a fast trot. Their armor jingled, a cacophony of bells. At one point, Gregor tried to quiet his metal scales with one free hand, but Einar shook his head. "Don't bother. The ants are deaf."

"So they don't know we're coming?" Gregor asked hopefully.

Einar almost laughed. "They feel your movement through the ground. Every step you take is a clarion trumpet."

Suddenly they were engaged; ants swarmed from every tunnel on all sides.

"Keep moving," Einar warned. "To stand is to die." Then he turned around and jogged backward, his twin swords already engaging ants. Gregor had to do the same.

Explosions rang Christopher's ears. Lalania was shooting ants off the ceiling with her pistol. In the close confines of the tunnel, the sound reverberated, damped only when it washed over the mass of ants.

"If they can't hear us," she shouted, and then shrugged, reloading while juggling the lantern and jogging.

Christopher waved the smoke out of his face and tried to decide what to do. Einar had emphasized the importance of momentum. The party was moving slowly, the men in front fighting fiercely to advance, while behind Einar fought defensively, merely trying to hold the ants at bay.

"Hold up," Christopher ordered. Istvar sheltered behind his shield while Cannan took a half-step back, the better to use the big sword for cover. A breath later, a column of flame roared down, filling the tunnel but not spilling out along the confined space as real flame would.

As soon as it vanished, the men rushed forward, crunching over burnt shells to claim the twenty feet of cleared space, and threw themselves against the ants behind.

Christopher thought about doing it again, but the battle was over. A few ants stood their ground and died to Istvar's and Cannan's blades while the rest fled back into the side tunnels. The swordsmen let them flee, jogging down the tunnel as fast as their armor would allow.

"Save the rest for the big ones," Einar advised.

His point was well made. The divine flame had reduced the ants to charcoal, a hammer swatting a flea. Also, it made the air stink of acid. Christopher coughed and wondered when war had become a marathon in armor. He really missed his horse.

Suddenly, Cannan looked around wildly. He was jogging with his sword on his shoulder, thus swinging his head like that threatened his ears, but that did not seem to be the source of his distress. The hallway they were in appeared no different to Christopher, save that it had leveled out from its constant downward slope, but Cannan clearly did not like what he saw.

"Run," the red knight said, and put his words to effect.

Christopher, out of habit, glanced back at Einar for confirmation.

"Faster," was the Ranger's response.

Now the party pounded across the concrete-like ground. Christopher fancied he could hear a change in the timbre of the echoes of their footfalls. Then the roof fell in on his head.

6

A RISING TIDE

It was a false roof, the blocks of concrete plaster no more than a few inches thick. A dozen feet above the enclosed tunnel was a natural cave roof, complete with stalactites. As the walls tumbled down, Christopher could see the rest of the cavern, approximately eighty feet long and sixty or seventy wide. The ants had made a fake tunnel through a real cavern to lure them into the open where they could be surrounded and swarmed by the horde of black chitin rustling across the ground.

Ahead of them he could see more falling earth. Ants were closing the passage out. Lalania flashed the beam behind them, and he saw they were doing the same to the rear. Sealing him in a cavern with several hundred giant ants seemed like a pretty good trap.

Cannan and Istvar reached the collapsing exit too late. Half a dozen soldiers stood their ground briefly before being dismembered.

"Backs to the wall," Istvar shouted. "Form a half-ring." The ants would only be able to come at them on one level instead of two. They might be able to hold them off.

Cannan, surprisingly, did not obey. He clawed at the debris blocking the exit, throwing boulders to the side.

"That's a lot of ants," Gregor said, taking up his place in the ring.

"They are not the threat," Einar noted. "They are merely workers. The ants do not intend to defeat us by battle."

It was true. The carpet of ants advanced slowly, and Christopher could see they were all the smaller workers. Presumably they could try to drown the humans under the weight of numbers, but it seemed like a bad plan given that it had already failed when tried with soldiers.

A sibilant, liquid gurgling crept into hearing range. Christopher looked down and realized he was standing in a puddle of water. When he looked up, he could see the reflection of Lalania's lantern in the rising water.

Cannan kept digging at the blocked entrance with his bare hands.

"Should I use the lyre?" Lalania asked, clearly hoping the answer was yes.

"If you do, they will attack," Einar answered. "Their only purpose is to prevent us from opening the way. The water will be our doom."

"Theirs too," Gregor objected.

"The queen is desperate. She spends her peasants and her magic freely."

"Huh," Christopher said. "This was going to be my plan."

Cannan swore and stepped back. He had pulled a boulder out of the blockage, and now a stream of water shot out from the hole. The stream got bigger as the water wore away at the dirt.

"They have already flooded the other side," Einar pointed out helpfully. "Did you think to prepare water breathing magic?"

"Did you think to suggest it?" Lalania snapped back.

Christopher ignored them both and pushed closer to the center of the room. The ants paused at his approach. Many of them were now struggling in the waist-deep water. He raised his sword and cast a spell, most likely the same spell the ants were using. Originally he had thought to use this spell to drown the hive, but its area was too limited. It would only affect a small area . . . such as this cavern.

What could be raised by magic could be lowered by it. The water began to sink. The ants clawed gratefully at the ground as it reappeared.

Lalania came to join him, away from the blocked exit. One by one, the other men did the same, eyeing her curiously.

"Wait," Lalania suggested.

After a moment, several ants scurried to the exit and began tearing it open. When the party did not attack, a dozen more joined the effort. At the other end of the cavern, more ants swarmed the wreckage and soon began flowing out of the room.

The ants clearing their end made enough space to flee through. A couple dozen more joined them, but by then the rest had moved to the far side.

The way was now open.

"We are all men of rank," Istvar said. "We could have held our breath longer than any peasant. You could have had a room full of treasure for the mere price of waiting a bit and lowering the water when it was ready to harvest."

Einar seemed to agree with the Duke. "Do you think to extend mercy? Those workers are all doomed; they will die in agony and madness when their queen is slain."

"And yet," Gregor said, "for this moment, it was not necessary to slay them."

"None can say what the future will hold," Lalania said.

"Our death at the jaws of a thousand ants seems likely." Einar shook his head. "Quite possibly at the mandibles of those you have just spared."

Christopher shrugged. "At least we don't have to dig our way out."

Istvar laughed and pushed into the tunnel.

They moved more cautiously now. Christopher could feel the weight of the earth over his head. Hundreds of feet underground, the air was warm but not still. A steady breeze flowed through the tunnels. Einar used it in his navigation, following the breeze deeper into the lair.

They passed workers huddling in rooms off to the sides, but there were no more attacks. Then all at once, a swarm of workers rushed at them. Istvar and Cannan killed a dozen before they realized the creatures were simply trying to get past. Seized by intuition, Christopher and his companions chose to follow them. For a minute, the humans and ants fled together.

A deep rumbling roared up the tunnel they had just abandoned.

The breeze reversed and pushed hard at their fleeing backs as dirt and stone collapsed. Once the workers began fleeing into side tunnels, Einar called a halt.

"We are safe now," the Ranger explained. "There are at least a hundred yards of rubble between us and any possible entrance to the throne room. The queen yields whatever treasure you can claim from her subjects on this side of the barrier in the hopes that you will be satiated."

"If we start killing ants, they'll start fighting back," Christopher said.

"Surely you don't expect her to murder them for you and serve their heads on a silver platter?"

That imagery reminded him of the goblins and a series of mistakes he was determined not to repeat.

"Can we still make it to the queen?"

Einar considered. "There are yet surprises; we have not faced the queen's champion. How much spell-craft do you still command?"

"About . . . half."

Einar's eyebrows went up.

"I know the feeling," Istvar said to the Ranger. "For myself, I am depleted. I have spent everything healing Ser Cannan. Although the royal sword makes him deadly, it does not provide the durability of rank." There was an implicit condemnation in his tone.

Lalania, despite being covered in sweat, bug juice, and dirt, rose to Christopher's defense. "In the service of a healer, rank can be replaced. As you yourself have demonstrated."

Einar ignored the argument. "What little magic I possess is sufficient to find our way out again but no more. Thus, I conclude that we can choose to press on with middling risk."

"We could retreat and return tomorrow?" Gregor suggested, although he didn't seem to think much of the idea.

"No," Christopher said. Never mind that he never wanted to walk into a subway tunnel again after this. "That will just give her a chance to recharge, too."

"A wise choice," Einar agreed. "If we retreat now they will take that as a sign of weakness and fight even more fiercely to prevent our egress. I conclude that retreating also carries middling risk."

Gregor frowned. "I'm pretty sure if we press on they'll also fight more fiercely out of desperation."

"True," Einar said. "Hence, the risk."

"Lala, if you please," Christopher said. He finally realized they had been waiting for him to give the order.

She shook out her hair, as if her appearance would affect the quality of her performance, and handed the lantern to Einar. "Once I start, I cannot stop, lest the magic end. So if you have any questions of me, ask them now."

It felt like a challenge. Had Christopher really dragged her down here merely as a torchbearer? Was she just another magic item in his pocket?

"What questions should I be asking you?" he said.

"Many," she replied with a snort at his attempted sophistry. "But not that one." She finished unwrapping the lyre from its leather covering, drew in a breath, and struck the first note.

White mist rose up from the ground and streamed to the blockage. Soon the party was standing uncomfortably in the center of the tunnel while dirt and rocks flowed by on conveyer belts of mist. The ants launched an attack from the still open end, trying to silence the lyre. A dozen soldiers and a score of workers died on Istvar and Cannan's blades. Christopher got to watch this battle more closely because they were not running for their lives. Both men focused on killing the ants as quickly as possible so they could not be overrun. The ant chitin, which seemed so hard and durable under his feet, parted like cheese under the men's blades, especially Cannan's. The ants also fought without regard defense, lunging suicidally to inflict a single bite against an arm or a leg. They traded their lives to deplete the men's tael. When Christopher reached out and replenished Cannan with a minor spell, the swarm lost heart and melted away. The battle was over as quickly as it had begun.

Cannan strode among the still bodies, stabbing. Christopher thought he might be administering mercy until the red knight stabbed an ant head that had already been fully severed.

The red knight returned to his side. "You should know," he said, and held the haft of his sword up. Christopher could see that the large aquamarine gemstone set in the pommel was glowing with an inner light of purplish hue. The blade had collected the tael of its victims.

"I always wanted a sword like that," Istvar said wistfully. "It lends a certain dignity to the necessary aftermath of a battle."

Einar disapproved. "It covers an ugly truth with a pretty lie. Battlefields should be grotesque, lest they become too comfortable."

"Being surrounded by grotesquery dulls the senses," Istvar argued. "Men must retain the capacity to be disgusted."

Christopher was surprised at the sophistication of the argument. He was also slightly worried that this was not the place to have an essentially theological discussion.

Gregor ended the argument in his own special way. "Imagine if we could make a cannon do that," he said. "The best and worst of both."

Cannan grunted and pointed down the tunnel. Lalania had opened the way. The party walked through the restored rubble while Lalania stroked the lyre, making the white mist polish the stones to a dull gleam. Busy work for the spirit laborers to keep them bound to the calling for as long as possible. Christopher wondered whether they resented it.

They passed two other major tunnel entrances. The third one they came to was blocked with piled boulders slathered in still-drying concrete.

"This is our final choice," Einar announced. "The queen lies behir that hastily assembled wall."

Gregor fumbled at his backpack and produced a silvered whiskey flask. "Friea gave me this for emergencies. I think we should top up before we go through that door." He took a swig and passed it around. The rest of the men took varying lengths of drink depending on how badly their vitality had been depleted.

Christopher raised his hand to cast and then stopped.

"It's too dangerous. We have to vote on it."

"Why?" Einar asked. "Only your vote counts. We cannot do it without you, nor will we abandon you."

Lalania's mist began dissembling the wall.

"What if I make the wrong choice?" Christopher asked.

"Then we all die," Cannan said. "The next words out of your mouth best be a spell."

Christopher cast the aura detection spell. Lalania had been coaching him on how to interpret its results, which was just as well because she was currently occupied with the lyre. In this case, the results were obvious. The entranceway was covered in a blinding yellow glow of menace. He was developing a healthy fear of doorways. So many creatures seemed to enjoy layering them in deadly magic.

His dissolution spell worked; the glow winked out of existence. The wall fell in a final jumble of stones. Beyond he could see a large chamber opening off to the left, its importance revealed by a ceiling twenty feet high. A single worker ant stood in the revealed portion of the room, staring at them like a meerkat on lookout duty. Istvar and Cannan inhaled deeply and charged into the room. Christopher had no choice but to follow.

When he turned left, he caught his breath. A carpet of black stretched many yards to the back of the room. At the front of the carpet was an ant the size of a small elephant. To either side was a line of car-sized warrior ants, like the ones that Joaden had reanimated. Behind them the carpet sloped down to merely ordinary cow-sized soldier ants. At the far end of the room, dimly visible in the furthest reach of the lantern's light, was the queen, the size of a city bus, her ovipositor even now releasing a white-sheathed egg. She stared out at Christopher through glinting insectoid eyes with unmistakable intelligence. In his mind, the carpet transformed into a royal cape laid before the feet of a noble ruler, its hem of giant warriors like gems to show off her status.

Then the carpet crawled forth to claim him.

The room was checker-boarded in golden auras, although none as intense as the one that had lain across the entrance. The ants moved through the auras without concern. Gregor and Einar stepped forward to shield him and Lalania. The woman was playing the lyre in earnest now, but Christopher had no time to wonder why. The front line of ants was covered in a flickering aura only he could see, and the huge champion was wearing several layers of light.

As it charged, he cast the dissolution spell again. The coat of light went out, depriving the monster of the queen's aid, although it did not seem to care. It rushed forward and snatched Istvar up in its huge mandibles, squeezing with incredible force. Any ordinary human would have been instantly sliced in half. Istvar was, as he had noted, somewhat more durable. Nonetheless, his tael would not hold out long. A pair of soldier ants crawled on top of the champion, reaching out to bite at him.

Istvar struck back at his captor, severing its left-handed antenna. This seemed like a weak blow until Cannan stepped forward into its blind spot and severed the champion's mandibles with a great stroke of the royal sword. Istvar fell to the ground like an armor-plated ball.

The champion kicked out with its front legs, knocking Cannan and Istvar back, where they rolled up against Gregor and Einar. For a brief moment, the giant creature was not standing on top of his allies. Christopher called down the tower of flame.

The warriors and soldiers trapped in the column popped like corn kernels. The champion crawled forward, slightly on fire and smoking like a chimney. Istvar and Cannan scrambled to their feet and fell back.

The remaining warriors rushed forward, filling the gap, protecting the champion while it recovered. Pushing his luck, Christopher stepped back and cast the spell again, narrowly avoiding including Istvar in the blaze. When the flames cleared, they left behind only ash.

If only he could do this forever. "One left," he told his companions. Twelfth rank had its limits.

"Save it for the queen," Cannan said, and leapt forward to intercept the swarm of soldiers.

Two slender ants appeared above the carpet, hovering on rapidly beating wings. Christopher had not seen these before, but Lalania had when they had attacked the circle of fire yesterday. She stepped in front of him, sheltering him. Before he could react to this unchivalrous deed, a stream of golden darts flowed out from the ants, curved around Lalania, and slammed into his chest like bullets. They hurt but not as much as watching his tael leak away like a stabbed waterskin.

Around him his men were suffering from dozens of wounds. Cannan in particular seemed to be fighting on pure adrenaline. Christopher cast a high-level spell, one of the ones gained by his new rank. Healing poured into him, the excess streaming out to replenish the men.

Forty feet away, the army of soldiers formed a ladder. Soldiers flowed up to the ceiling. Now they came at Christopher's party on two levels again. The swordsmen could not keep up. Christopher reached out to his patron for help. In response, a ring of flashing blades of light surrounded the human party at a distance of thirty feet. Every ant that tried to pass through it was diced like fruit in a blender.

Again the golden darts streamed forward. They passed through the ring of blades, swerved around Istvar's upraised shield, which was looking the worse for wear, and struck Christopher. This was getting troubling, but he wasn't entirely certain how to stop it. Gregor, given a reprieve from sword fighting, unlimbered his carbine and started firing. One of the fliers fell.

Christopher knew it was coming before it happened, although there was nothing he could do about it. Flames roared down from the ceiling, engulfing his party.

Except that everything within twenty feet of Lalania was unaffected. Where the flames did not intersect that circle, they burned the ant remains with a sickening smell. This spell was the same as Christopher's. It would have killed the lesser members of his party outright and severely depleted the higher. Instead, it had triggered Lalania's null-stone.

Deprived of magic, the party stood in the darkness. Cannan's sword no longer glowed. Christopher's armor felt heavy again, his magical strength suppressed. Lalania stopped playing the lyre now that it was only music. The notes died away, buried by the sound of tumbling stone as the entrance she had been holding closed fell to the ant's assault, allowing even more of them into the chamber. Only the circle of flashing blades just outside the radius of anti-magic held the ants at bay.

Light flared again. Einar had relit the lantern with flint and steel. Apparently it carried a store of oil as well. The Ranger seemed always prepared for any eventuality. He diffused the light to a general circle so they could see how badly they were surrounded.

"Which one will fail first?" Istvar asked.

"The blades," Lalania said.

The Duke frowned in displeasure. "I don't fancy fighting from inside this field. We cannot heal, and Ser Cannan will no longer enjoy the advantage of his sword."

Christopher told them the bad news. "When the field drops, she'll kill Lala, Cannan, and Gregor instantly." Their rank was too low to survive a spell of that power.

"Possibly," Einar said. "We may hope she is out of spells. She has already spent much; her champion was layered in magic."

Lalania held her lyre out. "Christopher, you must carry this. Your tael will protect it, and I can be revived more cheaply than it can be replaced."

He didn't take it. She was wrong. The column of flame would consume her corpse and leave him nothing but ashes.

Instead he walked backward, cautiously, until he felt his strength return. He was standing between the two rings. Another step back would thrust him into the blades, which would ironically dice him as effectively as it had the ants. A step forward would return him to the temporary safety of the null-stone.

"Your blade spell will not last forever," a voice said in his head. "Then my children will swarm over you before you can cast again."

Christopher knew it had to be the monster at the end of the hall, but it sounded just like Audrey Hepburn.

7

TEA TIME WITH THE QUEEN

He shook himself together and answered her. "You don't believe that. We've already got this far, and I still have magic left. Plus we have tricks you haven't seen yet. I think we can win."

A pause before she replied. Not petulantly; she was too polished for that, although it had the flavor of dismay. "Why tell me this?"

With her alien form out of range of the light and hidden by darkness, he could not stop himself from thinking of her as a young princess trapped in court intrigue beyond her depth. "Why talk to me at all?"

"You spared my workers when you could. I thought . . ."

"You thought you could make a deal."

"I answered your question. Now answer mine."

Now he paused, trying to understand his own actions.

In front of him, Gregor was digging in his backpack. The blue knight fished out a grenade and heaved it into the darkness. A second later, they could tell where it landed by the explosion, the blast illuminating the ants it threw up from the floor.

"You fell short twenty feet at least," Einar said, and held his hand out for one.

Christopher could feel the queen's shock in his mind. "How can you summon fire from within the anti-magic field?" she cried. "This is not fair!"

"That's two questions," he said. "Which one do you want me to answer?"

Einar's throw was better. In the flash, they could see he had reached the queen. The effect of her pain lanced through Christopher's mind like he had physically slapped her.

"It does not matter. Now that you are in my presence, I can smell the taint on you. There will be no deal. You only wanted to witness my suffering."

"No," he said, disgusted and horrified by her words even without fully understanding what she meant, but got no further.

"Then listen," she said. "Whatever part of you is still capable of feeling, hear what you would destroy."

A hundred thousand voices rang in his head. A cacophonic din, the murmur of the crowd if one could be everywhere in the crowd at the same time. He staggered, overwhelmed by the sense of closeness, of standing at the edge of ten thousand conversations.

Individual voices began to resolve. Trivial details, gossip over the blandest events, the daily lives of creatures whose entire existence was concerned with work and community. Who bumped into who in the crowded tunnels, which year of food pellet was the best, which tunnel needed repair, what the weather was going to be like tomorrow. And one plaintive voice tore at his heart, asking what was happening, like a frightened child in the dark.

"Never you mind," came an answer from a dozen sources. "Mother will take care of it. She always does."

Sudden silence. Lalania had stepped toward him, reimmersing him in the field. All of them looked at him with concern.

He shared their concern. The experience had shaken him to the core. Nonetheless, he waved Lalania back. Still dubious, she moved away.

His head was empty again, save for the queen. He could feel her attention. Struggling with his composure, he tried to regain control of the conversation, his skin crawling. "What do you mean by taint?" Had the *hjerne-spica* cursed him with some lingering effect in that one meeting in the Gold Apostle's keep? But no, that had been their second meeting. The first was in the snow, and he had been unconscious through it. It could have done anything.

Her disembodied voice was uncertain as he felt. "You did not react as I expected. Perhaps you do not know. Perhaps you serve unknowingly."

"Pretend that is true."

"You are Their creature, Their tool. They have crossed your path and touched your fate. When I divined you just now, I saw the empty places in your pattern where great powers have pushed and prodded you to their ends. Your entire history is an enigma shrouded in mystery, warped by unseen hands to some unrevealed purpose. How can you not be aware of this?"

He knew all of that. He had just thought they had failed. They had sent the ring to break his mind and broken Cannan instead. They had sent the Gold Apostle to torture him and the King to execute him, and now both those men were dead. Now they waited for him to open a path to Earth so they could consume that entire planet. He intended to see that they would fail at that, too.

On the other hand he suspected she was better at divination than anyone in his realm. Nobody else had ever mentioned empty spots and patterns.

Her voice was resigned to an infinite sadness. "Had I known I would not have avenged myself for the lives you took. Yet it would not have mattered. They send you where They will. I have communicated your status to my Empress. She does not desire conflict at this time. Therefore, your master need not fear retribution for what you do here today."

So she was being cast off by her own people, merely at the mention of the *hjerne-spica*. That was a power he would have been terrified by, if he weren't already.

"Nonetheless, I am free to defend myself. I will destroy you if I can and hope that your master turns its attention to other tools. It is the only option open to me."

He felt her turning away. "Wait," he said desperately. "I don't have a master."

She almost laughed. "We all have masters. Even the Ur-Mother serves at the whim of necessity."

He said the only thing he could think of to keep her talking. "I'm going to kill mine."

"Before or after you kill me?"

"Neither. Unless you make me. You are not my enemy."

"Of course I am," she said. "Your kind and mine must always contend, for the world is destined to belong to us. We will use it so much more efficiently than you. We will end suffering and waste, the lust of the hunter and the terror of the prey. All the planes of the Great Wheel shall fall to us in time. My daughters . . . I suppose I should say now, my nieces, down through the ages will see this glorious day. I regret only that I was of so little aid to our holy crusade."

He felt an involuntary pang of sympathy for the Wizard of Carrhill. Talking to religious zealots was definitely taxing.

"Okay, that sounds like it's a ways off."

"True enough," she conceded.

"In the meantime, we're here. I've got a *hjerne-spica* on my back and a war on my southern border. You can help me with at least one of those."

"You started this war. You invaded my realm and killed my warriors. And then you did unspeakable things with their corpses."

"I didn't do that. My predecessor did."

"From my perspective, there is no difference. The fact remains that humans from your lands slaughtered and despoiled my people. In exchange I took the souls I was owed, along with a small increase for my troubles. Did you expect me to do nothing?"

"I didn't expect anything because I didn't know you existed. If you had asked, I would have reimbursed you."

She paused, surprised. "Really?"

He thought about it. "Probably. Well, maybe."

"Instead you have lain waste to my realm. Half of my army lies dead, and my children shiver in their chambers, waiting for madness. Is this the concept you call justice?"

He shook his head. "You don't get to lecture me on justice. You killed innocent people because other people hurt you."

"And you slaughtered those who only defended their home from armed intruders."

She had him there. But he was not going to apologize. It wouldn't help.

"We have about five more minutes before those blades come down. Then we're going to fight, and one of us will die. If you have any way out of that, now's the time to bring it up."

"You could choose to walk away," she suggested. "I could choose to let you."

The rest of his party was listening to his half of the conversation. It was just easier to speak out loud. He closed his eyes because he did not want to see their reactions. "You named yourself my enemy. How does leaving you alive help me?"

"It does not," she conceded. "And yet it could. You need never face me in battle again. I will not intrude on your lands if you do not intrude on mine. I will let you keep the souls you have already collected and return the rest of my dead children to the larders without prejudice. And I will give you a tool against Them."

He had come here looking for monsters. Their tael would move him closer to the rank where he could challenge the *hjerne-spica*. Instead he had found arguments. He should not have listened. He should have fought in silence, thinking her just a foe to be destroyed, just as she said she was. As Lalania would no doubt tell him, it would have been the normal thing to do.

Instead, he did what he always did. "What can you give me?"

Now he could afford to open his eyes. Only Istvar seemed disappointed. Einar was calculating. Gregor was relieved. Lalania was amused. Cannan was stabbing at ant corpses just outside the circle and draining their tael with his sword.

"What you could not get anywhere else. It may not help; you may never thank me for it. But it will be one thing They will not expect you to have. What you make of it will be up to you."

He could not refuse. The *hjerne-spica* knew every move he could make. Only here, inside the cloaking spell of the ant queen's wards, could he hatch surprises, just as Alaine had told him secrets at the bottom of the goblin's keep. There was a lesson in that. The foes he battled offered resources other than tael. He would need all of them.

"Okay," he said.

"You swear it, by your patron and affiliation?"

"I do."

"Then I swear by the Ur-Mother: truce and a tribute. Come forward. Bring your null-stone if you please. You might not survive the journey otherwise, and I would rather not have to reset all of my traps afterward."

He stepped forward into the circle, where the queen could not read his mind.

"You made a deal," Gregor said.

"I did."

Einar cocked his head. "Have you reclaimed the bodies of my kin so that we may return them to the cycle?"

"No," Christopher said. "I'm sorry, but they're gone. The ants eat . . . everything."

"To be honest, we already knew that. Yet we thought we might at least gain vengeance. How shall I go to my people and tell them you have made a deal instead?"

Istvar growled. "I find myself also indisposed. You bleed the realm for every scrap of tael, and yet you will leave millions in the ground for the sake of mercy?"

"She promised me something to fight the *hjerne-spica* with. What good does it do me to gain rank if at the end it just eats me? What good does that do any of us?"

"Half the kingdom still doubts such creatures are real. Will you parade this fantastic weapon through the streets to convince them otherwise?" Istvar asked.

"No, of course not," Lalania said. "He'll keep it secret and expect the rest of us to make up a story that satisfies the people."

Christopher thought about stepping back outside the circle. The ant queen's conversation had been less painful.

Gregor shook his head. "The time for reservations has passed. We all signed on for this ride no matter how perilous the road."

"Your faith is commendable," Istvar said stiffly, "but it is not my faith."

"And yet, when you pray, does Foresetti guide you from this path?" Gregor shot back.

An uncomfortable silence followed. The blades whirred softly one last time and faded away.

"The gods give us less direction than we would hope," Istvar finally said. "As you already know. Yet I have chosen. I will tell my people that the Saint took what he was entitled to and no more."

"I will tell my people he is a squirrelly devil whose abuse we must suffer yet a while longer." Einar grinned wolfishly. "We have said the same of kings for generations."

"And I will tell the people you made the queen beg for mercy. Pray do not correct the record." Lalania shivered despite the heat. "Now what do we do to get out of here?"

Christopher waved them forward. The sea of ants parted as they walked across the long cavern. The queen's great bulk gradually came into focus, towering over them, growing from suggestive shadow to solid nightmare. Up close Christopher could see that her legs were not to scale. They did not even reach the ground.

A small, freshly formed ant, still shiny and wet, wriggled out from underneath the queen, holding something small and round. It paused just outside the circle and held the object up in offering.

"It wants you to step outside our protection," Lalania said. Her tone suggested this was an absurd request, tantamount to the lion asking the trainer to insert his head in its mouth.

At this moment, most people would have questioned the wisdom of such an act. Perhaps it was a trick to get Christopher close enough where her mandibles could reach him. Despite the fact she could not walk, her massive head had considerable range. Maybe she had a spell that only worked at point-blank range. Against this proposition was the fact that she had let Christopher bring all his swordsmen into striking range. She was at as much risk as he was.

Of course, neither she nor he had even considered the issue. His affiliation was White; hers was Yellow. They could be trusted to keep their word. Even the goblins had kept their word, after a fashion. The ulvenmen had been too proud to lie. The *hjerne-spica* had told him only true things, however misleading. The only dishonesty he had faced in this world had come in human form.

He stepped forward, out of the safety of the circle. Her voice was in his head again, no louder than before.

"You can now say you have stood in court with a Formian Queen. Few of your kind ever hold this distinction."

It was like a sight-seeing souvenir. Another magnet on the refrigerator, another supernatural beast to mark off on his bingo card. Dragons and elves and now giant ants. And of course, the *hjerne-spica* in the center of the card, the one space he would have preferred to not fill.

She apparently could detect his skepticism. "Should you ever meet another of my kind, you may find the distinction useful. But I confess the probability of that is vanishingly small. Honesty compels me to acknowledge that you will almost certainly lose any confrontation with Them and die screaming before being repurposed from tool to host."

"I haven't lost yet," he said. "People keep underestimating me."

"You underestimate Them," she said ruefully. "As we all do. They see to ends even the Ur-Mother cannot scry. As much as I sincerely wish for your success, I can give you no help other than plain and simple advice: avoid the obvious, the reasonable, or even the possible, for They will have foreseen all of those."

"And this," he reminded her, pointing at the gift.

"And this," she conceded. "Whether it can be of any value to you, I cannot say. If you learn to tolerate it, you may gain a momentary edge in a physical confrontation. It is up to you to leverage that into advantage, for this is the only gift I can give you. At worst I can tell you they will not expect it; the substance is incomprehensibly difficult to obtain."

The small ant shuffled forward.

"As with most things, start small and work your way up. It will always hurt, but in time it may not incapacitate. I myself have suffered the regime, although I will probably never face Their touch."

He took the lump from the small ant's grasp. It was a small pottery vial sealed with a plug so well-fit it did not leak. An artifact made solely for function, without a single thought for appearance.

"Don't thank me," she said before he could. "You will regret it later. Now go and do not return. I do not wish your taint to encompass me; I do not wish the web of divinations to weave my thread across your weft."

Their newly hatched guide led them unerringly up through the same tunnels they had come down. Halfway out the null-stone field disappeared. The device had a limited number of uses, but there was no way to tell how many remained. There wasn't even a way to be sure it would work the next time. It was activated by magic cast at it or its wearer; trying to detect magic on it would just trigger the effect.

With its absence, the rest of their spells came back. The magic swords resumed their glow, and Christopher's armor got a lot less burdensome.

The entrance had been collapsed and hastily restored since they had used it. The ant picked its way through the rubble. At the edge of the warding effect, it sidled to the side and waved cheerily at them as they walked past.

The squad of soldiers crouching behind earthen fortifications outside the tunnel mouth lowered their rifles. Christopher looked out over the cannon barrels still pointed in his direction.

"My lord Saint?" asked the sergeant, standing up in confusion. "Are you victorious?"

"Sure," Christopher said. "Let's go with that."

8

PLAYING DOCTOR

H is soldiers were disciplined. They did as they were told, withdrawing their blockades of ant tunnels back into the camp. Nonetheless, they communicated their confusion and disappointment. The army had suffered serious losses, a dozen men Christopher could not revive because acid had ruined their corpses. He added them to the growing stock of soldiers who would require the more expensive revival, the one that worked from as little as a fingernail.

This spell was still denied to him. Although he was now the same rank as Saint Krellyan had been, he served a different patron. The priests and priestesses of the Bright Lady were better at healing but worse at everything else. As a priest of Marcius, a lesser aspect from her pantheon, Christopher could cast a few spells that Krellyan had never seen. And he could throw around columns of fire like nobody's business. At the moment, he would have traded it all for a way to hide from the faces of his men.

Istvar was worse. He talked. "You could have gained a rank from this. Yet you march home with nothing to show for the sacrifices of your soldiers. If you think the army is dismayed, wait until you face the families of your mausoleum. They have been waiting two years or more for the resurrection of their husbands and fathers."

"Two years in which you have drained the realm just to reach this rank," Einar added. "How much longer do you expect the nobility to let you sequester every scrap of tael? If you are not going to exert yourself to climb the ranks, why should they hold you on their shoulders?"

It wasn't a total loss. Cannan's sword had brought out a healthy chunk of tael. To anyone else, it would represent promotion through multiple ranks. To Christopher, it was barely a drop in the bucket.

The price of rank doubled with every step; the distance from twelve to thirteen was as great as the distance from commoner to Saint. He had only reached twelve after devastating three nations: the ulvenmen, the goblins, and arguably the human kingdom itself. Absent the slaughter of civil war, tael only accumulated when people died of old age. And the spread of his policies and his promotions of healing priests had actually slowed the natural death rate. He had made up for this by denying the nobility their share, promoting only lower ranked priests from the White and the Blue, and consuming the rest of the tael himself.

He had avoided the immediate and obvious rebellion by pointing to a destination. When he achieved sufficient rank, he could open a gate to Earth and bring over all sorts of wonderful toys. This would make the common folk happy. It would not particularly make the nobles happy, as they were already diminished by the effect of guns and cannons. Better guns and bigger cannons would only lower them further. Unfortunately, some of them were starting to figure this out. The fiction was that once he achieved his goal, he would return the tax rate to the normal arrangement. He had never actually said this because he wasn't allowed to lie. But to anyone with half a brain not hidebound by tradition, it should have been obvious that empowering the commoners even more would not be the pivot at which the nobility regained their privilege. Luckily for him, half the brains of the kingdom were concentrated in the College of Troubadours, and they were on his side.

There still remained one mathematical detail. He would need to achieve five more ranks to command magic potent enough to travel to Earth and return. Late at night, he had done calculations on scraps of paper and burned them when he didn't like the results. At the current rate of production, he would die of old age long before he reached his goal.

Destroying the ant nation, eating every one of their souls, would have gained him at best a rank or two. Even if it had raised him four ranks, it would not have mattered. The final rank alone represented the death of a million sentient beings. If he murdered every living thing within a thousand miles, he would still fall short. Not to mention the inevitable descent into madness.

Paradoxically, the impossibility of the task freed him. He could not achieve his goals by conventional means. Hence, he must seek another path. Now if only he could find it.

To be sure, that path included murder. One way or another, he would have to kill. But there were creatures he wouldn't mind killing. The *hjerne-spica* were at the top of that list. Conveniently, as creatures of immense power, they yielded as much tael as whole civilizations. All he had to do was decapitate a fistful of the most fearsome monsters to escape anyone's nightmare.

He looked over the two nobles, past them to the men tearing down tents and packing wagons, and said nothing. There were few places he could speak openly and fewer people he could speak to. Ironically, the ant queen had been one of them. He already missed her.

Lalania spoke for him. "Our lord does as he must. Surely we all have learned that by now. He has always marched to a different drummer, yet success speaks for itself."

"The unmarked path is always more profitable, until it isn't," Einar said. "Disaster can lay around the next corner as easily as treasure."

"It is not us you must convince," Istvar said. "I have already committed my lot, however much I may regret that from time to time. There are many Green lords who still sit on thrones. To date they have not tried to subvert your rule. That may change if you appear to weaken."

"Perhaps they should not sit then," Einar suggested. "If Christopher lays claim to the tael of the kingdom, he still takes only the traditional portion from the hunt. Let them adventure in the Wild and bring home their profits."

Lalania wrinkled her nose. "And when they trespass on some other realm? Such as the very one we now march away from? Shall Christopher answer for every raider and brigand we export?"

"If he answered traditionally he would be drowning in tael." Istvar shrugged. "Perhaps the Rangers can find us a target acceptable to Christopher's sensibilities. Such as another ulvenman nation."

"Those things don't grow on trees," Einar said. "For the record, we have no known neighboring states. Well, other than this one, apparently."

"They are out there," Cannan stated. He was standing next to Christopher, as always, as close as a shadow. "You just have to travel far enough. As Niona and I did."

The Ranger's face was hard when he finally answered. "Had you come to us with your report, we might have made you one of us. But you did not."

"Had I done so, a great many things might be different. I do not need you to tell me that." Challenging words, said without a hint of challenge. Cannan was already back to scanning the perimeter for threats, his part of the conversation finished.

"I'm not sure it matters," Istvar said. "I know you have reinvented the humble wagon, Christopher, but there is still a limit to how far we can project force. Soldiers must be fed, and we need their hands to harvest the crop."

He was trying to build a steam engine, but the things weren't as simple as they sounded. A railroad across the kingdom would surely be good for the economy. One deep into the wilderness might let him send an army against some distant target. True, the idea of laying rails on the march might sound counterintuitive, but he had Lalania and the lyre. He imagined her astride a railroad engine, the white mist out in front laying tracks as fast as the train ran. It made a nice cartoon.

He laughed.

"My lord?" Istvar said politely, although with the Duke even politeness carried a backing of steel.

"Sorry," Christopher said. "I was thinking of something else."

"As we should be," Lalania said. "We have our marching orders,

Sers. Mine are no less onerous than yours. Yet our lord requires it, so it shall be done."

Without further comment, the noblemen walked away. Lalania turned to him and lowered her voice. "Perhaps you were thinking of the results of our latest endeavor. I confess I have questions myself, although humor was not the affect I would have chosen."

"Come to my tent tonight," Christopher said. "I think I can answer them."

Lalania stepped warily through his tent, like a cat on shredded paper. He had sent Cannan away on an errand and waited for her alone, lying in his cot, already out of his armor. From any other, it would be an invitation. He wondered whether she were frightened that it was or disappointed that it would not be. His own feelings on the subject were not to be trusted, so he didn't.

"I need your special skills." He winced at the flash in her eyes, so quickly buried by thespian discipline. "Not those," he said, his tongue clumsy. "I mean . . ." Unable to figure out how to extricate himself, he just skipped to the end. "You know what to do with this," handing her the clay vial.

"Who do you want me to kill?" she said, her voice forced into lightness.

"Nobody," he answered, striving to match her tone. "It's for me."

Her eyebrows went up in appreciation. "You understand what you are signing up for?"

"Not really." Finally something he could be honest about. "I know it will hurt. But if I don't go through with it, the ant adventure really was a failure."

"I cannot heal. Let us wait until we are in the presence of the Cardinal, at least."

"No. It won't kill me, if you start low enough. I don't need a doctor. I need someone who understands poison. That means a bard. I need someone I can trust to keep a secret. That means you."

"You are also trusting the ant queen. To a vast extent."

"Shouldn't I?"

She smiled at him. "The first time you ask for my advice, and you already know the answer. I shall consider it the success of my tutelage."

"Then let's get started. I don't know how long it will take to recover, and I'd rather not try to explain why I can't get out of bed in the morning."

Her smile gradually faded as she concentrated on her task. She opened the vial with the delicacy of a jewel heist and studied it. Eventually, she removed a pin from her hair and briefly touched it to the contents.

With her other hand, she pulled off the leather band that held her hair in a ponytail.

"Bite this," she instructed. "You can't regenerate teeth yet."

When he was ready, she smiled at him apologetically and put the pin against his bare neck.

For a moment he was back in the inn, poisoned, paralyzed, and surrounded by fire. Except this time he was on fire. The pain bloomed from his neck, engulfing his entire body in searing heat. He tried to scream, but his jaws were locked shut. Every muscle in his body activated all at once, fighting each other to a stalemate.

Above him Lalania's eyes were wide with horror and fear. In the back of his head, he could hear the voice of the animated suit of armor that served as avatar to his god. It offered him release from the paralysis; he could, by divine favor, move for a few minutes if he wanted to.

It would not be release from the pain, though. In his current state, being paralyzed was the best defense of dignity. He had once been tortured to death, and yet now that experience seemed pale in comparison. If he could move, he would only shriek, weep, and soil himself. Or worse, he would cast a healing spell and completely undo the entire point of the exercise.

He clung to the idea that he could end the pain at will, a life raft in a sea of red mist. Gradually, the mist faded to black.

⬥

Light flooded the tent. Karl stood in the open doorway, staring down at him with disapproval. "Why are you still abed?"

Christopher croaked something unintelligible.

Karl frowned and walked away, letting the tent door drop.

He struggled to sit up. It took several tries before he could force out the words of the healing spell. Afterward the soreness was gone, although he still felt like he'd been run over by a truck. One of the big ones, with eighteen wheels.

Cannan watched carefully, sitting on the edge of his own cot. The big man said nothing; presumably Lalania had informed him of the night's activities.

When Christopher finally left the tent, he was careful to disguise how badly he felt. Soldiers began stripping it down as soon as he stepped outside. The rest of the camp was already gone, packed into wagons for the journey home.

"How do you feel, my lord?" Lalania asked him as she handed him a bowl of cold porridge.

"I didn't sleep well," he admitted.

"Not usually what I hear after I leave a man's tent," she muttered.

"Careful with that kind of talk."

She glared at the rebuke but said nothing. The army believed that his chastity was the source of his power. He was pretty sure that was absurd; none of the various supernatural entities he had dealt with had ever inquired about his romantic activities. However, the proposition remained untested as Lalania was the only woman on this planet who interested him in that way, and she had come to respect his devotion to his wife. If that bond weakened, he feared he would lose the heart necessary for the impossible task ahead of him. Like healing the poison would only invalidate the exercise, falling for Lalania would end his current pain at the expense of making a mockery of everything he had suffered so far.

In a way, then, the army was right. He went to take his place at the head of the column, passing men who looked the other way rather than let him see their disappointment. Royal was waiting for him. The huge warhorse snuffled at him, its affection undiminished by the events of the last day and night.

9

GAME THEORY

O ver the next weeks, they developed a routine. Lalania would come to his room in the castle every few nights and dose him. The pain never lessened, but in time he learned to deal with it. The paralytic effect began to slowly diminish. When he could move again after only an hour, she would nod in approval and the next time increase the dose.

The change in protocol did not go unnoticed. Christopher saw the way common soldiers looked at Lalania behind her back. She had long been a favorite of the men, generous as she was with her magic, her songs, and sometimes her affections. At the same time, she had always been their greatest fear. If Christopher took to enjoying the company of harlots, he would cease to be the transformative figure to whom they had pledged. As just another ruler, a conventional king, he would still be a thousand times better than the last one, but the commoners did not care. They dreamed of freedom, not merely the absence of tyranny. The hopes of the long dispossessed could not be bounded by pragmatism.

She responded by becoming almost prim. Her hemlines got longer, and her hair was tamed into a matronly bun. This stilled the soldiers somewhat, but he could still feel their attitude reflected in his interactions with the nobility, ripples spreading across a pond. He had made his career out of being utterly unconventional, and now the merest hint of conventionality made people pause and reassess. Could he be toppled? Could his holy quest be diverted, delayed, or canceled altogether? Was there room at the margins of his absolute law to still seek profit and promotion?

So far it was only calculating looks and occasional inappropriate conversational pauses. The White Church, still under Cardinal Faren's iron hand, served him as loyally as they had served Saint Krellyan. The worst of the Dark lords were systematically being replaced with Bright vicars. Invariably, the disposed lords chose to take their chances in the Wild, marching off with a handful of loyal retainers in search of adventure and therefore treasure. Realistically, any one of them could stumble across some ridiculous long-lost artifact and return to destroy him, but he had to let them go. There were some traditions he dared not defy. Besides, he could never bring himself to murder people for nothing more than profit, even as much as he ached at watching the tael in their heads wandering off to vanish in the great dark forest.

Then one day, Lalania reported an unusual fact. The last lord to depart had left behind a fair amount of property in the hands of some of his retainers instead of selling it all off for portable wealth. This was the sort of thing one might do if one expected to return within a few years. Christopher's reign had apparently acquired an expiration date.

"What should I do about it?" he asked her.

She shrugged. "Traditional tactics suggest you allow a plot to develop against you—encourage one even—so that you can ferret out the ringleaders, whom you then hang as an example to the rest."

"I can't do that," he said, but she already knew that.

"In which case you must simply prepare for trouble. Unless you can hasten your final goal."

"I can't do that either," he said glumly.

"We should step up our security protocols. Your castle is shockingly open to infiltration. There are still poisons you should fear. Or possibly spells whose trigger must be delivered manually."

Neither of those seemed likely to him. By now the assassins of the kingdom should have learned to stop expecting poison to work, and the only two spell-casters of note were the Wizard and the Witch, both of whom knew he controlled an artifact that blocked magic. Or rather Lalania did.

"I don't need more security. I just need you."

She smiled. "Sweetly worded, but there are limits to what I can do. Yet there are limits to what the College can do, too. If we add agents in the capital that perforce means removing them from the provinces. And I would rather not be caught by surprise in either field."

An idea began to form in his mind, half-shaped and misty. "Could you do more with more rank?"

"Always," she said with a saucy smirk. "But we cannot pretend that rises to the bar of necessity you have established for promotion."

The idea condensed, opaque.

"And yet it is my right to decide."

"It is," she said cautiously.

The silver vial hung heavy around his neck these days, although it was entirely psychological. Tael had no weight. He pulled it out from under his tunic and screwed it open. Inside were the winnings that Cannan's sword had harvested, a solid lump that expanded to the size of a pomegranate when he took it all out. In this case, he poured out a smaller portion of precise quantity. It formed a tiny sphere in his hand, shining bright purple where the torchlight caught it.

Cannan, ever-present, glanced at him instinctively and then scanned the room on high alert. Lalania, the only other person in the room, managed to look both hungry and flirtatious at once.

"Is this enough?" he asked, unnecessarily.

"It is," she agreed again. "It is cruel to make me argue against my own promotion, yet foolish to proceed. To raise me to Jongleur can only muddy the waters. Uma is Friea's undisputed heir; you would throw the College as well as the kingdom into confusion with your intent."

"On the contrary. You have argued for your case." He handed her the lump before he could change his mind. Once the tael left his hand, he knew he had done the right thing. Whatever came next, Lalania had earned it.

She paused, her hand halfway to her mouth. "Tongues already wag.

How shall they wave when I receive gifts from you? I cannot dress any more demurely without being mistaken for a widow. And I cannot keep this secret for very long. It will grant me a new rank of magic, which I will eventually use."

"Use it right away," he told her. "Leave your agents in the courts of the country lords. And leave the gossip to me."

He watched her consume the purple ball. So did Cannan, the spectacle drawing his eyes away from watching for danger. It was a simple act fraught with the significance of life and death. In a single stroke, he had doubled the vitality of the woman and tripled her power. By his rough calculations, she was now a fourth-story figure: he could toss her out of a window on the fourth floor and her tael would be sufficient to let her walk way without a scratch. Cannan, although only third rank, was even more durable thanks to his profession; Christopher was somewhere around the fifteenth or sixteenth floor.

Once the tael was safely gone beyond recovery, Lalania frowned. "No good will come of this," she warned.

"No," he said, "I suppose it won't."

The idea taking shape in his mind formed a grinning leer. Good wasn't the intent.

~~~

A week later he added fuel to the fire. He called his pet witch Fae and her coterie of apprentices to court. The woman had always been a sharp-featured beauty; now, with her cherubic two-year-old daughter in tow, she was a veritable Madonna. Her apprentices had mastered the art of fashion and no longer dressed like a peasant's idea of a seductress. Instead, they dressed like actual seductresses. All of whom pitched at him for all they were worth even while they curtsied modestly in his presence.

"I've decided to promote you for your service to the realm." The witches refined his sulfur. He had promoted them before, advancing them along the apprentice track. Today he handed each of them enough tael to reach the first true rank of wizardry.

The look on their faces was more powerful than all of Lalania's art. Adoration beamed out, replaced by rapture when he nodded and they gulped down the tiny purple pellets.

"You are free of my tutelage," Fae told them, hiding her resentment reasonably well. "Sooner than any apprentice ever dared hope. And yet not without merit. Our lord's wisdom seals your rise."

"Not entirely," Christopher said. "I would prefer you keep an eye on them for the time being. To that end, I have a promotion for you as well." He handed Fae a substantially larger ball of tael.

She was too calculating, too cynical, to give into simple adoration. Yet the invitation in her eyes was no less real. He had just promoted her two ranks, opening a new level of magic. The damage she had done with just the first level made this a seriously questionable act, but the ghost of the strategy in his head smiled on it.

"You reward us beyond our service," she whispered. Only he could hear her despite the crowd gathered in the throne room. "You must know we would serve you however you desire. Trial our true feeling against the artifice of your troubadours. Let us shower you with our personal gratitude."

It was a heady compliment delivered in a husky voice of desire. It was also relatively easy to resist. Fae scared him, and her girls evoked the same feelings a passel of tiger cubs did. Cute, but you wouldn't want to be around them when they grew up.

The strategy took over his mouth and formed words. "Come to my chambers sometime," he whispered. There were at least a dozen people in the room who would have read his lips, and that only counted the ones who worked for him. He added an unnecessary condition solely for the eavesdroppers. "Discreetly, if you please." Fae didn't need to be told; it was the nature of wizards to keep secrets.

Beside him he felt Lalania's smile freeze. Her jealousy sent a little thrill through him, which was far more discomforting than all of Fae's innuendo.

It was several days before Fae took him up on the offer. She had sequestered Sigrath's old apartments in the castle and seemed to be establishing it as a second residence. With their promotions, the apprentices could now handle the powder mill in Knockford, leaving Fae free to take up the role of court wizard. That was a position he could not deny her, but he was still surprised to turn around in his own bedchamber at night and find her standing there.

Cannan had his sword out in a heartbeat, raised to strike. The woman ignored him, her face serene above the flimsy lace pretense of a dress she wore.

"My lord," she said, bowing low.

"How did you get in here?" Christopher asked. "Did anyone see you?" He wanted to add "in that ridiculous outfit," but decided not to introduce the topic.

"I assure you, my lord, I was unseen. Your bards picked over Master Sigrath's possessions quite thoroughly but could not deny me his spell-books. Your benefice already manifests itself."

He was pretty sure that was a complicated way to say that she could now turn herself invisible. Everything about the woman was complicated.

"That's great," he said, and handed her a bathrobe. "Put this on. You must be cold." It was always cold in the castle.

"If you insist," she answered, taking the robe without looking at it.

"That she comes alone implies she also evaded the bard," Cannan observed. He was glaring at her.

"The lady is skilled," Fae conceded in a way that made it clear she was about to backhand the lady with a compliment, "but few are skilled enough to defeat magic."

That was the point of his strategy. His enemies were drowning in magic. He wasn't going to beat them with skill.

"Tell me about divinations," he said, sitting on a chair next to the fireplace. She took another chair and folded the robe across her lap.

"An odd choice, Christopher." She cocked her head at him, and he almost laughed. The very instant he wanted something from her, their relationship reverted to a first-name basis. "Divination is more oft associated with divinity. For the arcane it is generally limited to inspection of the here and now."

"Scrying isn't about the here." Keeping up points with her was both instinctive and necessary in any conversation.

She smiled condescendingly. "I meant here as in 'on this plane.'"

It was also hard.

"But I assume you mean foretelling," she continued. "It is normal for the head of state to demand a generic divination every week. I would assume you do it yourself, though. Or perhaps the Cardinal?"

He did let the Cardinal do it. The old man had volunteered and understood how to interpret the results better. Faren had assured him that if the realm were going to be destroyed, he'd have a week's fore-notice, though anything less dire than that was likely to slip through the net.

"I do mean forecasting. How does it work?"

She looked at him for moment. "Not as well as one would hope. A week's advance is normally the limit. At best it reveals the probable course of events; should someone else divine that you have divined their plan, they may well change their plans and thus invalidate your foreknowledge. At worst the entity you contact has no knowledge of the affairs that concern you. Gods and demons have vast sight, yet it falls far short of omniscient. Events can be concealed by high-rank magic; facts no longer in the memory of the living may be unknown to even the greatest power. But why haven't the bards already explained this?"

He sighed. In a minute she was going to lecture him for revealing secrets. Namely, that the College could not do forecasting, which is why they couldn't answer his questions.

"They did," he said as truthfully as he could. "As much as they know. I wondered what a wizard's take on it is."

"My take is that it's not worth the risk. For you to chat with an extraplanar entity is business as usual. For us it is fraught with peril. We do not wish to be servants or allies of such creatures. They do not wish to reveal anything for free. Binding a demon to physical service is straightforward and relatively safe. Asking it for advice is asking for trouble."

"I think the Wizard of Carrhill did it once."

"I am not surprised. He takes inordinate risks."

Christopher thought about the woman's precious toddler, sleeping elsewhere in the castle, and looked at her dubiously.

She colored, slightly. "I concede the point. Being in your presence seems to provoke rashness."

As always, she found a way to make it his fault.

"A week? That doesn't seem to leave room for decades-spanning prophecy."

"Prophecy is a different matter. The gods can make promises about the future because they have the power to make them come true regardless of what anyone else does."

He hadn't thought of it that way.

"Have you been exposed to a prophecy?" she asked. She aimed for coy, but her naked hunger for secrets pushed it into lustful territory. Not a good place to be with her dressed like that.

"I don't think so." Marcius had offered him hopes, not prophecies.

"Then count yourself blessed."

He harrumphed. That was not a description anyone would assign to his place, wedged between dragons, elves, evil squidlings, and inscrutable gods.

"But I trust you did not summon me here to discuss spell-craft. We could do that at court." With an artful shrug, she managed to make her dress even more revealing. "Surely you have other topics in mind."

"Not really," he said. He looked away from her to stare into the fire, unable to insult her to her face. Especially because it would become a lie if he kept staring at her.

"If not me, then let me summon one of my girls. Or all of them. It would mean much to them. To any woman."

"I'm not—" he started, but she interrupted him.

"You are reasonably strong, acceptably handsome, and incredibly wealthy. Your meteoric rise is a beacon of virtue, the gods own stamp on the quality of your character. You are kind to the point of bewilderment and lethal beyond imagination. You are the stuff of dreams of every fresh-blooded girl on this plane."

The heat of the fireplace beat at his face. He blurted out the only thing he could say, the simplest truth. "I don't want to be. I just want to be me."

She stared at him, much as she had stared at the mysterious and powerful ring he had once asked her to destroy.

"Nothing you have ever done or said is as mystifying as that."

At this point it was pretty mystifying to him, too. He feared it might just be habit.

"And yet," she said, every word dragged out of her grudgingly, "there can be no greater defense against divination. Whatever wellspring drives you resists the analysis of the sane and sober. It stinks of divine providence. Only one force can hide secrets from the gods."

Tired of walking into her rhetorical traps, he simply waited.

She smiled at him. "Another god, of course. Your Patron works through you."

I am not your plaything. The memory of the words echoed in his mind. How much he had in common with his human enemies; how little he shared with his nonhuman allies.

Fae stood up, wrapping the fluffy robe about herself. "I presume you wish my discreetness to discreetly fail. This is a service I can render, although it pains me that any would be foolish enough to think my secrets can be plundered against my will. You need not worry; I will play my part as instructed. I fear you too much to do otherwise. As do all who serve you. Only your foes are protected from the terror of your mysteries."

She turned to Cannan and acknowledged him for the first time. "If you would be so kind as to see to the door, Ser."

Cannan glared at her much as he had at the Wizard of Carrhill, back in Lalania's tent years ago. When he turned away long enough to open the door, she vanished.

After a moment Cannan spoke. "How long am I supposed to hold this door open?"

Christopher held up his hand in a pause. There was no reply. After a moment he said, "I guess that's good enough."

Cannan closed the door. "Just to be clear. I'm not taking this one off your hands. You don't pay me enough for that."

10

THE BRIDGE

The remains of another season swirled around his horse's feet, maple leaves in many colors swept along by a brisk autumn wind. A crimson leaf blew from the ground and clung to his boot. He glanced down in melancholy. The years were beginning to pile up; he felt the weight of them on his memories, pressing them into flat images.

The present was alive and vibrant. He was stronger and healthier than he had ever been on Earth. He still sparred regularly with Cannan and Gregor, Karl kept him in the exercise yard, and the simple acts of everyday life were so much more active here. Leadership could not be asserted from a desk in a world without telephones. He had to personally see to problems in the field, visit his delegates in the flesh, and traverse an entire kingdom.

This should have been easy because he had many ways to fly. Unfortunately, all of them were limited to two or three people at a time. He had made a promise to his army long ago that he would not leave them behind again. Given all he expected of them now, it was one promise he dared not break. So he traveled the countryside on horseback, accompanied by dozens of armed and armored cavalrymen. He stood in the saddle for hours as his huge warhorse trotted over distances that would have taken minutes in the leather-cushioned luxury of a car.

Royal was in his prime. The horse was as healthy as . . . well, extremely healthy. The dedication of the palace grooms was the best care an animal could have. When that failed, there was always magic. The destrier loved to run at the head of a herd, snorting and stepping high. Christopher had inquired discreetly and been told he could expect another four years before age would begin to slow and weaken the beast. It felt like a deadline.

He didn't dare ask how many more years before age would affect him. The people of the kingdom generally underestimated his age, which Lalania assured him was a benefit. Growing up in modern comfort had left him soft but also unscarred and unused, and Krellyan's regeneration had removed what little scars he had earned. Here, the rigors of preindustrial life that made people so strong also wore them out early. Despite the fact that he could not regenerate teeth or limbs, he still had potent healing magic. He could expect to be a swordsman long past the time any professional on Earth would have to retire. Perhaps two or even three more decades.

A long time. Too long, for those flattening memories to endure; and yet, not long enough. A century of ruling would not bring in enough tael to achieve his goal. And he was pretty sure the kingdom didn't have a century's worth of patience.

An avatar of that impatience waited for him at the bridge. His troop had run cross-country for the sake of security and the animals. Royal, like all horses, hated the new concrete paving that Christopher was pouring all over the country. It was a mixed blessing. On the one hand, the draft horses that moved every pound of food from farm to town and city no longer had to struggle against grasping mud. On the other hand, the pavement rang hard under their steel-shod hooves. Christopher was not sure which was better for the animal's long-term health. Not that it mattered; the roads effectively increased the food supply of the realm as fewer crops were lost to transport and spoilage. The welfare of the animals would never trump the welfare of the people who owned the animals.

He dismounted and slowly led Royal onto the paved road, waiting for his troop. Although he rode at the front of the column most of the time, whenever they came to a chokepoint like a bridge or hedge-gate, half his men would go through first. Christopher had learned to respect thresholds.

In this case, they held back. The man at the bridge was a nobleman. He had the right to speak to Christopher directly. At Christopher's approach, he stood straight and clasped his hands behind his back.

"Well met, my lord," the young man said, inclining his head in respect. Rangers did not bow.

"Well met, Ser D'Kan," Christopher replied, although the pleasantry might well qualify as a lie. This meeting, so far from the formality of court, could only be bad news.

"Ser Cannan," the Ranger said, acknowledging the red knight at Christopher's side.

"Get to the point, boy," Cannan said. The words lacked sting; the two men had made their peace years ago. Their conflict was only habit now.

"Why should I have a point? Can not a nobleman ride the length of the kingdom for the sake of pleasure? Can not a servant meet his lord in the field only to pay his respects?"

Ironic questions. Christopher didn't bother to speak.

"Indeed," D'Kan said, as if Christopher's silence were answer enough. "Even the roads are a trial now. Peasant wagons take precedence over warhorses. Much is changed."

"The price of bread is down seven percent," Christopher said.

"Pity the bakers." D'Kan shrugged, his tone admitting he did not really care about bakers. "Yet no doubt they will absorb the loss and keep baking."

Actually, the bakers were happy because the cost of their ingredients had fallen at least ten percent, but D'Kan was not here to receive a lesson in economics. He was here for something else.

"They will," Christopher said, "as far as I know. But if anyone knows differently, they should tell me."

"'Know' is a strong word," the Ranger said. "Intimate. Suspect. Fear. These are softer words, if you are interested in them."

"I am." Christopher tried not to growl.

D'Kan dropped the act like a wet blanket. "Rank was ever hard to earn; now it is impossible. Young men watch their lives pass by and wonder how they can qualify for the peerage before they are too decrepit to lead. Young women note that their service to their faith must be justified by arcane procedures and standards they neither understand nor accept. It is all fine and well for the old to counsel patience because they have either achieved rank or given up on it. For the rest of us, we see only opportunity marching away with each passing day. Discontent brews upon itself like ale fermenting in a cask. Left too long, it will explode."

"How long?"

"I am not a brewer. I cannot read a recipe with any certainty. Yet parties of young hopefuls push the edges of our maps of the Wild, seeking treasure not yet sequestered by your law. With it comes risk. Risk that the adventurers will not return. Greater risk that they will. Nothing feeds ambition like success."

One result leds to angry parents, who were ranked enough to cause him trouble. The other led to greater ranks for the people already causing the trouble.

"I assume you already know the state of your realm," D'Kan said, resuming the mask of a polite young man. "I only introduce the topic by way of courtesy. I and several others plan to seek out the Cattlemen of Ser Cannan's past adventure. If there were any messages you care to send, Ser, I would endeavor to deliver them."

Cannan smiled in grim amusement. "There was an outrider named Ragnar. He is honorable enough and may attach some respect to my name. Your sister once healed his child, for which he will still be grateful. For the rest, I can offer you nothing you should not already know."

It felt like very little to Christopher, but D'Kan seemed satisfied. Cannan had armed the Ranger with information without laying restraints on how he used it. A neat trick that Christopher had not yet mastered: helping people without also binding their choices to his own ends.

"I should offer you something, too," Christopher mused aloud, uncertain until the words left his lips.

"Our arrangement has been satisfactorily concluded," D'Kan said. "We owe no debt on either side. Everyone understands that you do not play favorites when handing out ranks."

The boy used irony as subtly as a cattleprod.

"I do as I must," Christopher said. "As I expect everyone to do." He fished out the silver vial from under his chainmail tunic and screwed it open. Cannan watched him through hooded eyes again while D'Kan stared in frank curiosity.

Christopher handed the Ranger a small lump of tael, just enough to promote him to the second rank. The boy had it halfway to his mouth before he stopped to question.

"And the price of this?"

"Suppress rebellion as long as you can. Buy me as much time as possible. Oh, and survive your adventure."

A smile flitted across D'Kan's face. "This gift will certainly improve the latter odds. But for the former, I do not know what I can promise. In sheer point of fact, I cannot even guarantee my own faith. At some point, it must necessarily become obvious that you have left the path the gods laid out for you, and both duty and desire will force me to corrective action. As you must surely agree."

"I do," Christopher said. "We just disagree on when."

D'Kan stared at him. "How shall we settle on a time?"

Christopher looked back at the troop of armed men waiting a respectful thirty yards away. They loved him, but they followed someone else. "Ask Karl."

"You saddle him with much." D'Kan was as inscrutable as he had ever been, his face a closed and disciplined mask as the tael disappeared within. "A commoner that could make himself king with a word."

Christopher shrugged and turned back to his horse.

Later, safely ensconced in the private quarters of his castle, Lalania came to visit him, bringing admonition with her nightly dose of poison.

"You have provoked jealousy and compromised the voice of your staunchest defender among the Rangers, who now looks like a purchased songbird. He was foolish to accept a rank from you; how much more foolish must you be for having offered? What were you thinking?"

"It's what an ordinary king would have done," Christopher said. "Isn't it?"

Lalania stared at him. "It is. And yet . . . how is that relevant? You will never achieve your goal by being ordinary."

"No," he agreed. "What else would an ordinary ruler do?"

She lowered her eyebrows. "Promote the last of your servants who has not received a rank from your hand." With a flourish of her hand, she included Cannan in the conversation, where he stood against the wall as still as a column of stone. "Ser Cannan has been loyal beyond measure and gained not a shred of profit, which many feel reflects poorly on your character. It is a common complaint among those who respect Cannan for his strength, of which there are more than you might guess. Yet to promote a warrior who commands not even a scrap of magic would contradict your own precedent. The knights of the kingdom bark now; how they would howl then."

Christopher reached for his vial. Cannan frowned.

"This mistake I can at least forestall," Lalania muttered and jabbed him with the poisoned pin.

The fire, as always, but it was an old friend now. He merely flinched.

Lalania stared at him. He realized that he had moved. He could still move; he stood up from the edge of the bed.

She flung the contents of the vial on him, emptying it. Every droplet burned like boiling oil. His arm lashed out and caught her hand, instinctively.

"Careful," she admonished. "Should you brush against me with poison still on your skin, I will not thank you for it."

He let her go. "I guess it's done."

"It is. You enjoy a rare status that I will not give a name to, lest ears past or future are listening."

"Then it's time." He opened the silver vial and extracted a healthy lump of tael.

Cannan paused him with the force of his glare. "You know my terms. I will not step an inch off the path we tread."

Once, Cannan had forced Christopher to accept rank before he realized the cost. Now their positions were reversed. Christopher could not overpower the man, not without using magic. But he had a more potent weapon.

"I know," he said, and held out his hand, offering Cannan the tael.

Improbably, the man looked to the bard. She breathed in and out slowly, considering for the space of a long breath. Then she nodded, fraught with emotion that Christopher could not read.

"Go on," she said softly. "Whatever else comes, you have earned it. What comes next, you may require it."

Cannan surrendered to the combined assault. He took the lump and held it, wonderingly, until the novelty exhausted him. In his case, the briefest instant. The tael disappeared into his mouth.

"I suppose we have done enough for one night." Lalania picked herself up to leave. "Although not as much as I had hoped." She touched Cannan's arm tenderly before slipping out of the door.

The big man looked disappointed, which seemed an unusual reaction to gaining a rank.

"I didn't realize you enjoyed her company that much," Christopher joked, trying to lighten the mood.

Cannan's face took on a shape that Christopher had never imagined. It looked like a rock trying to blush.

"Oh," Christopher said, too surprised to keep his mouth shut.

"You spent many hours paralyzed and dead to the world," Cannan said, shrugging unapologetically. "There was little else to do."

11

WINTER OF DISCONTENT

He watched the rebellion grow like mold climbing up a cellar wall. The nobility were openly insouciant at court, constantly declaiming on their many and varied services to the crown and demanding commensurate reward. The commoners' discontent was less obvious, but he could see the resignation creeping over them, the glow of hopeful revolution fading in the cold light of winter days. Trouble bloomed at last in the form of an angry petitioner in the livery of his own castle servants. He saw the figure marching up the carpet with determination and hastily sat back down on the throne, abandoning the fleeting relief that court was over, and composed himself to receive a tirade.

When the peasant woman raised her face from her deep curtsey, he realized who it was. After all, he had just seen her at lunch: his first friend and roommate, manager of his kitchens, and Karl's wife.

"Helga?" he blurted out, surprised.

Lalania had already moved off the dais, assuming the formal business was done for the day. She paused, looking at him for guidance.

He waved the bard away. Helga could come to him any time. She didn't need an audience.

"I seek royal justice," the young woman said, her voice cracking in nervous shame.

Christopher was torn. If she was truly making a formal case, he owed it to her to follow procedure. On the other hand, this was ridiculous. He waved everybody out, letting them know the official court was closed. The crowd began moving toward the exit.

"Of course, Goodwoman," he said. "You can speak freely here."

She gathered herself to speak. "It is a complement of privilege. I mean, a complaint . . ."

Christopher interrupted her butchery of legalese. He could barely stand it when it was done right.

"Helga. Just tell me what the problem is."

A switch flipped, and Helga was suddenly a furious hellcat.

"Your witch! Your witch is the problem. She has already cast her spells upon my husband. Now her spawn seeks to ensnare my son."

The children were barely three years old. It seemed unlikely that one of them was working magic.

"Helga—" he started, but she cut him off.

"What has that devilspawn to do with my boy? She follows him everywhere! Why can she not find some other child to haunt? Hasn't her blood taken enough from mine?"

Christopher waited for her to catch her breath as she trembled in unfamiliar rage. He had noticed the children playing together. Once he had found them in the throne room, completely unsupervised. They had stared at him with curiosity, wondering why he was interrupting them. He had wondered where their nannies were. Both parties had left without answers.

"He seeks her out, too," he told Helga. "They like each other."

"Because he is enspelled!"

"I don't think its magic," Christopher said gently. "Just nature."

"You see it too! You know that harlot already casts a net for him!"

"I don't mean like that," Christopher blushed. "I mean they recognize each other. Like brother and sister." Better they should be raised that way now rather than later. It would forestall any Greek tragedies.

"But they are not!" Helga protested. "What of your vow of truth, that you should encourage such a lie?"

Christopher opened his mouth, but there were literally no words to say. He closed it again.

Helga clapped her hands over her face, stifling a scream as the fact washed over her. She shook with grief and rage, so fragile that he dared not even comfort her.

Her hands came away, balled into fists. Her voice was low and hoarse. "Why did you not tell me before?"

An excellent question admitting of no easy answer. It was a subject no one had discussed, so he had assumed it didn't need discussing. For once he was the person explaining the obvious, and he didn't like it. He excused himself as best as he could. "Because the knowledge would bring you pain."

"Then why did you tell me *now?*"

In sheer point of fact, he hadn't, although that defense was clearly inadmissible. "Because not knowing would cause you greater pain," he said, hoping it was the real reason and not merely cowardice.

Helga hugged herself and wept quietly. Christopher reached out for her, half rising from the throne, but she turned away from his hand.

"Does Karl know?"

Christopher sank back into the throne, ashes in his mouth. "I have never told him." It was the least truthful answer he could give and remain within his vows. "He has never spoken of it to me."

"The one thing I could give him that no other could. And now I find she has stolen that too. Yet you reward her with rank, and Karl gets nothing. Everyone around you rises but never Karl." She was sobbing openly now, but when he leaned forward, she shrank back.

Lalania had slipped up behind, returning to the scene of disaster. She caught Helga by the shoulders and hugged. Helga melted into her warm embrace and buried her face in the bard's blonde hair.

"The fault is mine," Lalania said, and for once Christopher agreed. "I should have told you years ago, dear Helga. I did not think it mattered. He has never acknowledged the child, and she has never laid a claim. I assumed soon enough there would be other children."

"She cursed us," Helga sobbed. "Nothing works, and I thought it was me. But it was her. She will not let me have a daughter of my own."

Christopher's eyebrows shot up in alarm. Lalania, with Helga's face safely in her shoulder, dismissed the notion with a roll of her eyes.

"Mistress Fae does not command such potent magic. Yet perhaps there is something that needs to be done. We shall ask the Cardinal. If that fails, there are medicines in the College of Troubadours that men have never bothered to study."

He sank back in relief. Lalania could fix it. Until he saw her face. Whatever the answer was, he wasn't going to like it.

One of the priestesses had returned, drawn by the sounds of sobbing. Lalania sent Helga off with her to see the Cardinal. Christopher waited warily while Lalania chose her words.

Finally, she shrugged and spoke bluntly. "It is Karl. That man has ridiculous self-discipline."

Christopher tried several different questions in his head, but all of them were absurd, so he left them unspoken.

Lalania explained, grudgingly. "I don't think he wants more children. So he has been . . . performing carefully."

Cannan, who as always stood at Christopher's shoulder as silent as a pillar, spoke up incredulously. "For three years?"

"He is a stubborn man," Lalania said.

Cannan was not satisfied. "How can Helga not have noticed?"

"He is also a skillful man. I doubt she is left in a condition to notice anything." She arched her eyebrows, trying to make a joke of it. It didn't help; both Christopher and Cannan winced at the implicit comparison. "Oh, stop it. This is not about either of you." She turned her attention to Christopher. "You must have a talk with Karl. I cannot guess why he has made this choice and would not dare broach it with him. But it is not fair to Helga."

Guilt fell onto Christopher like an avalanche. There were plenty of reasons for Karl to fear the future, and everything Christopher had done for the last two seasons multiplied them.

He put it off a few days, then a week. After the second week, he could no longer bear to evade Lalania's accusing gaze. When he found himself standing in a training yard, watching Karl watching cavalry men putting their horses through paces, he spoke up.

"Helga came to me with a problem."

"I have already told her to drop the matter. As guilty as the witch is, the child is innocent."

"Not that," Christopher said.

Karl's face was a warning sign with "NONE OF YOUR BUSI-NESS" stamped all over it. He stared at Christopher, amazed that anyone would dare to bring up such an intimate matter. If it weren't for twelve ranks of supernatural power, continuing this conversation would earn Christopher an epic beating.

He hunched his shoulders and bulled through. "A wise man once said, to have children is to give hostages to fortune."

"Yes," Karl said, as dry as a desert. "The future is ever uncertain."

"Never more so than now." There, he had said it; the elephant in the room stretched out its trunk and roared.

"True."

Christopher stared out over the training yard, afraid to look at Karl when he spoke. "Do you trust me?"

For a long moment, Karl simply stared at him. Then he turned to the training field and strode out into the mud, calling corrections to the horsemen.

There was a time when Christopher would not have understood, when he would have demanded a concrete answer. He had changed. It was not just the strange effect the rank seemed to have on his social perceptions. Years of command had taught him that some questions should not be asked, and some should not be answered. It was the Heisenberg principle of leadership; merely to acknowledge the issues changed their shape.

Karl had no choice. The man could not be more committed than he already was. To speak would have implied that it was even possible for him to doubt Christopher. Ironically, to say "Yes" could only have meant "No."

Yet it was necessary for Christopher to have asked. The question told Karl that Christopher knew he was doing wrong. To assume Karl's loyalty would have been to lose it as surely as demanding it would have. Like a chess match, he had to push his pawn so far but no further. He had to leave room for the future to shape itself to his ends.

Every move had costs, however. This one had made him a liar. The promise he had given D'Kan was worthless. Karl would never betray him.

The rest of the kingdom was a different matter. Faren's weekly divination warned of a minor incursion on the western border days before it would happen. Christopher should have dispatched Gregor or Torme to deal with it, but he was tired of doing what an ordinary ruler would do. Instead, he did what a stupid ruler would do and went himself.

Not alone; an entire company of cavalry followed him. Eighty men on horseback with carbines and half a dozen multibarreled rocket launchers on wheels. The launchers were shorter range than a cannon but much lighter to transport. The speed of his troop meant he could set out only the day before. By the time the city figured out he was gone, he was already halfway to the border. After a cold night camp, they were back in the saddle all day, reaching the expected trouble spot just as the sun was going down.

Cannan came with him, of course, along with Lalania and four priestesses of the Bright Lady. The troop was led by Major Kennet, one of his first recruits. The boy had grown into a frightfully competent young man. Lalania had spent the journey flirting with him and apparently had won him over. While the soldiers laid out their ambush, picketing the horses in a little forested hollow and digging a line of foxholes, she lectured Christopher with Kennet at her heel like a well-trained dog.

"We are in agreement: you must not reveal yourself until the enemy principles are identified. If this is a trap, you must run away. By the way, it should be a trap. Your head is the single most valuable object in the kingdom. Lopping it off would be a prize worthy of a dragon."

"The realm can replace a company," Kennet agreed solemnly. "It cannot replace a saint."

"Faren said it was minor," Christopher said, trying to find a plausible excuse for his presence.

"Then we should be able to handle it on our own," Kennet said.

"Agreed," Christopher said. "I'm just here to observe." It was close enough to the truth. His real goal was to not be on the throne while nobles glared at him and commoners avoided eye contact.

Lalania was having none of it. "If you wanted to watch, you could have scryed the battle. That is what any normal ruler with your resources would have done. Your mere presence denotes command, and command has its privileges. Specifically, the right to plunder. By leading this mission yourself, you have denied the Lord of Montfort any claim to the tael. He will view it as a theft rather than a favor."

Montfort had been slow to commit to a side and hence had mostly missed the civil war. Christopher had never figured out if that meant he should reward Montfort for not opposing him or punish the lord for not being a supporter. "I'm allowed to respond to threats to the realm," Christopher argued.

"A threat you just declared as 'minor.' And therefore, by definition, within the competence of the local lord."

"My lady," Kennet said earnestly, "this is the first significant incursion during the Saint's reign. We set precedent here. Defense of the realm is a national matter, not some lordling's adventure."

Lalania glared at the young man. "You can stop helping now."

"Yes, my lady," he said politely. With a crisp salute, he marched off to see to the disposition of the rocket launchers.

She turned her glare to Christopher. "You've ruined all of them. No one ever called me 'lady' to my face before you came along."

"Well now," Christopher started, and then bit his tongue. He was about to mention the fact that Lalania was older now than she used to be, which might account for why men treated her with more respect. This would not be wise. He had come here for a battle, not a war.

"It was always there," Cannan said. "You bards only played at blurring the line between noble and common. They only played along because they had no choice. Now . . . now they think they have a choice."

She ran her fingers through her hair, dislodging a handful of dirt and gravel from the road. With a grimace, she agreed. "True enough. I never thought I would appreciate the overweening pride of the nobility before. But now blindness saves them. If they had a clue about the faces the common make behind their backs, they would reach for a whip, the commoners would reach for a rifle, and you'd have a problem genuinely worth your time."

A pair of soldiers approached, carrying carbines. "My lady," one said, his voice barely above a whisper, "the Major has called for silence."

Lalania put her hands on her hips and glared at the rebuke. Christopher turned away to stifle his laugh. Night fell; the lightstones were stowed away, and the men were invisible in the dark. With their stillness, the normal forest sounds began to return. An owl hooted in the distance, answered by several crows. The herd of horses was far enough away that Christopher could not hear them. In any case, they were probably going to sleep, much like his own was. Royal stood with his head hung low and his eyes closed. The warhorse was disciplined enough to remain quiet and valuable enough to keep at hand. He was still saddled after the long ride, which would cause blisters. Fortunately, that was a problem Christopher could easily solve.

The two soldiers sat down and made themselves comfortable,

cradling their guns. Cannan silently joined them, squatting on the ground. Lalania paced about, trying to keep warm without making a sound. Every time Christopher moved a muscle his armor rattled, and the entire group would stare at him. When he sat down on a stump, he made so much noise that Royal briefly opened one eye. After that he stayed still. His tael wouldn't let the cold do any real damage to him regardless of what it felt like.

Several excruciatingly boring hours passed by in silence, giving Christopher ample opportunity to reflect on all of his mistakes to date. Chief of which, at the moment, seemed to be the decision that sitting in a cold forest all night would be better than staying in the city and having a nice hot dinner.

A light flashed, fifty yards to the front. Christopher's stomach flipped. They didn't actually know what kind of monster to expect. The last few hours had allowed his imagination to supply any number of horrific options. He prepared himself for the roar of gunfire.

"Ser?" a voice called out. A lightstone revealed itself. In the circle of illumination, Christopher could see three armored horsemen. Major Kennet and two other soldiers stood up and advanced.

"Name yourself," the lead horsemen commanded gruffly.

"Major Kennet," the young man answered. "On border patrol. We did not think to see you here, Ser. It is Viscount Conner, is it not?"

"It is," the horseman replied. "And I did not expect to see you, either."

Christopher let out a disappointed sigh. He had come all the way out here to face an interesting and new monster rather than angry nobles, and now he was facing one he already knew. Not a friend but technically an ally and in the employ of a neighboring lord. He had learned respect for the man's competence during the war, if not his friendship. Presumably Ser Conner had already defeated the monster and was on his way home. Lalania had warned that divinations were not guaranteed.

Beside Christopher, Lalania whispered a furious curse. He looked at her, but in the dark she was only a silhouette that communicated nothing.

"You were on adventure, were you not?" Kennet asked, the distant conversation clear in the still forest. The major seemed well briefed on local conditions.

"I am," Ser Conner corrected. "And I do not intend to return until I am prepared to restore the kingdom to its traditional ways."

"Yet you are here now," Kennet said coolly.

"I find myself only a few souls short of my next rank. Before I journey further into the Wild, I intend to avail myself of the kingdom's resources one last time."

"The Saint will not sell you tael to carry into the Wild," Kennet objected.

Christopher was suitably impressed with the political acumen of his army officer. Lalania, in contrast, seemed to think it was a terrible response. She darted forward to intervene, racing through the woods silently.

Cannan rose and took a half-step after her, then stopped and turned to Christopher. Before he could ask what was going on, it went.

"I do not intend to buy," Ser Conner said, and with an effortless motion drew his sword and decapitated Kennet. "Yours will do." One of his companions uttered a spell, and the other two soldiers collapsed instantly.

Lalania stopped running. "Dark take it," he heard her swear, and then finally the sound of thunder. Rifles blazed from all over the forest. Conner's two companions fell; the man jerked from the sting of bullets and reared his horse. In the flash of fire and smoke, lanced by countless shots, it pawed the air and died.

Man and beast fell to the ground. Conner took cover behind its corpse. Half a dozen men advanced out of the woods. Before Christopher could call out a warning—the knight would kill anything that got within sword reach—two men threw grenades.

The blasts forced Connor to his feet. The rifles cut him back down. A priestess dashed forward to attend to the fallen soldiers. They were already rising, woken from their unnatural slumber by the din.

Christopher stopped running. He had started when Kennet fell. Now he stood next to Lalania, robbed of urgency and bewildered. "I don't understand," Christopher said. "We came here to fight a monster from the Wild. But Ser Conner was one of us."

"Ser Conner no longer thought of himself so," Lalania said. "Thus, neither did the spell."

12

A DISH BEST SERVED COLD

He could not remember whether this was the second or third time he had brought Kennet back. That seemed like a detail he should recall. Probably Kennet knew, but he didn't feel like asking. In any case, the man was back at his duties within two days of having been murdered.

Lalania was unhappy with the entire affair. "It looks like a trap," she complained. "As if you had laid out bait."

"I didn't do anything," Christopher objected. In the end, his role had been purely observational.

"Which makes it worse. Like a lion watching its cub maul a rabbit, ready to pounce should the prey risk escape."

Christopher frowned at her. "He wasn't a rabbit. He was a murderer looking for victims." Unstopped, Ser Conner would have undoubtedly slaughtered dozens of peasants for the tael in their heads on his way out of town. Instead his tael was in Christopher's vial, thanks to the Cardinal's warning.

"Yet if you had made your presence known, Ser Conner would have stayed his hand and would still be alive today."

"I thought I wasn't supposed to go out there in the first place."

"And yet you did. This is a stark reminder that knights are merely a harvest of tael to you. Conner was Green and he still felt driven into the Wild. I will be surprised if we have any knights left by year's end."

They were sitting in the throne room again. It was the best place to have a private conversation lately, as traffic had been drying up. The nobility had stopped complaining as much, which was worrisome because it meant they were plotting more. The common petitioners had also slowed to a trickle for reasons less clear.

He looked around the empty room. "Where is everybody? Am I becoming less popular?"

She shrugged. "Treywan almost never had commoners at his court. Nobility is normally far too capricious for the small folk. You are achieving your goal of being perceived as ordinary."

"This . . . can't go on much longer."

"On the contrary." She tilted her head at him. "It can go on forever. So it has always been; so it shall always be. Your rank is enough to hold the throne, as it was for Treywan. Your rifles only make it obvious. It is clear that you will not rest until you have reduced every profession save for the priesthood, and yet there is nothing anyone can do to stop you."

She pirouetted on the long red carpet that stretched from the throne to the huge double doors, making a show of the emptiness. "It's been years since we had a ball. If you're going to be normal, at least we can dance."

"So . . . no rebellion?"

Cannan wandered over to a chair and sat down. "There are never rebellions. The throne changes hands through duel or assassination. Your civil war was a function of your theology. Just an extended argument between you and the Gold Apostle."

Lalania spun, still dancing. "Peasants are what wars are fought over, not with."

"Until now."

She stopped and stretched. "Half the kingdom thinks your rifles will stop working when you die. No one is going to use peasants against you."

His efforts to spread the scientific worldview were definitely a work in progress.

"We should not sit here and wait for them to strike." Cannan sat with his massive sword standing between his knees, point against the ground. Christopher hated when he did that; the blade left gouges in the stone floor. Sometimes Christopher would use magic to repair the stone but only when no one was looking. "Identify your enemies and destroy them first."

That was the problem. Christopher didn't know how to find his enemy.

"Without cause? You forget his affiliation." Lalania's lecture struck home; Cannan grimaced, acknowledging that preemptive murder was not really the sort of thing Christopher could justify. "And whom would you have him slay? Knighthood already withers; the other churches beg for scraps."

"I can think of two places to start," Cannan said. "At least one of which has given me sufficient cause."

The red knight was obviously referring to the Witch of the Moors and the Wizard of Carrhill. Christopher sighed. He actually liked both of them despite their respective inscrutability and moral flexibility.

"If you can think of two, then two can think of you." Lalania bowed, ending her performance. "Take a care of what dinner invitations you accept."

<hr/>

When it came, it was at the hands of a friend.

Christopher was riding down the winding road from the spire of Kingsrock to the plains below. Royal needed regular exercise, and Christopher was always glad to get out of the city. For a day trip like this, he could get away with an escort as small as Cannan and six cavalrymen. He would never be out of sight of the spire; if worst came to worst, he could just fly back to the castle for reinforcements.

There was of course the danger of a magical attack, but he had taken precautions against that a while ago. He wore Lalania's amulet under his tunic. It was a calculated risk because he would have to take it off before he could cast spells on himself—such as the flight spell. On the other hand, it would stop his instantaneous and immediate destruction by a variety of horrific spells.

It would also keep the Witch and the Wizard from doing anything he would have to kill them for.

Thus, he watched the sparrow approaching him with curiosity. It flew around his horse several times, working up the courage to come closer. It might be a lost pet looking for rescue or a spell-trigger of arcane death. The first possibility stopped him from having it shot, although in retrospect that was a poor decision.

When he held out his hand, it landed on his gauntleted fist and chirped at him.

"It's carrying something," he said. He cupped his other gauntlet, and the bird dropped a feather in his palm. Then it took to the air again, circling.

Cannan rode closer and plucked the feather from Christopher's hand before it blew away on the wind. "D'Kan's token. He invites you to meet; the bird will guide you. I did not think he could do this trick. His explorations must have been profitable."

"Should we follow?"

"Of course not," Cannan snorted. "The boy has outgrown his boots if he thinks he can summon a Saint to his whistle."

"On the other hand, he might have something to say." Their last meeting had been impromptu, discreet, and informative.

"Or he just wants to brag. Ignore him and he will come to court, if he has anything of value for you."

The thought soured Christopher. The last thing he wanted was another surly noble in front of his throne.

"I think we should go," Christopher said.

Cannan shrugged and tapped his heels to his horse. Royal surged to keep ahead, and the cavalrymen perked up their horses to follow, all of them chasing a sparrow across the fields.

After a mile, the bird flew into a copse of trees. Kingsrock was still visible behind them, and the sun was high and bright in the sky. Christopher and the men dismounted at the edge of the woods, loosening the saddle straps so their horses could rest. They took off their helmets for the same reason. One of the men passed around a skin of wine; Cannan took a swig and handed it to Christopher.

"Well met, my lord." D'Kan strolled out of the trees to greet them.

Cannan eyed him critically. "For a Ranger you spend an inordinate amount of time in Civilized lands. One might almost think you like it."

The Ranger smiled superciliously. "I don't have a mattress strapped to my back. Yet."

The red knight's eyes narrowed. Christopher was slightly taken aback and mildly impressed. It was a sophisticated insult, subtly implying that Cannan had become utterly domesticated and soft. D'Kan had grown sharp thorns.

"How was your adventure?" Christopher asked before Cannan could continue the sniping.

"Mildly profitable." D'Kan turned his smile on Christopher, who discovered he did not like it all. This new version of the young Ranger was not an improvement. "And you? How have your fortunes faired in my absence?"

Christopher had made a handsome profit off Ser Conner's death, but he didn't really want to count that as a win. He shrugged.

"You should go adventuring," D'Kan suggested. "You could put your fire sticks to good purpose. Instead you sit around waiting for old people to die."

"You forget yourself, Ser," Cannan said seriously. "Curb your tongue."

D'Kan shook his head disapprovingly at the red knight. "You should have counseled him to finish the ant queen. That alone would have bought his next rank."

"I'm not really interested in your opinion of my foreign policy," Christopher said, starting to get angry himself.

"I know," the Ranger said. "More's the pity. Well, I tried."

Cannan, frowning thunderclouds, stepped forward to chastise the Ranger.

The boy spat in the big man's face.

Christopher's heart leapt in his chest. Such an act could only be followed by violence. He was pretty sure the Ranger was about to die. At the same time, alarm bells were booming in the back of his head, belated and hurried as if the monks responsible for the noonday ringing had slept through lunch.

D'Kan flicked his hand and numerous arcane bolts leapt forward, sparkling like bottle rockets. The missiles pierced the cavalryman, killing all of them instantly.

Cannan had not moved, standing as still as a statue.

Christopher did the only thing he could. He cast a spell on himself, a simple blessing, the first and fastest spell he could think of.

His armor sagged at his shoulders as the null-stone triggered. He did not notice because he was watching D'Kan's face come apart.

Without magic, the disguise was not at all convincing. The mass of tentacles carefully folded and camouflaged was barely identifiable as a human face, let alone as D'Kan. The parts that made up the lips writhed; sound came out, shaped into hissing words.

"I suspected as much. My thanks for delivering the artifact; it is not the sort of thing I care to leave lying around."

Christopher drew his sword.

The *hjerne-spica* appeared to laugh. The sight was horrific, a bowl of snakes with the tremors. "I cannot decide whether this is wisdom or madness. While it is true your magic is worth nothing against me, magic was your only possibility of retreat."

Only a few years ago, Christopher had fought his first duel. A reasonable and peaceful person from a civilized society, it had never occurred to him that he would one day stand before a man who wanted to kill him. He had been terrified, his tongue as heavy as lead and as dry as sand.

Since then he had fought against fanged man-beasts, creatures of rotting flesh, mindless hordes, shadows of darkness, trolls, dragons, and giant ants. All of them had been his enemies, intent on his death and destruction. None of them had gazed at him with such heart-stopping malice. He had forgotten how savagely fear could bite.

And yet. "I'm not . . . retreating."

"How so? Surely you must understand I am displeased. I set you to a task that any simpleton can see you will never achieve. You take too few risks and offer too many mercies. Your mortal frame will crumble and fail long before you gain the rank you need. Now I must consume you, and regret the time I wasted on your career. A bad bet; a seed that will never flower."

The creature approached, walking around the paralyzed form of Cannan, its hands spread amicably. "In my defense, you seemed so promising in the beginning. What went wrong?"

"Nothing." It was hard for Christopher to speak in the face of nightmare. He felt like a child again, accosted by a bully in the skin of a hulking adult. "This was my plan." He raised his blade high.

The malevolent yellow eyes stared at him, calculating, then dismissive. It had mapped all the possibilities and found them unthreatening. One tentacle lashed out, absurdly long and thin, and struck him across the cheek.

The familiar fire, the poisoned agony. He stood stock-still.

"Failure is always a bad plan," the *hjerne-spica* said, and stepped closer, thick tentacles reaching out for his face.

Christopher hit it. His blade sliced into the creature's face, shedding flopping bits of tentacle.

"The only plan you would not see through," he grunted, because he wanted it to know he had outsmarted it.

The *hjerne-spica* sprang back, hissing, drawing D'Kan's twin swords. Christopher followed, striking down again, only narrowly turned aside by the short blades.

"Clever," it taunted as they lunged and struck at each other. The sound of steel rang in the air, punctuated by the wet squelch of blades cutting flesh. "At first I assumed you foolishly expected the favor of your patron to spare you paralysis. Of course it cannot reach into the null-sphere, and you would have been laughingly dismayed. Tell me, how did you become immune? Or were you always thus; has the race of man departed from its seed-line so much in all these years?"

Christopher was wholly focused on the fight, so much so he didn't have the energy to lie. "Ants," he mumbled, sweeping low. The creature's block did not reach; Christopher opened up a gash on D'Kan's calf. The wound splashed blood and then stopped, sealed by tael.

The blades might be mundane, but the combatants were not. They still had the unnatural vitality of their tael, even inside the anti-magic zone. It was an interesting conundrum, one of many Christopher did not have time to consider. Spinning under his last strike, the *hjerne-spica* passed through his guard and stabbed him under the arm its way past, neatly avoiding his armor. This would have killed a mortal man. It made Christopher take note. The ploy would not work again.

"I should have known," the creature complained. It almost sounded like a whine. "I should have been informed." Dimly Christopher noted that he was winning the fight. His armor and vitality seemed to be a match for the light frame of the Ranger. He was slowly pulling ahead on points, and points counted here.

"Maybe," Christopher said, his mind seeking any opening into its defenses, any thrust that would strike home, "maybe they didn't want to tell you."

It pounced in a hissing spray, tentacles and short swords weaving in hypnotic patterns. All of the training Christopher had done in this world paid for itself now. He ignored the threat and leaned into his own blow.

The blades stabbed into his face. One pierced his left eye and stuck. The other skittered across his skull, shaving off hair in its wake. Either blow should have been fatal. Instead he stepped back, drawing his long blade in a cut, and severed the creature from its body at the neck.

It flopped across the ground with startling speed. He sprung after it; to let it outside the range of the null-stone would be fatal. A lucky thrust pinned it to the ground. He reached up with one hand and pulled the shortsword out of his eye, although he still could not see out of it. Kneeling over the squid-like body, he grabbed handfuls of tentacles and sawed at them with the shortsword. The creature flailed and lashed, trying to blind his other eye. He turned his face left and right to avoid the attacks but did not retreat. He did not need to see to finish the job.

Eventually, he realized the thing had stopped moving. It was hard to tell because his hands were on fire where he had touched it. He could barely distinguish his fingers, and his face felt like a frying pan.

Doggedly, he gathered up the remains and cut each tentacle in half again. There did not seem to be anything to the creature other than tentacles. Even the eyes were on the end of suckered, slimy ropes. Both were gray and lifeless now. In the midst of the mess, he found three more eyes, much smaller, like unopened flower buds.

Something grated against the sword, notching it. A gnarled, hollow spike of dull purple metal. It looked organically grown rather than machined or forged. He held it, wondering what its purpose was, afraid he already knew.

The null-field vanished.

His heart paused for a few beats. Behind him a horse whinnied. Royal, for once held in abeyance by fear. Nothing else happened; the *hjerne-spica* remained in pieces on the ground.

He placed the spike in the middle of the butchered calamari and cast a simple orison. Tael began to collect on top of it. The ball grew and grew and grew. It did not stop until it was the size of a cantaloupe.

He looked up into Cannan's eyes. The man was still paralyzed, but the message was unmistakable. Christopher sat back and began to shove the tael into his mouth a handful at a time.

After he was finished, he staggered to his feet. The horses shied away from him, frightened by the *hjerne-spica*'s smell. Christopher realized he dared not touch anything with his poisoned hands.

He had magic again, however. He burned through three healing spells restoring his tael before he realized they weren't quenching the fire. It was hard to concentrate through the pain. Through sheer force of will, he brought Gregor's face to mind.

"I'm at the birch-wood south of the city. Send help. Bring a washbasin."

13

GHOSTS

Success cured all ailments. When the long-dead started walking out of his mausoleum, the tongues of discontent were stilled. The act of generosity bought the loyalty of the common; the display of power cowed the noble.

The *hjerne-spica* had elevated him to his thirteenth rank and halfway to the next one. It was the single most profitable act he had ever committed. Another dozen bowls of calamari, and he could go home.

The next ones would not be so easy, however. They would surely know what happened and take measures. The trick would not work a second time. However, he did not particularly worry that they would murder him in his sleep. After all, he was back on track. The project looked feasible again.

He had been unimpressed with the various additional ways to kill people that his last rank had brought. As usual, half the spells from this new rank were also dedicated to killing things, but these were starting to get seriously frightening. He had just gained the ability to raise the dead from a fingernail, and with it came a spell that would obliterate a foe fingernails and all. He could regenerate the men with crippled faces and missing limbs; he could kill a small crowd with a word. But only if they were Team Evil. A bomb designed for the righteous, it only killed enemies.

And the ability to control the weather. He had already known the weather system was unnatural. Now he could get his hands on the controls. Praying for rain had become a legitimate agricultural policy. There would be no more droughts as long as he had time to work magic across his realm.

He had also gained in wisdom, although this was probably less a

result of rank and more a product of experience. This time he asked
before bringing the Ranger back from the dead. Standing in the castle's
dungeon, where King Treywan had kept victims and Christopher kept
bodies he couldn't revive yet, he cast the spell that summoned the shade
of the deceased.

"There is still time for me to return you to the High Druid," Christopher told him. "Or I can bring you back again."

"From this?" the ghost said, looking down at his headless corpse.
"Has your power grown so great that you can revive even the despoiled?
Does my sister now walk the plane again?"

"Not so much," Christopher, wishing he could lie. "I still need a
component." Niona's corpse had been reduced to ash. Not by a spell but
effective all the same.

Beside him, a glistening track crawled down Cannan's face. Christopher ignored it because there was nothing else to do.

"Then . . . no." The ghost of the Ranger sighed, looking so much
older and wiser than he had as a living man. "My mother's heart is
already torn. To let you snatch me again from the judgment of our faith
would shred it."

The High Druid would return D'Kan to life. Just not in a human
body. It seemed a cruel fate for a handsome young man.

"We don't have to tell them," Christopher suggested.

"How your morality flexes when burdened with the weight of your
sins." The ghost shook its head. "Should I be flattered that you would
lie on my behalf?"

"Well. No." Christopher was hemmed in, brought up short by the
judgment of his own faith. He could keep silent, but he could not lie
when asked directly. That path had proved its weakness with Helga.

"Nor could I lie when facing the families of the rest of my party.
The creature ambushed us on our adventure, when we had barely
started. I watched my friends devoured alive by the monster, one after
another. It released their paralysis only when they could no longer fight

or flee, solely so that they could give voice to their pain. They are gone now because they chose to be my companions. I brought them to death because I chose to be yours. That I alone should live again seems a burden too great to bear."

"Can we find them?" Christopher knew it was stupid as soon as he asked.

"Of course not. Its spell-craft is at least as competent as Cannan's. It left nothing for the High Druid to work with and taunted us as it did so."

"I could . . ."

It cut him off. "You could carve up my mind and my memories as you did Cannan's? No, I think not. He can sacrifice his soul to bring my sister back. I have done enough; do not ask this of me."

The ghost folded its hands together and faded out of existence.

"He is not wrong," Cannan said quietly. "The druids are riven; their faith hangs by a thread. Niona may well lose her druidic powers when you bring her back. Such a fate would be torture for her."

"We'll fix it," Christopher assured him. "Kalani came back as an owl. It doesn't seem to be a problem for druids. If we have to kill Niona and reincarnate her to keep her profession, then we'll do it. That will be the easy part."

Cannan shook his head gently and sadly. "You always think you can talk everybody into anything. I know this, and then I let you do it to me anyway."

Christopher shrugged. "Talking is my only weapon. Rifles just kill people, and all of my foes have better magic than I do. All I have to bring to the game is a different perspective."

"Don't tell Lala," Cannan said. "You know how she feels about theologians."

Talking, however, was risky. There were secrets too dangerous to speak out loud. Christopher was going a little crazy with the constant sense of being watched at every turn. When he started planning a trip to visit the ant queen, solely so he could sit inside her protected nest for a few hours, he realized he had to do something.

Fae knelt before him, dressed in formal wear that was barely more chaste than her lingerie. "You summoned me, my lord?"

This time they were in the throne room, although once again it was empty save for his sword-bearing shadow and Lalania.

"I need a private place to talk. Lala says that's a thing wizards can do."

"It is, my lord, but I regret it is beyond my power. I would require many more ranks to obey your command."

He wasn't going to spend that much. "Can the Wizard of Carrhill do it?"

"Yes," Fae said, unable to mask her disapproval. "If you trust him to cast the spell."

"I don't," Christopher agreed. "But Lala says you could do it if he prepared the materials."

"That is an expensive way to achieve your result. And it carries a risk of failure, with the possibility of doom for myself."

"Do you want try?"

She glared. "Of course I do. To work such magic is the purpose of my life."

Lalania had also said that Fae would not have the skill to compromise the spell in any hidden way, as the Wizard might. He hadn't planned on bringing that up. Now it looked like he wouldn't have to. Fae clearly understood she was being used and didn't care. She would do it anyway.

<hr>

A week later, he stood in the castle vault. The room contained only a large table and a dozen chairs. He didn't have any treasure to store.

His gold was spent faster than it came in, and he usually wore the two magical artifacts he owned, his armor and the bullet-proof cloak. The lyre had spent years under a dusty cover; now it was always with Lalania. He suspected she kept it under the covers with her when she slept. It had always been a crime that Treywan had left magic items unused. Christopher didn't know how much of a crime because he didn't know what most of those items were. They had all disappeared with the Gold Apostle, who himself had been disappeared by the *hjerne-spica*, which had already demonstrated its appetite for magic. Somewhere at the end of the chain, there should be quite a pile of the stuff.

So far they had only taken things into the vault, so the allegiance of the guardian gargoyles had not been tested. Lalania assured him they were magical constructs, not real creatures, and only activated when someone tried to leave with something they hadn't brought in with them. They would not spy on him. Thus, the vault seemed an appropriate choice for a private conference. It was immune to mundane surveillance, the right size for the spell, and information was the only thing of value he produced. So now he watched Fae marking off the boundary of the room with mystic powders. Eventually, she was satisfied she had done it right and bowed before him.

"I am ready at your command, my lord."

He had already cleared his schedule for the day. This posturing by her was merely to remind him that failure was on his head, not hers. "Go ahead," he said, trying not to be annoyed.

She unrolled a scroll purchased from the Wizard of Carrhill for a small fortune. Christopher could have brought two men back from the dead for its price. It was a lot to pay for a single day of privacy. There was also a one in three chance that Fae would miscast the spell, thus wasting the scroll, although Lalania assured him that the chance of anyone dying was small.

As she read from the parchment, the words burst into flames. By the time she dropped the flaming scraps, they were so small they were consumed before hitting the floor. The dust scattered around the room sparkled briefly and then disappeared.

"Did it work?" he asked.

Fae smiled like a well-fed cat. "Of course, my lord."

Lalania pointed to the guards standing outside the open door. The men had horrified looks on their contorted faces. Christopher realized they were shouting, but he couldn't hear them.

"Hey," he ordered, "calm down."

"They can't hear you either," Lalania said. She walked quickly to the door and then stopped, putting both hands across the threshold. The men on the other side stepped back and pointed their rifles. She waited until they lowered them before stepping all the way through.

Christopher could see they were not entirely comforted by her silent explanation. He joined her.

"My lord!" their sergeant exclaimed. "Are you all right?"

"Of course. It's the same room." He looked over his shoulder as he spoke and stopped midsentence. Behind the door was a cloudy gray wall. "Oh. Okay, that looks pretty bad." Curious, he stepped back into the room.

The room was as he had left it. Fae smiled contentedly at him.

The sergeant bravely followed. "Oh," the man said, slightly disappointed. It took a bit of courage to step into that formless void, only to find a perfectly ordinary room on the other side.

Lalania came back in. "I said, should we send for the others now?"

"Did you bring what I asked for?" Christopher said instead.

She looked at him, preparing to be annoyed. With one hand, she pointed briefly to the other end of the room, where a leather sack sat on a chair. He had not noticed her sneak it in, which was kind of the point.

"Go and get the rest of the command staff, please," he told her.

Lalania frowned sourly. She knew she was being cut out of the fun. Christopher hated doing it, but he wanted to ask questions, and he didn't want Lalania to hear the answers. He was already worried about keeping them secret in his own head, which was protected by many more ranks than hers.

"As you command, my lord." She didn't leave right away, however.

"Thank you, Mistress Fae," Christopher said. "You can go now."

Fae wasn't any happier than Lalania about being dismissed.

"Of course, my lord. You need but speak and I obey." She bowed again, too deeply.

Christopher turned to Cannan. "I think I'll be safe enough in here. If you could wait outside and explain it to people when they show up? It's a bit disconcerting seeing that gray cloud instead of a doorway."

If Cannan objected to being reduced to a doorman, he kept it to himself. With a minimal nod of his head, the big man walked through the door. The women followed him, unable to stop themselves from throwing Christopher one last glance of displeasure. When they were gone, he sat down and relaxed.

Moved entirely by senseless spite, he made obscene gestures at the guards still staring into the room. They did not react, of course, since they could not see anything. He swore for a bit in English. It felt good.

"Okay," he muttered to himself. "To business." The rest of his staff would be showing up soon. He put the leather sack onto the table and opened it, scrunching down its edges to reveal the leathery strips bunched inside. He took the purple spike out his pocket and added it to the pile. Then he summoned the creature's ghost.

Spectral figures were supposed to be frightening. The pale shadow of this creature was like a painting of a nightmare, evoking the memory of fear and hatred without the meat of it. Christopher stared at the remnant of the architect of so many deaths. He should have felt elated at its current state or at least satisfied. Instead, it was inadequate, as if an alien horror were insufficient to explain all of the evil around him.

As always he hid from his fear in flippant small talk. "I didn't know if this would work."

The ghostly ball of tentacles spoke in his head, as it had the first time they had met, in the Gold Apostle's castle. "As the spell compels me to honesty, I must confess I would not have known either. No one in the history of the world has ever desired to speak to one of us alive. Why would they speak to us dead?"

"Because you can't lie here?" Christopher guessed.

"We never lie," the ghost said. "The truth is always so much more hurtful."

Christopher was pretty sure that was a lie itself, which, given that the spell was supposed to command honesty, was pretty worrying. However, he hadn't asked a direct question, so perhaps it was just wriggling through a loophole.

"I know there are more of you." *Hjerne-spica* never operated alone; Friea the Skald had told him that somewhere there would be a nest, thousands or tens of thousands of years old and guarded by enslaved monsters of every description.

"There are," the ghost responded.

Christopher paused. That probably counted as two questions asked and answered. He got a lot more now than when he had used this spell to talk to Pater Stephram, but there was still a limit.

"They sold you out. They knew I had a plan, and they let you die unwarned." He stopped because he did want an answer to this one.

"Unconfirmed," the ghost said. "Perhaps they assumed I was capable of managing my own district."

"That is possible. But you don't believe it."

The misty white tentacles wreathed in agitation.

"I do not."

"So you died, to me, a lesser creature. A simple human of high rank."

Despite their alien form and lack of substance, the tentacles communicated disdain. "Moderate rank."

"Of moderate rank," Christopher agreed, although the thought was discomforting. He could do a lot of scary things. It was disturbing to think there was worse waiting. "It must be humiliating. You must want revenge."

"It is. I do." The creature could not resist scoring easy points and racking up answered questions.

"You used me as a tool once. Do it again. Set me on a path to achieve your ends."

"I do not have ends now. I am dead." Those weren't answers, however. He had broken through; the creature was talking to him.

"I found your death profitable. I would like to kill more of you. Tell me where your nest is, and I will attack it."

The ghostly eyes blinked. "So it was madness after all. You are insane. And you must know, coming from one of my kind, that is saying something."

"I know, right? I barely defeated you. No way can I fight a whole nest. They'll eat me alive. And you'll have your revenge."

It stared at him slyly. "And if you have another clever plan? If you consume my nest through unimaginable trickery?"

"Then they deserve it. Just as they left you to my devices, so you can leave them. Failure is its own justification. If they are no more worthy than you, then why should you protect them?"

The tentacles jiggled obscenely. "To think my kind are called duplicitous. Your logic justifies any end so long as it accords with your desires. Perhaps we should reconsider our devotion. The White would seem no less constrained than the Black."

Christopher smiled grimly. "My logic is my problem. You have enough logic of your own to understand I won't do this lightly. You have to give me something more than just the location. You have to give me a fighting chance. A secret weakness, a back door, the disposition of the guards. Something."

"Do you not trust to the power of your sky-fire?" It was baiting him now.

"Not for this. I need more of an edge."

"You will march an entire army into the nest if I show you how to open the door?"

Christopher paused. He wasn't bound by the spell, but he still didn't think he was allowed to lie. "If necessary." That was vague enough to leave plenty of wiggle room later.

"But at least you will take your retinue, yes?" It was asking for a promise.

"Okay," Christopher said. "Sure." He probably would have anyway. "Why is that so important?"

"Because I want you to watch them die. What I did to the Ranger's companions was merely a field exercise. What the Masters can do in the heart of the nest will break your mind."

Its tone turned to glee. "Now, my end of the bargain. Travel fifteen degrees east of true north for three hundred and seventeen miles and four hundred and twenty-one yards. You will find a tunnel entrance hidden by magic and guarded by spell-craft. Carve this sigil upon your flesh, and you will be allowed passage without harm or alarm. From there, a few hundred yards underground will bring you to the lair. After that you will die but not before you realize how utterly you have out-smarted yourself."

Christopher ignored the barb, desperately trying to memorize the shape the creature had traced in the air with tentacle. He repeated it several times until the ghost signaled its approval by lowering its tentacles.

"Give me more," Christopher demanded.

"Strike before winter's end. The sigil is changed every year. Take my trephine. The Masters will use it to summon my ghost so I can laugh at you. Of course I will not remember this meeting, but it will undoubtedly torment you all the same. Until we meet again, my lord, go in fear." It folded its tentacles together in a complex pattern. As each one went behind another it vanished, until there was nothing left at all.

Christopher sank back into a chair, exhausted.

"What's up?" Gregor said, coming into the room. "Dark take it but that gray door is unsettling."

Christopher hastily closed the leather bag, hiding its contents. "Just a spell I was trying."

"Did it work?"

"I don't know yet."

The rest of his command staff arrived. Gregor and Torme commanded armies and were also the only two other priests of the church of Marcius; Cardinal Faren ran the White Church, which had almost doubled over the last two years now that its kindness was no longer viewed as weakness; Lalania, his liaison to the College of Troubadours which was also the national spy service. And last, Karl, general of the armies and the only man in the room who had no rank at all, and yet he was more valuable to Christopher than all the nobles of the realm combined. Cannan waited outside, choosing a role as bodyguard rather than advisor.

Missing were his allies: Duke Istvar and Lord Ranger Einar, Friea the Skald, the Witch of the Moors, and the Wizard of Carrhill. A number of lesser lords had sworn fealty to him, but they knew they served as employees, not equals. Hence the constant defections to the Wild. A life of adventure was an option for men and women of high rank. Christopher had almost emulated them once, flying his horse above the trees with Lalania on the saddle behind him, lured to seek out some new place where treasure lay in heaps without the snares of the kingdom lain upon them. Duty had brought him to ground, but now he had relieved these lesser lords of their duty. Lalania was right; he would be lucky to have any left soon.

The woman put her elbows on the table and clasped her hands. "Speak, my lord, and tell us why you have called us here at great expense to the realm."

"Why did we need all this rigmarole?" Gregor asked. "I thought we knew how to detect for scrying. You just look for that little ball thingy." He referred to the tell-tale, which appeared like a hazy ball of light. It could be hidden by a skilled practitioner, which is why rooms built for conferences were plain and as empty of furniture as possible.

"We can indeed account for those who would spy on us now," Lalania explained patiently. "But what of those who in the future would like to look in on this conversation? How shall we see a tell-tale that does not yet exist?"

"You can do that? Scry the past?" Gregor looked alarmed. "We're not even safe once we stop talking?"

"I cannot do that. But it can be done."

"But not here," Christopher clarified.

"Correct. What we speak here is hidden even from the gods. If you wish a plot that will not be forewarned by the Cardinal's divinations, lay your plans here. Although once you give an order outside this room, you may well set into motion events that can reveal the future."

"So we can plan . . . but we can't do anything about it," Christopher mused. "I can tell you that there are undoubtedly more monsters like the one I killed out in the birch-wood, and that we must make a plan for defeating them; but we cannot train tactics, stockpile weapons, or move troops without giving it away."

"Normally we would not involve mundane troops at all," Gregor said. "Normally we would practice and stockpile here in this room and then move with the speed of flight when we struck."

"We won't do that," Christopher said. "We can't beat them on our own. I'm going to ask for help."

"So you called us here to instruct us to do . . . nothing?" Torme asked.

"Are you complaining?" Faren asked. "I for one have plenty to do as it is. If you are unoccupied, I can find tasks for you."

"I find the conversation profitable," Karl said. "If the rank at this table is not proof against this threat, then rank will not save us. Thus, we need not fear the loss of rank we bleed into the Wild. The army grows into the space they leave behind. We used to turn away ten applicants for every new position. After the border affair, we turn away twenty. The realm will trust its future to divine magic and firearms."

"So no more adventures for you," Faren told Christopher. "At least until after I am dead. Something to look forward to, then."

Christopher bit his lip, unable to respond. He'd just made a deal for another adventure.

Faren tilted his head back and swore loudly.

14

ELVES

The days slid by. Christopher tried to be patient, knowing that the entities he wanted to talk to did not operate on human time. Still it was hard to tell whether he'd made enough of a ripple to attract their attention. And the end of the year was approaching.

Walking through the castle yard, Cannan spoke to him in a low voice. "There is a hawk watching us. It has circled three times."

Christopher sighed. What was this obsession with birds? He looked up at the sky. The hawk waggled its wings and flew down to land behind the stables.

"Another trap we're going to walk into?" Cannan asked.

"Always," Christopher grumbled.

Here in the castle grounds, Christopher could travel without a posse. Thus, he and Cannan managed to enter the stable yard alone, save for the dozen grooms working throughout the area.

A woman wrapped in a hooded plain brown cloak was waiting for them on a bale of hay. When they approached, she pulled back her hood, revealing a pretty face framed in white hair.

"Lady Kalani!" Christopher said, surprised.

"Saint Christopher," she greeted him. "I hope the day finds you content."

"I didn't expect you."

"Why would you?" she asked, the picture of innocence. "I happened to be in the area and thought I would call on you for old time's sake."

"Sure," Christopher said. "Of course." Apparently he was supposed to make light conversation in case anyone was listening. "Did you get permission to work with the ulvenmen again?"

"No," she said, sadness flitting across her face. "That story did not end well."

Cannan seemed to detect something in her choice of words. The man had spent a lot of time around druids, so he understood them. "But it did end?" he asked.

"Most definitively." Her face froze before it grimaced, and she changed the subject. "I understand you gained another rank."

The compliment applied to both of them, so Christopher wasn't sure who should respond. Cannan remained silent, however, which left it to him.

"I did, thank you. It's quite a story."

"I would like to hear it," she said seriously. "Although perhaps not here in a stable."

"Have dinner with us tonight," he asked. "We can talk after."

"If it please you," she answered. "I shall."

<hr />

Kalani was mildly disappointed to find that D'Kan was no longer in his service. Christopher was surprised she remembered the boy. When she found he had been reincarnated rather than revived, she frowned.

"I thought you would approve," Christopher said. "Isn't it the elven way?"

"It is the price of our curse," she said. "We do not ask anyone to emulate it. We would take elven form again after death if it were possible for us."

"Maybe you should go out there and set them straight," Christopher suggested. "The druids seem to think they're following your example."

She looked at him dubiously. "You advised me against the ulvenman project, yet I assure you teaching wolves to say please is vastly simpler than explaining to a community that generations of their faith have hinged on a mistake."

"On that we can agree," Lalania muttered.

Mistress Fae did not usually attend his dinners, but this was a special occasion since they had a guest. Now she reminded him why he didn't normally invite her.

"Our lord changes the faith of our realm. Generations of false churchmen fall into line; the people embrace the White with both arms." The witch spoke it as a challenge, which Christopher thought was wildly unfair as she herself had never shown a speck of interest in theology.

"Christopher does it by shooting people, which is beyond my ability," Kalani replied evenly.

"Oh look, dessert," he said, waving to the waiters to hurry up and bring it. "It's called ice cream. I invented it. Although it's better in summer." It would also be better with chocolate. He'd tried describing the flavor to Lalania to see whether she could replicate it with her magic, but it never came out quite right. Eventually he stopped the experiments when he realized he wouldn't know whether she got it right. It had been too long.

"After dinner," he said, when it looked like Fae would keep going despite the distraction, "I'd like you to prepare the conference room again. If you don't mind."

"Of course, my lord," she said, staring daggers.

～∞∞～

He and Kalani were alone in the vault chamber after Fae had completed her ritual. The elf stood, admiring the gargoyles. "They are skilled work," she told him. "Only a few hundred years old."

He leaned back in his chair, disappointed. "So they're original." The kingdom itself was only a little older than that. It was a depressing thought; it meant that Varelous the Arch-Mage, founder of the realm, had been the high point of the kingdom's sophistication. In all that time, they had never equaled his magic.

"Sorry," she said. "I did not realize you knew the kingdom's age. In our field notes, it says this is a controlled truth for your realm."

He stared up at her for a long moment. Finally, he felt he could speak without growling. "Are there any other secrets I should know?"

"Hmm. No, you invalidated them. The Iron Throne's subversion of the Gold, the suspicion of direct *hjerne-spica* involvement."

"A bit more than a suspicion."

"Which is why I am here. Forgive me, I would have been happy to visit you solely for the company, but the truth is that I was dispatched to investigate."

"Fair enough." Christopher could hardly take offense. He had been happy to see her for his own selfish reasons.

"So you did it?" She hid her excitement under a layer of reserve. Apparently discussing death and destruction wasn't supposed to be fun. The naughtiness was positively flirtatious.

"I did," he said.

"An astonishing feat for one of your rank."

Christopher found her honest appreciation far more alluring than the artless seduction she had tried the first time they had met. This was getting out of hand. Especially when he realized that no one could ever know what they did or said here.

"I cheated," he said, trying to deflate himself.

"There is no such thing when dealing with *hjerne-spica*," she laughed. "Even we are allowed to lie without compunction to their horrid faces."

"It told me they never lied."

She cocked her head in disbelief.

"While it was under a truth-spell. I talked to its corpse."

"Why," she said in amazement, "would you do that?"

"Because I wanted to make a deal."

She sat down heavily, staring hard at him. At this point, he had very good odds of either seducing her or getting himself killed. It was hard to tell which.

"It told me the location of its lair. And the password for entering."

Understanding flooded across her face. "And you would like to sell the information." Despite the mercenary accusation, she didn't seem any less impressed.

"Sort of. I know I can't do it alone. I was hoping to persuade Alaine and Lucien to help."

She laughed, skeptical and unnerved at the same time. "Lucien wouldn't walk into a goblin keep with you, and this is a thousand times worse."

"Oh," he said, crestfallen. "So that's a no?"

"On the contrary. My mother will leap at the chance. If your information is genuine, the Directorate will pounce on it. You may not appreciate their zeal, however. Understand that they will consider the destruction of your entire kingdom acceptable collateral damage for an operation of this magnitude."

"Um," he said. "Is that likely?"

"I assume not. Yet you must know the truth. Do you still wish to proceed?"

The kingdom was going to be destroyed by the *hjerne-spica* anyway, once they were good and ready. Christopher would rather deny them that. He nodded.

Her excitement was unsuppressed now. "Give me something to convince them with."

He traced the sigil in the air. She got it in one try.

"Does that mean anything to you?" he asked.

"Not at all. But when I show it to mother, she will either laugh at me, or she will get that look she gets when she thinks you don't know what the Dark you're getting yourself into."

Christopher knew that look well. He was glad he wasn't going to be the one exposed to it.

"And," Kalani said delicately, "your price."

"I have to go along," he said. "I have to bring my retinue." She looked exceedingly dubious, so he explained. "I kind of promised to do that as part of the deal. I'm not sure what happens if I break that. I'm worried it will invalidate the password or something."

"Probably true," she agreed. "Very well. They will explain that you will be in great danger. Then they will let you do as you like. If you are part of the attack force that implies, you will reap the regular rewards. For a man of your rank, that is probably half a share—out of many."

"Is there likely to be a lot of treasure?"

"There is," she said. "Although there might not be. The raid might fail or only be partially successful. The cost might exceed the gain. We know nothing of the size of this nest; it could be three young egg-mates playing at being Masters or it could be a dozen full clans with ten-thousand-year-old elders."

Christopher pulled himself together. This was no time to surrender to greed. "What I need is my seventeenth rank. And a free hand out from under their control. The rest . . . I don't care about the rest."

"You drive an easy bargain." She looked at him with concern. "Too easy. It smells like a setup."

He shrugged. "Alaine will understand."

She smiled wryly. "Still playing at secrets, even now? I know the answer. You wish to reach to your own world. You wish to be the path-maker for your people. Against that glory, what are a few ranks here or there?"

That was not what he had meant. He had told Alaine that she did not have the power to return him to his wife. Watching her with her forbidden dragon boyfriend, he assumed she would understand that some things were more important than power.

Kalani turned away but not before he saw tears in her eyes.

"Forgive me," she said, before he could react. "I am sick with fear. Everything you say is everything I ever wanted to hear. It all seems too neat and tidy. It is too beautiful to trust and too precious to pass by. It shakes me to my bones. I feel as if this one act will unleash a future I have hoped for all my life but never dreamed of because it is too large for the imagination."

"Well," he said, casting about for something comforting. "We still have to defeat the nest. If that fails, nothing changes."

She shook her head. "How contrarian, that failure should seem like the less fearful option."

From that comment alone, Christopher understood that, however many years she had been alive, she was still young.

"You can't speak of this outside this room," he said.

She winced at the obviousness of the rebuke. "Fair enough, as I was about to warn you of the same. Perhaps we should stop treating each other like tyros. After this you will truly be on the stage of the world. The rank you seek is uncommon even among elves. Far more so for other peoples."

"What about among *hjerne-spica?*" The one he had killed had been equivalent to a seventeenth rank, going by the tael it had yielded.

"Oh, no. All of them are Legendary. They come that way from the egg. But I was not counting them as people."

"Hold on." Christopher sat up straighter. "If every single *hjerne-spica* is a legendary spell-caster, how is it they don't run the whole damn world?"

She looked at him with curious sympathy. "Your answer is in two parts. First, to create an egg is as expensive as promoting you to that rank and thus requires the decimation of whole civilizations to achieve. Hence, their numbers are limited by necessity."

He paused, trying to process the magnitude of her words.

"And the second part?"

With a gentle shrug, she said, "They do."

Kalani was gone in the morning, her room empty and neat. She had made the bed before she left or perhaps never slept in it. One window stood open, looking out over the three-story drop to the courtyard.

Christopher could do nothing but wait. He had been doing plenty of that, but this was worse. He had thought that the elvcs were at war with the *hjerne-spica*. It appeared that they were more of a resistance force. Saboteurs fighting to weaken the ruling class, rather than an invading army. That cast humans in the role of oppressed citizenry. If the *hjerne-spica* were a traditional government, they would simply replace the nest and severely punish the entire region for its rebellion.

However, Kalani had said it was expensive. It might take them decades or even centuries to produce new overlords. He had to believe that two hundred years of freedom was worth a war.

He took to riding out of the city almost every day. He kept hoping for more birds to contact him, and if nothing else, Royal loved the exercise. The trips seemed to inspire his people, too. They all but cheered him on the way out and back in. Cannan finally explained that they thought he was going "on adventure," and they were hoping he'd gain more rank by killing random monsters around the country-side. The sheer disconnect between that view and reality was too large to bridge.

In the end, adventure came to his castle. A wandering band of minstrels, a dozen men and women of various ages dressed in the motliest collection of outfits he had seen outside of a Salvation Army store, capered at the castle gates as he rode in for dinner. He tried to ignore them; Lalania arranged for whatever entertainment was appropriate for state dinners, and he was learning to stifle his impulse to give random people money.

But as his horse passed the small, shabby wagon that served as the troupe's impromptu stage and probably their home on the road, he saw a woman caring for the donkey in its traces. She looked up at him with a face that dared him to comment on the ridiculousness of it all, if he happened to feel suicidal.

The eyes and hair were the wrong color, the ears hidden under black curls, but there was no mistaking Lady Alaine's minatory glare.

Royal stopped moving of his own accord. Christopher scrambled to play his part. "Ah." He turned to Cannan, who was staring at the troupe suspiciously. That didn't mean anything, however, because he stared at everyone that way. "Maybe we should have a show tonight."

Cannan gave off staring long enough to be amazed. "This lot? Lala would have them strung up. They're not even in key."

"Pardon me, Ser," said the smallest one. She appeared to be a child of nine or ten. "We are only practicing. Once we come together in tune, we will put on a show worthy of lords."

"Um. Who's in charge?" Christopher asked, looking at the back of Alaine's head. She had turned around and was ignoring the conversation.

"Today it is my turn," the little girl said. "I shall broker our wages and our services, if it please my lord."

"That's the oldest trick in the book," Cannan told him. "They think you will be more generous with a child."

"'Tis no trick, Ser. It really is my turn." She faced Christopher and curtsied. "And I shall not cheat you, my lord. I offer a night's work, with all the amusement, diversion, and dare I say wisdom we have to offer, for a flat fee. Seventeen silver pennies to make your dreams come true, at least for a little while."

Cannan rolled his eyes. "That's a ridiculous price."

"It is," she agreed. "And yet it is what was offered."

Christopher grit his teeth. Elves were as bad as troubadours, always speaking in codes. "Sure," he said. "I accept. I'll send my bard out to show you where to set up."

The girl curtsied again and stepped out of his way. Christopher and his cavalry escort rode past them and through the gates. His guts clenched in anticipation. Anything that could make Alaine that unhappy was bound to plunge the depths of misery.

15

SHOW AND A DINNER

The troupe performed with disparate skills. The little girl did a dreamy, languid dance that might have been sensual if she had been older or if the movements had been at all comprehensible. Several of the others sang like angels; one had trouble hitting the right notes. Half of them played a variety of musical instruments, again ranging from rank amateur to virtuoso. Lalania sat through the whole performance with a fake smile cemented on her face. The audience applauded politely when Christopher did, but he could tell many of them were wondering why their tax dollars were being spent on this.

After the show, the troupe was given a table at the end of the room. Christopher was amazed at the quantity of food that went to their table and disappeared. Then they went out to the stables to sleep.

Their sheer ordinariness made him wonder whether he'd made a mistake. He leaned over to Lalania to ask.

"A normal lord," she said conversationally, although her voice was pitched so low no one else could hear, "would send a footman to invite one of more attractive members up to his chamber."

"Should I do that?"

"You're not that normal. Not yet, at least. You can go look in on your horse. Everyone knows how you favor the beast."

He put down his fork. His appetite had not recovered yet. "Only if you come with me."

"I would be delighted." Her false smile had not budged.

So it was a party of three that eventually wandered into the stable. Christopher, Lalania, and Cannan, the usual group, although Lalania was sometimes absent for days. He seemed to spend most of his time around these two. Gregor, Torme, and Karl had other duties; they were often in the field training their regiments. Faren had a church to run, and Fae he avoided. Did this mean he could claim only these two as his retinue? The wording of his deal with the *hjerne-spica* was troublingly vague.

He fed Royal an apple, stroking the big horse's head. Eventually, the little girl from the troupe joined them.

"Did you like my dance?" she asked with the guilelessness of a child.

"It was unique," he said truthfully. "Although I'm not sure what it meant."

"Meaning is a secret revealed only by long acquaintance. Perhaps you should join our troupe for a while."

He chuckled. "Sadly, I have a kingdom to run."

She looked up at him. "Kingdoms are like sandcastles; they come and go with the tide. Wisdom lasts forever. And yet a wise kingdom lasts longer than a single tide. Your realm can spare a few weeks while you gain wisdom."

"Weeks?" He didn't have that kind of time to waste.

"Ambitious projects require ambitious plans." She smiled serenely.

There was a lot to unpack in that statement, including the suggestion that teaching him wisdom was an ambitious project, but Lalania didn't let him.

"You must take the concept seriously," the bard told him earnestly. "A good king knows when to indulge his subjects."

"Indeed," the girl said. "Take leave of your counselors tonight and slip out with us at daybreak to travel your realm in our company. We shall disguise you, so bring nothing but the necessary; your sword, cloak, and perhaps a nice tunic. We will teach you to sing for your supper, and you may learn surprising things about yourself."

Cannan stepped forward to glare down at the girl. "He goes nowhere without me."

"Of course," the girl agreed. "Although I have no hope of making an entertainer of you, still our hostler can use help with the donkey."

"And myself," Lalania said.

The girl nodded. "We could use a cook."

Lalania grimaced briefly before replacing it with a resigned smile. Christopher gaped at her. "Really? All this . . . really?"

She touched his face, glad for his sympathy. "Yes."

***

His armor and cloak were packed into a small chest. Cannan's scaled armor was folded and stuffed into a strong canvas duffel bag. Both their swords were wrapped in a thick blanket and tied up with string. He was wearing ordinary workman's clothes, scrounged up from somewhere deep in the bowels of the castle. Cannan had been the harder one to clothe; in the end, Lalania had to stitch two tunics together with magic to cover his broad chest. They stood in his bedchamber, saying their goodbyes.

"I don't like it," Gregor said. "I don't like you being gone, not knowing where you are or when you will come back, that you are going out with this lot, and that you have to travel like a beggar. I don't like any of it."

"That is rather the point," Lalania said. "These . . . people . . . are not particularly impressed with pomp and circumstance." She was wearing the plainest clothes Christopher had ever seen her in. Her only luggage was the lyre. "All those years you practiced humility will pay off now," she told him. "For a normal lord, this would be exquisite torture."

"If that minx tries to make me sing, you'll all know what torture is," he said.

Torme shook his head, agreeing with Gregor's displeasure. "We can say you are on adventure. That will buy us a season at most. Any longer and we will face difficulties."

"She said a few weeks," Christopher reassured him. "My patience won't last much longer than that. And in any case, the year's almost over."

Lalania cocked an eye at him. The rest of the room stared.

"Oh. I guess I shouldn't have said that last part. Well, there it is. If we aren't back by the end of the year, we won't be coming back."

Faren snorted. "You won't get out of it that easily. I will drag your corpse back onto that throne with my bare hands."

"I can't believe I'm not going with you," Gregor said. "How did this happen?"

"The kingdom needs you," Lalania said. "The Blue think you are on their side. They support the throne because they assume you look out for their interests."

Christopher couldn't help himself. He glanced at Torme. The man always seemed to be left out.

"He is needed, too," Lalania said. "The Green fear him. They assume he will see through their plots."

"You are too kind," Torme told her. "There are more important matters than my feelings. Christopher must name a successor in case he does not return. The nascent church of Marcius should not suffer rivalry for its leadership."

It shouldn't have been a hard decision. There were only two choices.

"Um. Torme?" He made it a question, in case anyone objected.

"Of course," Gregor agreed. "He outranks me in divinity. So much is obvious. But what about the kingdom?"

Christopher looked around the room.

"Not I," said Faren. "Nor, sadly, our esteemed Karl. The realm is not ready."

"The logical choice is Duke Istvar," Gregor said.

Christopher could not abandon his friend and everything they had built. "Karl can't be king, but he can choose the next king. Let Istvar or whoever make their case to him."

The man in question tilted his head. "I might prefer the life of a troubadour to that."

"Karl the kingmaker," Lalania said. "It has a nice ring. While you hold the army, you will hold the power to impose change. The College will be your ally as long as Friea runs it. You might have to bed Uma to keep her loyal, though. She's a bit . . . competitive."

It took Christopher a minute to understand she wasn't joking. The realization was not comforting; she would only speak so frankly if she were truly concerned they might not return.

"We should go," Christopher said. If he waited any longer, he might change his mind. He could stay here, live out his days making machines and justice, remain a saint instead of a legend. There was nothing left to threaten his throne. The troupe in the stable would destroy the *hjerne-spica* without him. His presence wouldn't matter. He could give away the location and stay safe and secure in the world he had built.

He picked up the wooden chest, heavy with armor, and walked out the door.

⌀⌀⌀

One of the men of the troupe had a go at the three of them with little pots of makeup and a pair of scissors. Surprisingly, there did not seem to be any magic involved, only skill. By the time the man was done, Christopher barely recognized his companions. He was spared looking in a mirror because there weren't any in the stable.

The troupe wandered out as soon as the castle gates rose, just moments after the sun did. The gate guards paid them little mind, perfunctorily searching the wagon and their backpacks for stolen goods and winking at the women. Christopher watched through narrowed brows, taking mental notes.

"Oh stop," Lalania said. "They're a hundred times better than they used to be."

Cannan grunted in disagreement. "They are lax."

"We are leaving, not entering. Where is the danger in that? They watched the lord of the castle personally let our group in. And in any case, there are no foes left to guard against."

"Rank always has enemies." Cannan spat on the ground. One of the gate guards noticed and looked at him. Christopher could see the man forming a sharp comment, thinking better of it, and deciding to let it pass. Another wagon approached the gate, and the soldier went over to it.

"Stop drawing attention to yourself," Lalania scolded quietly. "At least let us sneak out of our own courtyard."

Cannan laced shut the huge backpack the troupe had given him and swung it over his back. Christopher did the same with his considerably smaller one. The packs were stuffed with provisions from the castle kitchen. Christopher wondered whether they had been paid for. Lalania got off lightly, burdened only with the lyre in a leather covering.

He walked out of his own city unnoticed, invisible in plain sight. It had been a while since he had seen the city from this level. Normally, he was on the back of a horse. The city seemed closer and yet more distant, the cobblestones hard under his feet, the crowd in the street flowing around him without breaking their own conversations. Nobody stared at him. Nobody cared.

If the troupe had meant to teach him humility, they had already failed. He reveled in it. All through the town and down the long winding road that led to the plain below, he was just Christopher Sinclair. A tourist, gawking at the strange architecture, the unfamiliar costumes, the life of a city borne by little movements. An old codger sweeping the sidewalk in front of his shop. Men and women hustling to work. Three children playing tag throughout the crowd while their mother shouted at them.

"That was nice," he said at the foot of the spire of rock that held up the city. "Thank you."

"We have yet to begin," the girl said, amused. "You can call me Jenny. I shall call you Califax."

"Sure," he said. "Califax it is. Now which way do we go?"

"Ah." Her face fell. "I hoped you would have some idea."

"If you're looking for rich courts to play in, I would suggest north."

Claire smiled again, her mood changing as easily as a child's. "How far shall we travel?"

"Do you know what a prime number is?" He smiled back, pretending he was about to share a secret. "A number that cannot be cleanly divided by anything but itself. There are forty-five such numbers we must pass by 'ere we reach the forty-sixth. And with that many leagues we may find a court worthy of playing in."

She eyed him critically. "You don't actually know what a league is, do you?"

"No," he admitted. "I meant miles. Now are you going to keep criticizing or do you want to hear the rest of the riddle?"

"Of course," she said politely.

"Seventeen coins you were paid, but two were false. The true ones lean east."

She shook her head sadly. "You're really terrible at this."

It had taken him an hour to count out all the prime numbers to three hundred and seventeen. Consequently, he'd rushed the rest of it a bit.

"Let me know when you need another hint," he said, enjoying the walk. The sun was bright on the snow-covered fields, and his feet hadn't gotten cold yet. That was the weak point of his disguise. He was wearing peasant clothes, but his boots were fit for a noble. There was a limit to how much he would suffer for the sake of art.

By the time they stopped for lunch, the fun had stopped. Now it was just a terribly slow way to travel. He could still see the city in the distance, a lump of stone standing up on the horizon.

The troupe milled about, doing their own thing. Several practiced a juggling act while a woman tuned a lute. Lalania broke out pots and pans and cooked something hot over a blaze of kindling, Jenny watching critically to make sure the bard didn't cheat and use magic. Christopher sat on his pack and thought about taking up pipe-smoking. It would at least be something to do.

Cannan was at the wagon, helping Alaine rub down the donkey while it was out of the traces. So far the elf hadn't said a word to him. He stared at her, wondering whether he'd made a mistake. The sum total of his experience with elves was the woman and her daughter. He had assumed they looked similar because of the relationship, but what if they all looked like that? Maybe he couldn't tell one elf from another. He shouldn't apply a human template, as Lucien the dragon would have told him.

The elf looked up to catch him staring. The expression on her face killed his doubts. This was clearly a woman who had already exhausted her patience for dealing with Christopher. That meant she knew him well.

He realized he couldn't ask her where her dragon boyfriend was. Even if he figured out a suitably coded message, he wouldn't be able to understand the answer.

Jenny brought him a cup of hot soup. It was delicious in the way campfire food always is.

"Thanks," he said, cradling the cup in both hands.

"We will find a village to spend the night in. The others want to know what you can perform."

"I can do math tricks," he said between slurps. "And bad riddles."

"Neither of those seems appropriate entertainment for the peasantry. Perhaps I should find something else for you."

"Sure," he agreed. It was a relief to not be in charge.

When she came back to collect his empty cup, she brought him a lute.

"Um," he said. "Unless you want me to fix it, I don't know what to do with this."

"Just try it," she said. When he held it up, she frowned and corrected his hand position. "Now play something you like."

He couldn't even read music, let alone recall a song from memory. Playing a lute seemed a bridge too far. But Jenny's face was so intent, he felt compelled to try. He closed his eyes and thought of the fantastic intro to Heart's "Crazy on You." His imagination was so vivid he could hear the notes ringing in the air.

When the bass was supposed to kick in, he realized something was wrong. He could still hear the music, but it clearly wasn't in his mind because there was only the guitar track. He looked down at his fingers flying over the lute. He would have dropped the instrument in shock, but he liked the song too much. So he gave in to the moment, letting his hands do whatever they wanted.

When it was done, he discovered that his fingertips were bleeding. Magic might have granted him skill, but it hadn't given him the calluses of a professional.

"That was lovely," Jenny said, taking the lute from him and wiping specks of blood off the neck. "Don't heal your hands. We're not using spells today."

"Don't change the subject," he said, before she could divert him. "It's magic. I get that. But I don't actually know the song. Where did the notes come from?"

"You have heard the song before, yes?" When he nodded, she shrugged her shoulders. "Then it is somewhere inside you."

"Do you have any idea how many songs I have heard?"

"No," she admitted. "Your realm has a bardic college. Surely they know a thousand or more. Your realm is isolated, however, so I would not expect you to know more than those. And how many hours a day can you spend attending performances, anyway?"

He shook his head. A thousand songs was a single rack of a record store.

"You know how to make a stone glow like a torch, right?" He'd spent a fair amount of time casting that spell, back when he had been merely a Curate. "Imagine if you could make a stone play music. And then carry it around in your pocket all day."

"To what purpose?" she asked, mystified. "Light enables work, but what do you gain from constant music?"

"Amusement."

She wrinkled her nose. "It seems like a frivolous use of power."

He nodded. "Cardinal Faren would say the same thing. I would even agree with him. And yet, if you made pocket rock concerts, people would buy them."

"That sounds like the kind of logic that wizards used to invent trolls. And now the world is plagued with the creatures, while whatever warlord who first dreamed of paying for such a hideous tool is long since dead and dust."

Now she sounded so much like Alaine that he glanced up to make sure the elf was still at the wagon.

"That's one thing I know," he told Jenny. "Change can't be stopped. Swim with it or get drowned by it, but you can't stop it."

"Hmph," she muttered with a delicate shrug.

Alaine and Cannan were putting the donkey back into harness. The rest of the troupe was putting on their packs. Christopher joined them.

16

SHOULD OLD ACQUAINTANCE
BE FORGOTTEN

For the performance that night, he was given the worst job. They dressed him in motley, painted his face in ridiculous colors, and sent him into the crowd with a hat in his hands to solicit offerings.

Jenny, the little thief, played his song to wild applause.

Walking through the audience, two or three score of villagers layered in dirty, dull-colored linens, he was gratified to see no signs of hunger. They paid almost no attention to him, their eyes on the performances. He collected eight copper pennies, a loaf of hard bread, and a wedge of cheese wrapped in a handkerchief.

At the edge of the crowd, he witnessed a small drama. A stocky man was staring down a skinny teenaged boy holding hands with a pretty girl his own age.

"Shove off," the man said.

"You shove off," the girl said with spirit. "I came here with him."

The man snorted. "You're wasting your time. Just look at him. He won't come back from the draft. He hasn't got the fiber for it."

"That's not true," the girl said. "Everybody comes home from the draft now. Saint Christopher sees to it."

"Well, then, what's the point of that?" The man sounded truly aggrieved. "Should we breed our mares with any fool horse that can walk without falling down? The line will falter and we'll be reduced to flighty weaklings. Like this one."

An old man spoke over his shoulder, his eyes on the troubadours who were doing a juggling act. "He's not wrong."

"Aye," an older woman sighed, still watching the show.

"I don't care," the girl declared. "I made my choice."

The man took a step forward. "What makes you think it's up to you?"

Instinctively, Christopher put his hand to his waist. He froze when he didn't find his sword, remembering why he wasn't wearing it. He could knock this bully down with a dozen different spells, but he wasn't supposed to use magic. For that matter, he could easily win a fist-fight, thanks to his supernatural vitality, but again that would give away his identity. He was, ironically, more helpless than the first time he'd witnessed this little scene. One that must play out endlessly across this harsh world.

Before he could decide what to do, someone else intervened. A shorter, leaner man, younger than the deliberateness of his movements, stepped beside the burly man and placed a hand on his shoulder.

"It might not be up to her," he said conversationally. "But it's not up to you either."

The bully brushed his hand aside and squared his shoulders. "Walk away, Goodman," he said, low and dangerous. "This is none of your affair."

"Aye, it might not be. And yet here I am." The lean man stood with his hands at his side, not at all threatening. And yet, his stance was obdurate, a pillar of granite that did not challenge, but simply was.

The girl and her boyfriend had made use of the diversion and skipped off. The bully looked at the interloper, considering, but there seemed to be little point in pushing the issue now. He turned and stomped away.

A woman joined the lean man, stepping next to him and hugging him. "I wish you wouldn't do that," she said.

"So do I," he answered good-naturedly, putting his arm around her. "I just can't stand to see them pick on the kids."

Christopher stared. He knew this man. He just couldn't figure out from where. The man noticed him staring, and Christopher ducked his head and turned away.

Then it came to him. The last time he had seen this man had been three years ago, in a tropical swamp. Christopher had tried to shoot him. If he had succeeded, no one would have held him to blame. The man—a boy, then, barely older than the teenager he had just defended—had been making a game of torturing an ulvenman pup. Karl had dismissed the man from the army and sent him fleeing, all in the time it took Christopher to reload a rifle.

There was a story here. A private story that Christopher would never know. All he could do was watch the occasional scene from a distance and wonder at all the wheels that must have turned behind the curtains.

At the base of the city of Kingsrock, there was a field that held a thousand corpses. Men who had died for choosing to be on the wrong side of Christopher's theological dispute with the Gold Apostle. Men who might have turned out like this one, given time. Or like the bully; who could say? At that moment they had been enemies, whatever the wheel of fate might have made of them in the future, and now enemies they would remain, thanks to the permanence of the grave. He could never afford to revive so many.

He shuffled back to the wagon, where the troupe was taking their final bows. The crowd dispersed, and Jenny came over to check his earnings.

"Did you learn anything yet?" she asked.

"Nothing I didn't already know," he said. "And you?"

She inspected the contents of the sack. "I learned that you're terrible at this, too. Before you bed down, visit Jaime. He wants to talk with you."

He found Jaime beside a fire, sewing on a blanket. When Christopher squatted next to the gray-haired man, Jaime threw the blanket over both their heads. With a cheek pressed up against Christopher's, Jaime whispered, "Speak plainly what track we shall tread."

Jaime smelled of sweat, and his hair hadn't been washed in ages.

The man also did not understand personal boundaries. Christopher hurriedly repeated the words the *hjerne-spica* had told him. Jaime responded by whipping the blanket off and resuming his sewing. Dismissed, Christopher went to his bedroll. There was a pile of firewood he hadn't seen before, and Cannan was using it to build a fire that would burn hot and slow for the night. Lalania was still cooking dinner, so he sat and watched Cannan work.

"I'll stand the first watch," Cannan told him. "Although it seems unlikely we will face trouble tonight. The crowd was reasonably pleased; the girl didn't do that ridiculous dance."

"She stole my song," Christopher said. His fingertips were still sore.

"I think they expected more of an argument out of you." Cannan grinned wolfishly in the firelight. "I admit it is a pleasure to watch others crash upon the rock I have so long foundered on. Lala's enjoying it, too, I wager."

"Why would I argue?" Christopher wondered. "This is what I need to do. What would be the point of resisting?"

"Perhaps, for some, the journey is as important as the destination."

Christopher looked across the flames at the big man.

Cannan tilted his head in acknowledgment. "Not for us."

Lalania came to bed late, her hands cold and wet from doing the dishes.

⁓⧏⧐⁓

They walked for days, always heading north, stopping at a different village every night. Christopher was allowed to play on the magic lute, which won him applause for his one song. Cannan did a much better job of collecting money, looming over the audience like a giant clown and blocking the sight of the stage. Eventually, they paid him just to get him out of the way.

Christopher never seemed to have a chance to speak with Alain

She avoided him, and he let her. If they could not talk freely, there was no point.

The troupe seemed entirely comfortable with life on the road, although not with each other. Christopher witnessed several spats, three bouts of tears, one of which included Jaime, and a dozen awkward embraces. There did not seem to be any romantic couples despite the almost even division between men and women. Nor did anyone seem to claim the child Jenny. Indeed, they listened to her counsel gravely and respected her decisions.

One of the worst fights was over whether to grill or boil a chicken. Lalania stood helplessly while two men argued furiously, each holding a wing of the plucked bird. Jenny finally intervened and listened to the men state their cases for a while. Then she called Christopher over.

He obeyed with a frown. This was probably some kind of test of his philosophical mettle. However, he was hungry.

"What would you do?" she asked him. The two men stared at him, as if perplexed that his opinion could possibly be relevant. He largely agreed with their assessment.

"Who bought the chicken?" he asked. Both of the men started to speak, so he interrupted them. "I don't care about your arguments. Who bought the chicken?"

"Neither of them," Jenny answered.

"Then how it gets cooked is up to the person doing the cooking. Let Lalania decide."

The man on the left, a tall, thin man with a regal nose and thick curly hair so black it was almost blue, objected. "You are unconcerned with the principle of the matter?"

"It's a dead chicken," Christopher said. "What principles can be involved?"

The other man, short and portly and sporting an absurd handlebar mustache that Christopher had always assumed was fake, explained. "If it is boiled, we extract the maximum nutrition from the carcass. And we shall need all of our strength for the task at hand."

"To do so," argued the tall man, "is to leave nothing for those that come after us. Foxes could crack the grilled bones for the marrow and ants feast on the scraps."

His opponent immediately objected. "What do we owe the ants? What bargain have we sealed with them?"

"The ants play their part in the natural order of the world. If they did not exist, it would be necessary to invent them."

Christopher was sorry he had asked. "I reject both premises. The calories we gain from boiling are insignificant; the ants and foxes will do just fine without our chicken bones. The effort of cooking the chicken is less than the energy you've spent arguing over it. So: let Lala decide."

"How convenient," the short one sneered. "The decision will be made by your own faction."

"You could do the cooking," Christopher offered.

Lalania smiled in appreciation.

"Hmm," Jenny mused. "I expected you to cut it in half."

"Why? They're not the only ones eating it."

"It's not about dinner," the tall one said. "It is about principle."

"Look," Christopher said. "Sometimes a chicken is just a chicken."

Jenny looked up at him inscrutably. "Sometimes, though, it is not."

"Do what you want," the tall man said, letting go of the offending bird. "I'd rather starve."

"Starve then," the portly one spat vindictively. "You could spare a meal or two."

Christopher frowned. "He's the skinny one. You're doing it wrong . . ."

Both of them stared at him, confused and annoyed.

"Never mind," Christopher said. "Are we done here?"

"We asked for your judgment," Jenny said, "so we must respect your decision. Let the cook decide."

"*We* did not ask," the short one snapped.

Jenny shook her head in denial. "And yet he is here, my dear Oribus. We must play the hand we are dealt."

Both men left, equally angry. Christopher stared down at the girl. "Seriously," he said, "are we done here? Have I passed your tests?"

"The tests are not all about you," she answered. "But have we passed yours?"

He thought back over the trip. The troupe had been reasonably kind to the people they had met. They performed to the best of their ability, whatever that happened to be, which showed consideration for their audience. They treated each other with respect when they weren't arguing. They hadn't killed anyone and eaten their brains.

"Yes," he said. "Although it's a pretty low bar."

She nodded enigmatically and skipped away.

Two days later, they walked north through wilderness, no longer following track or trail. Christopher suspected they had left the kingdom. They camped that night in a forest without a fire, all of them huddled under the wagon for warmth, sleeping on and under the curtains from the stage.

In the morning, Christopher was awoken by elves.

<hr />

They were not quite the elves he was expecting. Alaine had cast aside her disguise, her hair white and her eyes violet again. She was joined by three others, all male, two of whom were wearing silvery chainmail of delicate weave and bearing long, thin straight swords. The armor looked too fine to be more than decorative.

But the rest of the troupe was unchanged. He had expected them to drop their act, but they sat around eating a cold breakfast, reacting to the elves no differently than they did each other.

Christopher pulled his boots on and stamped his feet, trying to warm up. Alaine noticed and started building a fire, piling wood together. While she was sparking flint and steel together, Jaime negligently flicked his hand from twenty feet away, and the fire roared to life. Alaine leaned back, her face neutral. Christopher trudged through the snow to enjoy the heat.

"That seemed a bit rude," he said.

Alaine was unconcerned. "The fire is lit. Does it matter how?"

"Of course it does."

She smiled innocently. "Sometimes a fire is just a fire."

Christopher decided to change the subject. "Lucien didn't want to come along?"

In response, Alaine rolled her eyes. Discreetly, demurely, muted almost to invisibility, but the most concrete sign of exasperation he had ever seen out of the woman. Christopher was too amazed at her lapse of sangfroid to follow up on the question.

The unarmored elf came over to the fire. "Well met, Ser," he said to Christopher.

"And you." It was the smallest possible response he could make. For once he would play his cards close to his chest, at least until he saw what the game was.

"Please, call me Argeous."

Christopher nodded, but did not offer his name in return.

Alaine laughed. "I see you have learned since we last met, Christopher."

"How shall I address you?" Argeous asked politely.

"Christopher will do," Alaine answered for him. "He was a terrible Califax, anyway."

Argeous nodded, accepting her judgment. "I want to confer strategy with you. And also my personal thanks."

Christopher raised his eyebrows questioningly.

"On behalf of the aid and companionship you offered my daughter," Argeous explained.

Confused, Christopher glanced over at the troupe, looking for Jenny to see whether he could spot the family resemblance.

"This should not be hard," Alaine said. "How many elves do you even know?"

"Wait," Christopher said. "You mean Kalani?"

"I do," Argeous said with a nod of his head.

"Then—you're . . ." Christopher looked back and forth between the two elves.

"He is Kalani's father," Alaine acknowledged. "Our association begins and ends there."

"Yes," Argeous agreed. "I'm sorry, is this an issue?"

"He wonders as to the nature of our relationship," Alaine said dryly.

Argeous answered seriously. "I assure you, Christopher, I have the highest respect for the Field Officer's leadership. We have all agreed to follow her lead in this matter."

Alaine was smirking. She was enjoying this. He was still getting off lightly, however. Lucien would have been howling with laughter.

"Maybe we should move on to the strategy portion," Christopher suggested. He looked around for Lalania and Cannan. The big man was right behind him, startling him again with his silent shadowing. The bard was at the wagon, filling frying pans with bacon. He waved her to come over.

Argeous nodded. "Understand you will not be the front line, and yet the situation will be necessarily fluid. Look to your own security primarily, although we would not take healing amiss."

"He means we can't spare anyone to babysit you." Alaine helped Lalania balance the frying pans over the fire. "Try not to get yourself killed."

A piece of bacon slid off a pan and fell into the flames. Christopher thought it was an inauspicious omen.

"I took some precautions," he said. "I left a scroll with Cardinal Faren. If you can get any part of me back to him, then he can revive me." Well, probably. Faren would have the same odds with his scroll that Fae had with the Wizard's, for the same reason. He'd only made one, however, because the scroll had absorbed a ridiculous amount of tael into the ink. "And eventually I can revive the rest of my people. Or yours."

"There is nothing you can do for any of us after the fact," Argeous said. "Let us hope it does not come to that."

"Okay. But you haven't told me what you want me to do."

Alaine shrugged. "Kill anything that isn't us. And don't get in our way while we do the same."

"I apologize for the lack of details, but we actually know very little about what is to come," Argeous said.

Jaime came over, drawn by the smell of bacon. He sniffed several times and then bent down to where Lalania crouched, tending the pans. The man shoved his head to within an inch of Lalania's chest and sniffed loudly. Lalania looked up in alarm at the intrusion. Neither Alaine nor Argeous reacted, which threw Christopher off-balance. Before he could figure out what to say, Jaime looked Lalania in the face, from inches away, and spoke seriously.

"It has but one more charge. Which is likely to be consumed on this errand, whither you wish it to or no."

Lalania put her hand up and gently pushed Jaime away to a more comfortable distance. "It's a bit late to leave it on the dressing table."

Obviously he meant the null-stone. Christopher had given it back to Lalania after the affair in the birch-wood. He was surprised; he had been told no one could know how much longer it would work.

"I could hide it for you," Alaine said neutrally, neither endorsing nor dismissing the idea. "And fetch it after."

Christopher shook his head. "I think you should hang on to it, Lala." It had already won three battles.

Jaime did not argue. He plucked the fallen strip of bacon from the fire and walked away, gnawing at it like a wolf.

"Your companions are ill-mannered," Lalania said to Alaine.

The elf laughed. "They are not my companions. They are yours."

"I thought you arranged this," Christopher said.

"Only from my end," Alaine replied. "And you have taken too long with breakfast. My companions are finally here, and we must be off."

A column of elves in gleaming chainmail marched silently out of the woods, three abreast and dozens long. They wore long swords and carried bows, sheaves of arrows peeking over their shoulders, and moved through the deep-packed snow without leaving a trace.

Lucien appeared, reaching over Lalania's shoulder to pluck a piece of bacon from the pan. "Dear bacon," he said. "How I have missed you."

"Oh," Christopher said. "You came after all."

"I was always here," Lucien said with a grin.

"You were a very convincing donkey," Alaine said with long-suffering patience. "No one could tell."

"Is it true? You did not suspect?"

Christopher thought about what he had seen. The donkey, pulling the heavy wagon without complaint, standing in the traces while they ate lunch, munching on bags of dry oats. Leaving behind little piles, as horses do, while walking down the road.

"No," Christopher said. "I never would have guessed."

The dragon in the shape of an elf smiled happily.

"Put your armor on," Alaine told them. Cannan immediately stomped over to the wagon, tossing aside the three cloaks he had been wearing.

One of the newcomers offered Alaine a stuffed burlap bag. She pointed to Lalania instead. "We are of a size," she explained, "and I think you will need it more than I."

When Lalania stood up, two elves began efficiently stripping her out of her winter gear and the leather armor underneath. Christopher would have objected, but an elf was gently pushing him away.

Cannan threw a dozen folding chairs and a sack of wigs out of the wagon as he dug up their bundled gear. Two elves helped him put on the scaled armor, barely pausing at its ancient design. They did the same for Christopher as soon as Cannan was dressed.

Alaine brought them hot bacon stuffed in cold bread.

"I hope I chose the right spells last week," Christopher said. He had not used magic since then, so his head was still full, but he might have liked to make a different selection. "I was expecting an hour to prepare."

Alaine stuffed the sandwich into his mouth. "That is a bad habit you must disabuse yourself of. Also, consider it is time they would have to prepare as well. They may even now know something is afoot, although they cannot yet know what. Once we chose to strike, it had to be within the hour."

Lalania joined them, tearing half of Cannan's sandwich out of his hands. She was wearing the silver chainmail of the elves and a self-satisfied smirk. It looked good on her, and she knew it.

"Now that," Cannan said wistfully, "is chainmail."

One of the women of the troupe approached them with a makeup jar in one hand and a brush in the other. She handed the jar to Alain and pushed Christopher's chin up. While she held him there, she painted something on his throat that stung. When she was finished, he almost reached up to rub at the pain but stopped himself just in time.

"Don't worry," Alaine said. "It won't come out for days."

The woman was painting on Cannan's throat. Christopher recognized the symbol he had learned from the *hjerne-spica* and taught to Kalani. Lalania went next, wincing at the sting; Alaine showed no reaction. When the woman was done, she dropped the paint pot as if she had forgotten it ever existed and walked away.

Christopher noticed that elves and people were disappearing. Argeous was next to two trees standing close together, his hand on one. Elves walked between the trees but did not come out the other side.

Here, at last, was a gate, although not between worlds. It would take them the rest of their journey in a single step.

The rest of the troupe shambled past, heading for the trees, dropping cloaks, hats, and, in one case, shoes. Jaime smiled crookedly at him. Oribus, the short man from the chicken argument, leered as he walked past. Jenny caught Christopher's hand. "Be careful," she said.

"You be careful," he retorted automatically.

"I will." She smiled up at him, and in that instant he wondered how he had ever believed she was a child.

Lucien poked him from behind. "I have been assigned the rearguard," he grumbled. "Let us not make it the home-guard. The gate will not hold forever."

Christopher trudged toward the trees. The noise was no more than expected from an armored man walking through snow, but in this company, it was the loudest sound around. Lucien opened his mouth to object, and Christopher cut him off.

"I've got this," he said, and cast his silence spell. Now he moved in a blanket of dead quiet. Lucien was reduced to pantomime for his commentary, which Christopher could ignore by not watching.

He strode up to the trees and walked between them.

On the other side of the twin trees was also a cold, snow-laden forest, although the air was thinner and the trees were covered in pine needles instead of bare branches. He could see the last of the troupe walking into a narrow cave entrance in the side of the hill, Jenny in the rear. The entrance was naturally camouflaged; he only noticed it because an elf in chainmail was directing people into it.

When he reached the entrance, the elf held a flask up to his lips and tilted it, feeding him a shot of light wine. Behind him Cannan and Lalania did the same. No one else drank, however. As he stumbled deeper into the cave, the darkness in front of him became transparent. The elves had thoughtfully provided for the three members of the group who could not see in the dark. No more lanterns or lightstones. He was playing in the big leagues now.

"Finally," Christopher grumbled. "For once we'll be on equal terms with the monsters." Of course no one heard him because of the silence spell. He wondered whether Lalania could get the recipe.

At least in the cave it was only cool, not freezing. They wound through narrow passages over clean stone. The passage was not easy even though someone had taken care to cut out the worst of the stalagmites. Jenny scampered along in front of him. He would have been horrified at following a child into battle save for that brief moment before the gate. None of these people was what they seemed. Unfortunately, no one had told him what they were.

The cave floor sank beneath them with every step. Once again he was descending into the bowels of the earth. The journey lasted long enough for Christopher to become thoroughly sick of narrow tunnels. He ducked under a low-hanging lintel, and when he stood up he was staring into an alleyway full of small bodies slaughtered by swords. Jenny stood in the middle of the carnage, watching him.

17

UNDER THE DOME

H is stomach twisted. He had done his share of fighting children. He had come here to kill squids, not . . . whatever these were. He let the silence spell elapse and opened his mouth to object, but a second look robbed him of words.

They weren't human. The heads and bodies displayed scaled, thick reptilian tales and long-fanged snouts. They bore short spear-like weapons and crossbows, some still clutched in lifeless hands. Leather armor covered their torsos, studded with bronze rings.

"They are not juveniles," Jenny explained. "Merely small."

Cannan pushed past him, forcing his way to the front. He glanced over the bodies. "Dragon-kin," he said. "Smarter than hobgoblins. They will have set traps. Stay behind me." The big man started running down the alley.

Lalania huddled behind Christopher as Alaine and Lucien slipped past.

"Oh!" Lucien said, shocked.

"I'm sorry," Jenny said, and Christopher realized she had been waiting for the dragon, not for him.

"Do not be," Lucien answered. "I know who to blame." He strode after Cannan with grim purpose.

"They are not really dragon-kin," Alaine explained softly. "Just an affectation. Yet they are innocent enough in their own way, unlike those horrid goblins. However, for our purposes today, the distinction is non-existent. They will attempt to kill and eat us just as vigorously." She hustled after Lucien.

"Why are we in an alley?" Lalania asked. "Did we go through another gate?"

"No," Jenny said, "although close enough. Look up."

Christopher did so and flinched at what he saw. Above him was a dull metallic purple dome that peaked at five hundred yards high and stretched two miles wide, covering an entire city. It curved down behind them; they had crawled under the lip. The buildings on either side of the alley were ordinary enough, stone and slate slapped together without an eye for tight joins. The road underfoot was cobbled in brick and marginally smoother. Over the tops of the ramshackle buildings, the farthest part of the artificial purple sky was at least a mile away. In the distance, he could see taller buildings as grand as Greek temples. Flying over the nearest was a long golden-hued dragon. The dragon raked the temple with fire and the marble cracked, flame washing blackened bodies out from between the columns.

"A demi-plane," Jenny said. "Left over from the first age of the gods. Light knows the *hjerne-spica* would never pay for so much adamantium even if they could afford it. Only the gods would be so profligate." Her face was wreathed with disgust. "Who knows how long they have sheltered here, protected from divination and direct assault by that indestructible membrane. We may yet have a sharp contest."

There was a series of explosions in the distance.

"Just to be clear," Christopher said, because no one had made it explicit. "That dragon is on our side, right?"

Jenny laughed at his ignorance. "Yes, of course. Today all dragons are your friends, although Oribus would gladly eat you any other day of the week."

"Incoming!" Cannan called from the mouth of the alleyway. He ducked back behind the wall and held his sword in both hands. "Trolls." Lucien stood on the opposite side of the alley and flexed his hands like claws. Alaine drew her long, thin sword.

Jenny gave Christopher one last inexplicable look. It might have been warning, or compassion, or something else entirely. Then she turned to face the incoming threat and began to stretch.

The front half of the girl rushed down the alley while the back half stayed in place. The stuff in between was made of snow-colored dragon. When her wings unfurled and beat down, they reached over the tops of the buildings and drove a wind screaming through the alleyway, collapsing one of the buildings under the pressure. With a second beat she was airborne, a dozen yards above the ground, and the last bit of little girl flowed into the tip of a long white tail. He had thought Lucien was huge in his true form; Jenny dwarfed the green dragon. She was white all over, but the edges of her scales caught the light and sparkled in muted rainbows. This was an effect all the more astonishing because there was hardly any light to speak of, only the illumination of the distant burning buildings. Without the elven potion, Christopher would have seen none of this.

He discovered the limits of the potion when she breathed down on the street beyond. The world flared, the light too bright to tolerate, and he had to turn his head aside. When he could see again, Cannan was alone at the end of the alley.

"Come," the big man ordered, waving in impatience. Christopher and Lalania obeyed.

They moved out into the street, stepping over a dozen charred corpses of trolls. Cannan stabbed at some as he ran by, draining their tael into his sword, but he left more than he harvested, moving quickly.

"Incredible," Lalania muttered. "We are literally jumping over my fifth rank in our rush to be killed by something else."

A hundred trolls would not buy Christopher his next rank. If they won, there would be plenty of time to harvest later; if they did not, it wouldn't matter.

The sky was full of dragons now, a dozen of them wheeling up and down across the underground city. Most were blue or green, with only one white and two yellow.

"We need to find cover," Cannan growled. "They will send a task force to seal the breach against reinforcements. We do not want to be here when that happens."

"Turn left," Lalania said, pointing ahead. "At the next street."

"How can you possibly know which way to go?" Christopher huffed as they ran.

"A city is a city. We want to be away from the edge but not in the center."

Cannan ran around the corner and into a dozen of the small lizard warriors. There was a furious battle as they stabbed at him with their forked spears, and he mowed them down like grass. Christopher moved to join, but Lalania held him back.

"Spell up," she said.

He started casting. After a while, Cannan finished and came over to receive a few spells as well. Christopher felt that everyone in his party should enjoy the energy protection field today. The chance of suffering friendly fire seemed enormous.

Only one small spell was necessary to replenish Cannan's tael from the battle. Lalania frowned at the expense anyway.

"We cannot all wear mithiril," Cannan said, sounding defensive.

"Let us not spend ourselves against petty targets," she answered. "The elves can weed what the dragons miss. Somewhere out here there should be a target worthy of your sword."

They turned at the sound of large feet, running in panic. Half a dozen trolls swept down the street, passing Christopher and his party without a glance. Behind them ran a pair of armored elves, one firing a bow as she ran. An arrow to the leg would cause a troll to stumble and fall, whereupon the other elf would decapitate it with a sword that flashed with searing light as it cut. The battle turned the corner and moved out of sight. When Christopher went to look, the trolls were lying headless on the ground, and the elves were nowhere to be seen.

"You know all of those elves outrank me, right?" Cannan asked Lalania.

"Show-offs," the bard muttered. She shook her head. "I'm still right.

Between Christopher's spells and that sword, you are a dagger poised to strike. It should not be wasted on small game."

"You want to find a squid?" Christopher asked.

"Erm. Perhaps we should not aim quite so high. How about a bishop? The dragon-kin must have priests who will heal the same as any other. Let us disrupt their supply."

They moved from street to street, putting distance between themselves and the tunnel entrance. Cannan kept a dozen feet ahead, in case there were traps. He peeked around a corner and immediately sprinted back, waving for them to run.

"Here," Lalania said, her hands jiggling the door of a brown stone building. It opened, and Cannan dashed inside. Christopher followed, ducking his head to fit through the low door. Lalania slipped in and pulled the door shut.

Christopher found a peep-hole in the door. He had to kneel to look through it. Outside a swarm of several hundred dragon-kin rushed down the street. Behind them came a regiment of much larger lizard-like humanoids. These were at least seven feet tall and covered in metal scaled armor that looked surprisingly similar to what Christopher and Cannan wore, and they carried massive halberds, small tree trunks with a sharpened anvil on the end.

He turned around to tell his friends that the defensive task force had arrived. Cannan stood with his sword held high, ready to strike, staring at a dozen of the small dragon-kin on the other side of the room.

These dragon-kin were not armored. They were barely armed, with a mixture of weapons like long knives and a rolling pin, and shuffled in an aimless mob, pushing each other forward.

"Lower your blade," Lalania whispered.

Cannan let his arms drop to his waist. The dragon-kin stopped advancing. Lalania raised a finger to her lips. All of them stood in silence until the heavy sound of marching passed down the street.

Christopher pushed the door open and ducked outside. Lalania and Cannan came out after him, and together they all ran around the corner. Just when he thought it was safe to say something, it started raining crossbow quarrels.

Cannan ducked, trying to hide his head behind his huge sword. Half a dozen bolts rattled on his armor. Lalania was struck square in the chest, knocking the wind out of her. The bolt bounced off and landed at her feet. Another bolt clipped her hair, and Christopher distinctly saw a blonde lock fall to the ground.

Up the street there were at least a hundred dragon-kin. The second rank was already stepping forward to fire.

"Behind me," Christopher said, and stepped forward, standing up straight and tall. Cannan sheltered in his wake, struggling to make himself small. Lalania hid behind the big knight.

It was quite unnerving watching the cloud of sharp, short bolts flying directly at him. Every single one missed, thanks to the cloak. They landed to either side, sparked against the cobblestones in front of him, or sailed over his head. He did not thank Master Sigrath, not even silently.

The dragon-kin went through three complete rotations, each bowman firing and moving to the rear of the line to reload. By the time they gave up and retreated, the street was carpeted in quarrels. The dragon-kin suddenly broke and ran, disappearing down a side street. Looking for something they could kill, no doubt.

"Should we chase them?" Christopher asked. As he moved forward his foot rolled on quarrel and he almost fell.

Lalania had recovered enough to complain. "A regiment of commoners? There must be hundreds of them here. What difference would one more or less make?"

"They're archers," Christopher said. When she continued to frown, he explained. "They might be able to hurt the dragons."

"Let us hope not," she said with a shudder. "Otherwise we are completely lost."

"Ballistae," he said. "Siege engines. Maybe there." He pointed toward the city center, where stone structures stood commandingly over the lesser buildings.

"They are not you," Cannan said. "And even you never successfully brought a cannon to bear on a dragon."

"Not guns," Lalania hissed, peering forward. "Magic."

Sparkling rockets blazed from the top of a stone tower, lancing out and stabbing a golden dragon in the sky. The creature banked and turned, swooping toward its attackers. It must have cast a spell because the next wave of arcane missiles splashed harmlessly off. Just before the dragon came into range to breathe, a vast storm of missiles shot up from the ground around the tower. They overwhelmed the shield, and the beast was pierced a hundred times.

It broke off its attack, howling like a freight train, diving for cover, and wheeling away from the deadly bolts. More came; the dragon sagged as it fled, and Christopher realized it would not make it to safety.

From above fell the white dragon, its terrifying roar rumbling across the city and reflecting off the dome above. Despite the noise of battle and the distance, Christopher could hear a furious ringing, chimes and gongs being beaten to within an inch of their life. Obviously the countermeasure worked; arcane missiles continued to streak up from the ground. The white dragon's shield also failed, and the bolts began striking home. Again the creature could not close the distance; it breathed out a vast white cloud and used the cover to change direction, diving back to where the gold was now far enough away to escape the bolts.

"Why didn't we think of that?" Christopher asked.

"It's not music," Lalania snapped. "It's magic."

"Look," Cannan ordered. He pointed with his sword.

The cloud had not worked. Somehow the bolts kept coming through the distraction, hammering the white dragon. It sank lower and lower, seeking cover, and finally fell to the ground, only a hundred yards from the tower.

Cannan was already running forward. Christopher ran after him. If Lalania wanted a useful target, this was it. The large lizard warriors would not need crossbows to kill a dragon on the ground. They could use their massive halberds.

Lalania ran past him. Christopher realized Cannan was slowing down, waiting for him to keep pace. The bard did not. Soon she was fifty, then a hundred yards ahead. Christopher ran as fast as he could.

"Go after her," he panted.

Cannan shook his head in denial.

Up ahead a wall began crawling out of the rubble. Lalania was putting the lyre to work. Christopher could see her standing in the middle of the street, playing. Dragon-kin began to rush at her from the surrounding buildings.

All of them died in a hail of arrows. Elves appeared from the shadows, covering Lalania, screening her. They fell back to the wall she had built just as Christopher and Cannan reached it.

"Priest," one of the elves said, "Come." He turned and ran behind a huge stone warehouse. It didn't sound like a request, so Christopher and his party followed.

The white dragon was lying the middle of a pile of stone and timber that had once been several two-story buildings, a jetliner after a crash landing. Christopher could hear battles raging all around the perimeter, held at bay by Lalania's wall and elven swords.

Argeous stood at the dragon's head, arguing with it. "You must be away, my lady. Our position will be overrun soon. Lizardvolk halberdiers approach from behind to crush us against the anvil ahead."

"I cannot," came the answer in a deep bass that Christopher nonetheless recognized as having the same essential quality as the child Jenny's speech. "The darts will pierce me if I rise."

"Then transform, and I will transport you to safety," Argeous implored.

"I am out of shapes for the day. In any case, as a human child, I can offer this battle no more assistance. As a dragon, even on the ground, I can still contribute."

"Or flee, and live to fight another day."

The dragon rumbled in what could only be a chuckle. "I do not have so many days left. This may be my last fight regardless."

Argeous was beside himself with grief. "The Stone Legion waits for you. The world cannot lose you forever. It is unthinkable."

While Christopher lacked the healing power of the priests of the Bright Lady, he made up for it in rank. He now had a very high-level spell that he had never really considered casting before. It seemed ineffective in terms of cost. A single casting of it would heal anyone completely, but he could use a spell of that rank to inflict an awful lot of damage, and even the hardiest person he knew—which was to say himself—could be healed with a handful of lesser spells. However, it looked like he had just discovered a cosmic loophole. It was time to see if "anyone" meant what it said.

He pulled off his gauntlet and touched one of the dragon's huge scales. The size of a car door, it was smooth and warm, like heated glass. He chanted the syllables of his spell. White magic gushed from his hand, splashing against the dragon before being absorbed. The release of so much energy made him dizzy.

The dragon turned its head to look at him, the vitality in its eyes testifying to the effect of his healing. "Thank you, Christopher. I will see that your magic is put to good use."

"It changes nothing," Argeous shouted. "You must still flee."

"I still cannot. The arcanists wait on the other side of that wall. They will slay me before I can climb out of reach."

"Dragon-kin casters?" Cannan asked, a calculating look in his eye.

"You cannot go where I cannot," the dragon said gently. "They will riddle you with half a thought."

"I'm counting on it," Cannan said. "Captain, give me six good men."
He held his hand out to Lalania while he spoke.

"Oh Cannan," she said, wincing. "There will be other foes than magic."

"And once the dragon is in the air, she can deal with them."

Argeous snapped his fingers. Six elves detached themselves from the wall and stood around Cannan, eyeing him critically. They had dropped their shields and carried a sword in each hand, although not all of them were male.

Lalania took the null-stone off and draped it over Cannan's neck. She kissed him and stepped back, biting her tongue.

He laughed at her. "Make me famous." He turned to the elves. "Stay within twenty feet of me or die." Then he charged around the wall, followed by the silver-clad elves.

Nobody else dared follow him. They stood in tense silence until Aregous grinned, his gaze on the ground, although Christopher understood he was using magic to see on the other side of the wall.

"A fine and proper distraction," Argeous said, and the white dragon sprung into the air. The downbeat of her wings drove them all to the ground. As her head cleared the wall, she spat fire on the other side. Some arcane bolts still lanced her, but not enough, and by the time Christopher gained his feet, she was gone.

"We must move," Argeous said. "The lizardvolk still come."

Eight elves were carrying huge shields, constructed on the spot out of ordinary shields and magic. They used them to create a portable wall for the others to hide behind. Christopher, Lalania, and Argeous were in the center, flanked by the score of elves who had surrendered their shields. Together the crowd moved out from behind the wall and pushed into an open field.

The field had once held crops, although Christopher did not recognize them and could not imagine what kind of plant grew in complete darkness. Now it held a battlefield. The crops were burning, their light reflecting off mud slick with blood. Corpses lay everywhere in various stages of dismemberment or cremation. Small dragon-kin dashed about in confusion, occasionally emitting sparkling bolts that failed to pierce the shield-wall. The elves would dart out and skewer anything that got within a dozen feet. Slowly the wall moved forward, picking its way over the broken ground.

Through gaps in the shields, Christopher could see their destination. A thick knot of figures battled in the middle of the field, more continuously rushing to join the scrum. He could see the large halberdiers mixed in with the dragon-kin, and here and there trolls loping eagerly to the smell of battle. At the center was a black hemisphere, twenty feet high and across. The null-stone activated, its magic blocking his potion-derived night vision. The men inside could not hold out against this flood of bodies. Christopher desperately wished for an artillery section or at least a rocket launcher.

He fell to his knees, tripped by the elf next to him. Lalania fell into his arms, narrowly missing being impaled on his sword. Around him the elves were going to ground, pulling the shield wall above them for protection from the sky. He glanced up and understood why.

Winged death was diving on the field in a complex swirling pattern, a dance with dragons instead of ballerinas. They raked the ground with long burning sweeps of flame. Christopher had prayed for artillery and been rewarded with an air strike. The elves huddled under their shields and hoped no one missed. Christopher crawled closer, snuggling up against a silver-clad body with undignified intimacy.

After a dozen breaths, Argeous spoke. "Now." The elves cast aside the shields, leapt to their feet, and charged the center. The burning field was ironically dimmed; the fire-strikes had consumed everything in their path instantly, leaving only gray ash. There was still a battle raging, however. The dragons had taken care not to splash the black hemisphere, and the creatures on the edge continued to fight inward, heedless of the death around them. At least until the wave of elves crashed into them from behind.

Christopher climbed to his feet and helped up the elf he had been lying on. It turned out to be Lalania. She wiped mud off the lyre.

Argeous was the only elf left beside them. He raised his hands for a spell, looking down the street they had come up. Christopher turned just in time to see a column of halberd-bearing lizardvolk get torched by the white dragon rocketing overhead. She moved with tremendous speed and vanished into the cloud of smoke rising from the field.

"Let us find a more defensible position," Argeous suggested. The lizardvolk, or at least the ones not already dead, were running around like headless chickens on fire, but Christopher could see them slowly reorganizing their diminished numbers back into a battle group.

The three of them went to join the rest of their company. Two elves staggered out of the black sphere dragging Cannan between them. He was a mess, covered more in blood than in his armor, which was missing most of its scales.

"I fear he will expire when the rage leaves him," one of the elves said.

"Probably," Christopher agreed. He reached down and touched Cannan's wild-eyed face. The man tried to bite him. Christopher ignored the feeble threat and started casting healing spells. "Anybody else?"

A number elves presented themselves. Christopher shared out what he dared to spare. Cannan recovered his senses and stood up under his own power.

"I cannot see so well from inside the sphere," the big man said. "It made fighting somewhat more challenging."

"How much longer will it last?" Argeous asked. "We could still make use of it."

"The rest of an hour," Lalania said. "Go on, take it. I was told this was its final charge, and as Cannan noted, we are blind inside."

"Thank you," said an elf from the center of the sphere. Up close, Christopher could dimly see through the null-stone effect by the light of the fires. The elf held the amulet aloft and a dozen more gathered around him. Together the group moved off at a full run, heading for the center of the city.

"We lost one," Cannan said quietly.

"I know," Argeous said, walking over to where the sphere had been. In its absence, Christopher could see a silver-clad body lying on the ground, its well-formed, finely featured head half-severed from its fine white neck.

"Help me strip her," Argeous told Cannan. "Quickly now."

The man and the elf rolled the body out of her armor while Christopher watched, disturbed. He had thought the elves too disciplined for such battlefield antics. Argeous surprised him, though. Once the woman was uncovered, the elf produced a dagger and began to cut her underclothes open. Before Christopher could object, Argeous moved on to cutting her body open, dragging a huge gash across her torso just under her breast. The elf shoved his hand inside, searching. His fist came out bloody and clenched around something small enough to hide in his palm. Christopher guessed this was the focus of the spell that automatically reincarnated elves when they died. Kalani had let that fact slip once; he imagined it was the sort of thing elves preferred others did not know, so he pretended not to see. Argeous touched the dead girl on the forehead with his other hand and whispered a cantrip, draining her tael into a purple stone. Both items went into a pocket inside his cloak as he stood up.

"The armor is for you, Ser," Argeous said. "Your own has suffered, and we do not have time to repair it." The elf ignored the dead body, as if it were no more than a log on the field.

"Let's find another place to change," Lalania suggested, changing the subject before Christopher could broach it. Cannan bundled the chainmail under his arm and they went forward, following the path of the other elves.

18

FIRE AND FURY

Christopher was not sure they were going in the right direction. The buildings ahead were being subjected to sustained fire strikes by wheeling dragons. On the plus side, he didn't really need the dark-vision potion anymore because the heart of the city was well lit now. In the negative column, however, had to be accounted the sad fact that buildings kept falling down around them.

One of the golden dragons felt the destruction wasn't fast enough. It landed on a tall tower a hundred yards away and began gutting it with huge claw strikes. After a few moments, the tower gave way. The dragon followed it to the ground, spreading its wings at the last minute to land gracefully.

A smaller dragon, a green one, joined it. Together the creatures flayed the ground, tossing up debris and bodies in a wild spray. Three more circled overhead, occasionally flaming targets that moved to threaten the landed dragons.

"I must leave you now," Argeous said. "My role is about to begin. We have found the heart of the lair."

Before Christopher could speak, the elf simply vanished.

A massive ball of white exploded in the face of the two digging dragons, freezing the moisture out of the air and sending snow sparkling down. The gold shook it off and roared, then dug harder. The green drew back and staggered off, crunching smaller buildings in its wake. It was replaced by a much larger blue dragon. The new dragon breathed into the hole they were digging with a stream of light that blinded like an arc-welder. Even at this distance, Christopher could feel the static discharge of electricity play over his skin.

A small group of elves hurried past. Alaine was with them, dressed in silver chainmail covered in blood. She glanced at the bundle under Cannan's arm.

"Use it well," she told him. The elves ran on, heading for the excavation.

Cannan stepped out of the shreds of his armor. Christopher put away his sword and helped the man into the chainmail, although he needn't have bothered. It slid on like a second skin, held in place by the smallest possible number of straps and catches.

"Are we winning?" Christopher asked. "It feels like we're winning."

"This has all been preliminary. The true battle is only now joined." Cannan was staring at the dragons in the distance. "You should go. But I fear Lala and I are outclassed."

"I'm practically out of spells," Christopher said. "I did a lot of healing. Without magic, I'm just another sword." He strongly suspected that even with his rank he was no match for the elven swordsmen.

"If I still had the lyre I would be able to help," Lalania grumbled. Christopher could tell she hated being out of the spotlight.

"I think you did just fine with it," he told her. "You saved a dragon's life."

"We all did," she said. "It took all three of us."

In the distance, the excavation erupted. Sparkling bolts lanced out of it, larger than the ones Christopher had seen before. If those had been rifle shots, these were cannon. Dozens and dozens of them ripped into the blue dragon. It rose up, standing briefly on its rear legs. Christopher could see the bolts tearing through its body and coming out bloody holes on the other side. The dragon clawed at the air, trying to gain purchase on nothing at all, and fell heavily to the side. There was no mistaking that fall. It was dead before it hit the ground.

Five more dragons rushed in, led by the white. With them in a group, Christopher could assign a sense of scale. The white was considerably larger than the rest. All of the dragons pounded at the ground, tossing up paving blocks the size of small cars. The rain of debris began destroying the surrounding buildings. Dragon fire and spell energy poured back into the hole.

Then it stopped, suddenly. Three dragons shrunk out of sight while the others watched intently.

"The elves have gone in," guessed Cannan.

Elsewhere in the city, dragons still roamed, burning and swooping. They seemed fiercer than before, if that were possible to imagine.

Two dozen halberd-bearing lizardvolk marched around the corner. Hissing and spitting, they charged. Christopher drew his sword and held his ground next to Cannan. Lalania ducked behind the remains of a wall, her thin blade in hand, waiting for a chance to stab someone in the back.

"Something for swords to do, then," Christopher muttered.

The three of them huddled in the basement. Half-collapsed, the stone wall facing the street actually lying in the street, it still offered a defensive position. Christopher summoned up the last of his magic to heal the bleeding gash across Lalania's face. It might not have been the worst of their wounds, but he could not bear the thought of her wearing a scar for the rest of her life.

"Bloody trolls," Cannan grunted. "I should have brought hand grenades."

"I should have brought a cannon," Christopher said. "But there was no place to hide it on that stupid wagon."

"I should have brought a silk pillow," Lalania retorted. "So I could put it over my head and be spared your petty misgivings."

"Or lunch." Christopher's stomach rumbled. "You should have brought lunch. I think the elves forgot we have to eat."

"We are in the middle of a city. If you need food, we can surely locate some."

He was out of magic, though. He couldn't make sure it was safe to eat. For that matter, he didn't want to know what they ate around here.

"Do you still have spells?" he asked Lalania.

"No," she sighed. "I ran out an hour ago."

Cannan frowned. "We have not seen an elf in some time. Perhaps we should consider retreat."

Assuming they could find their tunnel and win through whatever forces were there, they would just find themselves in a cold forest hundreds of miles from anywhere. "How would we get home?" he asked. "The elves were our ride."

Lalania pinched her face. "We need only survive until you renew. Then your magic can heal us, feed us, and transport us. How did you forget this?"

For all his reliance on magic, when he got tired, his abilities seemed to slip his mind. It was like trying to count change in a foreign language. At the end of a long day, you always fell back to your native tongue.

"It's been a long day," he said.

"Then let us end it," Cannan said. "We have delayed long enough. We should approach the lair and see if the war is won."

That seemed like a bad idea if it hadn't been. On the other hand they could still see the occasional dragon flying overhead, so presumably their side hadn't lost.

His stomach rumbled again. "Okay," he said. "Let's do that."

They picked their way carefully through the rubble. What little opposition they met seemed more interested in running away than fighting. Only the trolls fought for the sake of violence, and the supply of the regenerating creatures was steadily diminishing. The prevalence of flame probably had something to do with that.

A green dragon, one of the smaller ones, passed overhead and then banked to come around again. It found a street wide enough to land in, on account of the buildings on both sides being smoking ruins. The dragon waited for them to make their way over to it.

"I am glad to see you still alive," Lucien rumbled. "The Masters are dead; the field is ours."

"Nobody told the trolls," Christopher said.

"No," Lucien agreed, "nobody told them. They will have to be rooted out and burned, one by one. A tasteless, thankless task. That will probably fall to me."

Christopher had noticed that Lucien was, in fact, the smallest of the dragons present. Considering that not too long ago Lucien had been the biggest creature Christopher had ever seen, that was quite a change in status.

"What about the lizards?" Christopher asked, thinking of the household his party had spared.

"They are already fleeing. A tragedy in the making. They are ill-equipped for survival above ground; it has been untold generations since any of them have seen the sun. They will starve, and drown, and die of a thousand dangers. Unless they find civilizations to loot, in which case they and many others will die by violence."

Christopher had once had his house invaded by mice when a neighbor, notorious for his lack of housekeeping, had moved away. The animals, used to a steady diet of abandoned pizza boxes, had come looking for new markets once their unwitting benefactor had decamped. As annoying as the mice had been, they did not arrive with crossbows and magic.

"They should stay here," Christopher suggested.

"Orbius would eat them all," Lucien said. "For that matter, most of the others would too. Jaime's destruction has burned through all of their good will."

"But not yours?" Lalania asked carefully.

The green dragon sighed, a long and windy affair that knocked over a loose-hanging door. "I cannot help but think of Kalani and the ulvenmen. Goblins are irredeemable, but dragon-kin might not be."

"Have you mentioned this idea to Alaine?" Christopher asked.

Lucien snorted, emitting a cloud of smoke the size of a small wagon. "I may be the smallest dragon here, but I am not a hatchling. I know better than to bite my own tail."

Christopher nodded, thinking how unwise it would be to tell your girlfriend that you thought her daughter was right.

"Which is why," Lucien continued, "I want you to say it for me."

"Our lord is not known for his diplomacy," Lalania said sweetly. "Perhaps, therefore, not the best choice."

"On the contrary," Lucien said, lowering his right wing to the ground, where it formed a ramp onto his back. "She already expects the worst of him, and hence he has nothing to lose. Come now, let us be off before the trolls let hunger overcome their survival instinct."

Christopher looked dubiously at his companions, each of whom was looking at him with the same expression.

"It can't be any worse than your cloud spell," Cannan said with resignation. He climbed onto the dragon's back, trying to find handholds among the scales.

As it turned out, Cannan was wrong. There was a very large difference between driving a fast car without seat belts, seats, or doors and being a passenger in that car driven by someone else. Particularly when that someone was Lucien. The dragon didn't fly so much as make a large and extended quarter-mile long hop with the help of his wings. They went up with a sickening lurch, clawing at his scales for dear life, only to have their stomachs thrown into their mouths when he fell into a dive and swooped to the lip of the excavation. Christopher lost his purchase at the last moment and fell the last ten feet, landing in a clanking heap.

Lucien looked down at him curiously. Christopher picked himself up while his companions dismounted, looking as green as the dragon. Jenny lay curled up like a cat a dozen yards away, a mountain of white wearing a Cheshire smile.

"Argeous," she announced, "we are ready."

The elf floated up out of the gaping hole the dragons had clawed into the ground. The rest of the dragons gathered around, landing on the ground in a large circle around Jenny. Oribus, the larger yellow one, perched on the remains of a tower, where he could look down on the rest of them. Several members of the troupe, still in human form, followed Argeous out of the hole through various means. One flew, carrying another, and one simply climbed the raw earthen walls.

Alaine was the only other elf to join the meeting.

"We have not made a full accounting," Jenny said. "There are still minions to harvest and buried secrets to uncover. Yet the bulk of the treasure is taken and ready to be divided."

"What need of council?" Oribus said. "We had an agreement. Simply stick to the terms."

"Of course," she answered. "Your part was honestly done, and I intend no change to your share. But we have an unusual situation. One of our party made a deal for a fixed amount, which might have seemed fair before but now seems ungenerous."

A blue dragon spoke with a rumble. All of the dragons rumbled; they couldn't help it. They were simply too large to make any other kind of sound. "We are not in the business of generosity. Nor should we discount the wisdom of allowing the greater part of this tael to pass to the greater good."

"Indeed," Jenny said. "And yet, what were the precise terms?" She looked to Alaine, who seemed mildly surprised to be called on.

"'My seventeenth rank. And a free hand out from under their control.'" The elf did that annoying elven thing of quoting Christopher in his own voice.

Oribus shrugged, causing several bricks to fall off his tower. "The Masters are dead. No hand is freer than that. Pay him his rank and have done."

"But more may come. This demi-plane, as grotesque as it is to gaze upon, will remain a lure. It is simply too strong a position to leave unattended. Nor, as we all know," she said, looking at Christopher when she spoke, making it clear that her words were for his benefit, "can we destroy it. Such a task is not within our power."

"I can open a gate and flood it with lava," Argeous suggested. "Not destroyed, but uninhabitable."

The white dragon shuddered, making the ground itself rumble. "What a compounding of the crime. First, that the gods should spend tael thus; second, that we should cast it aside. It is spent; let us at least make something of its sacrifice."

"What do you suggest?" the blue dragon asked with a certain amount of exasperated suspicion. Christopher had been in a similar situation once, when he called a council to try and convince Karl to take a rank and it had not gone as he intended.

"One of us should occupy the demi-plane and claim the domain. Thus ensuring our partner his free hand while not wasting an opportunity."

Oribus shook his head, dislodging more bricks. "Among us only you have the stature to be a domain lord. Any lesser creature would just be bait. Yet why ask? You can claim it if you like, and none can stop you. Even if we cared to."

"I will not," Jenny said, and suddenly the air took on a gravity that made it hard to breathe. "My days are truly numbered. I will go with Argeous and take my place in the Stone Legion."

The dragons twitched their tails and murmured, a purring of grief, vibrating the ground with a subsonic keening that did not reach the ears but made the tears flow. Christopher wiped his eyes and noticed with astonishment that the elves and the troupe did not bother. They wept openly.

"Desist," Jenny said. "Remember that we have companions present." The pressure wave receded, though it did not take the sadness with it.

"Yet it does not change Oribus's facts," the blue dragon said brusquely.

"The fact is that we have a staggering amount of tael. We could make a domain lord, if we so chose."

"I will not surrender my share," Oribus cried out, offended to the core.

The other yellow dragon signaled his agreement by breathing fire into the air.

"No one is asking you to," Jenny said to both of them. "But we have here ten good dragons and a hundred elves."

"Nine," Oribus objected.

"Jaime's share is still claimed, and I shall dispose of it as I see fit."

The yellow dragon hissed with laughter. "To think you sold me on that provision for the sake of my own profit. If we do not reduce the shares for those who die, you said, then we will not be inclined to let each other down, you said. And now you spend a double-share."

"The policy is sound," the blue dragon declared. "As witnessed by your continued existence." It turned its head to Jenny. "How shall we determine the recipient of such largesse?"

"If it please you," she said, "I have a suggestion. Lucien led us to this prize; it was his foresight that made this moment possible. He does not shudder uncontrollably at the sight of that hideous dome; he looks on the dragon-kin as something to save. And he is young enough to make use of this power for a good long time."

"I am younger!" Oribus cried out, even more offended than he had been when he thought he was about to lose his share. Christopher was surprised; the yellow dragon was clearly a whole size category larger than the green. In what biology did that make sense?

"And when you are Green I will make the same argument on your behalf. Well, not I, since I will not be here on that grand and glorious day; but some other, in my place, will do as I have done."

Christopher looked over at Lucien, hoping for clarification of this confusing argument. The dragon had his wings folded together, as if he were trying to make himself small enough to disappear.

The blue dragon snorted at Lucien. "The change will do you good. Time to stop cavorting around with that elven girl and take your responsibilities seriously."

"That Lucien already has a working relationship with the elven Field Officer for this domain is also a positive," Jenny agreed.

"So that's what the kids are calling it these days," the blue dragon observed.

"I cannot," Lucien said, in as close to a squeak as a creature the size of a city bus could make. "I am not ready."

"None of us are ever ready," Jenny said sadly. "If you say no, of course we will respect your decision and not hold it against you."

The blue dragon bared his teeth. "Speak for yourself."

"If you agree," Jenny continued, "we will offer you what counsel and aid we can. Oribus and Lethanial will swear to silence; your new position will not be known outside those here today. You will have some time to grow into your shape before They attempt to reclaim the demi-plane."

"That will cost extra," Oribus said.

The blue dragon bared its teeth at the yellow, who wisely shut up.

"Enough debate," one of the other blue dragons said. "I have other commitments to meet. We know enough to choose. I agree to the proposal."

A green spoke up. "For Jaime and Jenny's sake, I also agree."

One by one, each of dragons signaled their assent, save for the two yellows, who gnashed their teeth in unvoiced outrage. The last to vote was Lucien.

The green dragon looked at Christopher with bemusement. "How dreadfully you punish your friends. What fate must hold for your foes beggars the imagination." He turned to Jenny. "You know I cannot deny you this, my lady. I will accept your charge and execute it to the best of my ability."

"Of course you will," she said. "We all do."

19

GOODBYE

"**I** am not entirely certain what just happened," Christopher said.

The dragons had dispersed. Jenny and Lucien sat far away on the largest remaining building in the center of the city, having a private conversation. The others changed back into human form and made their farewells, awkward and tender at the same time. Oribus and Lethanial were at opposite ends of the dome, each sulking alone. They apparently had to wait on Jenny's spells to renew before she could give them a shape small enough to creep out of one of the handful of tunnels to the surface.

The elves were also packing up, getting ready to leave. Alaine had come over to check on Christopher and his party. Since it might be the last time he saw her for a while, Christopher wanted some answers. In particular, the battle seemed anticlimactic for the culmination of his great quest. Things did not feel as resolved as he thought they would. He wanted to make sure that wasn't just his ego complaining because he had not been at the center of the action this time.

"The future is always uncertain," she answered. "The past is unclear. Why should the present be any different?"

Lalania was no more satisfied with ambiguity than he was. "What is a domain lord," she demanded, "and why did we acquire one?"

"You always had one," Alaine told her. "You just didn't know. To be honest, it would behoove you to forget. He cannot intervene in your personal affairs without risking his greater mission: to keep this entire domain free of *hjerne-spica*. A task so important I would have assented to Oribus taking the role if necessary. Although you would not have appreciated his reign."

"So there won't be a Black Harvest," Christopher asked.

Alaine looked around at the rubble and shrugged. "Other than this one? Not unless you cause it."

He narrowed his eyes at her. "I was told I had a free hand. So I'm going to finish my task."

"Apparently you understood some part of the proceedings after all. Yes, you may continue with your scheme. Yet do not forget my promise to you. It still holds, every word."

"Okay, but what can they do now? I mean, what's left to go wrong?"

She looked at him expressionlessly. "Anything and everything. You play for an entire plane as a prize. There are no rules to such a game."

"Which of you rules us?" Cannan asked with a glare. "Field officer or overlord?"

"'Rule' is a poor term. We each have certain responsibilities, which usually do not impinge on your concerns. I have been patrolling this domain for . . ." She stopped herself. "For a very long time. I will, presumably, be here long after you are gone."

"Longer than Lucien?" Lalania's barb thrust home, wicked and clever.

Alaine stared at her. "Yes." She turned back to Christopher, clearly finished with the topic. "You can stay here until your spells renew or even until your rank manifests if you wish. After that you should make your way home."

"About that," he said, but Alaine was already handing him a leather satchel. When he peeled back the cover, he almost fainted. The bag was full of bright, purple tael, flowing like oil but weighing nothing. It was worth many more times than the entirety of the kingdom he ruled. Indeed, he could buy dozens of kingdoms for the contents of that satchel.

It also represented the souls of millions of sentient beings. The gods only knew how they had lived and died over the centuries that the *hjerne-spica* had ruled this patch of the world. Dragon-kin and lizardvolk, humans and goblins, ulvenmen and trolls, and probably whole species he had never heard of. Loving and hating, fighting and making peace, raising children, writing poetry, carving a living out of a hostile world . . . and all to wind up in a sack.

"They divvied your share out by magic. You will find it is precisely the required amount," Alaine warned him. "Including what Cannan has already sequestered in his sword."

"So we two go home empty-handed?" Cannan said.

"That was the deal your lord made with the dragons. I would not lightly set it aside. He needs to learn to make better choices or you need to choose a smarter lord."

"We are not displeased," Lalania said loyally. "I at least have a song to sing."

"No you don't," Alaine said. "Every word of description of this place is like an arrow to Lucien's side. All it can do is give some future dragon-slayer clues. You are sworn to silence as much as Oribus and Lethanial. For the same reason, you should refrain from visiting, discussing, writing, or thinking about the demi-plane."

"Sure," Christopher agreed. Once he opened a gate to Earth, he wouldn't need to visit his new overlord. Lucien would come visit him.

She turned her stare on him. "You are not the only one discomfited by today's events."

"Oh come now," Lalania said. "Your boyfriend got a big promotion. Sure, he won't have as much time for you, but think of how the other girls will swoon over your match."

Alaine looked at the bard, and for a moment Christopher was genuinely worried. Getting into a cat fight with an immortal was not likely to end well.

"Something we share," she said at last with bitter compassion. The elf nodded her head and walked away.

Lalania stood as still as a statue, cheeks burning red.

Cannan finally spoke. "It occurs to me that the elves are also going home with nothing. They gave their share to the dragon, if I understood the discussion. And they suffered losses. I regret my churlish words."

"You are not alone," Lalania murmured.

Christopher sympathized. He often felt the same after talking with Saint Krellyan.

"Hey," he said. "Do you know what this means? I think I can bring Krellyan back. All I need now is a name."

"That will change the shape of war," Lalania said. "The worst kind of death will become an inconvenience."

"Not entirely. It's horrendously expensive," he confessed. "But imagine what we could accomplish with two saints."

Cannan's eyes smoldered, an entire forest of hopes on fire.

"Assuming the books in the College are right," Christopher qualified, trying to dampen the expectation he had just birthed.

"A legitimate concern. Our books are based on rumor and conjecture because there has never been a legendary figure in our realm," Lalania said, and then her hands went to her face. "Oh gods Bright and Dark, and now I understand why. That is the trigger for the Black Harvest. That is what They wait for. When anyone reaches a rank actually capable of challenging Them, then They strike. When the harvest is worth the labor and yet before it becomes too difficult to grasp."

"So if I had succeeded in my original plan of earning this rank," Christopher said slowly, "I would have destroyed the kingdom. And everyone in it."

He looked across the rubble-strewn field to where Alaine was shouldering a backpack. He had words to regret, too.

Cannan grinned, big and toothy, a wolf in lion's clothing. "Yet we harvested them instead. Enough of regrets. Whatever price we paid, whatever mistakes we made, we are here now. We are victorious beyond all imagining, and all our dreams will come true."

Christopher reflected that his future was not likely to be quite as neat and clean as Cannan's. Yes, both of them would get their wives back, but Christopher would still have a kingdom to run. Unless he could pawn it off on Krellyan. Now that was an uplifting thought. He started to grin.

"I suppose it is only fair for both of you," Lalania said. "My greatest dream was to win back the lyre of Varelous. I can see I should have dreamed larger."

Cannan looked around, his eyes more acquisitive than Christopher had seen in a long time. The man was for once seeking something other than threat and danger.

"I don't trust the food," the big man said, "but alcohol is alcohol. Somewhere in this Light-forsaken city, there must be booze. A celebration is in order."

Something was tapping on his forehead. Christopher groaned and brushed it away. The tapping came back. He tried to open his eyes, but nothing happened. In a panic, he sat bolt upright, which was a terrible mistake. The tapping was replaced with a brutal, dull pounding from inside his skull while his stomach sloshed back and forth like a wounded animal.

"Why can't I see?" he moaned.

"Because it's dark," Jenny said, from somewhere close by. "And the potion wore off."

A light gleamed, a pearly white torch flame hovering over her open palm. Christopher looked around, marveling at how much the motion hurt his head. Cannan was slumped on the ground like a dead thing, Lalania using his huge calf as a pillow. Broken clay jugs lay scattered around them, and everything smelled like cheap beer.

"You should pray," the little girl said. "When you can cast again, summon sustenance for yourself and your companions."

Off in the distance, he saw a flare of fire.

"Lucien is hunting trolls. Fortunately for you, none dared come close in the night. I will never understand this human need to distance yourself from your emotions at the moment of your greatest triumph. Your lives are so short and yet you still need escape from them."

"Maybe we need escape because they are short," Christopher grumbled. "Maybe it's that deadline we are trying to forget."

She tipped her head. "Perhaps. I cannot quite grasp it even so."

Christopher remembered that she was under a deadline herself.

"I thought you were going with Argeous."

"I can make my own way," she said. "I needed the night to refresh my shaping. And Lucien and I had much to discuss."

"There are things I would like to discuss."

She smiled at him. "I am sure there are. And yet not with me. I retire from the board; I cannot set pieces in motion that others must catch. Nor will you find Lucien a willing conversationalist, for the opposite reason. He is too new to his position to make commitments. What to you might seem like simple pleasantries could rebound to his future misery."

Christopher put a hand over his mouth and belched. "So far talking to me has been profitable for him." The words were as sour as they tasted.

"Profit and misery are distinct quantities, as I think you already know." She pushed at the empty satchel with her toe.

Christopher had drunk far too much last night, especially on an empty stomach. The release of tension was only part of it. Although tael induced a magical appetite, he had gagged at the feast. Fistful after fistful of souls, all filtered through the twisted tentacles of the foulest creatures the world could produce. The booze had brought on the courage necessary. But not self-discipline; he could smell the stench of vomit on his clothes. He had thrown up at least three times. Each time, Cannan had handed him another drink and driven him on.

It would take another four days for his new rank to manifest itself.

Then he would have new powers. Ironically, he wouldn't need artillery anymore. He would be artillery.

"Orbius and Lethanial are already gone," Jenny said. "You will never see them again. As for the elves, I cannot say. And Lucien will speak for himself from now on."

"What about you?" Of all the immortals Christopher had dealt with, Jenny was the only one he actually felt comfortable with.

"One soon learns not to predict one's own future. The results range from disappointing to tragic."

Christopher steadied himself, putting his hands on the cool, wet ground. If he was going to say anything to her, now was the time. "I'm sorry about Jaime."

She bowed her head. "As am I. He still had a life to live."

"Can I . . . can I revive him?"

The little girl laughed so hard tears fell from her eyes. "I believe you would try. What a fine game it would be, if pawns could summon queens back to the board."

"But they can. All they have to do is get to the last rank."

She frowned. "Hmm. I thought I knew the rules."

"They might have changed over the years. When did you learn to play chess?" He said it too casually, and she smirked at him.

"Never you mind about that. So it appears our allegory has run its course, and we should follow. Pray now, and I will take my farewell of Lucien." She put the light down on a brick, where it continued to gleam.

Christopher tried and failed to make himself comfortable. In the end, he just ignored the aches and irritations and forced himself into the meditative trance.

When he rejoined the world, Lalania was sitting in front of a small fire, her hair hanging in a blonde, dirty mess. Cannan lumbered up, dropping broken bits of half-burnt timber.

"Don't look at me," she grumbled. "Or I'll have to erase your memory."

"Please do," Christopher said, his head still swimming. "But first, let's eat." He cast the spell that summoned food out of nothing. The magical provisions were bland to the point of tastelessness, which at the moment was a blessing.

He was considerably higher rank than he had been the last time he had used this spell, and the quantity of supplied food was correspondingly greater. They made a good start on it anyway. Halfway through Lucien joined them in elven form and put away a healthy portion himself.

Afterward Christopher felt more stable, if still not fully human. He watched Lucien tempt a dragon-kin out the darkness with a loaf of brown bread. The creature crept forward, groveling and squeaking. Christopher realized he could not tell whether this was some helpless peasant or one of the arcanists who had almost slain Jenny.

"I dare not speak of debt," Lucien said, watching the creature eat. "Yet objective fact marks how our paths have intertwined. Who is to say they will not do so again someday?"

"We can talk freely here, right? Jenny said something about the dome blocking divination."

"Yes," Lucien begrudged. "You, at least, can speak your mind. I do not know that I can answer, though."

"I'm not going to open a gate to Earth right away. I need to put some safeguards in place. Also, there are a few other things I need to do first. Promises to keep."

Christopher exhaled slowly. "But when I do, things are going to change. I don't know how to explain it to you, so I'll just tell you this. Whatever you think of me and my strange ideas, understand that there are seven billion humans with their own strange ideas. I won't be able to contain them all. Not that I would even try. Things will . . . change."

"Incredible. I cannot imagine how your plane sustains so many, especially since I infer your world is, like most human realms, a fractious and disunified place."

That was a fair description. Charitable, even. Christopher nodded. "And the focal point of this infection of chaos will be my newly acquired domain." Lucien smiled wryly. "It is good we do not speak of debts."

Cannan spoke up from across the fire. "Will you call on us if you are attacked?"

"If I think you can help. Yet the obverse does not obtain; you cannot call on me unless the enemy is from outside the domain. I apologize in advance for the imbalance."

The big man shrugged. "Every peer makes the same bargain with a king. In any case, it will be others in the domain who cannot call on you for protection from us."

"All these years you struggled for your private miracle," Lalania said, "and now that the prize is within your grasp, you reach further. You would conquer every acre we can see; you would make Christopher an overlord in all but name."

"And why not?" Cannan said. "We did not make the rules, yet we must play by them. Well enough, then. Play we shall."

"Let's focus on first things first," Christopher said. He felt dizzy and not just from the hangover. He had put everything into this quest, and now it was almost over. What would he do afterward? Build an empire? Hand the kingdom to Krellyan and retire to a cottage?

Or . . . return to Earth. Would what the world make of him, a middle-aged atheist who carried a sword, served a god, and brought people back from the dead?

Jenny's words echoed. There was no point in predicting his own future. It wouldn't turn out like he expected, no matter what.

"We should go. Torme will be getting antsy." The end of the year was only a week away. The anniversary would mark his fifth year here. He stood up.

Lalania joined him, stretching uncomfortably in her chainmail. "Now I remember why you shouldn't sleep in armor."

Cannan grunted, scratching at his own. "It's better than any other. Lighter than Christopher's steel mail, and yet it turned the halberds like plate."

"It is definitely an upgrade," Lucien commented. "Elves rarely do things by half-measure; you will find it already has the highest rank of enchantment."

The three humans shared a look.

"Empty-handed, indeed," Lalania said, exasperated beyond measure. "How is it possible to hate someone who is so generous? Yet I would scrub that woman's mouth with a wire brush and lye if I thought I could get away with it."

"Do not say that in her presence," Lucien warned. "She might well let you. The price of a stray word is often high; imagine how much you would pay for an intemperate action."

"I was hoping we had seen the last of her," Lalania confessed.

"That is up to you. Should you require contact with me, Christopher," Lucien said, turning to face him, "send to Alaine. She may not always be available, but more so than myself due to the dome. Please do not visit unannounced. It would be a security risk, and also my defenses might unintentionally cause you some discomfort."

"You, too," Christopher said. "Drop by anytime. Don't be a stranger."

Lucien smiled in appreciation of the irony. They declined a ride to the edge of the dome, preferring to walk. Lucien, back in dragon shape, circled overhead, and thus nothing harassed them on the journey.

Outside, staring up at the wintery noonday sky, happy to see the sun despite its cold shoulder, Christopher turned them all to mist and led them home.

They landed on the roof of the castle. Lalania had to employ her skills to open the stairway door because it was locked from the inside. Dirty, disheveled, and tired, they tried to sneak back to their quarters but were invariably discovered by a servant. Much hue and cry later, Christopher relaxed in a hot tub of water and washed the stink of vomit off, a plate of bread and cheese within easy reach. Squires were seeing to his armor. It was good to be king.

He deflected a succession of questioners with noncommittal grunts, but Cardinal Faren was too sharp for that. The old man sat on the edge of his tub and helped himself to a slice of cheese while interrogating him.

"Your companions came back better dressed than when they left. This implies your venture was successful. Sooner or later you must tell us how successful."

That was precisely the topic he was trying to avoid. "Ask me again . . . in about four days."

Faren choked on his bit of cheese. Coughing, he recovered himself. "Now I wish I had access to the Cathedral library. Much has faded from the memories I laid down as a naive and hopeful youth."

"That goes for two of us," Christopher said, wondering how to pick up a chunk of bread without dropping crumbs in the bath.

"I suppose we will find out in due time. Meanwhile, put a leash on your guard dog. He was once as stoic as a statue; his sudden reanimation is scaring the serving girls."

"I'll take care of it. In about four days." Christopher decided to share his hot water with the bread and chewed on a flaky crust.

The old man picked up the plate of food. "Helga has prepared a special dinner in light of your return. Don't spoil your appetite."

"No danger of that," Christopher said, nonetheless watching the plate travel away from him. The bath was more comfortable, so he stayed there a bit longer.

Later, dressed and clean, he went down to the stable to visit his horse. It seemed odd that he had been there less than two weeks ago, although admittedly the long ten-day weeks of this world. So much had changed.

Cannan stood behind him, radiating coiled energy.

The horse snuffled, shoving at Christopher with its big hairy head. "Patience," he murmured, scratching its forehead. "We'll go for a fine ride tomorrow, I promise."

Lalania came into the stable wearing a professional demeanor and her silver chainmail. She looked fantastic in it, which probably explained why she was wearing armor inside the castle. Normally only soldiers and Cannan bothered.

"We have a surprise guest," she said. From the carefully neutral way she spoke and stood, as if someone was just behind her even though there was no one there, he deduced it had to be an invisible wizard. Presumably the one from Carrhill; Lalania wouldn't have called Fae a guest.

"Welcome," Christopher said, facing the woman and her unseen companion.

"Really?" grated a voice behind him with the sound of chains sliding on chains. "You welcome your death? How droll."

Not just a tone of voice; actual chains lashed out and wrapped his body, crushing and tearing at his flesh, binding him. Lalania's face was a mask of horror, and Cannan was already moving to attack when the world exploded in fire.

The Wizard of Carrhill was revealed at the entrance to the stable, a dozen yards behind Lalania, wearing his black robes and expression of unhinged rage, already mouthing the words of another spell.

The barn was burning down around them. Cannan and Lalania had been knocked to the ground by the blast; the Wizard's fireballs were far stronger than the wand of fire had been. Yet Christopher's energy shield was better than it had been, too, and all three of them were still wearing it from the day before. The shields absorbed the blast, leaving only a few loose flames to leach at them after burning out.

Christopher was not on the ground because something was holding up. The chains were trying to squeeze the life out of him. He invoked the special privilege due to a priest of a god of Travel and stepped out of their grasp, letting them slide off like loose clothes. It was important to have his hands free to cast because he needed to block the Wizard's next fireball.

As the pea-sized ball of flame streaked toward him, he cast his dissolution spell. The flame winked out, and the Wizard behind it cursed dementedly. Only the words "null-stone" were comprehensible.

Cannan was up and at his side, striking behind him. Christopher risked a glance over his shoulder and wished he hadn't. A thing stood there, eight feet tall and roughly man-shaped, wrapped in a profundity of black iron chains. Its eyes glowed red in its horned head while it struck at Cannan with long clawed hands. The chains moved around like tentacles, striking at both men. Cannan's sword carved through them, its enchanted edge parting steel like twine. The creature shrieked in outrage and transferred all of its attention to the big knight. It stood in a pile of burning straw and timber without seeming to notice, so Christopher deduced it must be fire-proof.

He was stuck in a dilemma. If he drew his sword or cast a spell, the Wizard would throw another fireball. If he did nothing, Cannan would undoubtedly lose to the demon. The big knight already had chains wrapped around one leg, limiting his movement.

Lalania gave him an opening by stabbing the Wizard in the face, having snuck up beside him in the smoke. The man jerked his hand and sparkling bolts flew out, lancing her. She staggered, caught her footing, and stabbed him again. Christopher did the smart thing and cast the silence spell at the Wizard's feet, robbing him of any spell that required speech to cast. While the Wizard dodged and weaved, trying to escape the zone of silence without getting skewered by Lalania's blade, Christopher summoned help from Marcius. Before he even saw what creatures the god had sent, he turned around to help Cannan.

He had to waste valuable time enchanting his sword. There was way plain steel would hurt this monster. Cannan lost the use of an to the engulfing chains, still hacking away with the big sword in one hand. Christopher sprung into action, striking at the binding chains. His enchanted sword was not as sharp as Cannan's, but it was sharp enough for this. Chains parted under the magic-enhanced blade, spiting links. Cannan, freed, leaned in and struck at the monster.

Together they drove it through the burning building, leaving a trail of bits on the ground, not all of which were made of metal. Eventually, they forced it into a corner and butchered it. When it died, the fleshy substance turned to foul-smelling mud while the chains fell like puppet strings suddenly cut. Then they rushed back to save Lalania.

They found her standing over the body of the Wizard, stabbing it repeatedly with her rapier. A huge white lion crouched on the ground, its fangs sunk into the Wizard's shoulder, holding the corpse in place.

Lalania was cursing violently but futilely in the silence. Cannan grasped her hand. She struggled for a moment, then turned into his chest and buried her face, shaking in fury and grief.

The lion dropped the mutilated body. Christopher could see it had bitten the shoulder half-off. It looked up at him with apologetic golden cat eyes and dissolved into white mist. He let the silence spell go with it, and the sounds of the building burning roared back in.

People were coming, bearing buckets of sand and water. Fire was a true danger to the castle and, by extension, to the city. Christopher and Cannan set aside their swords for buckets and went to help, leaving Lalania to deal with the body.

In the midst of the wreckage, Christopher's heart wrenched. His horse, his beautiful horse, was a formless lump of charred barbecue. A dozen other animals had died in the blast, their stalls obliterated. Nothing made of wood or flesh remained intact; even the low stone wall at the foot of the barn was scattered about like broken toys.

Death was no refuge from Christopher's wrath. Shoot first and ask questions later worked for a man who could invoke ghosts. Christopher waited several days for his wrath to subside, fearful that he would waste the spell simply hurling invective at the man who had betrayed him. Such petty vengeance would be futile; the ghost, as Faren had explained long ago, was not the man, nor would the man revived remember what the ghost endured. Not that this man was in any danger of revival. Even if Christopher offered, the Wizard would have to be a fool to accept.

"Why?" he demanded of the wavering mist in front of him. In death the Wizard's self-image seemed even less formed than it had been in life.

"Had I let your rank manifest, I would have had no chance." The voice was dry; it stabbed at Christopher with the memory of their intellectually engaging conversations.

"How did you even know?"

"The privacy spell was compromised. Your witch lacked the skill to detect it. Thus, I knew what treasure you had found. More to the point, I knew what deal you had made. So much wealth, and all you would take is a pittance. And nothing for your retinue! What ego, what selfishness, what a vast waste of resources. You could have transformed the kingdom; you could have made royals of your allies; you could have made legends of your friends. You could have made a legend of me."

Christopher knew it was futile to argue with a ghost, but it was still more productive than cursing. "I am going to transform the kingdom."

"Only in your childish dreams." The ghost sneered, the effect somewhat diminished by its current transparency. "You seek to overturn the patterns of millennia with your outlandish ideas. And yet the world you are trying to change remains the same at its most fundamental level. Tael is what it is, and we have adapted our lives to the shape it makes of reality. You think time is on your side, but it is only the tide waiting to turn. Your idiocies will splash against the wall of ages and fade away like a bad stain."

Ghostly hands spread, trying to summon the grandeur of its vision. "In its place, I would have raised a kingdom that could stand, according to a plan as old as Varelous himself. Your head alone would make me an Arch-Mage. I would take the throne and command your armies and rule as tradition demands. A national school to encourage wizardry to replace the knights you drove away. A pacifistic church of healers to fill the space of the militaristic churches you destroyed. The only fly in the ointment were those cursed druids, and I figured I could just ignore them."

"What made you think this assassination would even work?"

"You did," the ghost said. "You made it clear that the null-stone would defend you against my spell-craft. So I crafted a plan that would make it an anchor-stone around your neck. The field would have left you trapped in the demon's chains, denied the privilege of your patron; Ser Cannan's sword would have been mere steel, unable to sever them as they choked out your life. My fireballs and arcane missiles would have done for your pathetic retinue, if they dared to leave the field to attack me. If they did not, then the demon would have eaten them all. Without enchanted weapons it is nigh-indestructible."

Christopher shook his head. "How many damn demons are there, anyway?"

The ghost considered. "If you mean by kinds, I know of seventeen, not counting animating spirits. If you mean by numbers, I assume infinite. That counts as two questions answered. Now ask the rest and let me return to dust."

"It was a stupid plan."

"It was not without flaws," the ghost conceded, wobbling its misty head. "I did not anticipate that all of you would be shielded against fire, although that would not have mattered if the demon had dealt with you. I did not even consider that you would be without the null-stone. Yet I cannot regret it. It was clear that I would never gain another rank under your reign. I had no choice."

Christopher felt his face curling in disgust. There were always

choices. It was the lowest kind of cowardice to deny one's own consequences. With nothing else to say, he said what he felt. "You killed my
horse, you worthless bag of dirt."

"Could you rephrase that in the form of a question?"

"Do you feel sorry that you killed my horse, you worthless bag of
dirt?"

The ghostly figure shrugged. "No." The mist faded, the spell spent,
his questions asked and answered. He had learned essentially nothing.
The only lesson here, that greed overcame all decency and common
sense, he had already known.

20

HELLO, HELLO, HELLO

On the fifth morning after, Christopher sat at his desk in the royal suite, holding his hand in a candle flame.

It hurt every bit as much as one would expect. The skin blackened and cracked, and then healed thanks to his tael, over and over. He did not move his hand because he had made the choice not to move his hand. He could feel the rank he wore, scaffolding running through his mind: hard and unyielding like polished crystal. Somehow it augmented his mental faculties, his self-discipline and insight.

At the same time, it did not prevent him from making stupid decisions. Like letting his palm burn. He moved his hand away and picked up the bowl of water and ink-stone, warmed it over the flame, and finished signing the stack of orders and decrees. Even a legendary saint had paperwork to do.

He had decided to start with the least controversial decisions, work his way forward, and see how it went. Today he would bring back Saint Krellyan. It was hard to imagine how anyone could object to that.

At breakfast Cardinal Faren was as distracted as Christopher had ever seen him. Christopher, with the clarity of his rank or perhaps just self-reflection, understood. Just because Christopher could invite Krellyan back did not mean he would come back. Perhaps the saint had had enough of this world. Perhaps he was happier wherever he was now.

They went down to the remains of the Cathedral to do it. The lot sat empty, weeds peeking through the snow. Faren had moved the church headquarters into the castle, and no one else had the temerity to build on the land, at least not as long as Faren was alive.

Christopher stood in the snowy grass and chanted the words of the spell, flanked by a large crowd. Duke Istvar was there, his face struggling between skepticism and hope. The crowd wore a lot of white. All of the lesser priests had come from the neighboring counties. Only the Vicars stayed at their posts.

This spell was expensive in a way the other revival spells were not. It cost more, of course, but the cost went up based on the rank of the recipient. Such progressiveness was unusual for magic. In this case, it meant the spell was staggeringly expensive because Krellyan had been of very high rank or at least what had been considered high rank a week ago. The cost bankrupted Christopher and the White church and all of the Blue lords whom he had to beg for tael. It was not without value, however. This spell brought the dead back without the usual tax of losing a rank. Krellyan would come back as powerful as he had left.

Like with the other revival spells, a private vision opened for Christopher. He looked through a crack in the world to a formless white void where a naked man stood, bemused.

"I see you have prospered," Saint Krellyan said, apparently unconcerned with his lack of clothes.

"I am higher rank, yes," Christopher said. "But we still need you. Faren in particular needs you."

"How it must have torn his heart to see me die." Krellyan shook his head in dismay. "I can guess because I know how I felt, merely anticipating his. He was always old in my eyes, though when I was young, he was no older than I am now. But the fear did not bite until he crossed the age limit. So now you will bring me back to witness what I most dreaded. Unless, can it be that this new magic breaks that barrier?"

It was hard to argue people into coming back to life when you couldn't lie. "No. It doesn't change that."

"How long have I been gone?"

"Three years. We lost Svengusta and the Vicar of Cannenberry." Christopher realized, too late, that while he could not lie, he did not have to volunteer depressing information.

"So few," Kreyllan mused. "I am grateful for that. You may have to remind me of that gratitude once I step across the threshold."

Christopher held out his hand. "The gratitude will be mine."

Krellyan took his hand and stepped into the real world. The crowd burst into howls of grief, all the more potent for their long distillation. The sobbing turned quickly to singing as the priests hugged each other with such frenzy that many of them fell to the ground.

Faren was already down, his head on a stone while he wept. The naked saint reached down and pulled the old man to his feet.

"We should have brought a robe," Faren sobbed. "We didn't know."

Christopher hurriedly took off his own coat and wrapped it around Krellyan. It felt like a symbolic move.

"I assume I have much to learn," Krellyan said.

Torme stood up from where he had kneeled. "The King and the Gold Apostle are dead. Saint Christopher reigns. Your return is unalloyed joy."

Gregor climbed to his feet. "That about covers it. Welcome back."

Duke Istvar joined them, picking his way through the insensate crowd. "Well met, again, Saint Krellyan. I confess my astonishment at the power your protégé commands."

"Not mine," Krellyan answered. "Father Svengusta's, I believe."

Christopher winced. Krellyan, in making the transition, had forgotten the sad news, and now someone would have to tell him all over again.

Istvar, hero that he was, volunteered, although the quality of his rescue left something to be desired. "Can this new magic return Pater Sven?" he asked Christopher.

"No," Christopher had to say again. "Like all other revivals, it cannot bring back the old."

"But it could restore Duke Nordland? And his wife?" Istvar apparently had ulterior motives.

"Um. I guess so." Christopher hadn't actually thought about that. "But it's expensive."

"Now that you have reached your goal," Istvar stated, "you will return the tax scheme to normal. In which case I assure you we will quickly raise whatever fee you demand."

And Christopher had thought this would be the least contentious act to start with.

"My lords," Lalania said, "there will be time for this discussion later. Let us get the Saint indoors before the cold undoes all Christopher's good work."

"We should have brought shoes," Faren said, a fresh round of sobbing taking hold. "We didn't know."

Christopher held the next ceremony with a reduced guest list. Only his advisors and immediate family attended. Niona's, of course, although the closest he had to family also came. Helga clung to Cannan, apparently under the illusion that he needed the support.

The next day, they were in the throne room, with the big double doors locked and barred. Lalania had come prepared with a fine soft velvet cloak. Lord Beric stood stiffly, formally armed and armored; his wife Lady Io comforted and cosseted a great eagle that rested on her arm. The bird seemed large for such a small woman to hold, but the woman was a druid and thus far sturdier than she looked. Christopher, thanks to his elevated rank, was only a little bit afraid of her now.

Gregor and his wife Disa were there as well, both wearing a somber but hopeful expression. Cannan, in contrast, was a mess. Christopher could see the fear behind the big man's eyes, and he decided that perhaps Helga was onto something.

Though not as expensive as reviving Krellyan, the spell could hardly be called cheap. He had to borrow it from the druids with a promise to repay them at usurious interest rates. Nonetheless, it was one debt that Christopher did not regret. He called out to the lady Niona, using all of the names her mother and father had supplied, and was swamped with relief when the beautiful dark-haired druid appeared before him.

The backdrop was a forest, of course, although the lady was naked. She looked at him with surprise, and he suddenly realized that in her vision he was also naked. The spell was making the compulsion to honesty rather more obvious than necessary.

"Please come back," he said. "It was the ring."

"I know," she said.

"Cannan is here. He needs you."

"I know," she said again. "You would not call me otherwise."

Christopher held out his hand, his heart pounding.

She looked him in the face. "Answer me true, as you must do by the terms of this magic. If you were me, would you return to this world?"

The relief came flooding back. "Without hesitation."

She took his hand. The forest fell away behind her, replaced by the empty marble throne and the tapestries hanging on the walls. Cannan fell to his knees, his head cracking on the stone floor. The man trembled on the ground, his hands spread in supplication.

The eagle cawed loudly; Lord Beric wept openly. Lady Io was torn between joy and grief, the return of her daughter violating the terms of her faith. Lalania smoothly draped the cloak over the druid.

"Welcome back," she said, meaning every syllable. "You have been missed."

Niona knelt to her husband. Christopher didn't see what happened after that because he had to turn away. He only rejoined the conversation when Niona had hugged everyone else and finally came to him.

"Thank you," she said. "For saving both of us."

"Cannan did his part," Christopher said. "He saved a dragon's life. And mine, more times than I can count."

She nodded, accepting it. "D'Kan told me you met some elves."

"A bunch, actually. They're kind of scary."

She laughed in that earthy way of hers, and Christopher felt all his tension melt away. This one act justified everything else he had done.

"Are you still a druid? Because . . ."

"Even if I were not, it would not matter," she interrupted. "Some bonds are stronger than faith and power. I am, as it turns out, but I remain a wife first and foremost."

That was a nice sentiment for a man in his position.

"I know what you must be feeling," she continued, and he was reminded that uncanny insight was another feature of her personality. "I assure you love is stronger than circumstance."

Here she was, back from the dead with a husband guilty of her murder and a brother in the body of a bird, and she was trying to comfort him.

"We'll know soon enough," he told her. "Now go enjoy yourself. Bright gods but it's good to have you back." He hugged her and then let her go.

"You're fired," he said to Cannan. "The terms of our arrangement are complete. If you want a job later, you've got it; but for now, get the hell out."

Everybody left, Helga chattering away as they went, Gregor laughing out loud. Only Lalania remained behind.

"I think maybe I should give them some space," she explained. "Not that Niona would hold anything against me. But today is not the time."

He said nothing.

"No," she said, shaking her head. "I will not abandon you. Not for a king's ransom. I would meet this woman whose mere memory has put paid to all my arts if it kills me to do so. You cannot imagine how large she has loomed in my mind.

"Unless," Lalania continued, as if struck by a sudden thought, "you have changed your mind? This is quite literally your last chance."

He snorted, which was all the answer that deserved.

"Fortunately, I have grown used to failure," she teased. "You would know true suffering if Uma were in my shoes."

"I thought returning Krellyan would be the least controversial," Christopher said, changing the subject. "Now I have a tax revolt brewing and the lords we didn't replace with Vicars probably expect to keep their castles. Apparently I should have started with Niona."

Lalania laughed. "You only think that because you cannot see Lady Sigurane's face right now. She would claw your eyes out if she could. The druids are barely holding on; Niona alive again will crack them in half."

"That's okay," he said. "Kalani told us the elves would rather be revived than reincarnated. And Niona said she still had her rank. They can have both. They can get revived and still be druids."

"Perhaps," Lalania said archly, falling back into her role of telling him when he was wrong, "but Lady Sigurane cannot be High Druid when she no longer controls who lives a second life."

The political argument took his mind off tomorrow, which was the point.

This ceremony was private. He stood in his royal quarters, completely alone, for the first time in a very long time. Cannan had been a constant fixture, rarely farther away than the other side of a door. His oath was done, though, and now the man orbited another. No one else had the gall to intrude. Lalania had tried, heroically, but eventually she came to her senses. Christopher was not going to petition his wife with the young blonde woman standing at his shoulder.

The bard still had her hand in, choosing his clothes and trimming his hair as she did for court. He sat through the preparations in a daze, his mind elsewhere. He was desperately trying to remember who he was.

He had suffered from nightmares. Unusual in that he normally faced enough monsters during the day that they let him be at night.

The theme had been both mundane and heart-stopping; looking down at his watch and realizing he was late to pick Maggie up from work.

Never mind that he had never worn a watch and Maggie had her own car.

It had been five years. He'd vanished without a word for five years. It could have been two; he could have gone home years ago. He'd chosen to stay. It had seemed like a necessary choice at the time; his current rank and status implied it had been a successful choice; the fate of several worlds might even hinge on his having made that choice. Yet he feared looking into her eyes and trying to explain.

He had continued with his life, adapting to the world around him. What if she had done the same? What if she was already adapted to a world without him in it? If asked, he could only say he hoped she had. Nothing could compel him to wish five years of loneliness on the woman he loved. If she had found another, he could only thank the man for easing her pain.

Not that gratitude would stop him from competing for her renewed affection. He was prepared to compete quite strenuously, in fact, and now he had the resources of an entire magic-using kingdom at his disposal. He would put that up against anything an Earth-bound paramour had to offer. If she could forgive him for having chosen duty over love, then nothing less would stand in their way.

With his eyes closed, he chanted the words of the spell. It was many syllables long, and at the end curiosity won him over. He opened his eyes to see what it looked like.

The door to the hallway was gone. Instead the doorway looked into another room in another world. A room he did not recognize; it was not the house he had left. Maggie had moved, but the spell had sought her out, its ability to reach across the gulf of space apparently not impeded by a change of zip code.

He did not recognize the furniture, either. It was someone else's furniture. That someone might merely be Maggie after five years, unwilling to sleep in the bed he had abandoned. Or it might be another man's bed. Before his heart could stop, he spotted something familiar: a small framed painting hanging over the bed. Two birds, a crow and a robin in the same nest, a wedding gift from his artistic aunt.

She lay sleeping in the bed, alone, although the picture had already told him everything he needed to know. His knees sagged in relief, as if a great beast had released its claws and dropped from his back, to shamble away into whatever darkness it called home.

"Maggie," he said. He could only call out; he dared not step across the threshold. It would close behind him and that would be that.

She stirred in her sleep, throwing her arm across the empty bed. His heart seized again. Guilt and fear would give him a coronary if he let it.

"Maggie," he said, louder. "Wake up."

She sat up slowly and stared out at him. Always a practical woman, she did not shriek, cry out, or panic, but went right to the heart of the matter. "Chris?" she asked in wonderment, "why are you wearing a sword?"

"Oh." He looked down at his katana. If Cannan had been a shadow, the sword had been a part of his flesh. He had picked it up within days of having arrived; he had worn it, slept with it, fought with it, lived with it. The longest it had been out of his hands had been the very time he had wanted it most—the three days he lay in the King's torture chamber, slowly dying.

He took off the sword and leaned it against the desk.

"It's a long story," he explained.

"Oh honey," she said, "that doesn't matter. Come to bed."

His heart leaped at the invitation, and one foot moved forward of its own accord. With an act of will, he forced the other foot to remain still.

"I can't. I mean, you have to come here. I can't cross over without being trapped."

She looked past him to the great four-poster bed that he had inherited from Treywan and never bothered to change. She crinkled her nose. "A bit rustic . . . but whatever." After a moment, she looked perplexed. "I have to actually walk? What kind of dream is this?"

"It's not a dream," he said. "I mean, I know it seems like one." That had been his first assumption, too.

She slipped out of bed, wearing an old blue nightgown. It wasn't particularly attractive, but it made his heart leap in guilty pleasure. She wasn't dressed for company, obviously.

When she stepped across the threshold, she stopped and stared down in surprise. "The floor is cold. What an utterly superfluous level of detail."

"I told you, it's not a dream." He took a step closer, cautiously, his arms open, holding his breath.

"Of course it's a dream," she answered. "When the insurance company paid up, I knew you were truly dead. They stalled for years because there wasn't a body, and I let them because I wanted to believe. Everyone told me to move on, and finally I tried. And now here you are in my dreams."

He did not get the chance to respond. She stepped into his embrace and kissed him.

"Oh Chris," she murmured, and the world spun around him. He could not remember now which was the dream and the real. He held her, being the person he had once been. Recalling the things he had once cared for, the fears he had once battled, and the hopes he had once chased. The man he was now stood aside, looking on; then his perspective switched, and part of him flinched to see her embracing a stranger.

"The dogs," he asked, shaking his head to banish the multiple viewpoints. "What about the dogs?" Intellectually, he knew they must have passed on in the intervening years; neither of them had been young. Emotionally, he wanted to know they had not been harmed by his vanishing.

"They were waiting outside the truck in the morning. That threw me for so long. Why didn't they stay with your body? But they weren't in the truck. I knew you wouldn't have left them running loose, even if you had left me. Then the rain came. The river flooded, and they called off the search. And it was all over except for the accounting."

A professional joke. What she always said at the end of every movie. Bizarrely, he remembered that they had been waiting on a sequel to some popular show. He couldn't even recall the premise of the show now. The very concept of caring about imaginary drama seemed hard to credit.

"I'm so sorry," he whispered, holding her tight. Memories surged and clashed within him, watching sword fights on the big screen, wielding a sword in a war zone. The sight of fake blood; the smell of real.

She kissed him again. "Let's not waste the dream." After a moment, she pulled back and reached up to his face. "Why is your nose straight? How shallow am I, to change you in my memories?" She ran her hand lightly along his face. Then down to his arms, tapping at his hardened biceps, her eyes crinkling and the edges of her mouth turning up. "So much shallower than I ever realized."

"Oh. Right." He had forgotten. It seemed unfair that he should look like a twenty-year-old when she didn't. Light headed with anticipation, he cast the regeneration spell and held her while she coughed up her fillings.

"What the hell was that?" she asked.

"Look," he said, grinning like a schoolboy, and led her to the mirror. Treywan had kept it as a status symbol to show how rich he was; Christopher kept it because it served as a useful focus for casting scrying spells.

She ran her fingers through her freshly shining red hair and stared. "Alright. No roots, even. This dream is picking up." Unselfconsciously, she pulled at the nightgown and it fell off, crumpling at her feet.

Christopher caught his breath. All of his conflicted thoughts faded to obscurity, banished by the light in front of him.

Maggie turned and preened in the mirror. "I haven't looked like this for twenty years. At least I am an equal opportunity objectifier."

He went over to her, reaching out.

"Your turn," she said. It took a little more effort to get him out of his court clothes.

She stared at him with wide eyes. He had to confess the truth. "I never looked like this before. Life here isn't comfortable and easy."

"Everything good is always hard." Something else she often said, although in wildly differing contexts. Wearing only a wicked smile, she stepped into his arms again, warm and soft.

"I have to warn you," he said as they stumbled together to the bed. "You might be in for a bit of a surprise. The first time, at least."

The regeneration spell was always a bit too thorough.

21

AU REVOIR

"**A**iieeee!"

The shriek snapped him awake. He bolted upright, reaching for his sword. It was missing from its usual place. At the far end of the room, a beautiful redheaded woman was standing in front of the mirror, screaming.

"Maggie," he said, "please stop screaming."

She whirled to face him. "What did you do to me? Who are you really?"

"It's okay. I can explain everything. Just calm down."

"Don't tell me to calm down," she snapped, but at a normal volume.

The door exploded, crashing inward in splinters. Six armored men burst through, swords drawn and shields raised.

Maggie shrieked again, covering herself with her hands.

"Oh," Gregor said. "My apologies. We . . ." The blue knight thought better of continuing. He turned around. "Get out!" he ordered the men who had come in with him. The squad retreated, one of the men gamely trying to lean the largest remaining part of the door upright. It fell over and broke into three pieces.

Christopher got out of bed. He picked up his cloak and went to wrap it around her.

She shrank back at his approach, stopping him halfway.

"Why am I still asleep? I woke up, but I'm still in the dream."

The obvious terror on her face stabbed at him. "It's not a dream." He hadn't been thinking. She had to deal with not only transdimensional travel but magic all at once. He had struggled with waking up not in his own bed; his discovery of magic had caused him to demolish a cord of wood.

"It's not a dream," he repeated lamely. "I fell through a gate. This place has magic. It took me five years to get enough power to reach you." He held out the cloak like a peace offering.

She took the cloak from him and wrapped herself in it, hiding.

He winced. "It has been five years, right?" He wasn't entirely sure time passed at the same rate on both planets.

She was weeping now. "So long. Why were you gone so long?"

He went back to the wardrobe and got another cloak for himself. "I told you. Life here is not easy." The castle was always cold, even in summer.

"Then why did you bring me here? Why didn't you just come home?"

The words bit at him. "I couldn't leave. I just . . . couldn't. I can send you home, though. Anytime you want to go."

"Will you come with me?" She looked up at him, and his will almost dissolved.

"Not yet. There's still something I have to do here. But it doesn't matter. You can come and go as you please."

She gave him that look, the one she did when something he said didn't add up. Accountants were always good at that, keeping track and balancing the books. He loved it about her; it kept him honest. "If it's so easy, why did it take so long?"

Hmm. How to explain rank? "I had to gain access to the controls."

"Show me." She turned to where her bedroom had been the night before, which was now the shattered door. "Do it again."

He had never been able to pull one over on her. She called bluffs like a fish breathed water. "It needs a day to recharge," he admitted. "I have to wait . . ." He wasn't actually sure how long he had to wait. There were no windows in the royal suite, situated as it was deep in the heart of the castle, and he hadn't invented clocks yet. He was starving, though. They had been in here quite a while. "Dogs, but I'm hungry. Are you hungry? Can we go get something to eat?"

She frowned at him. "I don't have anything to wear."

As if by magic, Lalania appeared in the doorway, her face staring at the floor. She curtsied low. "If it please you, my lady, I am at your service."

Maggie frowned harder, and Christopher shuddered at the bullet he had dodged. Explaining Lalania now would be difficult enough; doing it last night would have been disastrous.

"Why is that woman speaking Norwegian?" Maggie asked.

"Oh. Right." Christopher stepped over to Maggie and reached out his hand. She watched warily but did not retreat this time. He touched her face, casting the spell that granted understanding of all spoken and written speech. He lingered over her lips, remembering the night before.

"I love you," he said, in the local language.

She stared at him. "I understood you. But your mouth didn't match the words."

Another problem. Marcius had granted him command of the language as part of his rank. He wasn't sure how to do the same for Maggie. On the other hand, the answer would almost certainly be magic, and there was very little magic denied to him now.

"We'll fix it later," he said. "Lala, can you get Maggie some clothes?"

Lalania tipped her head lower. "With pleasure." She whistled, and half a dozen serving women tumbled into the room, stumbling over the broken door. They were carrying dresses and shoes and looks of antici-pation, eager to meet the woman who had held Christopher's loyalty for so many years. One of the serving girls was Helga, temporarily demoted from head cook to lady's maid. He counted himself lucky that Fae was not among them.

"Please forgive our lack of preparation," Lalania continued. "Saint Christopher's service has not accustomed us to the presence of a woman."

"He's no saint," Maggie said instantly.

Lalania looked up for the first time, studying Maggie's face. "My lady, by the terms of our world, he is that and more."

"And I'm no lady," Maggie answered. "Why are you talking like that? Norway abolished nobility two hundred years ago."

Lalania's face faltered, and Christopher laughed out loud. Anyone who could make the bard doubt herself was a force to be reckoned with. He would have fallen in love with Maggie all over again except that he had never stopped.

"They've forgotten home," he said. "I think they must have crossed over a thousand years ago. They didn't even believe Earth existed."

The bard's gaze snapped back and forth between Christopher and his wife. He felt a pang of guilty sympathy. He and Maggie shared so much context that Lalania could never be anything but an outsider.

Two men, their heads covered by sacks, inched into the room carrying banners on poles. The serving girls set the banners against the door, making the room private again. The blindfolded men slipped out, guided by helping hands, and Lalania invited Christopher to join them.

"Allow us to see to the lady's needs, my lord," she said demurely.

He couldn't think of any reason to object.

"I should go," he said. He probably had more paperwork. The stuff piled up faster than horse manure in a stable and was more unpleasant to deal with. Then he realized he wasn't wearing anything under his cloak.

"My lord will find another outfit in the next room," Lalania said. "Ser Gregor can assist you."

"Stop calling him that," Maggie said.

"Of course, my lady," Lalania said, curtseying again. "Shall I refer to him by name, at your command?"

"Call him whatever he told you to," Maggie replied, clearly sensing a trap. Or perhaps setting one herself.

Lalania made an apology with her face. "He has a bad habit of introducing himself as Christopher."

"That will do, then," Maggie said. "And you may call me Mary. Not lady. Just Mary. It's my name. It's just a name."

"If I may be so bold," Lalania said gently, "nothing is just a name here. Your husband has spent many years understanding our ways. Allow me to help you do the same."

Christopher's stomach rumbled, loudly. "I'll just . . . go," he said. He wanted to kiss Maggie again, but that would lead to other things, and those other things required energy, which was gained by food. Hence the compelling lure of breakfast as a step toward the future. Or maybe lunch.

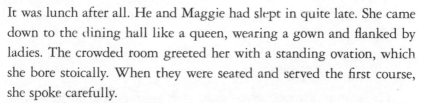

It was lunch after all. He and Maggie had slept in quite late. She came down to the dining hall like a queen, wearing a gown and flanked by ladies. The crowded room greeted her with a standing ovation, which she bore stoically. When they were seated and served the first course, she spoke carefully.

"My operating theory is that you have taken me on a Scandinavian holiday retreat in a historic castle, complete with reenactors. What I can't figure out is how we can afford it."

"Nothing about how we got here? You don't think you'd remember flying to Europe?"

She grimaced. "I assumed heavy drinking."

"The straight nose? The smooth skin?"

"Swedish massages."

He laughed. "That's way better than mine. I thought I'd been kidnapped and escaped after a bump on the head."

"And then?"

"Then I got into a sword fight. And everything went downhill from there."

She looked up at the ceiling, illuminated by dozens of lightstones. "Can I just say that gas lighting completely ruins the illusion?"

He leaned over and kissed her. It was just supposed to be a brief kiss, a moment of shared contact, an acknowledgment of her acuity, but it lingered. Eventually, the smell of roast beef drew him back to his plate.

The diners in the rest of the room broke into spontaneous applause again.

"They're laying it on a bit thick, aren't they?" Maggie asked around a mouthful of food. The beef was very good, and they were both famished.

"They are very happy to see you."

"Why?" Piercing, as always.

"Because I am very happy to see you." He grinned madly, staring at the side of her face. "Also, a lot of them expect it means a reduction in their taxes."

"We'll see about that," she muttered. "I mean, that's what I would say, if I believed this was real."

Christopher grinned even more widely. If people thought he'd wrought unbearable changes, wait until a CPA went over their books. They'd be howling at the moon.

"Oh, right," he said, remembering. "I remember how to convince you. Just wait until tonight. And then look up. This world doesn't have a moon, but it has stars. So many stars."

She stopped eating long enough to look at him. "You really mean that," she said quietly.

"I do," he said, meaning it all over again. "I'm the one who can't believe it's real. I spent so long fighting for this. I can't believe you're really here."

"I think I can convince you," she said slyly. "Just wait until tonight."

He ate faster.

Unfortunately, there was the rest of the day to get through. Christopher was the head of state, and as such the acquisition of a wife was a matter of politics. There was a long list of people who would be insulted if they weren't introduced. He knew it was a long line because it snaked back and forth across the throne room three times. He and Maggie stood because there was only one throne, and Christopher was avoiding sitting in it.

Saint Kreyllan was the head of the line. He smiled at Maggie and held her hand comfortingly. "I sympathize," he explained. "I myself am recently returned, to changes I could not have imagined in my wildest dreams."

"Or nightmares," Cardinal Faren muttered.

"Your husband came to us a poor petitioner. We took pity on him and the trouble he caused. And now we kneel to his throne, gladly, for all the good he has wrought. If I struggle with the transformation, how much more must you. And yet I see here the same man who once sat at my fire, begging me to send him home. A task beyond my considerable power; indeed, I thought it impossible." The Saint shook his head in gentle amazement.

Maggie nodded and squeezed the Saint's hand. Christopher put his arm around her shoulders and stopped himself from kissing her again.

Karl was next. "Sire, your sword," he said, holding out the scabbarded katana.

Christopher had forgotten to put it on that morning. He took it and draped the baldric over his shoulder. Only when he was finished did he notice Maggie staring at him.

"Why are you doing that?" she asked, her voice strained.

Karl answered before he could. "It is a badge of his office, a symbol of his god, and a tool of his profession."

"A tool?" she said, turning to face Karl. "Does he use it often?"

"As often as necessary, which is necessarily often. No throne is held without violence."

Christopher would have objected, but he was too surprised by Karl's sudden eloquence.

Maggie was shocked as well but by the content of the words rather than their form. "Are you saying he has hurt people? Even killed them?"

"Karl," Christopher got out, before being cut off.

"Thousands have passed under his blade; tens of thousands more have died at his command. It is why he rules. It is why we obey." The young man's face was as unsparing as stone, oblivious to Maggie's obvious distress.

"Maggie," Christopher tried again, equally futilely.

"You are saying he is a murderer."

Karl looked at her with something uncomfortably close to contempt. "Every one of those lives was a dagger aimed at my child's throat. The world is better that they are dead."

"Is this true?" she said, turning back to Christopher with wet eyes.

"Yes," he had to say, unwilling to elaborate. The full truth was so much worse.

Lalania stepped forward from where she had been lurking. Always ready to leap out of the shadows with a well-timed thrust. "It is the way of our world, Lady Mary. Here we fight or die. I have gleaned, from what little Christopher has said of your home, that it is not so there."

Saint Krellyan had not moved far. Now he added his support. "So much of what you did and said makes more sense now, Christopher." He spread his hands pleadingly to Maggie. "I myself have held the spear and killed to survive, as has every young man in this realm. None of us is innocent. Until you arrived, we could not even conceive of such innocence."

"Not just the men," Lalania said. "I do not wear my blade merely for show. This is our world; it is what it is. What you need to know is that Christopher has done more to change it than any other in history."

Maggie was surrounded on every side by a wall of thorns. Christopher wanted to hold her, but he was the sharpest vine of all.

"It's a lot to take in," she said after a moment.

Lalania nodded in concession. "Yet do not forget the reward. Half the men standing before you have already died; they live again only because of the power your husband gained. Our realm was oppressed by bad men and worse monsters, now vanquished because of that power. Our future no longer ends in an abattoir because of the creatures your husband has slain."

The bard might have indeed laid it on a bit thick. Maggie's face changed from existential dread to more immediate concerns. She seemed to notice for the first time how attractive the young blonde was. Lalania had worn her elven chainmail, perhaps to compete with all the armored men, and it really did fit like a glove.

"Okay," Maggie said. Christopher knew it wasn't surrender, just a truce; but it wasn't defeat either. There was an accounting yet to be had. Fortunately, he could trust her to add up the balance fairly.

They got through the rest of the evening without further incident. Maggie seemed to relax after they worked their way through the armed nobles and were reduced to important but weaponless commoners. One of whom turned out to be a recent visitor to the throne room although under different circumstances. Throd Mockmorten was apparently not only a wife-beater but also a guild-master. The man was no less lumpy and no better dressed than before, but he bowed his large frame with genuine humility. "A good wife is a treasure beyond measure," he said as he tipped forward, "and a well-married man is beyond wealthy."

"Woman," Maggie said.

Throd did not seem like the sort of man who expected to be corrected by a woman, even a queen. "Beg your pardon, my lady?" he said with a surprised expression.

"You meant woman, not wife. A good woman. A woman's existence proceeds her status as a wife."

Instinctively, Throd glanced at Christopher to see whether he would let this pass. Christopher responded by putting his arm around Maggie again. "She's always right," he said, thrilled for the chance to put the man in his place again.

When Throd had moved on, Maggie muttered, "Perhaps some people deserve to be hit with a sword once in a while."

Christopher felt his tension melt away. The line of well-wishers soon went with it as guards began ushering people out. Night had fallen, and night had recently become Christopher's favorite part of the day.

Maggie looked over at darkened windows, tall and narrow slits in the front of the great hall. "You said you would show me the stars."

He nodded. "Let's go to the roof. You can see half the kingdom from there."

They strolled through the castle, up winding stairs and narrow passageways, until they came out into the cold night air. Above them the sky sparkled with its profusion of twinkling lights, as bright as a full moon, although the light was white rather than yellow.

She gasped and turned into his arms. They stood, embracing for a long moment while her trembling subsided. Finally she spoke. "I still need to go back, at least long enough to call my mother. And let the office know I won't be in."

"It blew my mind, too," he told her. "I still can't figure it out. We must be at the center of the galaxy."

"That's ridiculous," she murmured into his shoulder. "There's a black hole in the middle of the Milky Way. And how could we get there? Even at the speed of light, it takes thousands of years to reach the center."

"I'm guessing physics is in for a bit of a rewrite," he agreed, remembering watching a dragon take the shape of a man.

Speaking of black holes, there was a hole in the sky at the horizon. The hole spread rapidly, and Christopher recognized the shape. Wings, but not dragon wings.

He pushed Maggie behind him, speaking the words of a spell and drawing his sword all in one motion. His blade began to shine with a light harder and sharper than the stars.

The demon vanished, only to reappear behind him. Christopher spun again, keeping in front of Maggie, chanting a different spell.

Maggie helpfully started screaming, or, as he preferred to think of it, raising the alarm.

It roared in some hideous language, the force of its words ripping at Christopher in a fiery wind. There were advantages to being of legendary rank. He shrugged off the assault and leapt forward, striking with his glowing sword.

The blade bit deeply into the monster's scaled flesh. It blinked, and then blinked again in surprise.

"I've learned since we last met," Christopher said. "No more dimension-hopping for you." Then he hit it again.

Its roar was of pain and anger this time. It struck back, its claws tearing deep furrows in Christopher's flesh that healed immediately. Without tael he would have been reduced to dog food just from that one attack. As Lalania had pointed out, there was a reward to all the killing he had done. He ignored the pain and thrust, trying to set up a chance to cut at its wings. He didn't want it getting away this time.

The demon responded by moving close and wrapping its huge body around him in a deadly bear hug. Unfortunately for the demon, that meant that it was within Christopher's touch. He stepped out of its embrace like stepping out of a coat, thanks to Marcius's special favor, laid his palm on the creature, and spoke a spell. The same white energy that had healed a dragon poured into the demon, stuffing it so full that Christopher saw white leaking out of its eyes and mouth.

It staggered back, smoking all over, lashing out with its claws. They hit like guillotine blades; the monster was not to be underestimated even at his rank. And he was unarmored, with only tael between his flesh and its talons.

Off to the side, he heard boots on the roof. Armed men were coming to help him. In the flash of light from their direction, he knew that Ser Gregor and his magic sword were among them. The creature turned to face the danger and released its deadly speech. Against foes of lesser rank, it would be instantly fatal.

The sound of footfalls vanished even while the mob continued to charge. He saw Saint Krellyan in its midst, his hand raised in denial. The Saint had surrounded his fellows with a sphere of silence, blocking the demon's words of power.

Christopher took advantage of the distraction to heal himself completely. It was overkill to use such a powerful spell on his mortal frame, but it was also quick, and he had only this instant's reprieve. Then he charged the beast again.

In desperation it leapt back on him, trying to drag him to the edge of the roof where it could escape while dropping him to his death or at least to significant discomfort. Marcius's favor still held; at Christopher's rank, it lasted for a good long time. This time when he laid his palm on the demon, white steamed out from under its scales as it writhed.

Now it broke and ran, hopping and spreading its wings. Christopher was glad not to be armored as he sprinted after it. A white lion charged ahead of him and pounced, bringing the creature to the ground. They rolled, the lion biting and raking, the demon's heavy blows spraying white motes like blowing snow across the roof. Krellyan had called for aid from the Bright Lady, although it might not last long against the demon's claws. Christopher took the opportunity to slice through a wing.

Krellyan sent in a wave of large white wolves to pin the demon down while Christopher hacked away. Gregor joined him. Eventually, the monster stopped moving and dissolved into black ash. Christopher knelt and cast one more spell, the smallest of them all, and watched a globe of tael grow in his hand. He was a rich man again.

"My lord," Gregor said at his side with a white face. "What the actual Dark was that?"

"Sigrath's demon. I have no idea why it stuck around or attacked now. Thanks for the assist."

"You did most of it," Saint Krellyan said, touching Christopher and healing him. Even in its death throes, the monster had been insanely destructive. "Yet I must disagree. Demons do not act on their own initiative. Someone had to have sent it."

"Well, it's dead now." Christopher surveyed the damage the battle had inflicted on his slate roof, which was surprisingly high. Both his blade and its claws had cut through the stone like butter, leaving the roof looking like crochet after cats had played with it. "And we made a healthy profit. Whoever sent it made a tactical error."

"My lord," Gregor said again, his face even whiter.

Christopher looked where the man was pointing. Maggie's body lay smoking in the ruins, charred almost beyond recognition.

His stomach lurched but only reflexively. This was all in a day's work for a Saint. Striding over to her corpse, he cast the revival spell.

Nothing happened.

He turned to stare at Krellyan, looking for answers. In response, Krellyan cast his own revival spell. The look on his face told Christopher it had failed.

He still had his most powerful revival, the one that required no more than a name. Brewing with anger, he chanted the long and elegant syllables. In his hand, he held enough tael to bring back the Saint a dozen times over. The list of names he knew for his wife was unambiguously precise.

Nothing happened.

Raging, he snapped out a different name. In a flash of light, his huge warhorse trotted onto the roof. He had not been able to justify the expense of tael before, but such concerns seemed wholly irrelevant now.

"I can bring my horse back. How the Dark can I bring my horse back but not my wife? How is this even possible?"

The people before him quailed, and he realized he was shouting. Let him shout, then. With the last high-ranking spell he had for the day, he summoned the person who should have to answer. As the last syllable died, he found himself again in the plain white misty field, stretching peacefully out in infinite dimension around him. In front of him stood the god Marcius, wearing an inscrutable face.

22

CALL OF THE FALCON

His blood still pulsed with the heat of combat. Pointlessly, since this place was not real, and there was nothing here to fight.

Marcius tipped his head. White-haired and yet young, handsome and muscular with sad ancient eyes, wearing chainmail that glittered like a rainbow in the imaginary sunlight, the god spoke with careful neutrality. "You must ask a question."

"Why." Christopher said, his voice thick and heavy.

"Because that is how the spell works."

His jaw was clenched so hard it was hard to speak. "Why can't I bring my wife back."

"Ah, that. Stay your avenging hand; understand I did not know until you asked me. My gaze is not always directed upon you, though you are now my highest ranking servant. Congratulations, by the way."

Christopher glared, his lip curling.

Marcius continued, politely ignoring his ill-tempered response. "The Lord of Death, known by your people as Hordur, has personally intervened. He sent the demon, which he could only do because you had met it before. So take a care of who you greet in the future. He now holds your wife's soul hostage on his own plane of Hel, the Underworld."

"How do I get her back."

Marcius quirked one eyebrow. "You don't wish to know why he has done so?"

"I don't care. Tell me what I have to do. And this time, be clear. No more games, no more cryptic clues, no more promises. No more deals."

"With gods," Marcius said by way of apology, "there are always games."

Christopher trembled, trying to contain his fury. "I did what you asked. I killed the *hjerne-spica*. You have no right to jerk me around now."

"While I can only cheer the destruction of one of those foul creatures, honesty compels me to note that I did not request such a task of you."

"You said you had something you wanted done," Christopher said, jabbing his finger in accusation. "You asked me for a favor."

"I did, and I still do. Yet I cannot intervene directly. Hordur is an elder god, one of the Six. I am a mere aspect, bound by the rules. I would say I lack the authority to make demands of an elder god, but the truth is that no one has such authority."

Christopher snarled. "I didn't ask you to intervene. You've never done anything for me before, why would I think you would now?" The god had promised him help once, and when called on revealed he hadn't actually needed any. "I asked you for information. The spell grants me a number of questions, answered truthfully to the best of your knowledge. Tell me how to rescue my wife."

Marcius looked at him with sympathetic eyes. "You already know. You must travel to Hel and bargain for her release, as in all the stories of your childhood. Although the details will be significantly different."

Of course they would be different since he had no intention of playing any more riddling games with oracular entities. "I'm done with bargains. How do I march my army to Hel?"

"The same spell that delivered your wife will open onto any plane, with the right key. Unique of all the planes, Hel is simple to find. A corpse, freshly slain between the start and end of the chant, will suffice. I concede that for our affiliation, that is not necessarily easy to obtain, but your realm manufactures criminals the same as any other."

"And then?" Because there had to be more.

"You will find Hel's defenses formidable. The demon you slew is native to that realm; their numbers are countless, not to mention the lesser forms and varieties. All the armies of Heaven would contend in vain against them on their own turf; we would tremble if they chose to invade ours. Your army will vanish like a raindrop in a volcano."

Christopher glared, and Marcius sighed. "Instead, you must travel with a small party, evade the majority of demons, and confront Hordur alone. His vanity at least makes this possible because he will want to toy with you and is incapable of feeling fear in the face of anything less than a flock of angels. Ironically, his personal avatar is perhaps the least dangerous of your obstacles, although obviously not to be disregarded. More famously, you must contend with the Mouth of Dissolution. It manifests as a floating sphere of impenetrable dark; whatever goes in does not come back out. Merely to touch it is to be destroyed beyond all magic's ability to repair, miracles nonwithstanding. And it moves at his command."

If the speech was intended to dissuade him, it failed. "Tell me how to defeat the Mouth."

"You must wrest control of it from Hordur in mental combat. Obviously, no mortal can win such a contest." Marcius hurried to the next part, sensing Christopher's impatience with this list of impossibilities. "Less obviously, a man of legendary rank does not exactly count as a mortal. Yet you are not up to the task. No offense, but the intellectual gymnastics required are more arcane than divine."

"So I will need to recruit an ally."

"Recruit seems like a weak word, given that failure to win this contest inexorably results in utter dissolution. You must find an ally who has nothing left to lose."

"I have someone in mind," he said, thinking of Jenny.

Marcius, as always, seemed to exist merely to foil him. "One last constraint: you cannot solve this problem by throwing dragons at it. Hordur would view even a single elder wyrm as a threat worthy of hiding behind his demon horde. Your Jenny is a flock of angels all on its own."

Christopher breathed out heavily. "So to defeat Hordur, I must first be underestimated, and second perform the impossible."

The god smiled encouragingly. "Such describes your entire career, does it not?"

"This is bullshit," Christopher said, shaking his head in denial. "Every part of this is a stupid setup."

Marcius did not deny it. "There are wheels within wheels. And yet, this is not news to you. You understood the nature of the game. You shaped yourself into the role laid out for you, when you could have gone home."

He looked at Christopher intensely, compassion and judgment mixed in equal measure. "Instead, you placed your wife on the board as a piece in the game. Are you so very like one of us now?"

Christopher raised his fist and stepped forward, angry enough to strike a god. But his hand did not fall. It was true, terribly true. On some level, he had understood that bringing Maggie over would be the next step in the drama unfolding around him. He had intuitively recognized that he could either get out of the game or play it to its conclusion. What he could not do was sit at the table for amusement.

"I'm not the only one to cross over from Earth. The next victim might have fallen for the *hjerne-spica*'s plot, and then they would have taken us unaware. My existence is a threat to Earth but also a chance to learn to defend ourselves. I had to try." Voiced, his defense felt vainglorious, and yet there it was.

"You didn't *have* to."

Christopher growled. "I *chose* to. I chose to believe that I was a better chance than the next random person. I chose to think more of myself than a name plucked out of a phone book. Or at least, no worse."

"We are all a product of our choices, and few of them survive rational scrutiny," Marcius said. "That your humility drove you to the heights of arrogance is not the most surprising facet of this multisplendored world."

"I will do it," Christopher said. "I will shove Hordur into his own Mouth. And I don't care what the consequences of destroying the god of death are. If you or any other gods care, then you get my wife back for me. Right now."

"I care," Marcius assured him. "Yet I am bound by the game as much as you. We both must play our hands as best we can and trust to luck."

"You are a god of Luck," Christopher said. "Doesn't that count for anything?"

"I am," Marcius said with sad resignation, "both more and less than either of us know." With an enigmatic frown, the god disappeared and the world of mist faded, leaving Christopher on his cold war-torn rooftop.

"What did the god say?" Krellyan asked, his brow troubled.

"Rubbish. As always." Christopher grunted from the depths of foul temper. "Also, I'm going to Hel."

He felt strung out, like a rope stretched too tautly between buildings, twin immovable points that nonetheless must somehow converge into a single future. The only way to relieve the tension was to move forward.

The Witch of the Moors stood before him wearing a respectful wariness. She had come quickly at his summons. He noticed that people now leapt to obey his commands with an alacrity that went beyond mere respect for the throne. He strongly suspected that they were afraid of him, but contemplating this fact did not advance his cause. So he didn't.

"I cannot serve, my lord," the Witch said. "My magic is arcane in nature, but I am not a wizard. It is a different approach to the same well of power, intuitive and personal rather than rational and academic."

"That rules out elves, too," Lalania said unhappily. "They also practice sorcery. Argeous will be no more help than our Lady."

What he needed was a proper wizard of high rank. He used to have one, but then he had to kill him.

"You could promote your own," the Witch suggested. She looked meaningfully at Fae, standing off to the side. As his Minister of the Arcane, the young woman was naturally involved in this discussion.

Christopher said nothing, lost in thought. This left it up to Fae to respond.

"I am not worthy." Fae did not stammer, but it was impossible to miss the reluctance behind the words. "The Wizard of Carrhill demonstrated as much. Even with advanced rank, I will never be the equal of this task."

Lalania waited a moment for Christopher to say something. When he didn't, she did. "Do not denigrate yourself, Mistress. This is no ordinary task. Varelous himself would blanch at what our lord asks. Or likely refuse. I have recently reviewed our legends of the plane of Hel, and none of them contains a successful attempt." Lalania had taken Alaine's words to heart and now suspected that what she used to think of as merely tales and songs were in fact coded truths about all manner of obscure things, such as demi-planes under the surface. "Indeed, the Mouth is generally presented as an intelligence test. As in, anyone intelligent runs away before they are consumed."

"You could revive the Wizard," the Witch said.

"No," Christopher grunted.

Lalania looked at him with concern before explaining to the Witch. "None of us trusts the man that far. He would turn on our lord in the heat of battle and make a deal with death itself for a promotion."

Still trying, the Witch offered another name. "You could revive Varleous?"

"No," Lalania sighed. "He lived a full life. He is beyond the reach of any magic now."

"I need smart," Christopher said, thinking out loud. "Not rank." He had a fistful of tael from the demon, enough to make an Arch-mage out of an onion if he wanted to.

"We can search the kingdom for native talent," Lalania suggested. "It will take time, but surely an adventure of this magnitude should not be hurried. We can reach out beyond our borders; there must be other human realms, and I suspect Alaine knows where they are."

Christopher shrugged. "If we're just looking for the smartest man in the world, I already know his name."

He stood up and walked out of the room, oblivious to the niceties of court decorum. Lalania dismissed the gathering behind him, mending fences without actually making apologies. She caught up to him just as he was about to close the door to his suite.

"Christopher, you are worrying people. Including me. Please do not do this alone."

Indifferent, he let her in, shutting the door behind her and invoking his spell, chanting out a name dredged from memory. The doorway now looked into yet another Earth-bound bedroom. Christopher was mystified why everyone seemed to be asleep when he called.

The target in this case was not strictly speaking in bed, nor asleep. A thin and wasted form sat in an electric wheelchair, reading from a tiny screen. The man was middle-aged, although he looked ancient, prematurely aged by the degenerative disease that he had famously battled for twenty years. His eyes raised to Christopher and Lalania. There was shock, of course, and skepticism, and concern. There was also a spark when his gaze fell on the pretty blonde bard, as there would be from most men. Christopher grimaced in satisfaction. He would use that, because he would use everything now.

The man moved two fingers, the only part of his body beneath his eyes still under his conscious control. He tapped at a small pad. After a moment, speech issued from a computer speaker on the wheelchair, ironically in a Southern California dialect.

"If she is a Valkyrie, then you must be Odin."

"I'm not a god," Christopher said. "But from your perspective, there isn't much difference. I cannot cross the threshold, so you need to wheel yourself over here."

More tapping. Everyone waited patiently. "You want me to participate in my own kidnapping?"

"I want you to participate in something far worse. You'll probably die. I'll probably die. But I was told I needed the smartest man in the world. If you are interested in playing chess with a god and winning, get over here before the door closes."

The man tapped hesitantly, thinking furiously even while he composed a response. Christopher could almost see the gears turning in the man's head, thanks to his supernatural perception of people's emotional state.

"I would like a change. Dice is not a particularly satisfying game."

The wheelchair lurched into motion. Christopher felt a smile crawl onto his face. It was remarkably easy to convince people to do impossibly dangerous things. All it required was a challenge to their pride, a pretty girl, and the complete lack of any other options. Richard Falconer was dying, had been dying for his entire adulthood. It had not stopped him from publishing ground-breaking physics papers or winning Nobel prizes. Now it would not stop him from recklessly rolling into an adventure he could not possibly understand.

Once Falconer crossed the threshold, Christopher knew he had won. There was no need to spell out the terms of their bargain. He strode forward, grabbed Richard's hand, and pulled him out of the chair. "You won't need that anymore," he said, casting the regeneration spell.

Choking, coughing, and trembling, Richard bent double before standing up and spitting something into his hands.

"I didn't know the British did fillings," Christopher confessed while he cast the translation spell on Richard. "I thought you people had bad dentistry."

"Madness, dream, drug-induced hallucination; whatever this is, I didn't come here for nasty stereotypes." Richard brushed Christopher's hands away and turned to Lalania, making a little half-bow. "Richard Falconer, my lady. Tell me how I can be of service."

Lalania flushed slightly under the force of that gaze. Falconer was a notoriously determined personality. Doctors had written him off as dead a decade ago, but he had hung on through sheer willpower just to prove them wrong.

"You may call me Lalania," she answered. "You will soon enough have rank of your own, and it shall be I who must bow and call you lord. If you meet my lord's requirements, that is."

"Direct and to the point," Richard said with satisfaction. "Skip on a bit, if you would," he told Christopher. "It's been a while, if you know what I mean."

Christopher backhanded him across the face, hard enough to draw blood from a split lip.

Richard's eyes flashed with fire. This was not a man who was used to be being abused, wheelchair or no. To his credit, and as Christopher expected, his intellectual curiosity trumped his emotional response.

"Explain."

"It's not a dream," Christopher said. "Sooner or later everybody has to bleed to understand that. I don't have time to waste waiting for you to figure it out on your own."

"And if I hit you back?"

"Go ahead," Christopher shrugged.

Richard did, instantly, and he put his back into it. Christopher did not bleed, of course; his tael saw to that. It hurt, but nothing like the nightly poison Lalania had administered, and in any case no pain could penetrate the shell around his heart. He remained unmoved and watched Richard nurse his bruised knuckles.

"If you want to hit me with a chair, you can," he told Richard. "I am a Saint; you cannot kill me without considerably more effort than that. I can use magic, like the spell that brought you here and the one that healed you. I am going to make you a wizard. You won't be as hard to kill as I am, or have as much magic, but you will be capable of falling out of a seven-story window and walking away from it. You will also be able to blow things up, fly, turn invisible, call demons, and make sandals." Christopher rattled off the things he had seen wizards do without really thinking through the whole list first.

"You expect me to accept all of this on the strength of a bloody lip," Richard said with completely understandable skepticism.

"I don't care if you accept it. I care that you do what I need. We are going to Hel, and you have a part to play. Lalania will explain. Once you understand, you will be fed tael, a mystical substance that grants supernatural powers. Fae will teach you the basics of wizardry, although I expect you to surpass her quickly. If you can't, then you are of no use to me."

Richard crooked his head. "And if I am of no use to you?"

"Then I'll find somebody else."

23

PARTY OF FOUR

One by one, Christopher called his subjects to this throne. One by one, they found ways to decline the honor he sought to bestow. Once upon a time, people had flocked to his side, hoping to join his retinue. Now that he was going to Hel, people shuffled and made excuses.

Lalania helped them. "There is no point in taking another priest. If divine magic will matter, you have as much of it as can be asked for. This is a traditional quest, or at least it must appear traditional at the outset, lest it fail immediately." He had told her everything Marcius had said. He was done with secrets. "Thus, you must form a traditional adventuring party."

He waited for her to continue. She looked a little sad at the loss of their usual banter. He could see that. He just couldn't bring himself to do anything about it.

"You need a rogue and a warrior. One to open doors and the other to fight what is behind those doors. You already have the priest to heal the warrior and the wizard to deal with the things that can't be killed with a sword."

"Richard is working out?" It had been a week since he had last seen the man, who it must be said took to the study of magic with a monomaniacal focus appropriate to the world's greatest theoretical physicist. Richard had read every book on magic in the entire kingdom in two days, without stopping to sleep, and was now at the stage of conducting experiments while his rank manifested. Christopher realized that Fae must be made miserable by the comparison, but again he couldn't seem to care enough to act.

"You could say that," Lalania said while looking at the wall. "Fae and I have kept him in hand, though, and his studies progress at a prodigal rate. He cracked the Wizard of Carrhill's personal spell-book code because it was faster than reading it with a spell."

"Where can I get a rogue?" He'd had a professional assassin once, but again, he'd had to kill her. "Does the Invisible Guild even exist anymore?" In the early days of his reign, he had hung quite a number of them.

"I assume so, but those of a rank to interest you must have already taken their chances in the Wild. However, all is not lost. There is another profession with similar skills, and they are already loyal."

He stared at her, wishing she would stop trying to be clever. Or expect him to be.

"The College," she said, exasperated. "I am talking about bards. You should promote me to a sufficient rank and take me with you."

There was a time he would have objected. There was a time he would have pointed out that he was probably marching to his death, and he didn't want to take anyone else with him.

He sat silently instead.

She took it as a positive sign. "Two more ranks would make me half again as hardy. I could finally withstand those ubiquitous barring spells. Ants and goblins would no longer require my pretense to be able to accompany you."

"And the warrior?" he asked.

Lalania considered. "Cannan is the obvious choice. He has a sword fit for a king, and he owes you more than his life. He will need more ranks, though."

"No." Christopher discovered that his despair had limits. Cannan had just been reunited with his wife. Destroying that was a price too high to pay.

She shook her head but not in surprise. "He will be crushed. He has waited for you to call him, secure in the knowledge that no one else has the courage to follow you to the gates of Hel. He thought you were merely magnifying his loyalty by calling him last and giving everyone else a chance to decline. He gloried in watching those of higher rank mumble and back away."

"No," Christopher said again.

Lord Einar had declined, asserting that his tracking skills did not extend to the Underworld. Lord Istvar had suggested Christopher revive Duke Nordland and ask him, which just sounded like an expensive way to get insulted to his face. Torme and Gregor were priests or half-priests, and thus superfluous. That didn't leave a lot of choices.

"One of those elves," he said, thinking of the silver-clad warriors.

"What possible inducement could you offer?" Lalania asked skeptically.

"A job well done." The god of death was breaking the rules. It seemed like something the elves should be offended by.

A page crept into the otherwise empty throne room to announce a petitioner. Christopher nodded absently. He had forgotten who else was due to appear and present a reason to avoid going on a suicide mission.

The person who walked into his hall was the last one he had expected. Alaine strolled up and tipped her head in nominal deference to his status as king. He was more powerful than she was now—Lalania and he had estimated her rank somewhere around ninth or tenth—but he still found her intimidating. She knew too many secrets and too many dragons to be taken lightly.

"I understand you are planning another adventure," Alaine said. "So soon after the last one?"

Christopher growled at the elf. On this subject, he would berate gods.

"Such is often the case," she said, not in the least concerned with his anger. "We reach for our most cherished dream, only to find it hollow once off the high shelf."

"The situation is rather different," Lalania said sharply. "Saint Christopher was satisfied with his dreams. Other parties intervened."

"I was not speaking only on Christopher's behalf," she answered. "Yet it is true that the law, such as it is, appears to have been violated."

"If you're here to do something about it, say so," Christopher said. "If you're here to tell me you can't do anything, I already know that."

"I am not here to tell you I cannot do anything," she said, sending an electric thrum of promise through Christopher's spine. "I am here to tell you what I can do. This is my domain, and as such, I take it personally when someone else trespasses on it. Also, we elves have no cause to love Hordur, and no desire to see you fail where so many others have. Thus, I must tell you: your wizard is not ready. He will lose."

"And?" Lalania said in challenge. Christopher held his breath, hoping for the best.

"And I have come to make him ready. Understand we do this for our own purposes; but at this juncture they coincide with your own."

"Will you give us a warrior too?" Christopher asked. "Apparently we need a warrior."

Alaine bowed her head in genuine humility this time. "I have been farther across the face of Prime than many, and to more planes than most. Yet I would add to my travels. If you will have me, I will accompany you."

<hr>

Christopher found himself begging for scraps to raise the tael for Lalania's promotion. Richard had consumed all of the demon's tael. He had lost all patience, however, and his requests for charity came out as demands. Only the fact that everyone expected him to never return from this adventure kept them from rebelling.

Krellyan was widely viewed as the soon-to-be occupant of the throne. Christopher found he did not care, either for or against. Not that it mattered because no one asked his opinion. In general, people avoided him as much as possible.

Even Cannan was gone, off to Niona's homeland. He had not left without making a statement, however. Alaine returned to court wearing his sword on top of her own silvered mail.

"It is a good sword," the elf acknowledged. The thing seemed too large for her, but that did not fool Christopher.

She brought Richard with her. The man looked diffcrent, tanned and worn into his new skin, at ease in his elven leathers. He also spoke the local language fluently.

"I understand the Lady Alaine will accompany us? And the bard as well? So it's a double date." He was too polished to leer, but the look he gave Lalania could not be mistaken.

She muttered under her breath, an aside for Christopher. "The man is insatiable. I wonder how Alaine fared."

"It was only a week," Christopher whispered back. The memory of Kalani's extremely casual approach to the topic made him squirm. He did not need to know more details.

Alaine apparently could still hear them. "A week for you and I. Not for Master Richard."

"Say what?" Christopher blurted.

"Time dilation." Richard stared at him with alarming directness. "The gate spell necessarily reaches through time as well as space. You reached twenty-five thousand years into the past to bring me here. All you have to do is stumble a bit on the return trip and Bob's your uncle. You're back just after you left, no matter how long you were gone."

Christopher narrowed his eyes, wondering if the man was making fun of him. "I don't understand."

Alaine smiled. "Now you have some measure of how the rest of us feel. Yet in this case, I can interpret. What he is trying to say is that Argeous took him to a plane where time passes differently. He has been gone for three years from his point of view."

"Oh. Sorry?" Christopher wasn't sure what he was supposed to make of this news.

"You needn't be," Richard said. "It gave me a chance to make a proper study of magic. Not that I don't still have questions. I imagine you must as well."

"He learns quickly," Alaine said, and her words carried a hint of warning. "The Directorate was impressed. In sheer point of fact, he surpassed their standards and won their respect."

"What she is trying to say," Richard said, "is that I am now of equal rank to you. They promoted me because they thought I deserved it."

Christopher raised his eyebrows in surprise. That was incredible generosity, especially for a creature that would soon fade from the long war the elves waged.

"Also because any less would result in failure," Alaine explained. "The Directorate was willing to make this investment because they think you have a chance to hurt our common foe significantly."

"They?" Lalania asked pointedly.

Alaine smiled at the barb. "It is true that I concur with the Directorate in this regard."

Richard rubbed his hands together in satisfaction. "The Directorate also provided me access to their library. Which I must say is quite considerable for a people who do not practice wizardry. These elves are like squirrels, caching all sorts of nuts against future need. Not quite what literature primed me to expect."

Christopher had more immediate concerns. "Did they give you any nice toys?" He still hadn't recovered the magical gear that had been looted from Trewayn's vault.

Richard shook his head. "I manufactured the apparatus necessary to my rank, but I turned down everything else. We can do better."

"I must also say that you have been offered better than myself," Alaine said. "We have a few champions of higher rank; any of them would be willing to take my place at your side."

"I turned them down, too," Richard said. "This mission depends on discretion as much as force, and I am concerned that any entity more significant than Lady Alaine would set off warning bells. As the local Field Officer, her presence is explicable; you, of course, are expected, the bard isn't high enough rank to matter, and I am too new to have a reputation."

"You seem to have taken it all well in hand," Christopher said.

Richard looked at him with a piercing gaze. "You called for my help and staked my life. I intend to succeed."

Chastised, Christopher bit his lip.

"To wit," Richard continued, "I need your assistance. If one of us opens a gate to Earth the other can cross over for almost three hours. I would like to acquire a few of our own toys."

"We already have the best from Christopher's forges," Lalania said, her hand going to the revolver she wore.

"No offense," Richard said to her with a fetching smile, "but I had more in mind."

Christopher could not take offense. It was objectively true that Earth had better firearms. It was also likely true that Richard would have advanced technology further in five years than he had. And the physicist probably wouldn't have a wife to be rescued, requiring him to run off and abandon his kingdom.

"Um," Christopher said, realizing he had not even considered the issue until now, "do you need to call home and tell someone where you are?"

Richard laughed, genuinely enough, but his eyes were still on Lalania. "What could I possibly say? I got up and walked away from my wheelchair to play with the fairies? People disappear all the time on Earth, for all sorts of reasons, but world-famous cripples don't just vanish without leaving so much as a fingernail. You should have prepared a corpse and set my bedroom on fire. If no one had looked too closely, it might have worked. Now the British tabloids will be exploding. Yes, I have family who must now be agonizing over my fate, but the daily medicine that kept me alive is not easily obtained. By now logic and reason will have confirmed my death in absentia. To disturb them with an incoherent phone call would seem the better part of cruelty."

He shrugged his shoulders disarmingly. "Scotland Yard is no doubt in a tizzy as well, but I doubt your mercies extend to them, nor could they be assuaged with a mere phone call either. Unless you were placing a ransom demand. That, at least, would make sense."

"You see what I mean," Alaine said ruefully.

Christopher did see. He should have made that phone call on Maggie's behalf, but he hadn't, for the same reason. What could he possibly say? To hear his voice when he was supposed to have been long dead assuring that his now missing wife was perfectly fine would only make her family crazy.

Especially since he could not force such a lie through his lips. Maggie was lost, and he did not know where or how. He stood up, driven by the same whip that had lashed him since that moment.

"Where do you want the gate?" His hand was already trying to trace out the spell.

"On this side, in your stable. Sympathetic foci can only increase the chance of success. As for that side, I have an address."

"You intend to steal horses from Earth?" Lalania asked. Apparently she understood him when he spoke of arcana.

Christopher had not understood it, but he had not asked because he didn't care. He started walking down the long hall, heading for the courtyard.

"Of sorts," Richard said to Lalania as they followed him out. "But why don't you come along and see? I'm sure you could make yourself useful."

Lalania blushed. "I know nothing of the situation you are entering. I would only be a liability."

Richard shook his head, although his eyes did not move. He stared at the bard like a man in a desert staring at a waterfall. "Nothing I can plan is beyond your improvisational skill."

Christopher exchanged a glance with Alaine. The elf looked back coolly, unconcerned with the little drama. He decided not to worry about it. Lalania had been dealing with this for her whole life; she had literally been trained for it.

"Give me the address," he said, interrupting some inconsequential flattery.

Richard handed him a slip of paper. While Christopher read it, his eyes having to refocus on the unfamiliar English lettering, Richard cast his own spell, summoning the white mist that Lalania's lyre produced. In its wake, his and Lalania's clothes were transformed into military uniforms.

"I liked that blouse," Lalania complained.

"Trust me, this suits you better, Colonel." Richard saluted her crisply, still managing to imbue every word and act with salacious intent. "I am your driver, ma'am. We are to collect a Wolf for Home Duty."

"Snap to it, soldier," she barked, throwing herself into the role.

Richard grinned, his eyes making a double-entendre out of her remarks, but what he said was, "That was perfect, but unfortunately it needs to be in English."

Christopher turned away from the gaping hole that opened into a paved alleyway in another world and cast the translation spell on Lalania.

"What am I supposed to say to anyone who comes wandering through here?" he asked.

"That's your problem," Richard said. "Go ahead and tell them the truth for all I care. You can hardly make a worse mess of it than you already have. Just keep it open until we get back. I don't fancy having to answer MI6's questions without magic on my side."

He raised his eyebrows at Christopher's obvious question, answering it before it could be asked. "You didn't know? Magic works as long as you hold the gate open. I will still be a legendary wizard over there for the next three hours. Why didn't you research this? I mean, I know you're an engineer, but this is at least technical."

"I had other things on my mind," Christopher answered testily.

Richard gave Lalania an appreciative glance. "I understand. No, wait, I don't." Before Christopher had to respond, Richard took Lalania's hand and led her down the alleyway.

Alaine stood at his side. "My experience of Earth natives is woefully small, yet I find myself drawing broad conclusions. Please tell me I am wrong."

"They're not all like us," Christopher said. "Most of them are normal."

She gazed through the gap. Christopher realized she might have wanted to go along. For that matter, there were things he would have liked to have asked for. A bar of chocolate, for instance. He began hatching a plan to send Alaine across to look for a corner shop, but it fell apart when he came to the part where she paid for it.

"Hang on," Christopher said. "How is he going to buy an army jeep?"

"It seems obvious that he intends to steal whatever he requires. He cleverly kept you distracted, precisely so you would not ask that very question. Although his affiliation is technically White, he is not quite as circumscribed as you are."

Christopher looked at her, remembering her promise to murder him and everyone he knew if he went astray. "And you?"

"No," she confessed. "We do not bind ourselves to gods. If I should fall and abuse my office, it is upon myself and my fellows to correct it. We will not lose our powers merely because we lose our way."

"That isn't necessarily a good thing," Christopher said, thinking of the value of a fail-safe. It was nice to know that if he went for Team Evil, he would at least be denied the spells he wielded in Marcius's name.

"It depends on whether or not you trust the gods."

He started to object, but his long-ago argument with Lalania came back to him. Instead, he asked, "Do you have reasons I should doubt Marcius?"

"Not at all," she said. "Yet that does not mean such reasons do not exist. It just means I do not know them."

He was glad that Richard was absent for this conversation. Gods were another thing he had not researched. In sheer point of fact, he had told Marcius to his face that he did not believe the god was being upfront and honest and yet continued to trust him completely.

"Wheels within wheels," he muttered.

"We have ridden the Great Wheel for longer than you can imagine," Alaine said. "In all that time, we have seen things that would beggar your dreams and terrify your nightmares. Yet I can tell you this: never before has the Directorate offered such rank to a mortal. He is truly a remarkable specimen."

With a flash, Christopher realized he had been rendered entirely obsolete. Richard had made it clear he could open gates too. And because he was from Earth, he could take over the role of guardian of the gate. Or target of the *hjerne-spica*. Whichever it was, this world no longer needed Christopher. He could go home now.

Except that he couldn't. There was no home left to go to.

He stood in his stable, stewing in anger.

Richard timed it close. Alaine had started to frown, meaning that her internal clock was running out. Christopher had found a hay bale to sit on, tired of standing after the first two hours. Servants had brought them wine and cheese, and a squad of soldiers waited just outside the stable doors with rifles and a cannon.

At least no one wandered by the rip in the world. Christopher wondered at the luck of that until he realized Richard must have done something to hide it.

Shortly after night began falling on the alleyway, he saw headlights. An open-topped jeep zipped around the corner and confidently drove through the gate, coming to a stop between Christopher and Alaine.

Richard saluted from the driver's seat. "Reporting for duty, General."

Lalania was sitting in the passenger seat, flushed with excitement. Christopher smiled to see her reaction to automobiles.

"Was it an eventful trip?" Alaine asked the bard, more archly than Christopher thought necessary.

"You're not one to talk," Lalania replied, before turning and pointing at the heavy machine gun mounted in the back. "Richard says this is for you."

"A bit of an upgrade over your bow," the man said, winking at her. He seemed far more relaxed than he had been several hours ago. Apparently action was good for the soul. Christopher itched to join them. Every moment of delay felt like nails being driven into his spine.

"When can we go?" Christopher asked.

"A few more details," Richard answered. "I need to show Alaine how to use the gun, which I imagine won't take long. And I need to teach Ell to drive, although she's already pretty handy with a stick shift. You and I will have our hands full with spells, and in any case, I bet your license has elapsed."

He had a pet nickname for her now. Lalania didn't flinch at the familiarity, so Christopher let it pass. There would be a time when he would have to account for all the wizards he expected her to keep on side. Not now.

24

ROAD TRIP FROM HELL

R ichard had loaded the jeep with supplies before returning. Extra fuel, boxes of ammunition, several assault rifles, half a dozen large automatic pistols, and a grenade launcher.

"For the small stuff," he explained as he showed Christopher and the women how to load and charge the rifles. He had spent a day teaching Lalania to drive the jeep. Alaine had only needed a quarter of an hour to master the machine gun. Christopher had watched it destroying a stand of trees and frowned at the inadequacy of his own armaments. His artillerymen had stared in slack-jawed lust.

"How do you know how to do all this?" Christopher asked.

"The internet," Richard replied. "You can look up manuals. Ell borrowed a phone while we were over there. The question you should be asking is how did these girls master these skills so quickly? You think it took you only a day to learn how to operate a motorcar?"

At least he knew the answer to this one. "Rank. It makes everything easier."

"Only to a limit," Richard said. "But yes. It does something to your mind. This truly fascinating phenomenon calls into question everything we think we know about consciousness. You'd think you'd be more curious."

"I saw a dragon turn into an elf," Christopher said. "That made me curious."

Richard shrugged. "The least interesting event I have witnessed. It's just energy. A staggering amount, but just energy. This . . . this is how our brains work. This is complex."

Christopher had finally had enough. "Look. While you were lounging around in an elven academy, I was fighting for my life. I didn't have time for abstract questions."

"As I understand it, you've been on that throne for a few years now."

Christopher sighed, all of the fight taken out of him when he realized how little he had changed the justice system of this world. "It had its own distractions."

"That at least I can believe." Richard was apparently trying to make peace in his own insufferable way. "But surely you noticed that people here, even people without powers, have tael."

"Yes," Christopher said. "I did notice that."

"Didn't you wonder what it is for? I mean, if tael lets you cast spells, Ell learn to drive a car, and Alaine jump out of a ten-story window, then what does it do for ordinary people? Why is it there at all?"

Christopher shrugged. "I don't know. It's just a feature of this world."

"Yes: a feature of this world, and no other. Which explains why you summoned me instead of Ramanujan."

"Who?"

Richard frowned at him. "Srinivasa Ramanujan. The mathematician. He died in 1920. You really don't know who he was?" He shook his head in dismay. "If you wanted the smartest man in the world, you should have revived him. I assumed you augured for a name, rather than simply relying on popular press reports. I had, until now, assumed my status as the greatest living intellect had been established by divine authority, not merely your stray recollections. But no matter. You cannot revive Srini despite the fact that he died young. Because he died without tael. There is no record of him in the cosmic database."

Christopher felt his blood turn to ice. "Is that why I can't reach Maggie?"

"Not at all. She died here. The instant she stepped across the threshold, she was infected. Should you open a permanent gate to Earth, everyone there will be infected within a heartbeat. Only the temporary nature of your gates so far has prevented it."

"That's an ugly word," Christopher said.

"Yet appropriate. Like a virus, it sits in our heads, doing nothing for us. A benign infection, if you will, but we did not ask for it, and it gains us naught. You and I only profit because we have *other* people's tael, as well as our own. As far as I can tell, our native quantity of tael only serves to register us with the magic system. We can be scried on, spied on, revived, and a select number of other effects less immediate than simple directed energy. For instance, no one without tael can be shape-shifted."

"You understand," Christopher said, scratching his chin, "that I had no un-taeled subjects to study."

"Another reason I took Ell to Earth. That sympathy spell she does, where she makes you think you're her best friend? That doesn't work. But she could still disguise herself. It's a bloody mess, it is. Like it's completely arbitrary."

That was something they could agree on. Christopher nodded his head in sympathy, but Richard shook his head.

"It only seems that way. There has to be an underlying principle, a purpose. If all that was necessary was cosmic tagging, that could be accomplished with a fraction of the standard amount. This is wasteful, and nature is not profligate without reason. Eventually I will figure it out."

"Great. That's great. I'm happy for you. Can we get back to the problem at hand?"

The man stared at him curiously. "What makes you think this isn't?"

Their conversation was interrupted by an explosion. Alaine had figured out how to work the grenade launcher.

"Not as effective as one of your fire strikes," she said with a frown aimed downrange where the logs they had set up as targets were lying in disarray from the blast.

"Except it works from within an anti-magic sphere. Which will prove useful, I think," Richard said. "Christopher and I will both prepare that particular effect."

"Is that where we're at?" Christopher asked. "Preparing spells?"
"We are," Richard confirmed. "We can leave in the morning."

The words did not comfort Christopher. He had already fought and won against impossible odds and lost anyway. Nothing had convinced him that this time would be different.

Karl shook his head sadly. "I cannot decide which I regret the most: letting you leave or letting you take that vehicle away. Why didn't you make any of those machine guns for us?"

They were standing in the courtyard while Richard checked over the preparations. He had made a list, although Christopher suspected it was merely a prop he could wave at people who weren't moving fast enough to suit him. The man did not seem like the kind of person who forgot things.

"They're hard. Also, you need smokeless powder or they get fouled and jam." Christopher sighed. "And don't even ask about the jeep. I bet it has electronic fuel injection. I can't even guess how to manage that."

"I can't believe you're going without me. Again." Gregor was trying to make a joke of it, but the truth hurt nonetheless. Disa clung to the blue knight's arm with a look of gratitude that took the pain away.

"I also feel the sting of rejection," Torme said. "Though I know I have no reason to be anything but grateful. Still, it is the adventure of a lifetime and hard to miss out on."

"It's not my idea." Christopher defended himself. "I wanted to take the whole army. Marcius told me not to."

"Good advice even if it didn't come from a god," Lalania said, joining the little knot of men. "I have made a study of our legends. Stealth really is the key. An army would attract a plague of demons. And even with machine guns, I think we would lose."

Christopher grunted. "I wouldn't be taking jeeps." It would probably take his merely mortal men several months to master the art of tank warfare, but Christopher would have gladly endured it.

Well, not gladly.

"As am I dismayed," Cardinal Faren said. "This feels too much like a capstone. With Krellyan restored to us, our world is as it was, only better. This reads like the end of our chapter in your life, and I am shocked to discover I do not want that."

There was a brief round of smiles at the irascible old man's confession.

"Yet do not let my words weigh on you." Faren reached out and took Christopher's hands in his. "We will finish the work you have begun. Karl's army will replace the knights. Krellyan's Vicars will replace the Barons. Your witches will teach us your chemistry. Your smiths will teach us your physics. Your bards . . . well, they will do what they always do, and we will try to ignore it as usual."

Helga bit her lip through her tears. "You are all talking like he will never come back. He always comes back. I was there, the first time, before any of you. He came back."

Christopher hugged her and then reached down to pat the child clinging to her dress. "Of course I will. No one else knows how to make a decent bowl of porridge."

They were ready: Alaine standing in the back of the jeep with her hands lingering over the machine gun, and Richard sitting in the passenger seat. Christopher wore his armor, sword, and cloak. Lalania and Alaine were in their elven chainmail, the elf with the big royal sword over her back and the bard with a rapier at her side. Lalania also had the lyre, which made Christopher a little uncomfortable because technically it belonged to the kingdom. Richard was unarmored, in only the light leather the elves favored. He was not unarmed, however; he carried a short-barreled assault rifle. All of them wore one of the heavy pistols he had brought back. The bullets for the pistols were huge, almost as big around as the rifles that Christopher had made. Richard swore they would stop a buffalo. Christopher, remembering the bull Karl ha killed, suspected that Richard had never actually seen a buffalo and certainly not what passed for large herbivores around these parts.

Vicar Rana intercepted him as he made his way to the jeep.

"Do not upbraid me for my superstitions," she admonished him. "They are the only comfort left to me these days, when my son makes bombs out of water and fire." Johm's first attempts at steam engines had a tendency to explode. "Just take this. Once before you marched in impossible danger, and I gave it to you then. Once again I do the same, in the hope of the same outcome."

She handed him a heavy bronze jar, the magic water bottle that could sprout a firehose indefinitely. It was, as he expected, the one marked with the sigil of Marcius. He had no idea how it would help, but he could hardly say no.

"Thank you," he said instead, "for everything."

One last petitioner waited for him: the Witch of the Moors, in a flowing white dress. "I am not entitled to this color," she admitted. "It is a symbol only. Yet you have won me over. My people will fare better under Krellyan's reign than mine. I may choose not to renew my sovereignty. At the least I will serve your Saint loyally."

"I would not go so far, my lady," Lalania said. "As Christopher has made clear, the realm still requires magic."

"You know I don't actually have any idea what you are talking about, right?" Christopher said.

The Witch smiled. "I know. As I also know you are under a spell older than magic. Go with my good wishes, and succeed."

He nodded, pretending it made sense, and hurried the last few steps to the jeep.

"I call shotgun," Richard said. "You ride in the back and keep our gunner alive."

Christopher climbed up to his assigned seat, checking his headroom. If Alaine swung that gun around too vigorously, he would get a knocking.

Lalania started the jeep. Christopher cast the spells that would last all day at his new rank, energy protection and strength. Both of them seemed likely to be helpful enough that he cast them on everyone.

Alaine handed each of the three humans a small potion vial. They unscrewed the tops and swallowed the contents. More of the elven night-vision magic.

"And a chaser," Richard said, producing a six-pack of beer. "It's traditional for road trips," he explained, handing them each one.

"It's warm," Christopher said after the first sip.

"Like I said, traditional." Then the man muttered something under his breath that might have been, "Bloody Yanks."

Lalania drained hers in one go, tossed it over the window, and hit the gas. The jeep lurched until she slammed on the brakes, throwing them all forward.

"Just checking." She grinned wildly.

Richard stood up, hanging onto the windscreen. He started chanting the gate spell.

Christopher looked around curiously. He hadn't paid that much attention to the preparations and wasn't sure what they were going to do for a key. His gaze fell on Major Kennet, who waved to him cheerfully. Christopher smiled and waved back, just in time to see Karl shoot the young man through the head with one of the new automatic pistols.

The boy fell, dead as a doornail, blood and brain spraying out from the blast. Christopher's mouth went dry. Richard finished his chant and the rift opened, jagged, dark, and foul, a stench blowing in from the plane of the dead. Ahead Christopher could see an entire decaying forest of rotted trees and dead moss. To the side, he could see Krellyan kneeling over the body. The Saint caught his eye and nodded reassuringly.

They had found a volunteer to open the gate. Fortunately, it was temporary duty. Kennet had been brought back so many times, he must be used to it by now.

As Lalania accelerated toward the rift, Richard threw his empty beer can out of the jeep. Christopher gratefully raised his to his lips, no longer concerned about the temperature.

The forest was sparse enough that the jeep could wind through it, crunching over dried leaves and through huge spider webs that stretched from tree to tree. Christopher's job was navigation; he had cast his compass spell and now held his hand pointing in the direction they should be going, regardless of whatever temporary detours Lalania had to make for the terrain.

Richard hummed a tune, his rifle in his hands and one foot up on the dashboard. "Should have brought some music," he said.

Alaine was unamused. "As if this vehicle does not announce our presence enough."

"I got one with the new mufflers." Richard shrugged. "The smell of horseflesh would be worse."

Christopher fished around at his feet, trying to find the rest of the six-pack.

"Why don't we fly?" he asked. He wanted to try the air-walking spell and see whether the jeep's tires could ride on little puffs of cloud.

"NO," all three of them said in unison.

"Nothing would attract the *bevinget* more quickly," Alaine said.

"That's our name for the winged demons," Lalania explained. "The other one, with the chains, is called a *kjede*. The Wizard of Carrhill's books were very informative."

"Oh," said Richard. "I just don't like heights."

"Those are only two out of many," Alaine said.

"Yes, but they're among the worst, right?" It was strange hearing Lalania ask for confirmation. And from an elf, no less.

"The *bevinget*, definitely. Some of the others are less obvious and thus more dangerous for it."

"I think," mused Richard, "that mostly we'll be dealing with the obvious today."

The land opened up, turning into a dry riverbed free of anything larger than a weed. Christopher felt a little homesick, at least until he looked up. The sky was black and starless but not empty. A dead sun hung overhead, giving off no light; the land was perpetually dark, the night never-ending.

Lalania accelerated, driving faster.

"Watch out for drops," he said, worried. "Or pot holes."

"You watch out," Richard answered. "Seriously. You have a spell for that, right? Can you put it on her?"

"No, that's me." Alaine kissed her fingers and then touched Lalania on the top of her head.

The bard immediately swerved, throwing them all up against doors, or in Alaine's case, the gunnery frame.

Richard put his seat belt on. Christopher did the same. Lalania, quite sensibly, already had hers on.

"Sorry," Lalania apologized. "I think that was a false alarm." She swerved again and drove past a gaping hole in the ground that bubbled with some foul substance.

"Um," Christopher said, his gaze having been directed outward. There was a crowd of skeletal figures, several hundred strong, running along the edge of the riverbank, black and yellow skin flapping from white animated bones.

"I saw them," Alaine said. "They won't catch us."

Ahead of them, the land began to move. Bushes and dirt rose up, falling off a giant rotting body of something five or six times larger than an elephant. It might have been a dinosaur, once.

Alaine aimed the machine gun but held her fire. Lalania downshifted and turned, spraying sand. She cut around the hulking beast and left it behind.

"I concede," Alaine frowned. "Horses would have been worse."

"I know," Richard said lightly. He had another can of beer in his hands.

"Where's the other one?" Christopher leaned forward to ask but then had to sit up and point Lalania in the right direction. "Take that fork."

She hewed around and sent them down a narrower channel. "No choice here," she said. "Hang on."

Corpses started popping up out of the ground, grabbing at the jeep as it went past. Most of them slid off or were crushed by the jeep's solid front bumper. One managed to hang onto the passenger door.

Richard hit it with the butt of his rifle until it fell off. One hand remained clinging to the side mirror, unattached to the rest of the body. Richard kicked it off with his boot.

"This is the little stuff." He scanned the sky. "We should see something bigger soon."

"Behind us," Alaine said. Richard looked over his left shoulder and sat up straight, trying to get a clear line of sight. Christopher had no chance; Alaine was in his way. Behind her he could see three winged creatures bearing down on them. Richard took a shot, the sound loud and sharp in front of Christopher's face. He watched the brass cartridge fly out, bounce off the windscreen, and fall by the wayside. Alaine shouldered her rifle and began firing, raining brass over the edge of the jeep.

"Slow down," Richard called over the gun shots. Lalania let the jeep idle down to a lower speed. Now Richard and Alaine had a steadier firing platform. He fired carefully while she blazed away. All three of the winged creatures fell, one after another. Alaine tossed her depleted magazine overboard and shoved a new one into her rifle. Richard scowled, apparently aware that his efforts had been completely unnecessary. Christopher was disturbed to see that none of the flyers had tried to retreat even as their wingmen died in the air.

"So much for unannounced," Richard needled Alaine.

"I did that for you," she answered. "The harpies have no interest in me."

The jeep slowed as it crawled out of the riverbed. Now they were on a long, flat plain. There was no cover here, and Christopher was glad the jeep's headlights were off. Any light would be seen for miles. Torches would be like fishing lures. At least the gunfire was only temporary.

"There's our bigger," Richard said, pointing ahead. Two small figures were drifting through the sky, slowly heading their way.

Alaine frowned. "If you would, Christopher."

He cast his weapon blessing on her machine gun, expending considerably more spell energy than usual. This one would last for almost an hour.

Looking forward again, he realized the small figures were in fact huge. They had only seemed small because of how far away they had been. They weren't far away anymore, and they weren't slow.

Richard was fixing earmuffs over Lalania's head. Christopher couldn't get the muffs under his helmet, so he just put his fingers in his ears. Alaine squeezed a dozen rounds from the big gun and then did it twice more.

As the jeep zoomed between the bodies, each the size of a small wagon and slowly turning into smoke, Alaine actually wheedled. "Surely we can stop. It would take only seconds."

"No," Richard said.

"Why would we stop?" Christopher asked.

"Those creatures are almost legendary," Alaine said, staring backward as they vanished in the distance. "A wealth of power unimaginable to mortal man lies on the ground back there, and this wizard of yours drives past it like a cheap taco stand."

"Stopping to collect loot is how people get killed," Richard said. "Ell's stories make that clear, as if common sense and history were not enough. We're not here to get rich."

"Says the man who was handed his rank," grumbled Alaine, but without heat.

"How do you know what a taco stand is?" Christopher asked, amazed.

"You don't have tacos in your kingdom?" Alaine answered, equally surprised. "Are you sure? I thought I had . . . never mind. It must have been somewhere else."

"Thank the gods Lalania can't hear this," Richard said. "We had burritos while we waited for the jeep to be brought up out of armory parking. She loved them."

"Now I know you're putting me on," Christopher said. "You can't get Mexican food in London."

"Listen, mate, it's a cultural haven. The most multicultural city in the world."

Christopher had to stop arguing so he could tap Lalania on the shoulder. He pointed vigorously, following the instruction of his direction-finding spell, and she swerved again.

Richard muttered an oath. He leaned over and flipped on the jeep's headlights. Then he cast the anti-magic spell and the world went dark, save for the cone of light cut out by the halogen beams.

Now Lalania drove through the night on merely mortal terms. She slowed instinctively, no longer guided by the trap-finding spell, but still driving faster than Christopher would have dared. He didn't say anything, however, because she couldn't hear him. Alaine was using the machine gun again.

The battle was not completely invisible. Columns of fire struck at the jeep, incinerating the decayed vegetation outside the sphere of protection. Waves of dark energy and at one point a giant hailstorm of mixed ice and flaming meteorites lashed around them. Christopher saw several of the huge winged demon forms pass overhead, and Lalania had to swerve around one that fell in front of the jeep while the machine gun tore into it.

A twelve-foot-long spear smashed through the windscreen and into Richard's chest. The iron tip came out the back of his chair, impaling Christopher's right calf.

"Dismiss the field," Christopher shouted desperately, struggling to remove the spear. He pulled his calf off it, ignoring the blood and pain, put both gauntleted hands together on the spear head, and pushed.

Richard gurgled, blood spilling out of his mouth. He must have said the right words because the darkness went away. Lalania stepped on the gas. Christopher finally got the spear out of the man and quickly cast. He kept his hand on Richard, letting the healing power flow as he watched an invisible meter in his head winding down his spell power.

"You see why ninth rank would have been insufficient," Alaine shouted in between bursts of gunfire.

The spear would have killed the lower ranked Lalania instantly.

"Nonsense," Richard argued. "He would have revived me. With less than a minute's death, I wouldn't have even lost my prepared spells."

The wizard leaned back and put his face close to Christopher to ensure that his words were heard. Christopher thought he was going to say thank you.

Instead, he said, "Your turn."

Cryptic, but Christopher understood. He cast his anti-magic sphere. Lalania cursed loudly at the return of darkness but was drowned out by the shattering roar of a hailstorm. Ice in chunks the size of watermelons smoked as it fell and exploded when it hit the ground. The ground outside of the protected sphere was torn and broken.

Some of that damage landed in front of the jeep. When the wheels hit the rough ground, the jeep bounced high. If Christopher had not been strapped in, he would have been thrown out. Another giant spear slammed into the jeep and passed through his thigh, sticking into the floor. If he had not been temporarily airborne, it would have gutted him and severed his spine. He hung onto it for support until they reached flat ground again. Then he pulled it out and tossed it aside, tael binding his wound before he bled more than a gallon or two.

The next spear was aimed at the jeep. It impaled the hood. The engine started coughing.

"Okay, now we stop," Richard shouted between machine gun blasts. "Here—no, there."

Lalania locked up the brakes, and the jeep started sliding. Richard pointed at Christopher and gestured imperiously.

Christopher did the bravest thing he had ever done. He unbuckled his seat belt and fell out of the jeep. It plowed on, without him, and then the engine died. The lights went out, all sound went away, and Christopher was alone in the dark surrounded by monsters. And without magic. The anti-magic sphere was centered on him.

He decided to stay on the ground and play dead. Maybe nothing would notice him. This did not work. A horse-sized, fanged, cat-like creature, although its mouth seemed to be triangular in shape instead of the traditional arrangement, came bounding up. He rolled over, his sword held out between him and the beast, but it was only a bit of steel at the moment. The creature ignored it and put one huge paw on his chest to hold him down while it bit off his head.

Gunfire erupted. The tri-part mouth writhed and then came apart. The animal staggered back and died, its head reduced to pulp by Alaine's machine gun. The jeep lights flared, and its engine raced as it circled around to pick up Christopher. Richard had used his magic to repair it.

"That's right," Richard said, extending a hand to pull Christopher into the jeep. "I earned honors at Oxford and went to an elven wizard academy so I could work in the motor pool."

They raced on, although blindly. Lalania could not see beyond the headlights, and Christopher could not use his direction magic. Alaine steered her instead.

"This part is obvious," she explained.

There were no more attacks. The machine gun was a weapon the enemy could not understand. There were defenses against it, of course—Christopher was wearing one of them, in the form of his cloak, which would have protected him from all those spears— but those defenses did not work without magic, as his recent encounter had demonstrated. Anything that got close enough to hurt them would be robbed of defense by the sphere and torn to pieces by the gun.

Lalania locked up the brakes again. The jeep came to a stop, idling, at the foot of a cliff that stretched up into the sky, beyond the range of his unenhanced vision.

"Now comes the hard part," Richard said. "Also, the weird part." He signaled with his hand, and Christopher dropped the field. That was the last of them. He and Richard could only master one each and still be able to prepare the gate spell.

With his night vision restored, he could see the cliff was five hundred feet high.

"You definitely want to strap in for this," Richard reminded him. The wizard cast a spell and nodded to Lalania. "Drive on, miss."

"It's a cliff," she said.

He pointed to a sloped bit at the foothill, steep but still navigable by the jeep. "Start there."

She drove over to the slope and cautiously edged forward.

"Step on it, girl," Richard ordered, and slapped her knee. The jeep lurched forward. Lalania grit her teeth and punched the gas, driving straight at the cliff, the jeep angling up sharper and sharper until it felt that it must tip over.

The wheels held. Even when the jeep was completely vertical, Christopher lying on his seatback like a bed, the wheels held. The engine whined and complained, the jeep slowing in its advance up the cliff side, and Lalania down-shifted.

"Might want to dump some weight," Richard suggested, throwing a jerrican of fuel over the side. Alaine made a quick inventory of her ammunition stores and threw several boxes out the back, which was now also down.

Everything not bolted down fell into the back, most of it hitting Christopher on the way past. He caught the almost empty six-pack by its plastic holder, its one remaining beer still intact. After a moment's contemplation, he regretfully threw it after the ammo boxes.

Alaine fired a few times while they drove up the cliff face. Fortunately, the machine gun was rigged for anti-aircraft fire, so she could aim straight up, which was now actually level with the ground. The various beasties thought better of pressing the attack and stayed away.

She also fired several times at the lip of the cliff, far above. Consequently, Lalania only had to dodge three large boulders thrown at them, one of them accompanied by a large troll that had been knocked loose by the machine gun. It flailed and wailed as it went past. Another dozen boulders fell, but they were launched blindly and fell harmlessly to the side.

When the jeep finally crawled over the edge, there was a crowd of trolls waiting for them. Alaine knocked down the front ranks with the gun, but they were already regenerating while their fellows leaped over them.

Christopher started throwing columns of fire. Richard added a few fireballs, and the problem went away.

Lalania advanced along the top of the mesa through the charred remains of the trolls, which blew away in a charcoal dust. A few hundred feet from the edge was a huge temple, vaguely Greek in architecture but on a giant's scale. Not a single column was wholly intact; there were chunks of marble the size of cars scattered about, and the whole structure was missing a roof. She drove up a flight of shallow stairs, the jeep bumping with each step, and came to a stop on a well-worn marble floor.

Illuminated in the headlights in front of them was a single human-sized figure, dressed in a black robe, skeletal hands clasped in front.

"WELCOME TO MY PARLOR," it said in a graveled voice, the weight of a thousand dead stones disturbed by a dreadful tread. Christopher remembered when the Wizard of Carrhill had pretended to be a terrifying undead monster. This was the effect he had been going for. Christopher vaguely wished the man could be here now, just so he could see how far short his attempt had fallen.

25

EXIT STAGE LEFT

A laine immediately opened up. She did not stop until the machine gun clattered to silence, its ammo box exhausted.

Christopher massaged his ears. The figure remained in front of them. The bullets had passed through it without effect. A marble column in the distance behind it slowly fell over, chewed to the core by the stream of lead.

"Can't blame a girl for trying," Richard muttered. "Bashki would have been proud." He got out of the jeep and stretched, raising his arms above his head and rolling his shoulders.

Lalania turned off the jeep and jumped out, throwing the backrest forward so she could extract the lyre from its steel box behind her seat. Alaine hopped down, landing lightly despite the armor she wore. Christopher was left to clamber out, his armor catching on the jeep frame and almost tripping him.

"YOU HAVE NO BUSINESS HERE," the black-robed figure declared in a voice that brooked no argument. Christopher almost found himself agreeing and ready to get back into the jeep, but the statement was not directed at him.

"I'm just sight-seeing," Alaine answered. "This is the closest I will ever come to your domain."

"ALL COME TO ME IN THE END."

"In a way, I suppose." Alaine was, incredibly, smirking. "But only because we will win. We will not begrudge you a few hours of hollow boasting. We will not hear it over our celebrations."

"Not even that," Richard said. "By that point in the process, you will no longer be a coherent pattern of energy. There will be nothing left to gloat."

"YOU CHALLENGE ME, MORTAL?" The voice did not register amusement or concern. It was vast and deep, beyond emotion.

"I do. Protocol demands that we negotiate first. Release the woman known as Mary Sinclair, and I will release you from my challenge."

"A WOMAN. SO MANY ANCIENT AND LEGENDARY ENTITIES DESTROYED FOR THE SAKE OF ONE MORTAL WOMAN. WHOLE CIVILIZATIONS DIED TO RAISE THE WINGS YOU HAVE STILLED. AND YET YOUR GREED IS SATISFIED SO EASILY? CHOOSE, THEN. TAKE WHAT YOU WILL."

Stone ground on stone. A dozen human figures rose up from the ground on circular daises of marble. They stood stiff and still as mannequins, scattered about the ruins at random. Christopher ran from statue to statue. Each was an impossibly beautiful woman, in the prime of life, completely naked and posed seductively. Their eyes were jet-black, without any white at all, which rather diminished their allure. None of them was Maggie.

He stopped at one, anyway. This one was male and merely very handsome. It was also familiar. Major Kennet, naked and yet whole, the damage caused by the pistol repaired. The young man looked good, aside from the black eyes.

"We need this one too." Christopher called out.

"YOU HAVE MADE YOUR CHOICE," the voice stated.

"No," Christopher said. "None of these is Maggie. I'm not even convinced they're real people. But Kennet doesn't belong here anymore than Maggie does."

"YOU SPENT HIM LIKE A COIN TO GAIN ENTRANCE TO MY REALM. WOULD YOU NOW ROB ME OF MY PAY? ARE YOU A THIEF, THEN?"

"You're not one to talk," Christopher shot back. "We're all rule-breakers here. Give me my people, and I'll go."

Another grinding sound. Another figure rose up out of the ground. Maggie, wearing only her long red hair. Christopher ran to her, stopping himself from touching her only by an act of willpower.

Her eyes were black. The sight terrified him.

"A TRADE." The voice should have had humor in it, or contempt, or something. Instead it boomed as flat and dead as the high plain. "PLACE THE WOMAN YOU BROUGHT UPON THE DAIS AND TAKE THIS ONE. FAIR IS FAIR."

Lalania's face blanched. Christopher shook his head.

"The deal is that you give me what I want, and I leave. You started this; you stole from me. You can't negotiate now."

"YOU STOLE FROM ME. MY FLOCK DEAD IN THEIR NEST. THEIR WICKED AND CURLING THOUGHTS STILLED. AN ETERNITY OF SILENCE."

"Then they shouldn't have attacked me." Christopher fumed. Arguing with a god was a waste of time. This was one of the few lessons he had learned since coming to this world.

"THEY SAVED YOU. WHEN YOU WOULD HAVE FROZEN IN THE SNOW. A MEANINGLESS DEATH BY RANDOM CHANCE. NOW YOU DEAL WITH GODS. IS THAT NOT WORTHY OF GRATITUDE?"

"Pay attention," Christopher snapped. "I already answered that argument. We've all done what we've done for our own purposes. Except you kept my wife from me when the rules of magic say you cannot."

"I AM DEATH. I AM THE RULES. THE RULES ARE ME."

"How bloody long is this going to go on?" Richard complained. He turned back to the jeep. "Where's that other beer?"

"I threw it out," Christopher said. He was a hundred feet away and had to raise his voice. "You said to dump unnecessary weight."

Richard boggled. "What part of beer spells 'unnecessary' to you?"

Kennent slumped to the ground. Grating his teeth, Christopher pulled himself away from Maggie and went to help the boy.

"Sir?" the young man said as Christopher pulled him to his feet. "I'm ready to go."

"Not yet," Christopher growled. "We haven't gotten everything we came for."

Kennet looked around, noticing the other people. "Why are the ladies here? Is this what revival is always like, and I just don't remember?" He looked down at his nakedness, but since there wasn't anything he could do about it, he just shrugged.

"This is not a normal revival. That obviously failed. That guy," Christopher jabbed his finger at black-robed figure, "is the reason."

"I HAVE A NAME."

"I need a gun," Kennet said, his face hardening. Christopher drew his pistol and handed it to the boy. Being naked was bad enough; being unarmed in this place would make anyone crazy.

"THEY DID NOT COME TO SAVE YOU. THEY WOULD LEAVE YOU BEHIND IF I GAVE THEM WHAT THEY TRULY WANT."

Kennet raised the pistol and fired. When Hordur didn't fall, the young man frowned. "I need a bigger gun."

"There's one on the jeep," Christopher said, "but it won't help." He walked back to Maggie, slowly, warily, while Kennet sprinted for the jeep.

"STOP, THIEF."

Christopher steeled himself and stepped onto the dais. He bent Maggie over his shoulder and lifted. In his arms, she became dead weight, her limbs dangling loose, no longer a statue. Just a corpse.

"VERY WELL. YOUR CHALLENGE IS ACCEPTED."

Out of the ground in front of Hordur rose a black sphere the size of a beach ball. It was truly, unforgivingly black. Nothing reflected from any part of its surface. Wind whistled continuously as it rushed in to fill the unfillable void; dirt crumbled into the shaft it left behind.

"Finally," Richard muttered.

"My apologies in advance," Lalania announced, "but it is what he requested." She bent her hands over the lyre and abused it, producing a remarkably good imitation of industrial techno rock.

Richard clasped his hands before him, his face set in anticipation.

The sphere began to move slowly, inexorably, toward him. His eyes darted back and forth like a chess master burning through strategies.

Christopher hustled with the naked corpse of his wife on his shoulders, trying to close the gap without getting near Hordur or the sphere. He saw Alaine draw her sword and stand with her back to Richard's. This was a remarkable act of confidence; the elf could not see the sphere's advance. If he succumbed to it, she likely would too.

Kennet was standing in the back of the jeep, reloading the machine gun. Apparently he had been watching during Alaine's lesson.

Christopher reached the jeep and dumped his wife's body into the rear seat. He flinched as her arm bounced off the backrest. He spent a moment trying to tidy her or cover her up. They should have brought a blanket. At least her eyes were closed now.

Then he went to guard Lalania, drawing his sword and casting a weapon blessing.

"What's the plan, sir?" Kennet asked him, pointing the machine gun at Hordur.

"The plan is Richard wins and we all drive home."

"Is there a plan B?"

Christopher thought about it. "Not really."

"Pardon me for saying so, sir, but that seems like poor tactical preparation."

"Preparation is a strong word. We didn't even think to bring a spare set of clothes. Or a blanket."

He looked over. Richard was not winning. The sphere continued to advance at exactly the same rate as it had before. The distance had fallen to two dozen feet. The man did not appear to notice; he stood his ground, concentrating fiercely.

Christopher knew there was no point in fleeing. The sphere would follow as fast as Richard ran, closing the remaining gap at the same measured rate. Once engaged, the Mouth would not be denied until it was fed.

At a dozen feet, Christopher started to worry. At six he held his breath. At three his heart stood still.

"Oh," Richard said. "Is that it?"

The sphere stopped moving.

"My apologies. I should have seen it sooner. I did not think I would cross space and time to solve a Hilbert space."

The sphere moved back a foot and stopped. Christopher forced himself to breathe.

It lurched, suddenly, leaping two feet toward Richard before resuming its slow advance. It stopped again, only inches away, and Richard chuckled under his breath. "We solved that one a few years ago. You really should keep up."

The sphere began moving backward. Hordur raised his skeletal hands.

"IMPRESSIVE. BUT NOT UNPRECEDENTED."

The sphere paused briefly and then resumed its retreat.

"OTHERS HAVE WON THIS GAME. THEIR NAMES ARE HIDDEN BECAUSE THEY ARE NO LONGER MORTAL."

Richard continued to concentrate. Christopher was distracted by a gurgling sound. He looked around and saw Kennet flopped over the gunnery frame, his throat slit. Hordur leapt from the back of the jeep and bent down, disappearing from view.

Christopher jerked his head around again. Hordur was still standing where he had been, the sphere gradually approaching him.

"Dark take it," he growled, and ran to look behind the jeep. While he was running, Alaine begin firing her assault rifle, spraying a wide area as if firing at something she could not quite see. Christopher ducked below the jeep, not wanting to get hit, before remembering he was wearing his cloak. He stood up again.

Hordur—the second Hordur—was facing Alaine, laughing. It was hard to tell he was laughing because he had no face, just a dark spot in a hood, and he made no sound. Still, the posture was clear enough.

Alaine charged the rifle with another clip and resumed firing. The bullets bounced off the black robe. She threw the rifle aside and drew her sword from where she had stuck it, point first, in the marble floor.

Hordur raised his hands, a dagger in each, like he was extending an invitation to dance.

Kennet was dead, his head hanging on by a thread. There was blood all over the jeep and Maggie's body. Christopher pulled the boy's corpse to a sitting position and held the head on.

"This is a normal revival," he told the boy as he cast the spell.

The young man's eyes fluttered to life. He fell back, exhausted and confused. Christopher left him and went to help Alaine.

The skeletal figure was absurdly adroit. It leapt and capered; gamboled, even. Christopher and Alaine chased it with their enchanted swords, trying to hit a wisp with a sledgehammer. The twin daggers were a net of steel they could not penetrate. Well, not steel; their swords would have gone through that like butter. The dagger blades were dullish purple.

Despite the enchantment on his sword, Christopher noticed that the blade was taking damage. A nick here, a gash there, every time Hordur blocked.

While they fought, Hordur argued with Richard for his life.

"YOUR COMPANIONS WILL DIE AND MY PUPPET WILL SLIT YOUR THROAT. TAKE YOUR WINNINGS NOW OR LOSE EVERYTHING."

The voice boomed over Lalania's hideous music. It was hard to ignore.

"YOU DARE NOT SUCCEED. IF THE SPHERE TOUCHES ME I WILL BE GONE. WITH ME WILL GO MY TAEL. IRRETRIEVABLY. TAEL ENOUGH TO MAKE YOU A GOD."

It should have been desperate or pleading. Instead it was the same robotic announcement.

"A CRIME AGAINST REALITY. TO DESTROY A BILLION LIVES FOR NO PROFIT. YOU WILL GAIN NOTHING. THE

WORLD WILL LOSE THE IRREPLACEABLE. ACCEPT MY SUR-
RENDER AND BECOME A GOD. RULE YOUR OWN PLANE
WITH YOUR OWN RULES. LIVE FOREVER."

Christopher risked a glance at Richard. The man did not appear to
react to Hordur's offer. This was incredible loyalty, far more than he had
a right to expect. He had offered a healthy body and a new problem set,
and the man had thrown away three years of his life without hesitation.
Turning down Hordur's largesse seemed almost uncharacteristic.

The puppet Hordur took advantage of the distraction to stab Christopher in the stomach, straight through his armor. Tael stopped the
wound from being fatal, but it still enraged him.

He tried to drop a column of flame on the second Hordur, but it
tumbled out of the way. When it rolled along the ground, he could hear
the bones clacking. Then it was back on its feet and blocking Alaine's
two-handed swing with both daggers.

In the jeep, Kennet had staggered to his feet. He was fooling
around with the machine gun again. Christopher doubted the gun
was strong enough to hurt Hordur, and in any case, the risk of hitting
Alaine seemed too great. It didn't matter, however, because Kennet was
pointing the gun downrange to where the other human statues stood.

Human no longer; they were growing wings and fangs, their skin
changing to different hues and tones, long forked tails whipping around
them as they stretched and moved. Still naked and attractive if you
were into that sort of thing. Kennet started shooting them.

The Hordur puppet was pushing its way toward Richard's exposed
back. Alaine took several dagger blows moving to intercept it. Christopher realized he needed to change tactics.

"Hold," he commanded, using the smallest offensive spell he possessed, the one that froze people like statues. It didn't work. He tried
again, putting the power of his rank into it.

"Hold. Hold. Hold." He chanted, burning through spells, as he
moved to put his body between the puppet and Richard. Over his head

streaked rounds of tracer fire as Kennet machine-gunned the winged demons ahead.

"HOLD," Hordur's voice boomed. "YOU DO NOT KNOW WHAT YOU DO. YOU CAN BE A GOD AND KEEP THE WOMAN FOR YOURSELF. EVERYTHING YOU EVER WANTED. LIVE FOREVER. HOLD."

"Hold!" Christopher commanded, and this time it stuck. The puppet froze. Alaine decapitated it in a single stroke. The body fell to the ground, a lifeless bag of bones. Above them wings stretched, the demonesses charging through the air. They went for Kennet first. He destroyed two more before they got him, shredding his naked defenseless body like hamburger with their razor claws.

Christopher and Alaine took advantage of the fact that the flyers had to land to maul Kennet's body. They struck from behind, cutting off wings and limbs with each stroke. The creatures clawed back, maddened and vicious, but his armor and tael held. Halfway through the battle, the female demons began screeching in terrible agony.

Richard strolled over and waved his hand. A dozen sparkling bolts lanced out, stabbing the last demon and stilling it. He spoke almost casually. "I'm thinking we should go. The sooner the better."

"Oh thank the gods," Christopher gasped. "You won."

"What?" Richard put his hand to his ear. He turned and caught Lalania's eye, signaling her to stop playing. She put the lyre down and burst into tears.

"Sorry, could you repeat that? I had Ell turn off my hearing. Figured it would be one less distraction."

Christopher said it again, but his mind was already moving on.

Alaine was stabbing the corpses of the demons with the royal sword, harvesting their tael. Christopher had to ask her for some of it.

"Stop. Dying," he ordered Kennet's mutilated corpse, putting it back together again with another revival spell. The boy sat up, reaching for something, and then fell over, completely spent.

"We are all in the bard's debt," Alaine said to Richard. "Hordur offered to make you a god. She chose not to let you hear that."

"Don't tell him!" Lalania cried out. "Why would you tell him?"

Alaine looked surprised. "It was a compliment."

"Hmm," Richard said.

"Few mortals would have refused such an offer." Alaine apologized, but to Richard, not Lalania. "I am glad we did not have to find out whether you were one of them."

Richard cocked an eyebrow. "Are you glad we did not have to find out if Ell was one of them?"

"I am. And yet, it was unlikely to be an issue. No one ever thinks of the support staff."

Christopher wanted to go comfort Lalania. He didn't. It wasn't his place anymore. "Behind every great wizard is a great bard," he said, paraphrasing a joke to amuse her.

"That's not how the saying goes," Lalania said, wiping her face. She quoted the correct form. "'Behind every great wizard is an apprentice waiting to kill him.'"

"Well, then," Richard said, carefully walking over to her. "I shan't get an apprentice." He held his arms open in invitation.

"Fae will be displeased." The bard was trying to make the conversation light.

Richard was not helping. "Mistress Fae's pleasure is no longer my concern."

He kept advancing. She stood perfectly still until he touched her. Then she collapsed into his embrace, whispering apologies. He silenced her with a kiss.

"He is not wrong," Alaine said, ignoring the unfolding romantic drama. "We should go. The destruction of a god cannot fail to have unfathomable fallout. As much as I would like to profit from it, I do not care to face a swarm of hungry *bevinget* on the wing. They will seek either revenge or glory, or perhaps merely the tael they assume we have won."

"Was it true?" Christopher asked, his voice held low. "Was the offer real?"

Alaine looked at him. "Of course. As was everything Hordur said. The history of a billion lives are snuffed out as if they had never existed. All that was left of them was tael, and now that is gone. They can never be reclaimed."

He looked to where the sphere hung in the air, still swallowing the wind. "What if he had put Maggie in there?"

"Then she too would be lost to all time. Yet he did not. Nor could he; to do so would have surrendered the only leverage he had over you. Though I do not know why the god of death desired to have leverage over a mortal in the first place, so do not ask."

Richard was pressing Lalania into the driver's seat, trying to untangle himself from her grasp.

"What else does it mean? The god of death is dead. Isn't that going to . . . change things?"

Alaine climbed back into the gunnery frame, an ammunition box in her hands. "Probably not. It has always been elven philosophy that the gods are unnecessary, mere ornaments encrusted on the proper shape of the world. Now all will see if we were right."

Christopher took his place, careful to buckle in. He leaned over and strapped Maggie's cold, dead body into her seat. Richard held the lyre rather than disturb him by trying to put it back into its box. Lalania started the jeep's engine.

"You don't seem too worried," Christopher said to Alaine.

"I trust the wisdom of our sages. It is having to explain all of this to my daughter that I fear. The young are ever in a hurry."

"Why would the death of a god make Kalani impatient?"

Alaine smiled down at him, having finished reloading the machine gun. "Because she will be eager to slay the rest."

26

YOU CAN NEVER GO HOME AGAIN

Christopher had only met Marcius three times. Never in the flesh, yet Christopher trusted to his judgment of the god's character as projected into his dreams and hallucinations. In retrospect, that might not be wholly justified.

On the other hand the god was the source of his power. Power he still needed, for a short while longer at least. Discovering that the elves were the enemies of that source put him in a difficult position.

Alaine had warned him never to thank her. The elves did what they did for themselves.

Yet they were clearly White. Their actions had to be directed toward the greater good for all, or else everything he'd learned about this world was wrong.

And everything he'd learned in his own world had taught him that unrestrained power was the enemy of good. To be held accountable was the flesh and blood of morality. Maggie had approached her work as a holy mission to uncover truth and assign responsibility. What people did with their money never bothered her; what mattered is that they admit, to themselves and the world, where the money went. This was a surprisingly unpopular position, and Maggie had become accustomed to frank discussions with CEOs and millionaires. It was also one of the things he loved about her.

If no one held the gods accountable, then they could not be moral. It was as simple as that, and Marcius had confessed that no one had the authority to make Hordur follow the rules. And if they were not moral, they could never be Team Good. Tools, perhaps; allies or friends, even; but not principals.

It was a conundrum. Christopher decided he didn't really have to deal with it, though. As soon as they got off this infernal plane and revived his wife he could afford to take a dispassionate view. There was still room in Johm's shop for another engineer.

Getting off the plane was a nontrivial problem. They could see winged forms approaching, sensing the vacuum in the current power structure. Richard renewed his climbing spell, and the jeep plunged down the cliff face, dangling them all from their seat belts. Driving up the cliff had been strange; driving down it was terrifying.

"Pump the brakes, sweetie, or you'll burn them out." Richard spoke with the trepidation of any man telling his girlfriend how to drive, but also with the apprehension of a man hurtling down a five-hundred-foot drop. Where the engine had struggled to pull them up, the axles now squealed with the effort of letting them down slowly.

Not too slowly, however, as Lalania and everyone else watched the demon host arriving out of the corner of their eyes.

"They can catch fire?" Lalania looked with concern at the floorboard, worried that her foot might suffer.

Richard slapped himself on the forehead. "Of course. Why didn't I think of that?" He handed the lyre back to Christopher so his hands were free to cast the energy-shielding spell on the jeep.

Christopher now had to keep the dead Maggie, the unconscious Kennet, and the irreplaceable lyre from falling out. It kept his mind off the approaching demons.

The squealing lessened, and the brakes held. They rolled down onto the plain with only brutal bumping and jostling. Lalania stepped on the gas.

Alaine used the machine gun liberally, firing at long range. She was less interested in killing than in keeping foes at bay while the party returned to the spot they had entered from. Richard had made noises about how the plane of Hel was "tidally locked." They could not locate the gates at will; instead, each opening had to correspond to a location on Prime. The problem was that Hel was small and Prime was huge. Missing by a single mile would dump them thousands of miles away from the kingdom. Given that they had two legendary spell-casters, an elf, and a machine gun, that probably wouldn't be fatal, but it would be inconvenient. Especially if the gate opened in the middle of an ocean.

"Trouble," Lalania announced. The plain in front of them rose up, and for a moment he thought the ground was erupting. The truth was hardly less terrible. A cloud of insects a hundred feet tall and a mile wide swarmed into the air.

"Ignore them," Alaine ordered. "Do not so much as swat." She cast, touching each of them. "Take care not to crush one by accident with your body, lest the spell be undone for all of us."

"Dark take it," Richard said. "I hope it's not cockroaches. I bloody hate cockroaches."

They entered the swarm at high speed. Giant insects splattered against the windshield with sickening thumps, the wipers gamely throwing their corpses off but leaving the window smeared in ugly colors of green, brown, and black. Alaine hunkered down, mostly protected by the gunnery frame. Christopher ducked his head.

The cabin of the jeep began to fill up with bugs as large as his hand. Hideous wasps with three-inch-long stingers, weird black beetles that dripped acid, some alien worm-like things with three wings that looked entirely impractical. They began crawling on him.

It took a supreme act of will not to knock the creatures away. When he realized they must be on Maggie's body, he almost panicked. He closed his eyes. It was the only way he could remain still.

The jeep swerved back and forth, implying that Lalania was still steering. He could hear a thin keening and realized the bard was screaming with her mouth closed. It had the character of disgust rather than pain, so that was okay.

Eventually, they outran the cloud. He discovered this when cold water gushed over his head, which seemed inappropriate for the plane they were on. Alaine was washing out the jeep with the bronze water bottle, careful not to injure any of the insects in the process.

"That was creepy," Richard said. There was a many-legged winged centipede on the dash in front of him. He raised his foot but stopped and looked to Alaine for permission.

The elf carefully turned the unconscious Kennet over, looking underneath. "It's the last one," she said.

Richard's boot descended in a wet, pulpy squelch.

Lalania was breathlessly issuing a steady stream of obscenities, her hands in a white-knuckled death grip on the steering wheel. Richard leaned over and kissed her. The swearing stopped as she breathed in great gulps.

Alaine issued instructions, and the jeep plunged into the narrow river channel. Christopher assumed it was the same one as before, although there were no tire tracks. Something had erased all obvious signs of their passage. His direction spell was useless now; it could lead to the way in but not to the arbitrary and unmarked way out. They would have to rely on the elf's skills.

The jeep sped along the dry riverbed, racing toward giant moving figures in the distance. Above his head, the machine gun barked again and again, but the figures did not fall.

"This will take more ammunition than I have left," Alaine shouted at him.

They were close enough now that Christopher could see the dinosaurs were already dead, rotting flesh hanging from exposed and weathered bones. Destroying the hulking corpses with a machine gun would be like carving a turkey with a pistol: slow, messy, and surprisingly ineffective. He stood up, clinging to the gun frame for support, and began to chant.

Marcius's power was weak here, and the monsters were huge pools of dark energy. The jeep raced forward, hurtling directly into a T-rex that lowered its massive jaw to scoop them up. Lalania apparently expected Christopher to make the thing go away. He chanted, pouring out energy, until it exploded into a shower of black leathery bits just in time to let the jeep pass through. After that Lalania swerved to and fro, trying to avoid the beasts.

He destroyed three more and she dodged half a dozen, but the riverbed was simply too narrow. As she curved around a stegosaur, its massive spiked tail swung down in front of the jeep. Lalania locked up the brakes, but in the sand they had no grip. Christopher looked up for that heart-stopping instant when it was obvious they would crash. And then they did.

He picked himself up out of the sand. His tael was sufficient that a mere high-speed automobile accident was not terribly discomfiting. His companions were almost as durable. They were already rising from the ground where they had been scattered.

The jeep, however, was done for. It was bent at a ninety-degree angle and upside down. Alaine staggered out from underneath it, carrying Maggie's body.

Richard fired off a spell, sending sparkling bolts lancing into the dinosaur that had wrecked them. Christopher thought it was pointless to seek revenge against a dead thing. Then he realized the dead thing was stalking toward them. Richard repeated his spell three more times before it sank to the ground and stopped moving.

"I can't do that again," the wizard said, with only the slightest strain of tension. A few hundred feet away, another dozen dinosaurs trundled toward them, making the ground shake.

The group had drawn together, coalescing to Lalania's position where Kennet leaned on her shoulder and raved incoherently. The boy had miraculously survived with nothing worse than a broken leg. Christopher healed him and asked, "Anyone else?"

"I'll live," Lanalia said, her eyes on the dinosaurs. "At least until those things get here."

There were too many to destroy. Christopher cast a simple spell, making himself and his companions invisible to the soul-trapped abominations. He would have done it before except it wouldn't have hidden the jeep.

The monsters thundered past. Christopher knelt and picked up his wife's body from where Alaine had lain it, hefting it over his shoulders in an undignified pose. Kennet collapsed again, having endured too much in one day. Richard lifted the naked man in the same fireman's carry. It didn't look nice, but it was the only way to carry a body long distances.

"I am out of spells," Richard said casually.

"We could fly now," Lalania suggested to Christopher. "We are close."

Christopher could not stop himself from growling. Lalania raised her eyebrows.

"Not I," he had to say. He could turn them to mist, and they could flee easily. But a cloud could not carry Maggie's dead body.

The smell of gasoline wafted over him. Alaine was emptying a jerrican over the jeep.

"I would leave as little as possible for our enemy to study," she explained.

"There are thermite charges in the right locker," Richard said. "Hot enough to melt steel."

Alaine tore the locker open and started placing fist-sized white packages under the jeep in strategic locations. She wasted precious time trying to detach the machine gun from its mount, but the frame was bent and would not release. In the end, she strapped a charge on the barrel with a look that was suspiciously close to regret.

Richard turned and began walking toward the forest in the distance, Kennet over his shoulders. Lalania picked up the bronze water bottle and the lyre and followed him. Christopher hustled to catch up, dodging the blindly lumbering dead dinosaurs. Two steps forward, one step back, trying to get across the river without getting squashed. It reminded him of something, but he couldn't remember what.

Behind them a fireball blossomed, sending a thick column of smoke into the air. The fire burned so brightly that Christopher didn't need night vision to see until he reached the edge of the forest. Alaine was waiting for them there, the grenade launcher in her hands, her eyes scanning for any threats following them.

"Unfortunately, an effective signal flare," she said. "We should hurry."

There were corpses in the woods, but only man-sized. Christopher knocked them down with a wave of his hand. Alaine slung the grenade launcher over her back as she used her sword to chop up two of the triple-jawed hellcats, an exercise that left her bleeding real blood. He converted his flying mist spell to heal her. After that the retreat seemed to be going well until they entered a small clearing and found a *bevinget* waiting for them, its black-eyed fanged face smiling at them.

Christopher had no magic left, save for the one high-ranking spell for the gate. He could convert it into healing and hurt the demon, but then they would have to wait twenty-four hours for their spells to recharge before they could go home. That did not seem likely to end well.

The monster opened its mouth to roar, and Alaine shot it with the grenade launcher, straight down its throat. It hiccupped twice and then exploded from the inside out.

"Here is close enough," she said. "Open the way."

He chanted while she stabbed the dead demon with the royal sword. He could hear wings beating behind him, getting closer, but the gate could not be hurried. Alaine raised the grenade launcher and began firing into the distance.

The rift opened. Richard and Lalania sprinted through. Christopher spent precious seconds lifting Maggie's body before following. Alaine came through last.

Instantly, he shut the gate behind them.

"You could have let one through," Alaine complained. "We could have taken one more. I still have the launcher."

Richard was not amused. "Bloodthirsty much?"

They were standing in the beech wood where Christopher had fought the *hjerne-spica*. Christopher decided to have it cut down and turned into a parking lot. He had developed an aversion to the place.

"I don't even have a message spell," he said. "We'll have to walk."

⎯⎯⎯ ⌾⌾⌾ ⎯⎯⎯

Halfway to the city, a kind farmer paused his wagon, silently offering them a ride without taking his pipe out of his mouth. The party looked a sight, covered in blood of different colors, dirt, decayed moss, various burn marks, and carrying two naked bodies. The old man shrugged silently as if adventurers were too common to remark on. He spoke only to his mules, telling them to get along now with amiable authority.

Christopher wrapped his magic cloak around Maggie, trying not to notice all the scrapes, burns, and broken bones her body had suffered. He did run his thumb over her eyes, checking. The lack of black should have been comforting. Instead, the dry, lifeless corneas stabbed at his heart. She had never seemed truly dead to him until that moment.

Alaine stretched out on the load of straw, relaxing. "A good trip. The *huldrene* were profitable, and we bagged a *bevinget* at the end."

"You don't regret the loss of Hordur's tael?" Richard asked.

"Of course. And yet his destruction is prize enough to make me smile for many years."

"Speaking of profit," Lalania said while trying to clean her boots with a handful of the farmer's straw, "what you captured in that sword does not belong to you alone." The straw started smoking after coming into contact with a green discoloration on her boot, and she threw it overboard. The farmer frowned around his pipe. Lalania stripped her boots off and considered tossing them, too.

Alaine took the contaminated boot from the bard and inspected it.

She shrugged and handed it back, dismissing it as no longer dangerous. "True enough. Yet there are debts to be paid."

"You can take my share," Richard said. "And his. But Ell earned hers."

"And he?" Alaine pointed to Kennet, where he mumbled and shivered in the wagon. "As a company he is entitled to a single share to our many, and yet that alone will make him a minor lord. Is this also your desire?"

Lalania began looking around for something to cover the naked man. "That's up to Christopher. He disburses his company's portion."

"Don't we get to deduct the price of the jeep as an expense?" Richard asked.

Christopher's heart punched him in the chest. He put his hand on his favorite accountant's cold body and tried not to weep.

"Such picayune details are beneath our dignity," Alaine replied. She held her hand below the pommel of the great sword and whispered. A tangerine-sized ball of purple flowed into her hand.

The elf handed the treasure to the bard. Lalania stared at it, eyes wide. At the last minute, she turned to Christopher. "May I?" Technically, she still worked for him without a share or salary.

Christopher could think of nothing less important right now. He shrugged, utterly indifferent.

She swallowed the tael, hiding it behind her hand. "To think I have eclipsed the Skald without ever even holding her rank."

"My share also goes to the Directorate," Alaine said. "Technically, I should turn over these as well, but as I said some details are too small to obsess over." The elf displayed the two large dull purple daggers that Hordur's puppet had fought with. "They are adamantine, so we elves would only be discomfited by them. You might appreciate them as souvenirs."

"Go on," Richard said to Lalania as he took one. "We'll have a matching set to remind us of our first date."

Lalania took the other one, admiring it. It was harder than steel and sharper than a razor. "What makes you think I want to be reminded? The service was terrible, and the ambience left much to be desired."

The wagon rattled up to the city gates. The guard leapt into action, summoning a proper carriage and finding clothes for Kennet. They still called Christopher "Lord," which was nice. It had been less than a day, but he had already come to think of Krellyan as the ruler.

〜〰〆

He had slept only through force of will. The royal suite felt like a stranger's room. Maggie's body lay on a couch, covered by a velvet cloak, and for once he was glad of the cold.

He washed, dressed, and ate like an automaton, waiting for the moment when his spells would recharge. He slipped into the meditative trance instantly, seeking the relief of abstraction. When he opened his eyes, his room was full of people.

Lalania bowed. "Forgive us," she said, "but we have become very much attached to the Lady Mary in the short while we were privileged to know her."

Most of his court had crowded in. Alaine was not there, but then she wasn't really his. Faren and Krellyan were looking at him more than at the body. Gregor, Torme, and Fae stood silently in the rear. Richard was behind Lalania, half his attention on her instead, but even half of his formidable intellect was like a physical pressure.

They were here for him despite Lalania's words. They were worried about him.

"It will work," he told them. "There's no one left to oppose me."

"A concept that boggles the mind," Krellyan said with a shake of his head. "Divine avatars are occasionally defeated on our plane. This is an inconvenience to the god in question. Yet to destroy one on its own plane is a true death. To dissolve one into the void is incomprehensible. To do so to an Elder god defies description."

Richard smiled wickedly. "The Mouth is still where I left it. I think I need a new employer now. And as I understand the color scheme, there are at least two more you could do without."

"More than that," Krellyan said. "The Elders have their hosts of aspects, and the list of mortals who have ascended to demi-godhood is as long as the myths of our bards."

"Richard Falconer, god-killer for hire. I like it." He grinned at his own wit. "Ironically, it's not even the first time I've held the title. I wrote a book once that was denounced in much the same terms."

"Merely to jest of deicide makes my knees tremble," Krellyan said. "Surely we are not so exalted. Lady Mary will return, and we will go back to our lives, reaping wheat and brewing beer. The sun will rise and fall, and time will work its will upon our fates. As it always has. As it always shall."

Christopher found the Saint's words comforting. He could think of nothing more appealing than growing old with Maggie. Watching the children they would have play with Karl's. Teaching the kingdom how to live a better life, fueled by science and magic and the one quality that Maggie had that always eluded him. Patience.

Lalania handed him a silver vial. In it he found a nugget of tael, not the vast sums he had been used to dealing in, but still enough to power a spell. He said the words and touched her cold, white corpse.

Nothing happened.

He bent his head to her in grief. Dimly, he heard Saint Krellyan repeating the spell. Through a fog he perceived its failure, the shock through the assembled company, and voices raised in consternation.

A terrible suspicion bloomed in his mind, and he lifted his gaze, heavy and dreadful as a basilisk, to where Richard stood.

"I didn't see you kill him."

The words hung in the air, silencing all else.

Lalania spoke. "I did. I saw it. I saw everything."

Her words washed off him without effect. Christopher stood, his sword hanging loose and ready at his side. "How do I know you are not Hordur in disguise?"

Richard scratched his chin. "I am uncertain myself. How would I know I am not?"

"There is only one test," Christopher said, dredging from his memories. They felt old and deep, as if from the bottom of a vast gloomy pit. "I cut your head off and measure the tael that comes out."

Lalania stepped in front of Richard, tears running down her face. "No. I saw. I saw."

Richard put his hand on her shoulder, comfortingly. "Okay. That's fair. As long as you put it back on afterward, obviously."

It was such a Richard answer that Christopher felt his anger slide away. Hordur, ancient and cruel, could never have responded to a threat with a logical proposal.

"No," Christopher said. "I know who is to blame." He walked through the crowd, oblivious at their parting before him. Down the winding stairs and into the throne room, the castle suddenly empty before him, servants and soldiers hiding in doorways and alcoves at his approach.

Entering the great hall, he threw aside a spell. The doors sprung to life at his command and barred themselves, leaving him alone in front of the throne. He summoned Marcius, but this time he used the gate spell. He applied the syllables he had omitted before, and this time the target of his spell was compelled to step across the threshold as soon as it opened.

Marcius stood before him, in the flesh, unarmed save for a short oaken baton.

27

FAVORS

Christopher drew his sword and charged it. The blade shimmered with power, equal now to the royal sword. Sufficient to cut stone or steel or the skin of any supernatural creature otherwise immune to mere reality.

"I did what you wanted. I killed. And killed. And killed. A *hjerne-spica*, an entire *nest*, a *god*. I gave away my throne, raising up my own replacement. I surrendered my special status, summoning a man capable and willing of opening gates to Earth. I did everything you asked, and you still. Won't. LET. ME. GO."

He was shouting at the end, his words echoing in the great stone hall.

"No," Marcius admitted. "We will never let you go. The Formian Queen was only half-wrong. It is our taint lain across your fate. When I saw you in the court of the Bright Lady, I saw into your mind. I saw . . . possibilities. I took your life in hand and cast it like dice across the future."

Christopher raised the sword to strike, but it would not be enough. "Why? At least tell me why."

"Tell you?" Marcius said, and his voice was as sharp as the sword. "How can I *tell* you a hundred thousand years of experience? I have memories. So many memories. I remember watching my daughters taken by local warlords, my farm instruments dangling from my help-less hands. I remember hammering plows into swords, raising armies, marching on castles. I remember hanging tyrants from battlements. I remember the pain of loss and the thrill of victory and the stabbing truth that one cannot replace the other."

Marcius looked around the room, his anger still fierce but not aimed at Christopher. "And in those memories, I have green skin, scaly and thick. Or brown fur and clawed hands. Or pink and soft, or black or gray or yellow. I have tails and wings and extra arms and carapaces and hooves. It took me so many years to understand I could not have been all of those things. That I could not have lived all those lives. For eons I searched for the real one, for the memory of my first and mortal life before ascension. For the real memory of the real child I lost, the real injustice that set my life on a path of violence in the service of justice."

The room fell silent. Even in the depths of his rage, Christopher could not turn off his analytical mind. He answered the unspoken question. "You did not find it."

"No," Marcius agreed. "I could not find what did not exist. There was no real memory because there was no real me. I am a construct, a puppet made from whole cloth. I exist to give voice and power to your injustice. But I am not justice. I am a tool. A tool in the form of a living body that exists only to destroy life."

Christopher still held his glowing sword with its threatening light. "Sometimes killing is necessary."

"True. But not something you would have known five years ago. Not as you know it now."

"What has any of this to do with me? What has it to do with my wife?"

Marcius spoke conversationally. "There are real gods, raised up from mortality by the feast of souls. A surprising number of humans, although your kind has not been here terribly long. Other beings of other races. The Ur-Mother of the Formians. The ulvenmen's terrible demon-dog, who ironically is as trapped here as they are. No elves, obviously. No dragons or *hjerne-spica*, although the distinction becomes admittedly blurred there. Many of them have their own planes. Most serve their flock, doling out spells and recruiting new worshippers. Some wander the world for adventure, immortal and nigh-unkillable.

My fellow aspects of the Bright Lady all have real histories. Imagine my divine grief at discovering I alone was fake."

If anything could penetrate Christopher's blanket of anger, it was disgust. "So you want to die. Want to see what death is all about. Always the bridesmaid, never the bride. Etc. Etc. Etc." It was so self-pityingly Gothic, it made his lip curl.

"That is not a desire I am capable of expressing." Marcius looked at him again. "Self-destruction is outside my design parameters."

"And yet," Christopher said.

"Any yet," Marcius agreed softly.

"You asked me for a favor," Christopher said. "You promised me one in return. Tell me how to save my wife."

Marcius shrugged apologetically. "Hordur yet endures. What you did would have obliterated any lesser being, yet the Six are different. Normally deities travel from their own plane to yours via a spell that creates a projection. The destruction of that copy is expensive but not fatal. The countermeasure is to destroy them on their own plane, where you can strike at their real body. Some number of gods have already passed this way. The problem is that Hel is not the originating plane for Hordur. The Six all maintain home planes, exactly as any other divine being, and yet they are not actually on those planes. They merely visit them, as other gods merely visit Prime. This is a fact known to no one other than the Six. I can only tell you this because you already know. I am not even sure I knew it before this moment."

"So I go somewhere else, and kill him again," Christopher snarled. "Wheels within wheels."

"Yes. I cannot tell you where to go because I do not know. I cannot tell you how to kill an Elder because I do not know. I can only say you must pass through all the elemental planes, earth and water and air and fire, to the true and hidden abode of the gods."

Marcius stepped forward, holding the baton in one hand as an offering, not a threat. "And I can tell you that no mortal can open the way to that place."

"You are a god of Travel," Christopher reminded him. "You promised me a pebble to bridge the gap. You can open that door."

"Self-destruction is outside my design parameters." The god whispered the words in agony this time, as if he had broached too close to an open flame and been burned.

Christopher wasn't going to kill Marcius no matter how annoyed he was. He was not a butcher for hire. "You don't need a favor from me to die," Christopher said. "Just turn your back on an elf for five minutes."

"Those elves," Marcius said, almost as an aside, "know half as much as they think they do. And yet they are not wrong." He raised the baton and lightly tapped Christopher on the chest. "To slay a god is not lightly done, even when you have tricked him into presenting his true body and not a projection. To haul one through a gate and chop off its head leaves yet a corpse that can be raised, the same as any other. Short of the Mouth of Dissolution, only one method exhausts the possibility of revival."

"I don't care," Christopher said, but the god ignored him.

"A fact you do not seem to know: revival has its limits. Twenty-one, to be exact. No being can be recalled more than twenty-one times."

Christopher cursed under his breath. It turned out he did care. Somebody needed to convince Major Kennet to stop dying heroic deaths before he ran out of return tickets.

Marcius had more stray facts to offer. "I am not always manifest in my armor and sword. I have another function, after the battle, when I get to wield the rod of life. Well, *a* rod of life. It's not singular. You could make one, although it's absurdly expensive." Even *in extremis* the White had to tell the whole truth. Marcius prodded Christopher again with the wooden baton.

"I'm not going to kill you," Christopher stated, shrugging off his annoyance. The rage was still there, underneath, but he was saving it for Hordur.

"You know we are not allowed to lie," the god gently remonstrated. He stepped forward again, as close as a lover, his voice gentle and intimate. "There are other facts you do not know, other questions you should be asking. Why does Hordur single you out? What prompts an Elder God to dispatch a demon to your home? When did you become a foe worthy of the attention of the Six? Who whispers in Hordur's ear, bragging of your exploits and promises of more to come? How does Hordur even know your name?"

Ugly suspicions crawled through Christopher's mind, black chitinous spiders of rage.

"I," whispered the god. "I am the answer. I played you like a piece in the Great Game. A strategy so obscure no one guessed, played so subtly no one saw my hand adjusting the board. Under the cover of military strategy, I, bound to truth, learned to deceive. I learned cold calculus and the sacrifice of the few to save the many. I learned to strike swiftly without compunction, the better to serve the cause of mercy. I learned to make promises without reckoning the cost, to bind myself to the unthinkable. I learned that I was capable of acts that no one would have believed, least of all myself."

The god stretched out his arms and raised his chin, exposing his flawless white throat. "And now I stand before you, engineer of your fate and key to your freedom. The only path forward lies through me. The only chance that you will ever see your wife again lies through this door."

Christopher cracked like a fault line over roaring lava.

He lunged, shoving the glowing blade into the god's body. Its point entered under the chin and slide out the back of the skull, slathered red. The body dangled from the blade, a bloody puppet on a meat hook. Marcius was of divine rank. It took him a long time to die. Christopher stood with shaking hands wrapped around the hilt, the tsuba crushed against the fine white throat while blood poured around it and showered his fury.

The light went out of the god's eyes, quite literally. They had been glowing softly, as had the god's entire body; now it was simply dead flesh. Christopher lowered the sword, and the corpse slid off to lie in a heap on the blood-soaked stone.

There had been another transformation. Christopher's sword had changed; the blade was of dull purplish metal and had the proper pattern now, although it no longer mattered, as adamantium was already impossibly hard. A diamond was set into the hilt, partially exposed under the cord wrapping the handle. The cord was new, too, replacing the leather Dereth had mistakenly used so many years ago. The blade glowed with a soft white light, and the diamond sparkled with intense purple, reflecting the immensity of tael it now stored.

Christopher bent down and picked up the wooden rod in one hand. He touched it to the corpse, triggering a rebirth. The god coughed and sat up. Christopher brought the glowing blade down and cut from shoulder to breast. He hacked away while the god writhed in pain.

He did it all twenty more times.

Each time the god died easier, as his rank was stripped away. Each time was harder for Christopher, as the man he struck down grew more and more human. In the end, a dead peasant lay at his feet, no different than a thousand others in his fields. The floor was deep in blood. It splashed when he dropped the spent baton, now just a piece of wood. It squelched under his boots as he trudged over to the throne, trying to escape the spreading pool.

The doors went back to sleep, becoming inanimate objects again. They opened, and men entered cautiously. From the courtyard, Gregor and Torme, with swords drawn. From the interior doors, Karl and

Lalania, carrying assault rifles. Behind them were Richard and Saint Krellyan, hands raised to cast spells.

"I'm sorry," Christopher said to the good man in white. "I think I need to use this throne a while longer yet."

28

HMS *VIGILANT*

Becoming a minor deity was less transformative than one would expect. He still ate, bathed, and put his pants on one leg at a time.

On the other hand he ate a lot. Despite his mood, his body put away huge quantities of food, he sprinted up and down stairs, and he slept deeper but shorter than before. He was no longer young merely in appearance. The cold no longer bothered him. He was uncertain whether that was because he was immune or simply the hardiness of youth.

He also did not have to pray to the animated suit of armor for his spells. He could just take them off a shelf in his mind. Surprisingly, he still had limits, although they were multiples of his previous restraints. He could now cast seven gates a day if he wanted to, which was an absurd quantity of power, and yet far from infinite.

He saw auras around everyone, all the time. Their morality and their emotions flickered in a corona wreathing their bodies. In the past, he had tried to avoid spying on his companions. Now he could not help it.

The change hit Torme hardest of all. The man came to him the day after with an ashen face, flanked by Gregor and Cardinal Faren.

"I can no longer renew spells," Torme explained. "I have no divine connection. Nothing appears when I meditate."

Gregor nodded agreement. "The same for me. I know my first-rank magic is not terribly important, but I have become quite accustomed to it."

"I wonder how many other priests he left in the lurch," Christopher mused. Marcius had skipped out on his job and left other people to pick up the pieces. It seemed rather dishonorable.

"But you have taken his rank," Torme said.

Christopher stared at the man, trying to follow what he was getting at.

Faren chuckled, although his humor sounded hollow these days. Acts of deicide made the old man dizzy, it seemed. "You must speak your mind. He is too dense to guess."

"You could grant me spells," Torme explained. "I can pledge to you."

"No," Christopher said instantly.

"Then I am returned to a career as a knight, and a poor one at that. All I have left is my vitality." The man said it with such an air of acceptance that Christopher was stung to the core.

"It's not my place to pay Marcius's debts," he said defensively.

"I rather think it is," Faren answered. "Rank carries privilege but also obligation."

Despite being a god, there were still battles he could not win. In the end, he grit his teeth while Torme and Gregor knelt before him, reciting words of devotion.

Afterward, he could see Torme and Gregor's auras even when they weren't in the room, as if the intervening stone walls were irrelevant.

"Aiee," Gregor moaned the next day. "It unnerves me to hear your voice coming out of an empty suit of armor."

"There are probably other benefits of your new rank," Torme said. "Though they may require you to increase the size of your flock. In sheer point of fact, I had selected out a dozen novices who I thought adequate to the rank of Pater. I was going to broach the topic, but things became somewhat unsettled."

If Christopher had not returned from his adventures, Torme wouldn't have needed to. He would have been the head of the Church of Marcius, and the decision would have been his. Christopher could not fault the man for ambition. He was only doing what he thought was right.

Relentlessly, Torme carried on. "Now I approach you in a different guise, although the issue remains the same. I am, I believe, the head of the Church of Christopher. I wish to present candidates for the priesthood."

"Are you sure that's wise?" he tried to argue. "What if I die? Then even more people are left in the lurch."

Torme stared at him frankly. "You have already outlived the aspect of an Elder god."

In the end, he got away with only three because they couldn't afford any more promotions. Tael was in short supply. Every grain from Marcius's multiple deaths had been required to elevate Christopher; the diamond in the sword was empty.

The sword was another annoyance. It had remained transformed, constantly glowing and obviously supremely enchanted. Christopher would have preferred Marcius leave him a fresh rod of life as a divine icon. In any case, he had taken Travel as his domain, rather than the War, Luck, and Strength that Marcius had represented. As a minor deity, he was only entitled to one. A pair of flying boots would seem more appropriate, in addition to making him happier than a bloody sword.

The blade was a chain. It reminded him that he was still playing Marcius's game.

On the plus side, court duties went quickly. He could usually tell at a glance who was guilty and who was repentant. People stared at the glow coming from his sword and didn't even try to shade the truth.

He wanted to spend his time in a dull haze where pain could not reach him. He failed. His mind, sharp and agile, prodded him to help Richard during the day. His body, hungry and virile, disturbed his sleep every night. It was good that Lalania spent all of her time with Richard now. It was good that Richard was of sufficient rank and self-esteem that he lowered his brows in warning whenever Christopher stood too close to the bard for too long.

Christopher reminded himself that the wizard had already killed an elder god for far less provocation and stepped back.

"I want my wife," Christopher said. As he did a thousand times a day, although only a few times out loud.

"I want all the gold in your kingdom," Richard answered. "Print more paper and pass a law forbidding the use of coin. It will be more convenient and give you better control over the economy. Gold should only be used for foreign exchange."

Christopher did as he was bid. Because the kingdom had no foreign contacts, the gold piled up in his vault. There was a lot more of it than he expected. How this planet avoided massive heavy-metal poisoning was a conundrum that Christopher did not care about. There were other mysteries to solve.

Lalania turned out to be the key to one of those mysteries. Her new rank gave her insights she had not been able to access before. The songs and legends she had studied revealed new facts. Richard assured her that this was a mystical process, not the product of clever study, and thus she bore no fault for not having seen before. Christopher bit his tongue to watch the man shelter the bard's pride. He bit it harder, watching her glow under his words.

"You are certain he said them in that order? Earth first and fire last?" Richard asked.

Christopher lowered his eyebrows at being questioned like a wayward pupil. "Yes. I am certain."

"Those are the elemental planes," Lalania said. "I am surprised there is no mention of light and darkness. But then, Hel is normally equated with Dark. And we know that is a false lure."

"I don't care about some tourist itinerary," Christopher said. "Get me to the center. Where the gods really live."

"Of course," Richard exclaimed. "The center. Why didn't I see it before?"

Christopher glared at him. "You did. You're pretending I gave you the idea just now because you want me to feel like I am contributing."

"Thank god we can dispense with social niceties," Richard said.

"Literally, in this case." He chuckled. "That joke will never get old."

Christopher remembered that Richard might have been a god in his place and said nothing.

"Hel is indeed fake," the wizard lectured. His years in front of a classroom were obvious now. "So are the Halls of Light and the other four Elder planes. They are all actually located on Prime. This can be deduced once you realize the dimensional keys to each of those planes are symbolic rather than sympathetic. To go to Aelfhiem, you need something from Aelfhiem; to get to Hel, you need an act of theater."

"How do you hide Heaven on Earth?" Christopher asked, genuinely curious. He had never been to the Halls of Light and had no intention of going now, but they sounded nice. Surely their neighbors would have noticed. Presumably Hel was equally remarkable to whoever lived next to it.

"This place is much larger than home," Richard said. "Ten times the size, in fact. You can't tell because they went to great lengths to conceal the fact that its round at all. There's an illusion that makes the sun look like it's directly overhead, no matter what latitude you are at. It must break down at the poles, but that still leaves plenty of places to hide a continent as small as Hel. A little magic, a thousand miles of ocean without a sextant, and Bob's your uncle."

Ten times the diameter worked out to something like a hundred times the surface area. Richard was right; room to hide a whole planet if you wanted to. "Hold on," Christopher said, thinking it through. "How can this planet be that big and still have normal gravity?"

Richard smiled at him, and Christopher felt sympathy for Lalania. In the face of that beaming approval, anyone would melt.

"That is a fine question indeed," the physicist turned wizard said. "The answer is that the planet is hollow; otherwise we would be crushed by the sheer quantity of gravity from its center. It's a bloody Dyson sphere, except we're on the outside. Probably because they screwed the inside up, not understanding physics or biology. They started over on the outside once they discovered other planets and saw how it was supposed to work."

"So below us is a mirror of here," Christopher said. "Earth, then water; air; and . . . a tiny sun?"

"A fake sun, purely magical," Richard said. "In their vanity, they thought they should be the light of the world. To be fair, I'm not convinced the one up there is real either. It might be an illusion; I'd need to do more observations."

Christopher didn't care about the sun he could see. He cared about the one below his feet. "And inside this false sun?"

"Tael," Richard said with a grin. "Thousands of miles of it. If you were an Elder god, where else would you live?"

Layers of a planetary lollipop. With a creamy god-infested center.

Richard wasn't finished. "The gravity here is only about ninety-seven percent Earth standard. Aelfhiem was slightly less; the elves must hate it here. This brings up an even more fascinating question. Of the four planets I have been to, all of them were close to one G. How the Dark is that for a coincidence?"

"How could you breathe on all of them?" Christopher asked.

"Also interesting, although less so. Carbon-oxygen bindings are self-selective for complex life. Maybe one G is too; we don't know. But maybe somebody did."

Lalania pouted. "I don't understand what you are talking about."

For once, Christopher did the explaining. "He's saying that the universe looks intentional. Somebody set it up so that there were lots of planets with the same chemistry and physics. Because they wanted everybody to share common ground."

"Of course," Lalania said. "The gods created the world for us."

Both men spat an obscenity at the same time.

The bard blanched. "Your blasphemies were amusing when you were mortal. Now I find them unsettling."

"The gods created Prime," Richard conceded. "I'll give them that. Their fingerprints are all over this place. But the rest of the universe? No. Nothing I can stuff into a portable black hole can make a quasar."

"So there might be a real god at the center of all this," Christopher mused. "I mean, God. The Creator."

"Not anymore." Richard shrugged. "The universe might be designed, but it obviously isn't maintained. Whatever laid the ground rules for the Big Bang is long gone, consumed and disordered by the process. We can only mess around with the machinery; we can't change the fundamental rules. It turns out there's more machinery than we thought, but still. No spell will change Planck's Constant."

Christopher discovered that he had exhausted his interest in both theology and theoretical physics. "And you found the main control panel. Now tell me how to get there."

Richard put his hands together. "I have an idea, if you are willing to borrow a few more toys from Her Majesty's Government."

"Borrow?" Christopher said. The jeep they had stolen was a pile of slag on an alien planet. It wasn't going to be returned.

"When you open a permanent gate and extend magic to Earth," Richard said with sincerity, "no one is going to be complaining about the cost. Least of all the Queen. She knows full well the value of being the first to establish colonies in a new world."

Thus it was that Christopher found himself hovering above the river west of Kingsrock, casting a gate spell of epic proportions. Richard had given him a name and, more importantly, an excuse. He needed to compel the crossing, and he needed a reason to do so. Richard swore that his own brother would not resent being summoned to his side. It would be a violation of the man's will but for a good cause. Christopher bit his lip and hoped it would be good enough.

Not that there was anyone left to censure him. His powers no longer depended on the approval of another.

He chanted the words. The rift in reality opened up, spilling forth a deluge. Seawater shot out, flooding the banks and sweeping downstream, a gash the size of a building in a waterskin the size of a mountain. Borne on the waves came fishes, seaweed, and the long gray steel hull of a Vanguard-class submarine.

Christopher rose up to avoid being crushed and closed the gate behind it. The vessel settled in the dwindling waters, lying in the river like an orchid in a too-small pot. It listed to the left about fifteen degrees but stopped before falling over. He drifted down to the conning tower and waited.

Eventually, a hatch opened and a human face appeared. Christopher was surprised to see it was female and immediately chagrined at his surprise. Richard flew up from the banks and waved to the woman.

"Ask Captain Falconer to pop up for a moment, would you luv?" Richard said, his accent suddenly thick.

She produced a submachine gun and began shooting at Richard. Apparently the angle of the ship disturbed her aim because she missed. He flew behind Christopher, sheltering behind his cloak.

"We mean you no harm," Christopher tried to say. He didn't feel shouting would be dignified, so he had to wait until her magazine was empty to continue.

"Please summon your captain. His brother would like to speak to him."

The woman spoke incredulously. "Dr. Falconer?"

"Aye, that's myself," Richard said, floating out from behind Christopher. "How's Bob holding up these days?"

The woman fainted.

"Maybe we should go in," Richard suggested. "But you first. I don't particularly want a face full of nine-millimeter slugs."

By the time they reached the hatchway, unseen hands had drawn the woman inside. Christopher realized he shouldn't have worn his sword. It wasn't very welcoming. They dropped to the decking and clung to railings. More faces over gun barrels stared out of the hatch at them.

One of them was older, lined with authority and experience.

"Dick?" the man said. "What the bloody hell are you doing here, and what have you done to my ship?"

"Technically, it was him," Richard replied, pointing at Christopher. "If you're going to shoot anybody, start with him."

Christopher didn't get a chance to speak.

"We thought you were dead. Why the bloody hell aren't you dead?" the captain demanded, his outrage now personal.

"Not for lack of trying," Richard quipped. "It's a long story, and it's hard to tell over the sound of gunfire."

The gun barrels lowered. The captain staggered out onto the tilted deck and gaped in awe at the countryside. "I thought our instruments had gone screwy. But they're right. Where in the bloody hell are we?"

"Not Hel, actually, for which you should be grateful. I've been there, and I have to say it was not at all pleasant." Richard grinned and carefully worked his way forward. "It's good to see you, Robert. It's damn good." He held out his hand.

Captain Robert looked at the extended palm in wonder. "You look bloody good for a dead man." He clasped hands and shook, and then he pulled Richard into an embrace that threatened to dislodge them both. "Bloody good."

"Hi," Christopher waved to the other faces. One of them was the woman with the submachine gun. "It's not your fault you missed," he explained to her. "Magic."

He realized it was the wrong thing to say when she raised her gun and carefully squeezed off a shot at him.

"Belay that," the captain ordered.

"He's right, sir," she replied. "Our weapons don't work on him."

"Oh, they work," Richard said. "They work just fine. That's why you're here, in fact. An enemy of the Crown is in need of killing. I have MI6 clearance at the highest levels, Captain, and I'm invoking that authority to commandeer your ship for the good of the Commonwealth."

"Still talking rubbish, I see," Captain Robert said. "But come on in and explain. Lieutenant, put on some coffee. I imagine this explanation is going to take a while."

The crew were trained professionals. They continued to operate through the shock. Their captain asserted that everything was in hand, and they chose to believe him through force of habit. The captain was just as disoriented, but he knew he had to put on a strong face for his crew. Therefore, through sheer willpower, he walked without flinching under the alien sky and issued commands as if nothing had changed. Both layers, commander and commanded, pretended the situation was comprehensible and manageable, and because they did so, it was. The ballet impressed Christopher. His men had relied on him for courage in the face of monsters, but they had grown up with monsters. All they feared was death. These people were terrified for their sanity.

After several hours, they had gotten most of the crew out of the ship, about a hundred men and half a dozen women. An unknown number remained on board, guarding engineering and the arsenal. The rest were engaged in the problem of bringing their ship onto an even keel. Christopher watched Krellyan greeting the captain and trying to put him at ease while Richard squired his lady friend to his brother's disapproving glare. The disapproval seemed pro forma; the man could not help but appreciate the woman's beauty or her obvious affection for Richard. Christopher could see all of this reflected in their auras, in case it wasn't obvious enough on their faces.

He could also see that absent Richard's personal connection, Lalania's charm, and Krellyan's gentle authority, the entire affair would have ended as it begun: in gunfire, eventually deadly. The ship looked like a great beached whale, its conning tower the only thing breaking the illusion above the fins, and he could not see any obvious weapons or deck guns, but he knew the ship must carry awe-inspiring firepower. Richard wouldn't have asked for it otherwise.

Karl was another point of contact. He snapped a salute at the captain, who instantly recognized a kindred soul. The captain spoke to the young man with wary trust, knowing that he represented both honor and the focal point of any military threat. The captain apparently had decided to ignore the existence of the flying bullet-proof caped crusader. Christopher was happy to be out of the spotlight for once.

There was only one hiccup, when the Saint had to cast the translation spell on Karl so he could speak directly to the captain. Christopher could see the suspicion in the captain's bearing. He understood; it felt like being tricked, that a man could suddenly speak fluent English when a moment ago he pretended to be dumb as a post. The captain did not let his concern rise to his face, which again impressed Christopher. Marcius should have got himself a Royal Navy officer in the first place, and everything would have gone much more smoothly.

Karl summoned an army of draft horses from the city. The submarine crew noticeably relaxed at the sight. Horses they understood. Horses were the same in every world. Again Christopher could relate. He went to take his own out for some exercise. The beast needed it and so did his young body.

He rode alone. No one thought he needed an escort anymore.

By the time he returned, night was falling. The engineering operation had been put off until daylight. Christopher saw army tents in the field next to the river, set up for their guests to use. It was a clever compromise; it kept the navy men off the ship, allowing them to acclimatize to the new world, while not dragging them into the unfamiliarity of a foreign city. It also meant the entire crew would get to see the starry sky for themselves, silencing any doubters.

The captain agreed to come up to the castle for dinner. His crew lined up and saluted as he climbed into a carriage. They set their own guard on their camp, armed with submachine guns. Christopher rode over on his lathered, happy warhorse to where Karl was mounting up.

"You want to know why I didn't make any of those submachine guns for you, I suppose," he said.

"I assumed it was because you were cheap," Karl answered. "They consume ammunition like a soldier drinks beer."

It took him a minute to realize Karl was telling a joke. It took him longer to work out why.

"You like these guys?" he finally asked.

Karl nodded. "They are as mortal as I. And yet Master Richard, the most puissant mage this realm has ever known, looks at their vessel as if it could destroy the world. He speaks to his brother with sibling familiarity, but he addresses the ship's captain with respect."

Christopher looked over his shoulder and finally drew the conclusion he should have drawn hours ago.

The damn thing was nuclear.

29

SCANDALOUS

This world had a litany of evils that defied description. It had imported monsters from other planets to round out the list. Even so, Christopher was chagrined to have added nuclear warfare to the rolls.

He sat quietly at dinner while Richard and Lalania charmed Captain Robert. It was strange watching them work as a pair. It was stranger watching them employ Karl and Krellyan in their performance.

"But why steal my ship?" Robert asked. He had heard the tale of the trip to Hel and had suggested that a fleet of tanks would be more useful for a planetary invasion. Christopher agreed with that assessment, so he leaned in to hear Richard's answer.

"First and foremost, I need a nuclear reactor. And you have one of the very few portable ones in the world." Richard waved his hands in excitement. "There are certain experiments I am desperate to perform."

"You can't just crack open our reactor and mess around," Robert said. "It's not like dad's car. You won't be able to put it back together afterward."

"Restoring machinery is the least of my problems now. I have a spell that temporarily reverses causality—"

Lalania elbowed the wizard.

"The technical details are unimportant," he continued without missing a beat. "I can put stuff back together. What I could not do was refine an irradiation source, at least in any reasonable time frame."

"Richard," the captain said, trying to interject reason into the conversation, "they'll know. They'll see the core has been tampered with."

"Oh," Richard said. "The sub's never going back. At least, not in one piece."

The captain put down his fork and knife. His face went hard. So did his aura, its blue deepening.

Richard continued on, oblivious. "I have a list of extensive modifications I need to make. I don't think the Royal Navy will want it back afterward. Or will be able to afford it, for that matter. But first I have to do those experiments."

"You're talking piracy." Robert was not amused.

"I'm sorry, brother. But the fate of the world quite literally hangs in the balance. There are creatures here that would consume Earth, if they could find someone foolish or wicked enough to open the door. They now have over a hundred candidates. Even if we killed every man and woman in your crew and burned their bodies, those creatures could still make use of them."

The captain's mood was not softened by such talk. "Then send us back."

"It's too late." Richard seemed genuinely grieved. "They know. They're watching. Sooner or later someone else from Earth will cross over, and they'll pounce. Sooner or later they'll find a path. And then Earth will be doomed. All the guns in the world cannot withstand magic." The wizard turned to Christopher. "Show him."

The captain stared at Christopher, suspicious and skeptical.

"Bark," Christopher commanded, in Celestial.

The captain yipped like a dog. Then threw his hand over his mouth in astonishment.

"You see?" Richard said. "We have the advantage in the first encounter because they do not understand technology. But once they reach around it to the man behind, we are defenseless. Right now they are just noticing something has happened. They are slow to react; they are used to a long game indeed. Eventually, they will come for us in all their hideous glory, and we will lose. We could send you back to Earth; I could go with you. Perhaps with all of the force we have here in the castle, we could drag Christopher back. But that would only delay the inevitable."

"Perhaps delay is good." The captain was a trained strategic thinker. "Technology will progress. We'll be stronger. We might even learn this magic you talk about."

"Earth will never discover magic," Richard said with finality. "It only comes from here. And honestly, I am not entirely certain Earth has time to wait. There are a number of threats that could credibly destroy terrestrial civilization. Your submarine's arsenal represents only one of them."

"How will this help?" Robert asked the same question Christopher wanted to.

"There are untapped resources here. There is space, open and unclaimed wilderness. There are foes to scare the Communists into the embrace of the Monarchists and have them all singing kumbaya. The differences between the races of men will melt away when they see a troll."

"Not for long," Lalania said. "Men in other kingdoms employ trolls and worse." She was pretending to take Robert's side, the better to be convincing when Richard countered the point. Christopher thought it was a pretty good objection anyway.

"Sure," Richard conceded. "Eventually it will all go back to normal. But there will be an escape hatch, a way into another world. Even if we lose Earth, the human race will survive. And not as slaves for some monster. The monsters have magic; fine, we can learn it. Let them try and learn physics. I'll gamble our whole species on us winning that race."

Hearing his own arguments in the mouth of another made Christopher question himself. Did he sound so reckless? Had his position always been merely the precursor of invasion and conquest? Was he risking the fate of his world just for the sake of his wife? Or perhaps the fate of the entire cosmos; if humans lost this fight, the *hjerne-spica* would be empowered. They would not hesitate to make use of the worst aspects of technology. It might soon be elves and dragons facing nuclear weapons.

The wise course would be to open a gate and chuck them all back. Take the sub and submachine guns away. Leave the black powder for Alaine to clean up. Pack it in and go while there was still a chance to quit. Give up on his wife, who now lay dead because of his decisions, because of his obligations. Because he had not run home at the first opportunity. Because he had chosen power and glory over her. Because he had played at someone else's game.

He looked across the table to where Karl sat, rapturously absorbing Richard's talk.

He could flee thousands of light-years in a single step and still never outrun that face. Leaving was not an option.

Richard issued orders. Christopher followed them. The man was a certified genius, and he had a plan in mind that he was too wise to write down or fully reveal. Christopher, who had so long demanded blind trust from others, found himself on the receiving end.

The submarine was fully conquered. The squad of Royal Marines that held the arsenal never had a chance. Richard flew inside while invisible and put them to sleep with a spell. Christopher knew how they felt, from when it had been done to him. The Marines woke up in the same dungeon he had woken up in, although under considerably different conditions. The only torture was the local beer, which the Marines assured him was only fit for bathing in, not drinking.

In the middle of the night, they murdered a guard and snuck back into the submarine to set the reactor to overload. Richard knocked them out again, and Christopher revived the man they had killed. When the same guard served them breakfast in the morning, the fight went out of the Marines. They sat in the dungeon and drank his lousy beer.

Richard had Christopher open another gate to Earth. He took over

Lalania, Karl, and a squad of cavalrymen he'd taught how to drive. They came back with a dozen jeeps and an armored personnel carrier.

Captain Robert objected to the proceedings. "You're obviously hell-bent on a career of robbery, but don't compound it with kidnapping. Let my people go home."

Richard shook his head in denial. "If they walk through that gate, MI6 will pick them up within hours. And how will they explain the loss of their ship? A lie will get them imprisoned; the truth will get them committed. I'm sorry, but they're stuck here for a while. Once we're done with our little mission, we'll figure out how to establish trade and travel with Earth on a regular basis. Until then they're better off here."

"Prisoners of war have rights," the captain said stiffly.

Christopher intervened. "They're not prisoners. Okay, they are, but not of war. There's no state of war here. We'll pay for all this equipment eventually."

"Are you mad, boy?" Robert spluttered. Christopher didn't take offense; these days he was younger than Karl. It was disconcerting for them both. "Do you have any idea how much a Vanguard-class ship costs?"

"How much does a full course of cancer treatment cost?" Christopher responded. "I can cure twenty people a day."

"Then why aren't you?" The captain's challenge hit home, and Christopher grimaced.

Richard answered for him. "Because he must husband his power. Until we finish our task, none of us is safe."

"You have been less than specific as to the nature of your task," the captain noted.

The wizard shrugged. "You understand operational security. It's a need-to-know basis. I will tell you this much: I need your boat in operational order. I need your crew."

Robert squared his shoulders, his face set like a mule. "You cannot command them."

"You know we can," Richard said. "You saw, at dinner."

"No, we can't," Christopher said. "We will never be able to do that. Your people have to train my soldiers. That much has to happen. But no one will compel them to commit treason or suicide."

The captain raised his eyebrows at the last word.

Richard objected. "We have at least a thirty percent chance of success. I wouldn't call that suicide."

That did not comfort either the captain or Christopher. He tried to make the captain feel better anyway. "We'll pay your people for the training. I'll settle accounts with your government later."

"But why?" Robert asked his brother. "She's a beautiful ship, but her only armaments are torpedoes, which probably can't even target anything you have here, assuming you have an ocean to fight in. And forget the missiles—I only have half the codes. You'll never launch one."

"A problem, yes. I have some ideas, but I'll need to go off-mainstream again to implement them. I hope I can convince Ell to come this time. The elves are shockingly poor company. The women don't flirt and the men don't drink." Richard turned to Christopher. "I'll need tael, too. Staggering quantities of it. We need to go back to Hel and do a little hunting."

There were many things wrong with that plan. Christopher brought up none of them. "I'll call Alaine and let her know," he said.

Alaine did not come alone. She brought her boyfriend, who was not at all happy about recent developments. Lucien stared at him like a landlord at a particularly destructive tenant. In elven form, he was still gangly but now a full six inches taller. Sheer height made him intimidating.

"What is that *thing* lying in the river?"

Christopher considered several answers, including technical ones, and settled on the most truthful. "A mechanical dragon."

Lucien rocked back on heels. "Do you challenge me for the domain, then?"

It was a thorny question. "I don't," Christopher finally answered. "I'm not sure I can speak for others."

"I know you have ascended." The dragon was trying not to sound threatening. "I can smell it on you if nothing else. But understand I am also elevated. In terms of raw power, I still outrank you."

Christopher shook his head. "It's not me you need to worry about. I warned you that change would come. Richard is just the leading edge of that change."

The wizard in question joined them. "Excellent," he said, offering a welcoming hand to Lucien. "I have a favor to ask of you, Master Lucien."

The dragon stared at the hand and then at the man. "Is it not early in our relationship to be speaking of favors?"

"Oh, I hope not. We shall be fast friends, I think. Because the alternative is unthinkable." Richard, despite the smile on his face and the warmth of his tone, managed to be twice as threatening as the dragon.

Lucien looked aside to the elf. She shrugged helplessly. "He has the backing of the Directorate. I am in no better position than you."

"Friends, then," Lucien said, taking Richard's hand and squeezing it painfully. "Friends indeed."

Richard extricated his hand. "Wonderful. Because I would like to carve a chunk out of your roof."

The dragon smiled at the jest. "Help yourself. Take as much as you can." Nothing could damage adamantium except adamantium.

"I'm not being fair," Richard apologized and drew the adamantium dagger from his belt.

Lucien apparently recognized them because he glared at Alaine. She bore it stoically.

Richard ignored the social difficulty and plowed on. "I had an idea like this." He produced a mechanical iris for a camera lens and demonstrated how it opened and closed. "You don't actually need a solid foot of adamantium to block scrying. Just a thin layer when it's closed will do the trick. And if you ever decide you want to leave by a door the previous owners don't know about, you can just slide it open."

Lucien considered the wizard and his toy. Christopher watched in fascination as the dragon's intensely green aura flared and swirled, moving in patterns he could not grasp. Richard handed the iris to Lucien and turned his attention to Alaine.

"Up for another road trip?" He smiled with the light of the sun. The effect washed off the elf like ocean spray on a mountain.

"Now you want to get rich?" she said dryly.

"Yes, yes I do. This is all going to cost a lot, and Christopher is already broke."

"Did you bring me another machine gun?"

"I did," Richard said, "and more. But I'm worried about sending ordinary men over. I think the demons will vaporize them with a glance."

"I might have some friends who would be interested," Alaine said. "They will need to be paid, however."

"Halfsies?"

She considered. "It is unorthodox but not unthinkable."

The wizard turned back to the dragon.

"No," Lucien said with a heavy sigh. "If I accompany you, the *bevinget* will either hide or swarm. I doubt your weapons can deal with a hundred at once."

Richard looked like he was calculating. "Hmm . . . not yet. I was aiming for a dozen."

"Once you do this, they may well start to rank you as a dragon." Lucien's warning seemed only half-serious, as if he couldn't quite believe the wizard's brash talk. "You may never get a second easy hunt."

"Another price I must pay for my deal with Christopher. So many opportunities squandered because we are in a hurry."

Lucien handed the iris back to Richard. "I accept your bargain but only because I fear you would manufacture adamantium if I denied you access to mine. You understand why civilized beings object to the substance, yes?"

"I do," Richard agreed. "Once tael is frozen into adamantium, it is lost forever. To rob the future for a momentary advantage is a crime. Except when it is necessary. I hope you can see the distinction."

The dragon did not look convinced, but he did not argue.

※

Christopher's contribution to the raid was to open the gate. Apparently, he was no more welcome than the dragon; his divine rank meant merely stepping foot on the other side would set off alarm bells across the plane. However, he discovered that he could open the gate without a key. No one needed to die this time.

Richard and Lalania led a party of silver-clad elves over in vehicles. They came back six hours later, minus three jeeps and the bodies of four elves, although their soul-stones were recovered and they would be reborn soon. Technically, Christopher was entitled to a quarter of the wealth the expedition brought into his kingdom. He didn't mention it because Richard was already spending it all for him.

The next day, Richard and Lalania went back to Earth again for three days, the gate closing behind them this time. They had to rely on her skills rather than magic to avoid detection and arrest, a feat made possible because the bard had already learned English. Her profession gave her an advantage with languages, and she had recently obtained a high rank. They took a sack of letters from the crew of the submarine to their families and loved ones, along with three heavy chests of gold, and came back with two large trucks full of equipment.

Now Christopher had real work to do. Richard wanted a drilling head installed on the submarine, the conning tower cut off, and tank tracks attached to the bottom. Somebody had to design it all. Fortunately, they had a mechanical engineer to hand. It was an impossible task, of course, but where technology failed magic intervened. Christopher had once repaired his armor with a spell; he could weld steel with his hands now if he wanted to. He only did the hard bits, however. Richard had found a way to create a skilled workforce out of nothing, merely by the vast expenditure of tael.

The wizard gathered a hundred volunteers and promoted them to the highest level of the craft profession. Then he walked them through training classes he had downloaded off the internet. Within a week, they were as skilled as seasoned mechanics, having mastered their new craft with help from the tael. This was normally only done with warriors; a force of knights could be raised from soldiers in a day if you could afford it. But no one had ever wanted an army of craftsmen before.

Handing out promotions made Richard quite popular. It had the opposite effect for Christopher. Johm came to court to tell him of the cost, his aura writhing in bolts of green and yellow.

"He has stolen all of my apprentices and most of my smiths. Your factories are shuttered. Not that it matters. We have seen the new weapons. All the skills we have mastered are dust now. You will import what we can never match. Everything I have built is cast aside, mere toys for children. I have wasted my time and my life."

Johm had just built his first steam engine that lasted more than three days without exploding. Now he was competing with automobile engines.

Christopher found words he hadn't used in a while. "I'm sorry," he said, meaning it.

"It was always going to be thus, wasn't it? You were always going to leave me behind." Johm stood in front of him with empty hands and a broken heart.

"No," Christopher said. "That's not what I planned. That *thing*"— he waved at the river, where the submarine sat in the dry dock they had constructed, diverting the river around it—"is never what I planned.

So much of this is not what I had expected. If I had known this was the end, I would never have begun." If he had known the god of death would cheat him twice and Marcius would play the martyr, he would have gone home three years ago.

"Their skills are hollow. They can do what your mage wants of them, but afterward they will struggle to earn a living. Magic cannot replace hard work. What will you do with them then?"

Christopher had already paved roads for wagons. Now he had trucks. Richard and Lalania kept bringing them over from Earth full of supplies but never took one back. They were starting to stack up around the training yard. If he put them to work, the price of bread could go down again. "We've got all those vehicles. Somebody has to take care of them." He'd have to find a way to make his own gasoline, though. Importing basic energy resources was not a sound basis for an economy.

The smith's grief drowned his anger, and Johm spoke like a defeated prisoner. "I wanted to build. I wanted to design. I wanted to discover. But it all has been done before, and there is nothing new for me to invent. So you will make me handmaiden to someone else's genius."

Christopher found a smile. "Spoken like a first-year university student. Yes, all the easy discoveries have been made. But there's still work to be done. I have to turn a submarine into a drilling machine. Richard very helpfully gave me adamantium blades for the cutting part but never once considered where the cut rock would go. Something has to move it behind the sub so the sub can move forward."

Johm looked around the hall and for the first time seemed to notice how empty it was. They were the only two people there. Christopher, so long flanked by advisors and guards, was alone.

"We are fellows in exile, then," the smith muttered. "It does not leaven my heart, and yet I find I cannot hate you."

Having his company made Christopher feel better, though.

They pulled the same trick for the submarine crew. Christopher called for volunteers from his army, stressing the danger of the mission. He got a hundred men standing at attention the next morning waiting for orders. Of his original little troop from the village, only Major Kennet was among them. He was surprised and tried to make a joke of it.

"Charles wasn't interested in learning to swim?" he said to Kennet.

"Oh, no, sir," the soldier replied. "We drew lots, and his did not come up."

"I asked for volunteers," Christopher said, frowning.

"Yes, sir," Kennet replied. "We drew lots to see who got to volunteer."

All of them were promoted as craftsmen, which would conflict with their future career as knights, except none of them ever expected to be a knight. Kennet, who had already spurned any talk of promotion from the Hel trip since he had been rescued rather than rescuer, accepted this one, eager to take his place as a deck officer. Captain Robert was as impressed with the young man as everyone else always was.

Sacks of gold induced the submarine's original crew to teach the men the basics of maintaining and operating the ship. Much to Christopher's surprise, two dozen mariners asked to go along.

Captain Robert was not happy, but he did not say no. Instead, he assigned a condition: he had to go as well. "As if I would let you take my ship into uncharted waters without me." Then he convinced the chief engineer to join them with a simple argument. "Richard thinks he knows how to operate a nuclear reactor because he read a book about it."

The chief spat in disgust. "There will be more gold?"

"Sure," Christopher said. Gold was the least of the expenses he was incurring.

Richard left in the middle of the preparations, going with Argeous back to the time-dilated plane. He did not get to take Lalania, which clearly grieved him. She was traveling back and forth from Earth every few days, trading gold for the technological supplies they needed and staying one step ahead of the authorities. It wasn't as dangerous as it sounded. They were unlikely to shoot her on sight, and if they put her in prison, Christopher could just pull her out again.

Christopher got three wizards back the next week. All of them were Richard.

"There was too much work to do," Richard said. "I copied myself. They're only simulacrums; they have half my rank and cannot progress further. But for code-breaking, that was good enough."

The moral dimensions of this were staggering. None of the Richards seemed to care. All of them asked where Lalania was. For her part, the bard took the duplication of her paramour in stride, although for the next few days, Christopher saw little of her, and she always seemed to be exhausted.

Soon enough he had other problems to solve. The Lady Kalani showed up in his throne hall, doing her level best to connive her way onto his ship. Alaine, who was still unaccountably hanging around, flatly said no. Christopher, as usual, managed to make a bad situation vastly worse.

"Your mother said you would be impatient," he said with a smile. Whatever the punch line was supposed to be died forgotten when he saw the rage that flooded the girl's face.

"How dare you!" Kalani shrieked at her mother. Alaine weathered it like a boulder, but Christopher could see her pain reflected in the roiling of her flat, white aura. "You . . . you slattern!"

This seemed an odd choice of insult, given that Kalani had tried to seduce him within hours of their first meeting.

"We are in public," Alaine said, her voice held mild by the weight of centuries of self-discipline. The only people present were the two elves and Christopher, but then again, he was not family.

"That did not stop you from maligning me!" The girl was leaking tears.

"She didn't actually say that," Christopher said hastily. "I misquoted her. Please stop screaming."

"Understand I spoke in human terms," Alaine said.

"You do that a little too much, don't you think?" Kalani aimed to wound. Christopher winced but not for Alaine's sake. The woman was as tough as adamantium. The attempt to hurt her mother was tearing Kalani apart, though.

Alaine answered with measured words, fury buried in content rather than tone. "I have been awake for thirty thousand years. You do not get to tell me what is too much."

"Have you? How would you even know? You have thrown away so many things."

Alaine narrowed her eyes in confusion.

Christopher, in his infinite wisdom, tried to help. "I don't think you can complain. You weren't exactly a blushing rose when I met you."

This was a huge mistake. Kalani turned her contempt on him. "That was duty. It would have meant nothing to me; I would have forgotten it as quickly as I have forgotten that you declined. What she and that dragon do is *different*. They take animal form and they . . . they do it for *pleasure*." The girl shuddered, embarrassed to the core, and covered her face with her hands.

Alaine sighed, deeply unwilling to explain but compelled to. "We elves do not feel lust as other races do. When Aelph bought our immortality, he feared we would misuse it. He calculated the size of Aelfhiem and how many elves it could support, and he found the number wanting. Thus, we no longer seek out reproduction; the act means less to us than shaving does to you. He feared we would overrun our world and so put a leash on our desires. Instead, we have rather the opposite problem."

"That's stupid," Christopher said, outraged on behalf of all elves, everywhere. "There are far better ways to manage population growth. Sure, it's a problem, but it's a problem that can be solved without cutting things out of your brain."

"Aelph was a demigod, but he was not omniscient. He could not foresee all the consequences of his actions. As I am sure you understand."

Christopher couldn't even foresee the consequences of his conversations. "Is there some way to fix it?"

"Not without surrendering our immortality. Every few millennia, the question comes up for debate. The decision is always to leave things as they are. Kalani will eventually have to participate in that decision; she may find a way to forgive her morally corrupted mother then."

"Not that. I don't care about that," the girl whimpered, despite having done nothing but complain about it since Christopher had met her. The truth finally leaked out, borne on a whisper. "You had a son."

Alaine snapped her head around, a deadly adder ready to strike.

Kalani faltered under that feral gaze but could not stop. "You purged him. He died here, the true death, and you purged him from your memories. You chose to forget him." Her voice weakened with every word.

In a moment of insight, Christopher understood. He reached out to comfort Kalani. "She won't forget you. I won't let her."

The girl moaned from the bottom of her soul and ran from the room, weeping. It had the sound of a wound being drained, so he let her slip from his grasp and go.

"You make many promises," Alaine said flatly.

"I'll be around to keep them," he said. "I'm one of you now. An immortal."

"Tell me that again in ten thousand years."

He bowed his head in humility. "I agree. The only notion more fantastic than my living forever is imagining that someone as clumsy as I am could survive that long. There are still things that can kill me. Lucien, for instance. Or I suspect you, if you tried hard enough. I would ask your advice. Tell me how you made it so far."

She sighed again, this time in despair instead of dismay. "Your flattery is clumsy and yet more than my daughter offered. I have made compromises. I seek pleasure where I can. How many sunsets over the ocean have I seen? I do not know. I forget them, so that I may be surprised by their beauty all over again. Every thousand years or so, elves seek out seclusion for a period of days or years. We review our memories. We choose which ones to discard, which ones to keep. Our minds are not infinite; we cannot keep every moment alive. Nor need we; the knowledge of what I had for breakfast an eon ago is of no interest to anyone, least of all myself."

Her hands fidgeted with her sword belt. He would have thought her ashamed if he could assign that emotion to the obdurate woman.

"I can only assume I feared the effect of losing a child. It would have weighed on my heart; it would have made me hate this place. It would have dragged me from my duty. So I purged him, and his life, and his loss. In truth I often wondered why the Directorate had never before assigned me a mate. Yet I did not question because it was not my place to question and because I did not want to know."

She looked at him sharply. "Understand, few of us can indefinitely bear the eternal war; the death and destruction, the risks for so little reward, the inching of progress to a goal that is after all merely a cataclysmic battle for the right to commit genocide. Ten thousand years is considered fair duty for a field agent such as myself; then we can retire to the Stone Legion. To do so early is to risk being labeled *impatient*, the single worst word one can apply to an elf. We are transformed to statues to wait for the final conflict, when we will take flesh again to fight one last time. Aelfhiem is like a sculptor's studio, littered with statues of elves and dragons and other allies who wait for the call to arms. I am somewhat of a celebrity by virtue of my longevity. Both in choosing to stay awake and failing to be murdered. Now, perhaps, I perceive why so few are willing to match my record."

She paused, reckoning with the past. After a moment, she remembered the present and spoke almost apologetically. "I am sorry to be the bearer of bad news. You are a demigod; you will not need to forget. In time I will seem absent-minded to you. Yet you must know your immortality is not perhaps the panacea you hoped for."

"That's okay," he said. "Nothing lives forever. Even the universe will pass away someday. The point is getting to choose; getting to decide for yourself when you're done."

Alaine smiled in spite of herself. "You may yet make the long haul."

"We have to let Kalani come," he said. "She found me first, after all."

"To prove my love for my child, I have to subject her to the path most likely to destroy her? There will be no casualties on this mission; we have far too much power for that. We either triumph completely or are destroyed utterly."

"Hmph," Christopher said. "Every time I think it's the end, it's just another beginning. I'm almost curious to see how they'll cheat me this time."

30

EARTH, WIND, AND FIRE

Weeks passed as the expedition took shape. Richard was everywhere, and Christopher realized the man slept in shifts, sending his copies out to manage the preparations night and day. He could always spot the difference between the real Richard and one of his clones, but no one else seemed able to tell them apart.

Eventually, Lalania stopped making grocery runs as the submarine took its final form. Now the hard part began: pruning the guest list. After the success of the previously doomed mission to Hel, everyone now assumed Christopher was invincible. Also the vast quantities of tael that Richard had been throwing around were like a summoning spell, drawing would-be heroes out of the woodwork.

Karl and a squad of his best marines, of course. All the newly trained crew and the mercenaries he had recruited from the original crew, including the captain and chief engineer. Richard. or rather, Richards and Lalania. Alaine and Kalani, because he couldn't say no. Torme and the three new recruits to his church, again because denial would break their hearts. Gregor and Disa, because she convinced him he could not alone heal an entire crew. And, astonishingly, Cardinal Faren.

"I owe you this much," Faren said. "And not just you. Svengusta would have gone by your side; I am but a poor replacement in his honor."

Krellyan and the vicars would stay and run the kingdom. If Christopher never came back, few would notice. Duke Istvar had stopped asking for Lord Nordland's revival; apparently he had communicated with the Duke's ghost and discovered that the man did not want to return to a world without his wife. And his wife's ghost did not want to return to a world where her entire county, servants and friends and extended family, were cold ashes. Nordland swore to raise enough tael to summon every person the Lady could name; consequently, the Blue were happy to turn over the duties of government while they went hunting in the Wild. Christopher appeased his conscience by giving the blue knights assault rifles. It was a bad time to be a troglodyte; but then it was always a bad time to be a cave-dwelling cannibalistic monster on the border of a Blue county.

Christopher was able to refuse the remaining horde of adventurers because the sub could not support more people. He turned down every Ranger by pointing out that he already had a ranger and a druid, in the forms of the elves, and it would be an insult to them to suggest he needed two guides.

Cannan was one of the ones who fell by the wayside. The big man stared at him dangerously while he was told. Christopher looked into Niona's grateful eyes and did not flinch. Christopher also made Cannan take his sword back from Alaine by threatening to give the knight his own ridiculously overpowered glowing katana.

Cannan could not ignore the symmetry. "We are done, then, you and I. I came to take your sword, and now I flee it."

"We are still friends," Christopher said. "Always. But your life belongs to someone else now."

They clasped hands, which turned into an embrace.

"Take care of my horse while I'm gone," Christopher said. The horse was as unhappy as Cannan at being left behind. Niona would be the best possible companion. He kind of wished he was staying in Royal's place.

He turned away and climbed the ladder hanging from the submarine's side, the last to board. Standing on top of the vessel with Richard, next to the hatches that had replaced the conning tower, he looked up at the city towering over them. Richard's plan was to drive directly into the side of the mountain and then gradually slope down, until the sub was standing on its nose. Despite all their magic, they didn't actually have a way to manhandle the sub into that position; it weighed too much.

"I should challenge you," a voice said at his shoulder. He turned to find Lucien standing next to him, where a moment ago there had been no one. "Or beg a place in your company. And yet I can do neither."

"There is still a part for you to play, Master Lucien," Richard said. "This is an orchestra, not a hero's journey."

"I know," Lucien conceded, "and yet this vessel carries away my companion, trapped in the snare of your Saint's vanity. Only the fact that I am equally ensnared stays my claw. Yet I mourn for our future that could have been, however dull it would have been compared to this glory."

"I'm sorry," Richard said, "but I do not."

"Bring her back," Lucien said, "or you will. Yes, threats! For I am Green, for all that minx Jenny has wrought upon me. I can still be roused to insensate violence."

Richard shrugged good-naturedly. "No complaints here. I know that fury will soon serve us well."

Christopher was watching the mountain rumble closer. The blades on the front of the vessel began spinning, making a horrible noise. Richard eyed them critically but seemed satisfied.

Lucien stepped back, falling off the ship and transforming. He spread his wings and flew, circling the city. In dragon form, he was now truly huge, as big as Jenny had been. Christopher's city crowded the walls to see the sight of a lifetime. This was a send-off worthy of a legend.

"We should go below," Richard announced, clambering into an open hatch.

Christopher followed him, sighing as the heavy tracks chewed through his cavalry training field, turning it into broken and dangerous ground.

Life on a submarine was . . . boring. It was small and close, and there wasn't anything for him to do. Something serious broke once, and he almost got excited, but one of the Richards fixed it with magic before anybody even figured out exactly what the problem had been.

The days piled on top of each other. They ground along, traveling an astonishing four or five miles an hour through solid rock. The ship never stopped shaking; the sound of rock cracking and splitting rumbled everywhere, underneath conversations and into dreams. After the first three weeks, Christopher couldn't remember what silence sounded like.

Richard had cast some kind of gravity warping spell; inside the sub, the floor remained the floor, even while it was standing on its head, plunging into the earth. The wizard claimed that vibration dampening would have been too expensive, but privately Christopher suspected he just hadn't anticipated how annoying it would be.

Christopher hosted dinner every few days, spending his magic to summon food and give them all a change of pace from naval rations. Lalania put on truly inspiring performances. Gregor and Torme worked out in the ship's surprisingly well-equipped gym, discovering the attraction of body-building. Christopher joined them because he had energy to burn. How mortal twenty-year-olds survived on submarines without going stir-crazy mystified him.

There was also time to talk, and to think. Certain things became clear to Christopher now that he had a wider perspective. Faren and he finally had the kinds of theological conversations he had skipped by not being a novice.

"Hordur tried to bribe Richard with immortality. Yet Marcius didn't even mention it when he was trying to bribe me into killing him. As if it were the least important part of becoming a demigod."

Faren spoke carefully. "The Bright Lady tells us nothing lives forever."

Christopher smiled wryly. "She is right. The universe is not stable; it's either going to fly apart or collapse on itself. Eventually, it all ends in a fireball or cold soup."

"Immortality would seem to be a bit of a cheat, then. A lifetime lease on a house about to be consumed by a forest fire or subsumed by flood. No wonder Marcius didn't make it part of his bargain." Faren approved of the god's strict honesty.

"It's not as bad as that," Christopher said. "One of those fates is billions of years away, and the other trillions. Statistically, an accident will claim me long before then, demigod or no. For that matter, too many more days on this boring submarine and I'll be clawing to get out just like Marcius."

"I don't believe you." Faren shook his head. "I have lived a long and full life. I achieved everything I dreamed of. I loved and was loved. And yet, on any given morning, I find that I am not quite ready to quit."

"But you would," Christopher asked, cutting to the heart of the matter. "If the price of another day meant the death of an innocent, you would choose to quit. Even if that other had not yet been born."

"Especially if they were unborn," Faren agreed. "I have had my fun; it is only fair that another also have their turn. As I would hope others would chose for me, if I were the one yet to come."

"Hordur wouldn't," Christopher observed, perhaps unnecessarily. "He would hold on until the bitter end, until everything was cold and dead and merely a shadow of life."

"Indeed," Faren said. "So much is evident from his interior decoration choices."

"This is the supreme irony, then." Christopher chuckled because there was no other possible response. "The god of death fights for eternal life, or, rather, as close to eternal as possible. The elves and all the good guys fight for an early end to the cosmos. They want to burn it all down."

Faren smiled guiltily. "The legend of the phoenix. From the ashes the world is born anew. Our faith is that it is not mere myth, but an expression of truth."

"It is. If the universe collapses, a new one will be made from the explosion. If it fades to soup, then that's it. Nothing interesting ever happens again."

"And knowing this, how would you choose?" Faren asked him, as wary as a hare in an open field on a bright summer's day.

"The same way I would want others to choose if I were the one who had not yet had his turn."

This was the dividing line between Bright and Dark: those who would yield their place after having their fun, and those who would not. This was the meaning of the creed he had sworn, the great debate between the colors, the final conflict the elves fought for even as they acknowledged it would end in their death.

This was why Alaine had been hanging around. That was why she had let him live after their little conversation, when he had offhandedly said his goal was choosing when to die rather than living forever. She could whistle and a dozen dragons would come running to eat his face. Instead, she was helping him.

Another pop quiz he had passed without even knowing it was being given. If he wanted to make it to the end of the century, he would need to start paying more attention in class. That or spend less time around dangerous women. No wonder most gods spent most of their time hiding.

He went to share his insights with Richard. "That's what the tagging is for. Everybody gets to vote at the tipping point, when the universe has to decide whether to linger or die and be reborn. The tael is there to record the vote."

The wizard shook his head. "Still too much for that. There's enough tael in Karl's head to do magic if you put it all in someone else's." Karl had, amazingly, managed to avoid the latest round of promotions, even when Richard had promoted the original submarine crew so they could learn the local language overnight. Karl's job on the sub was soldiering, and he was already perfectly skilled at that. He and his squad were still commoners, although they carried modern assault rifles and wore magical elven chainmail.

"Also," Richard continued, "the elves are wrong. There won't be some discreet event. Reality is continuous; this vote is being constantly applied."

"Wait. You mean, like, every day? As in every time we choose evil we expand the universe a tiny bit, and every time we choose good we contract it a fraction?" Christopher boggled to see physics and theology so neatly unified.

"Poor Einstein." Richard shook his head in sympathy. "How could he guess that the cosmological constant changed based on whether or not he cheated on his taxes? I had grad students tear their hair out over the idea it had ever have changed; wait until they find out it changes all the time."

The man grinned. "On the positive side, I've got another Nobel lined up. I found dark matter. It's tael. The stuff is real, you know: it interacts with gravity differently than baryons, but it's still *physical*. It's quite literally the stuffing of the universe, existing everywhere and nowhere at the same time. Prime is unique only because here, at the center of the galaxy, there's enough gravitational tension to let it break out of its pocket dimension."

Christopher stared at him. "Explain, then, why this physical atomic substance clumps around sentient brains."

"Oh, no." Richard waved his hands, warding off the responsibility. "That's your department, Saint. That's theology."

<hr />

There were events. The submarine came under attack from elementals, animated constructs of rock and magic. There were weird and horrific monsters that lived down here, thousands of miles under the surface of the world, in caverns and tunnels.

For the most part, the submarine's armor kept them at bay. When they broke through, men with guns or swords would destroy them. Then Christopher would repair the rents in the ship's hull while Disa put the men back together. He began to feel a little like Richard: did he really obtain divine rank to be a glorified welder? But of course his magic undid the damage, which was far more effective than merely rewelding a patch.

The ship would lurch when they crashed through a cavern, breaking through the resistance of rock into open air. Alaine was steering the ship with her magic these days, trying to avoid the worst of these pockets. If they hit one large enough, it could do real damage as the ship fell forward. Richard was fooling around with a gravimeter, checking his calculations.

"How much longer?" Christopher asked, standing over his shoulder and trying to pretend he hadn't asked the question two days ago.

"Same as before. We'll get there when we get there. Can't be hurried, you know." Richard answered without actually paying attention.

"Why not?" Christopher asked. "For that matter, why don't I just gate us there? Skip all the stuff in between and pop's your cousin."

The wizard looked up from his device with horror on his face. "You're just asking this *now?*"

Christopher blushed. He didn't retreat, however, because he realized he really wanted to know the answer.

"The gods left defenses other than their cherubs with flaming swords." Richard had been calling the elementals that, although none of them had used weapons, flaming or otherwise. "While the boundaries between the elemental planes are arbitrary in the physical world, they're demarcated by a web of ley lines. Any travel through a gate leaves an invisible leash. This is why you can banish elementals from Prime; you can snap that leash and send them back. If we gated to Water, say, and tried to cross to Air, the web of ley lines would trigger our leash, and we'd be sent back to where we started from. By physically crossing the boundaries, we avoid that leash."

"Then . . . why won't the sub be sent back to Earth? It came here through a gate." So had Richard. So had Christopher, although his gate had been a rare but natural occurrence.

"Sent back to where now?" Richard smiled grimly. "There's an advantage to not being in the cosmic database. Because Earth does not have magic, travel to or from it does not create leashes."

It also explained why Christopher was not sent home the day after he had arrived. Krellyan had magically examined him and found nothing but an ordinary man.

The cosmic coincidence kept him occupied for the rest of the week. After that he started a nightly poker game, using steel washers for chips. Faren was terrible because he could not bluff; Torme was a sharp player with his inscrutable face. Gregor was just terrible. The various Richards sat in, playing efficiently but not particularly inspired. Alaine wasn't interested, but Kalani held her own, cautiously defending her chip stack with careful wagers. Things were almost getting fun until Lalania joined and cleaned them all out, three nights in a row.

<hr>

After five weeks, the ship finally broke through to open water. The relentless throbbing stopped, replaced by the gentle and reassuring hum of the electric generators, and everyone breathed a sigh of relief. Most of all the members of the original crew, who were finally in the element they were accustomed to. Richard had installed cameras around the outside of the sub, hidden by steel covers. Now that there was something to show other than rock walls, they were deployed and piped images to screens in the bridge and throughout the crew quarters. Admittedly, the images mostly petered out into a blue-green haze after thirty feet, but it was still more soothing than looking at nothing. Occasionally, there would be some grotesque fish-like creature that people gaped at. Alaine would tell them which ones were good eating, although nobody tried to catch any.

The elementals of this plane were helpless against the sub. Organized swirls of water, no matter how determined, could not damage the hull, although they made for interesting displays in the camera screens. They would cluster around it, trying to impede its progress. Eventually, they would slip down and get sucked through the propellers, and then they were no longer organized.

A giant squid as long as the sub wrapped itself around the ship in a tight embrace. Christopher could not tell whether the creature was hungry or just lonely, but it slowed them down, so a party went outside to dislodge it armed with magic water-breathing and swords. This consisted of all the high-ranks, save for Richard and Christopher, who were deemed too valuable to risk on petty battles. Christopher lent Torme his sword, hoping to put it to good use.

The adventurers came back black as midnight, coated in the squid's blood, laughing and joking at the danger they had faced. The two principals sat with Captain Robert on the bridge and tried to hide their pique at being left out. Richard in particular looked miserable watching Richard the Second wiping ink from Lalania's face.

"Everything I have seen on television taught me that landing parties were supposed to include the senior officers," Richard complained.

Captain Robert shook his head. "Only you could be jealous of yourself."

The sub cruised along at high speed. Robert still complained, asserting that without Richard's disfiguring modifications, the ship could have gone faster. They only turned the rotating blades on once, when another giant squid made the mistake of grabbing the ship by the nose. In ten short, comfortable days, the ship broached the surface of the water, straight up in the air like an orca performing in a water circus.

Much to everyone's surprise save for the Richards', the sub did not fall back to the water. It continued to drift through the air, suspended by the equipoised gravity of the huge shell of rock around them. They had all been told to expect this, of course, but the reality of it was still hard to credit. A party went out on deck to see for themselves.

The artificial gravity of the sub bound them to the deck. Richard warned them not to jump too high, however; they would break free of the field and drift off under their own power. Around them was mist, glowing white-like fog illuminated by a distant sun, yet thick enough that after a few moments they could no longer see the water they had left behind. The air was cool, pleasant, and not completely empty. Christopher could see a lump of rock as big as a small building. Moss grew on all sides of it, and a three-winged bird-like creature the size of a car came winging toward them, screeching.

"Whatever that is, it is brave to charge us," Richard said.

Lalania sniffed. "It is defending its nest. It has no choice."

Alaine was less generous. "It thinks of the vessel as merely another rock and us as prey."

The creature's home was falling astern. Captain Robert frowned. "It's going into the drink."

"Interesting," Richard said. "Eventually all of the rocks should wind up there. I wonder what keeps them out."

"Can we tow it?" Lalania asked. Another one of the creatures was screeching at them from the rock. "Save the birdy's nest?"

"I am sure there is a natural process sufficient to the occasion," Kalani said with the detachment of a zoologist. "Still, I wish we had time to observe."

The creature drew closer, opening and closing its three-part beak.

"Shoo!" Lalania shouted, trying to scare it off. It screeched at her and flexed three sets of sharp claws.

"That's not a bird, and it's going to eat you," Richard told her, drawing his pistol.

"Oh, stop being such a man." She started singing, a gentle, crooning lullaby. The creature slowed its approach and turned, circling the ship in a less aggressive manner.

Christopher reached out and caught a sailor who had fallen asleep and was in danger of drifting away from the ship.

"You're supposed to be my muse," Richard complained. "Now you're giving it away for free."

"I earned that last rank killing demons. You have no say in how I dispense my charms." She stopped singing, however, and the sailor woke up, his eyes crossed. He seemed grumpy at having his sweet dream interrupted.

The banter made Christopher lonely. "We should go back inside," he suggested. His previous encounter with an air elemental had taught him respect. The simple spell that had kept that one at bay would not work here, not on its own plane.

"In a second. I need to check the engines." Richard shouted commands through the hatch. Machinery creaked and groaned; the aft torpedo tubes opened, along with vents designed to funnel air through them. Jet engines whined, and the ship lurched to life. The bird-thing screeched and fled; the humans staggered and headed for the hatches.

Captain Robert did not appreciate his boat being turned into an aircraft. Svelte and swift in the water, it was clumsy in the air. It reached a surprisingly high velocity but not without cost. Steering was largely by accident; Richard had designed it to go in only one direction. No one had thought there were things that needed to be steered around. But some of the floating boulders were as large as skyscrapers; running into one at two hundred miles an hour would be worse than the Titanic hitting an iceberg.

The small boulders were bad enough. Richard withdrew the cameras behind their shields to protect them. They could be repaired but not replaced, and the boulder strikes were powerful enough to knock them clean off the ship. Ultimately they had to station a crew on the front of the ship with telescopes because people were easier to fix than machines. Christopher's worst fear was that a man would get lost overboard, in this vast expanse of nothing, while the ship plowed ahead, unable to turn around in anything less than a thousand miles. Everyone was armed with a pistol and strict instructions to shoot them selves if this happened. The lost he could not help; the dead he could summon by name. This did not apply to the elves, who were consequently banned from exterior duty, which was a real blow as Alaine was their best spotter.

A number of adamantium blades were knocked loose from the battering and went spinning off into the void. Richard shrugged off the loss. "We'll take the short way home," he told Christopher. "The abode of the gods is not in the cosmic database, either, for pretty obvious reasons. A gate from there will apply no leash."

It did mean that Richard was gambling everything on victory. There would be no retreat.

There were other irreplaceable losses. A boulder smashed into the front, jolting the ship and claiming a casualty of one of the Richards. Christopher went to help, but there was no body, merely a small patch of snow blowing away on the wind. The clone had dissolved back into its original substance.

He had a talk with the other clone. "You can't volunteer for dangerous duty anymore. I can't revive you."

"You can't revive any of us," the clone said. "At best you construct a new entity that has our memories and thinks it is us. Which, to be honest, is largely indistinguishable from what happens every night. Self is constructed moment to moment; continuity is an illusion."

Christopher decided to practice being divinely patient. He responded gently. "Nonetheless, most of us are attached to that illusion."

"As am I. But I already have a continuity; the essential pattern that you call Richard will continue even after this form is destroyed. As long as one of us survives, none of us can truly die."

"You're not identical," Christopher said. "Even if you started out the same, you must diverge as your life goes on. For instance, the other Richard would never engage in so much theology."

"I perceive you are insulting me in an attempt to preserve my existence," the clone replied. "That is kind but superfluous. We are in constant telepathic content; our experiences are shared, and thus we do not diverge into distinct entities. If I seem distracted at the moment, it is because the other Richard is currently engaged in very strenuous exercise, which I am also experiencing. Now if you'll excuse me, these equations won't differentiate themselves."

Christopher had just come from the gym. There was no one there. He decided, however, not to press the argument since he was clearly losing.

They crossed the plane of air in only two days. The mist cleared out instantly on the other side, like passing out of a cloud bank. The guide crew hastily shuffled back inside as the temperature rapidly rose. Ahead of them was a glowing ball of flame that filled the sky. The ship picked up speed, no longer concerned with collisions. There was still air to feed through the engines because the flame was illusionary, although the heat was real. Christopher was amazed at this final confirmation of the god's scientific illiteracy. They did not know that stars burned nuclear fires.

"They can't afford to know," Richard explained. "They don't want anyone else to know, and if they knew, someone might ask. Also, common sense suggests not surrounding your house with the only force that can destroy you. I told you tael was real matter. It's still vulnerable to leptons, if they're energetic enough."

Richard's most powerful magic came into play; he had enchanted the entire ship to be fire-proof. This had cost more than all the promotions he had handed out, but there was no other method to survive this leg of the journey. The outside temperature climbed to five hundred degrees. The crew could have survived for an hour or two at most while the hull absorbed the heat, but it was impossible to cool the vessel inside of a fireball. Like a tank hit by a Molotov cocktail, eventually the crew would have cooked. Instead they listened to the roaring of the flames battering at the hull and took a lot of showers. The thermostats said the inside temperature hadn't changed, but everyone sweated a bit anyway. Looking at the wall of fire didn't help; the crew tended to leave the external displays turned off.

"Now it's your turn," Richard told Christopher at the end of the next day. "There's a wall ahead of us that's not real. It is a shear in the fabric of reality, like the back side of a gate. Nothing can pass through it, neither magic or technology, matter or energy. No known power can punch a hole in it. If we hit it at four hundred miles an hour we'll crumple like a straw and then melt."

Christopher stood up from his bunk, where he had been vainly trying to sleep for the last eight hours. He put on his sword and armor and went forward to the bridge.

Captain Robert ceded his command chair, his face white with worry. This was far outside his call of duty. Christopher sat down in the chair, shifting to make his sword fit. The Royal Navy had given up swords a long time ago.

He put his hands on the controls. "I am a god of Travel," he said. "No way is barred to me."

The ship lunged forward. Silence fell; flames no longer beat at their hull. The sensors for the exterior environment spun or blinked according to their various failure states. The screens showed the ship floating in a purple haze without any sense of motion or direction. Sparks of light flashed, distant lighting in a summer storm, fireworks at twilight, giving the haze the look of a vast web.

Six human figures materialized on the bridge in various costumes: a sad and lovely woman in white lace; a suit of blue plate armor with a face-obscuring great helm; a dark-haired voluptuous woman in green silk; a waifish figure in blue and gold motley, face hidden behind an opera mask; a muscle-bound giant in red leather with a massive two-handed ax; a black, hooded cape hanging over fleshless bones.

"YOU AGAIN?" Hordur's voice boomed. "SOME PEOPLE JUST CAN'T TAKE A HINT."

31

FIN

"Some people can't stop cheating," Christopher said. "You've stolen from me twice. There will be no third time."

"DO YOU THINK SHE IS HERE, FLEDGLING?"

"I know she is." He was looking at the cosmic database itself. Every flash of light was a spell being cast, somewhere in the outside universe. Every flicker was a use of power, every strand a link connecting past and future. The shapes of transformed dragons were stored here in some inscrutable code, the memorized spells of wizards, the answers to prayers and divinations. All of magic and what it could do sprawled out around them, ten thousand miles deep. Somewhere out there was the connection that would bring Maggie back into being. Somewhere out there was the meaning of everything he had been and become.

"THEN SEARCH FOR HER. IT WILL ONLY TAKE A BILLION YEARS."

The woman in green threw a disgusted look at Hordur. "True love deserves better than foulness. I will help you, fledgling. We will find her while your blood still runs hot."

Christopher surrendered to the truth he had been hiding from, walls of denial plunging into the untroubled sea, swallowed whole, leaving behind a glacier of cold truth. "I didn't come here to rescue my wife."

The blue armor spoke, sonorous and grave but at least at human volume. "You have violated the home of the Six, which is forbidden. Hordur has sequestered your partner's soul, which is forbidden. Retreat, and we will compel him to release her. The balance will be restored."

The glacier sparkled but remained unmoved by the sun's light. "I didn't come here for justice."

The jester bowed. "You drive a hard bargain. We will throw in god-hood for her as well. Together you both may frolic across the eons as immortals."

"I sure as hell didn't come here for more *deals*," Christopher snarled, and the mountain of ice loomed across the skyline.

"A man of action," the red god said. "We will do battle. If you win, you can name your price. If you lose, you will at least die with glory, rather than being cast out ignominiously to disintegrate in the outer planes."

Christopher pursed his lips and did not bother to answer. Wind whipped along the surface of the ice without effect.

"Then what do you want?" the lady in white asked. Ostara, the Bright Lady, the patron of everything that was good and true, the soul of kindness itself. He looked at her, and the ice cracked, falling aside, revealing a man raising his hand to the sky. The man's face was bearded and shaggy and obdurate beyond the comprehension of ice and stone. The light of the sun burned his eyes, but he did not flinch.

"I'll have that second apple now," he said.

The assembled company of gods stared at him.

"I get it. I understand your perfect balance." He spread his hands, acknowledging what he came to destroy. "Bright and Dark, good and evil, order and chaos. It has a pure mathematical beauty that I can appreciate. It's all wonderfully symmetrical and so very abstract."

He leaned forward in his chair. "But the universe *is not symmetrical*. It exhibits chirality; it has preferences. When electric current flows, it always creates magnetic flux in the same direction. The amount of anti-matter is not equal to the amount of matter. The universe was created by a set of conditions that favored a particular outcome.

"And we mortals—we are not abstract. The messiness of life imposes its own order, its own rules. We call those rules morality. You never evolved; you never had to choose between cooperation and competition. You never had to trust someone else to survive. You never needed morality.

"This world was not created for you because you're not even real. You've cloaked yourself in bodies and memories, but they are stolen. If anything like you was supposed to exist, it was to help us. To act as a clearinghouse or central command for the controls of the universe, when we were ready to use them.

"But you woke up first. You were all alone. You divided the world into your abstract quadrants, derived from pure theory. You threw yourself into each role in equal strength. You locked us out of our inheritance and claimed it for yourselves.

"Even so, you were paralyzed. You could not decide the fate of the universe among yourselves. You thought it was because all of your parts were equal. So you played with mortals, a galactic game show. You chose teams and made captains out of prophets. We fight and struggle, while you keep score and rack up points, trying to gamble your way out of your logical impasse.

"The truth is that it was never your decision. Our predecessors are gone, utterly; nothing can pass through the eye of the needle of cosmic destruction and rebirth. But they left us something anyway. They rigged the game, laying the structure for the formation of the next universe. They made sure it would be a universe capable of organization, of life, of intellect. And they put their thumb on the scales. They made us flesh and blood and therefore *moral*.

"What they did not make us was mortal. You did that. There is tael enough in our heads to preserve us against the ravages of age. What the elves bought and paid for was always supposed to be ours for free. When a race arose to sentience, when it became capable of understanding the choice to be made, it was supposed to be granted the time to make a wise choice. We are to choose whether or not we want the universe to be destroyed, but only after we've had a chance to fully enjoy it.

"So that is what I want. To release the block on the tael in our heads. Yes, there will be problems. The elves will help; they can teach us how to cope with immortality. There will still be goblins to deal with, wicked and evil and now immortal; but again, that's an argument to be had between living creatures, not hyper-real mathematical constructs. Even the filthy *hjerne-spica* deserve their immortality, if they can defend it."

Ostara gazed at him with shining eyes. "To do as you ask would destroy us as discrete entities. The consciousness we employ is sustained by our theft. I do not know what would become of us if we let it go. Yet we would gladly do so for your sake. But we are three of six; as you have already noted, we cannot overrule the other half."

"I know," Christopher told her. "When you could not destroy your enemies, you made Marcius as a secret weapon against yourself. You thought if you died, then at least the stalemate would be broken. He failed; he could no more destroy you than he could destroy himself. But he found me."

"YOU WILL DO WHAT WE CANNOT? YOU WILL SLAY A GOD?"

"Not alone. Richard didn't tell me because he's got a habit of secrecy. I'm sure it will serve him well in his new career as a wizard. I worked it out anyway. The instant we passed through the barrier, we disappeared from the rest of the world. The elves took that as their signal. They attacked, on every front, against every known or suspected *hjerne-spica* lair, against every realm or church that wore the Black. They woke the Stone Legion, called in all the dragons, made a deal with the Ur-Mother, and who knows what else. They're throwing everything they have against your worshippers."

Christopher leaned over to make an aside to Alaine. "Tremendous courage, that. To assume we're doing our part instead of having been vaporized."

"THEY WILL FAIL. YOU TRICKED THEM INTO ATTACKING TOO SOON. THEIR ARMIES WILL BE CRUSHED. THEIR ALLIANCES SHATTERED. THEY WILL NEVER RECOVER THE STRENGTH THEY SQUANDER TODAY."

"They don't have to win," Christopher said. "They just have to make you fight."

The screens that looked into the void were flaring with lights, like a thousand Christmas trees on Christmas Eve. Every blink was a spell being cast.

Hordur laughed. "THE BATTLE IS EASY. THE ELVES USE NO MAGIC. THEIR DEFEAT WILL TAKE BUT MOMENTS."

"They're not using magic because Richard told them not to. Again, may I say, an act of incredible trust. Your followers are using magic, though. Just tossing the stuff around like there's no tomorrow. Meanwhile, the rest of you gods, you're just experiencing the normal requests for spells, right? Nothing out of the ordinary."

Computers whirred on the bridge, analyzing the data from the cameras. Christopher looked around. The rest of his crew were as still and silent as department store mannequins.

A bell chimed. The computers had reached a conclusion. Seven green lights lit up on the control board. A red button started glowing, pregnant with menace. It would launch his own harvest of black, although excision would seem to be a more appropriate verb. It would reshape the world on a fundamental level and make room for real change.

Christopher reached forward. His hand stopped inches away as paralysis seized him. He invoked the special dispensation of a god of Travel that freed him from all restraints.

Nothing happened.

"YOU ACCUSE US OF STOLEN LIVES. HOW MANY ARE IN YOUR HEAD?"

The weight of those he had consumed crushed him. Here, in the source of tael, his ill-gotten gains counted against him. It was a leash the gods could use against any ranked person. They understood it intimately because they had created the entire system of ranks in the first place. They were, after all, merely ranks without a person underneath.

Only heroes of legend could ever win their way to the abode of the gods through the layers of defense that surrounded it. Once there, they could do nothing without the gods' consent.

Karl stepped forward, pure and unsullied, unranked despite every plot Christopher had laid to elevate him. The red god raised his ax threateningly; the yellow one took off her mask and revealed a beautiful woman whose eyes begged for Karl's attention.

Silently, Christopher laughed. Fear and lust were perhaps the least effective weapons to deploy against Karl Treyingson.

"WE WILL MAKE YOU A GOD," Hordur tried.

If he could have rolled his eyes, Christopher would have rolled them right out of his head. There was only one thing less likely to move the young stalwart than an ax or a pretty face, and that was a promotion.

Karl pushed the button in contemptuous silence.

The ship shuddered. The screens flared out, overwhelmed by the glare. When they faded back in, they displayed seven blazing lights streaking away from the ship. The lights winked out, one by one, as the rocket engines did their job and shut off.

"WHAT HAPPENS. SPEAK, FLEDGLING. WHAT HAVE YOU DONE."

Christopher's mouth worked, although it was not entirely under his control. If it was, he would have remained silent, following Karl's awe-inspiring example. "The missiles are ballistic. I can't call them back, and you can't affect them; they're cloaked in anti-magic spheres. Although I'm guessing that wasn't actually necessary? You have no power here except through our ranks. Even so, probably Richard or I could have cast spells to interrupt. So it's good that's off the table."

Ostara shook her head in misery. "What does this accomplish?"

"Tael is real. You are a complex network made out of tael. The missiles are nuclear warheads; when they explode, they will destroy trillions of units of tael. We can't reprogram the network, but we can still smash it. Richard figured he could excise Hordur from the network or at least enough of him that he can't maintain consciousness. He gambled everything on Hordur being spatially localized, although as you can see he was prepared for a certain amount of distribution."

She stared at him, aghast. "And if it fails?"

"We've got nine missiles left. I imagine Karl will start blowing stuff up at random."

"SAVE ME. IF I FALL YOU WILL ALL FALL. WITHOUT THE BALANCE WE WILL ALL FALL." Hordur, the god of death, begged his fellow gods for life.

The screens flared to solid white, the light of an artificial sun temporarily blinding them. The gods assembled before him seemed paler and less substantial in the harsh illumination.

"The fledging has beaten you in combat," the red god said. "Far be it from me to rescue a weakling." He vanished into nothingness.

Another two flares as more missiles reached their target. The cameras struggled to recover.

The golden jester's face changed again. Now it was a man's face, old and lined and full of judgment. "Who will provide for our priests when we are gone?"

"Your networks are still physically there. Even if you disassociate, the spells can still be drawn upon. Hordur, not so much. His followers will find themselves cut off from most divine magic. That will tilt the balance in favor of the elves, who already play the game without divinity." By the time Christopher finished speaking, the gold man was gone.

"If I must die, I die for love." The green woman smiled and was gone.

The screens turned white again. The cameras gave up, saturated to exhaustion.

"The thing is fairly done." The blue armor bowed and winked out.

Hordur was disappearing by parts with each detonation. A chunk of his shoulder, a leg, his left arm. He jerked and staggered as if aware of what was happening. Then the rest of him dissolved, leaving behind only the remnants of his cloak to collapse on the floor. It turned to smoke and dissipated, wafting up to the whirring fans of the sub's environmental controls.

"Thank you," Ostara whispered. "Although you have earned more than just words." She did not disappear; instead, she transformed. The woman wearing the white lace dress was now a beautiful redhead with wide green eyes and lovely lips pursed in shock. Images and metaphors melted away from him, leaving only a man coming home to his wife after a long and unplanned absence.

Christopher stood up from the command chair, a grateful smile curling onto his lips, absent-mindedly laying aside his sword. He stepped forward, and Maggie leapt into his arms.

"Chris," she moaned breathlessly. "What the hell just happened?"

"It's a long story," he said, holding her close. "But we've got time now."

ACKNOWLEDGMENTS

Thank you to everyone who came along on this journey, which took so much longer than I dreamed and went to places I never anticipated. Special thanks to Sara, for making me rewrite chapter twenty until it worked, and to Rene, for giving me the courage to go where the story led. I have waited fifteen years to write that line about the second apple, and now that it is done, I find myself missing Christopher and Karl and the families they have built. But their future stretches out beyond mortal imagining, and mine lies here with all of you.

ABOUT THE AUTHOR

M. C. Planck is the author of the *World of Prime* series and *The Kassa Gambit*. After a nearly transient childhood, he hitchhiked across the country and ran out of money in Arizona. So he stayed there for thirty years, raising dogs, getting a degree in philosophy, and founding a scientific instrument company. Having read virtually everything by the old masters of SF&F, he decided he was ready to write. A decade later, with a little

Author photo by Dennis Creasy

help from the Critters online critique group, he was actually ready. He was relieved to find that writing novels is easier than writing software, as a single punctuation error won't cause your audience to explode and die. When he ran out of dogs, he moved to Australia to raise his daughter with kangaroos.